W9-AQR-274

# CONTESSA

# HELENE MANSFIELD

# CONTESSA

DOUBLEDAY & COMPANY, INC.
GARDEN CITY, NEW YORK
1982

All characters in this book, with obvious historical exceptions, are fictitious and any resemblance to actual persons, living or dead, is entirely coincidental.

Library of Congress Cataloging in Publication Data

Mansfield, Helene.
Contessa.

I. Title.
PR6070.H693C6   1982      823'.914   AACR2
ISBN: 0-385-17300-8
Library of Congress Catalog Card Number 81–43536

## Acknowledgments

Thanks to the staff of the Soviet Embassy, London, for their kindness when I went to ask about the cossack folk song "Stienka Rezin."

Thanks to Chappell Music, London, for allowing me to quote from "The Carnival Is Over."*

Thanks to the staff of the Prado Museum, Madrid; the Hermitage Museum, Leningrad; the organizers of the Spanish Civil War Exhibition in Madrid, 1980; the local staffs of tourist organizations and cultural organizations in Córdoba, Seville, Albacete, and Valencia; the staffs of the Bibliothèque Nationale, Paris, and the British Library, London.

Thanks to Count Graf for his memories of Paris in the twenties, and to the Marquis de Villaverde for his fascinating memories when we talked about the Spain of his youth (this took place in 1967). Thanks to two unnamed ladies who spoke about life after leaving Russia in 1918.

# CONTENTS

# CONTESSA

# PROLOGUE

## Paris, 1900

The ballroom of the Duchess of Chambercy's house was lit with crystal chandeliers from which a thousand candles threw pale amber light on walls painted with peacocks and cupids. Around the room two hundred men and women in evening dress were waiting for the principal guests to arrive. The orchestra leader fidgeted with his baton. Waiters and footmen stood rigidly at attention and society ladies spoke in hushed whispers.

At that moment the Prince of Wales entered with his wife, Princess Alexandra. The guests bowed and curtsied as the couple descended the stairs and walked along a line of people chosen for presentation. Eagle-eyed matrons examined the princess's flawless complexion and her emerald tiara. Men looked with curiosity at the prince and were impressed by the dignity of his bearing. Then, suddenly, the guests' attention was diverted to a young woman who appeared at the top of the staircase. A gasp of surprise rose from the assembly at this departure from protocol. The duchess looked toward her royal guests, amused to see that the prince was enjoying this unexpected interruption to his royal duties.

The girl at the top of the stairs was very young, with a heart-shaped face and silver-blond hair arranged in ringlets threaded with seed pearls, rosebuds and ribbon. Her eyes were violet blue with thick dark lashes framing them. Her dress was pink with a handspan waist and a tempting décolletage. She wore no jewels and the only decoration on the dress was a pair of doves that swooped with outswept wings from shoulder to breast. For a moment the girl hesitated, debating whether to withdraw. Then, conscious that she was already late, she walked down the marble stairway, fluttering her fan and blushing ingenuously as a wave of spontaneous applause greeted her. She curtsied to the royal couple before making her way to the corner of the room, where she was greeted by her hostess, the Duchess of Chambercy.

"My dearest child, I thought you were never going to appear, and now look what a sensation you have caused."

"I apologize for being late, madame. This evening everything has gone wrong. First my chaperon broke the heel of her shoe. Then our carriage wheel had to be adjusted when we reached the Rond Point. I do hope you won't tell Grandmama that I missed dinner."

"I shall only complain that you stole the attention from my distinguished guests."

As the orchestra began to play the first waltz, men sprang to their feet and soon the girl was surrounded by eager admirers. Guests who had witnessed her unusual debut began to gossip furiously.

"Who is that lovely young thing?"

"I'm told she is Russian, though she has been living in Paris since she was a child."

"I wonder why she was not present at dinner."

"My dear, Russians are *never* punctual."

The Prince of Wales was waltzing with his wife, though his eyes were lingering on the girl in the corner of the room.

"She's very young, isn't she, Alex?"

"Madame la Duchesse told me she is fourteen."

"What is her name?"

"Her name is Valentina. I don't recall the second name. She is Russian and the daughter of a grand duke. This is her first ball. Why don't you ask her to dance, my dear. I'm feeling a little tired from all that walking around the exhibition."

The prince returned his wife to the ladies of his party and made his way to the corner of the ballroom where the duchess was holding court. Nodding to his hostess, he looked with interest at her companion.

"Will you introduce me to your protégée, madame?"

"Of course, Your Royal Highness, I shall be delighted."

The girl curtsied gracefully as she was presented by the duchess.

"Mademoiselle Valentina Ivanovna Nikolayeva from St. Petersburg, His Royal Highness, the Prince of Wales."

"*Enchantée,* Your Highness."

"May I ask you to dance, mademoiselle?"

The music quickened as a Viennese waltz followed the sedate opening medley. Valentina smiled eagerly and the prince was moved by her innocence, her beauty and the dimple in her chin. Her perfume, a delicate blend of jasmine and iris, reminded him of women in the balmy days of his youth and he looked with affection at her, conscious that her manner was unusually knowing for one so young. He weighed Valentina's mouth with its Cupid's-bow upper lip and full, sensuous lower one. She was a tantalizing, exquisite creature; of that there was no doubt. The prince, noting that Valentina was blushing under his scrutiny, told himself he had best stop staring, and he began to converse politely.

"I hear this is your first ball, mademoiselle."

"It is, sir, and I am thrilled to be here. Madame la Duchesse was a close friend of my late mother. That is why she agreed to present me. I have been visiting this house since I was five; indeed, I used to pretend that I lived here."

"How long have you been in Paris?"

"I arrived on my fifth birthday, sir. Now I have almost forgotten Russia, except for the snow and the land that I loved. I remember Papa once pointing to the horizon and telling me that everything, as far as I could see, was ours. It is a moment I have never forgotten."

"Every Russian loves the land. It is part of the national character."

The prince led Valentina to a wistaria-covered terrace and taking two glasses of champagne from a passing waiter handed one to her.

"Was your father related to the Grand Duke Ivan Fyodorovich Nikolayev?"

"Papa *was* the grand duke; did you know him, sir?"

"I met him once, in Monte Carlo, if I remember rightly."

"Do tell me about my father. Since Mama died everyone shuns me when I ask about him. One would think at least that he was a criminal."

The prince sighed at the young lady's frankness. Ivan Fyodorovich had been one of the world's most dedicated gamblers, a Russian of charm and wit, a womanizer and a man destined for tragedy. The prince had met the grand duke in Monte Carlo in 1890, when the Russian had come close to breaking the bank. Within forty-eight hours Ivan Fyodorovich had lost not only his money but his estates in St. Petersburg and the entire family fortune. With nothing else to lose he had withdrawn from the Grande Salle and shot himself on the grounds of the casino. Conscious that Valentina was waiting for him to speak, the prince remembered her father lying in a pool of blood under a blue Mediterranean sky and wished he had not mentioned the grand duke. He did his best to be diplomatic in his reply.

"Your father was a fine man. He was handsome, charming and popular and I have no doubt he inspired many of his contemporaries to jealousy. If he had a fault, it was that he liked gambling too much for his good. But all of us gamble in one way or another, don't we?"

Valentina sipped her champagne, pleased to have learned something of the father she barely remembered. Before she could ask further questions, the prince suggested a polka and soon they were in the middle of the assembly, talking animatedly as though they were old friends. When the prince returned Valentina to her hostess, the young Duc de Noailles engaged her for a dance. The duke was followed by the writer Jules Renard, the Duc de Gramont Caderousse and the painter Kees van Dongen, who asked Valentina to sit for him.

"I intend to paint you as the spirit of springtime, surrounded by violets to match your eyes. Does the idea please you, Mademoiselle Nikolayeva?"

"I am flattered by your interest, sir. Perhaps you will call on my grandmother to ask her permission."

By eleven o'clock Valentina had been invited to a ball, a hunting party, a séance and a series of four-to-fives. She had been christened "an enchanting angel" by the playwright Edmond Rostand and *la femme la plus délicieuse du monde* by the actor Lucien Guitry. Dreamily she sat at the duchess's side, watching the guests dancing, their smiles formal and fixed as though nothing in the world could ever disturb their composure. The clock struck the half hour and the duchess asked her protégée if she was enjoying the ball.

"I have loved every minute of it, madame. I can hardly wait to tell Grandmama all I have seen and heard."

"You will always remember this evening, my dear. Women never forget their first ball and the first time they fell in love. Now, it's almost time for the last waltz. To whom are you going to give it?"

The Prince of Wales bowed. Valentina curtsied. Then, as the guests watched, he led her into the haunting melody of the dance. Gradually other couples joined them on the floor and soon the room was full of wafting feathers, intoxicating perfume and the tempting rustle of taffeta. The prince looked quizzically at his partner, assessing her as he assessed every woman he met. Was she a temptress in the making? Had her entrance been carefully contrived to attract his attention? Or was she one of those women who are unaware of the effect they have on people around them? He concluded that there was no deliberate calculation in Valentina, only the promise of sensuality so potent it was almost tangible. He looked into her eyes and asked about her future.

"Is it your intention to stay in Paris?"

"It is, sir. I adore Paris and have always been happy here."

"What do you love about it?"

"I love the chestnut trees in the boulevards and riding in the Bois every Sunday. I love skating in the Palais de Glace and visiting the country to collect fruit from Monsieur Ivanov's orchard. I am hoping to marry a Frenchman someday and to have a fine house in the Bois de Boulogne. Then I shall be a true Parisian."

"A Russian Parisian, surely?"

"A not-so-very-Russian Parisian, sir."

Dawn was breaking as Valentina rode home with her chaperon. The night sky was streaked with pink and yellow and the streets smelled of poplar leaves after a shower. She was thinking of one of the young men she had met that evening and the compliment he had paid her: "Today I saw the Palace of Electricity at the exhibition. It had fifty thousand colored bulbs and mightily impressed me, but you have outshone everything and put the wonders of the exhibition out of my mind. I do hope you will not mind that I have fallen in love with you, Mademoiselle Nikolayeva. . . ." Valentina smiled, delighted at the prospect of making every man in Paris fall in love with her. When she was older she would take time to consider the proposals she received. Then she would choose the handsomest, strongest, kindest man in the city and marry him. They would have a dozen children to warm their later years and she would look back on the flirtatious early days of her life with amusement.

Elizabeth Fyodorovna, matriarch of the Nikolayev family, watched as her granddaughter handed her wrap to the maid. She thought how lovely Valentina looked and how happy. Then she sighed. How was she going to tell the child all that had to be told?

Looking through to the salon, Valentina was surprised to find her grandmother waiting up for her. She ran and knelt before the old lady, kissing Elizabeth Fyodorovna's cheeks and chattering about the ball.

"Flora broke her shoe and we arrived late, Grandmama, but no one minded and the Prince of Wales danced with me three times. A painter called Kees van Dongen asked me to sit for him and we have so many invitations I don't know how we shall *ever* find time to answer them all."

"Is Madame la Duchesse well?"

"She is, Grandmama. And she asked me to give you her best wishes."

"What a good friend she has been to this family."

Suddenly Valentina noticed that her grandmother was looking pale and tense. Kissing the wrinkled hands, she asked tenderly, "Are you not well? Shall I ask Flora to bring you something to drink?"

"No, my dear, I am just getting old. God knows why I am still alive when my body is as worn as that old carriage we keep having mended. I waited up for you because I have something important to tell you."

"Could it not have waited until tomorrow?"

Elizabeth Fyodorovna touched the silver ringlets and the rosebuds in her granddaughter's hair. Then she took a deep breath and explained what she had been at pains to conceal for so long.

"There are some things which you must be told, now you are no longer a child. Firstly, you are *Russian* and all your family is Russian. It is a fine family of the most noble line. Your father loved you and your mother, but he loved gambling more than anything in the world and in the end he died for it. After his death I discovered he had lost everything he owned at the tables. Our lands, our palaces and most of the family jewels had been placed at the disposal of the fiends who had encouraged him in his obsession. Your mother and I came to Paris to live because we could not bear the thought of remaining in poverty where once we had lived in splendor. That, my dear, is why we had to leave St. Petersburg."

Alarmed to see tears in her grandmother's eyes, Valentina remained silent. The old lady continued.

"When we first arrived in Paris we lived well. Then, when Nadya had sold all her jewels and I all of mine, we were forced to learn economy. During your mother's final illness she was fortunate enough to be befriended by a Russian gentleman who happened to be visiting Paris. He had been one of Nadya's suitors in the days of their youth and no doubt she wished she had married him instead of your father."

Stung by this comment, Valentina protested.

"The Prince of Wales was complimentary about Papa."

"The Prince of Wales is a gentleman; how else would he have spoken? Now, where was I? After your mother's death your schooling, your expenses and those of this house were taken over by the man who had befriended Nadya, though he was not rich by the standards of our family. Three months ago he died, leaving me a small annuity which will enable me to keep the house in which we live but which will not permit me to launch you in society. I have therefore taken the only step which will ensure your future and I shall be obliged if you will abide by my decision without argument."

Valentina rose and looked apprehensively down at the old lady sitting so proudly by the fire.

"What have you done, Grandmama?"

"I have agreed that you will marry Count Korolenko, who is one of the richest men in St. Petersburg. You will leave for Russia in the morning."

Stunned, Valentina gripped the mantelpiece, her face paling with shock.

"But I have never met this man!"

"You will meet the count when you arrive in Russia. First, you will spend a year in the Korolenko Palace, which is situated on the Nevsky Prospekt. There you will learn how to manage the household and then you will be taught the count's ways by his sister, Yekaterina Vasilievna. When you are sixteen you will marry the count and settle in the palace in which you have been living."

"How old is the count?"

"He is forty and as wise as you are inexperienced."

"I will *not* marry him, Grandmama. I will *not* be sent like a parcel to Russia to be trained in the ways of Russian society. I want to live in Paris and I have always wanted to live here. How could you consider sending me away? Why could you not have arranged a marriage for me with a French gentleman of means?"

"You are Russian. Your ancestors were leaders of Russian society. How can *you* wish to deny your heritage?"

"I do not wish to go to Russia, Grandmama!"

"Would you prefer to train as a seamstress or as a nursemaid?"

"This is nineteen hundred, Grandmama. Is it really so unreasonable to want to marry the man I love?"

Elizabeth Fyodorovna spoke resignedly.

"I have no money left, my dear. What little I had was spent on that dress you are wearing. I arranged for you to attend the ball because I wanted you to have something special to remember in the years to come. Guard your memories well, Valentina, for this is the last you will see of Paris, perhaps forever."

Tears fell down Valentina's cheeks and onto the satin of her dress. She spoke in a whisper.

"You say you love me yet you are sending me away to a country I cannot remember to marry a man I have never met."

"The alternative is poverty and at best marriage to a Frenchman in trade."

"I would rather work as a seamstress than go to Russia."

"You are Valentina Ivanovna Nikolayeva. It is not for you to have such low ambitions. You will leave for St. Petersburg in the morning. There will be no further discussion about it."

Valentina ran to her room and threw herself onto the bed. Her fists were clenched and she wondered how it was possible to be so happy and so sad within the space of an hour. When she had stopped crying, she sat up and listened to the sound of a vendor calling his wares in the street below. Wistfully, she walked to the window and looked out on the city she loved. The chestnut trees outside her window were heavy with pink blossoms. There were yellow roses in the garden and forget-me-nots bordering the path. In the road cyclists were mingling with ladies in elegant broughams, gigs and automobiles. Valentina smiled despite her sadness as a carriage drawn by three Percheron horses blocked the way of a mounted guard of the Chasseurs à Cheval, their swords dazzling in the sun, their white plumed hats fluttering in the breeze.

As she sat in the high-backed chair gazing out at the busy scene, her eyes misted with tears and she could see nothing at all.

All day the distraught girl remained in her room, refusing to eat and sitting tearfully at the window. Convinced that the step she had taken was for her granddaughter's good, Elizabeth Fyodorovna made no attempt to reason with her. Still, she felt empty and despondent. Without Valentina the house would be as silent as the tomb. Without her granddaughter's joie-de-vivre there would be nothing to look forward to, no light at the end of the tunnel of approaching poverty and ill health. At first Madame had planned to return to Russia with Valentina, but the count had been adamant that his bride be sent alone. He gave as his reason for this strange request the fact that he wished his fiancée to have nothing to remind her of her years in Paris. It had taken all Elizabeth Fyodorovna's diplomacy to persuade Korolenko to allow Miss Knatchbull, Valentina's English governess, to accompany the child. She had lied to the count about Miss Knatchbull, telling him that the Englishwoman had only just joined the household and could therefore not remind Valentina about her years in Paris. She had also omitted to tell the count that in addition to English Miss Knatchbull spoke Russian, which would be needed when dealing with servants of the lower orders in St. Petersburg, and French, which many of the aristocrats of the city chose to speak instead of their native tongue. Elizabeth Fyodorovna sighed. Had Valentina forgotten how to speak Russian? She thought of the Tsar, who spoke English with his family, a newly fashionable choice of many of the more widely traveled aristocrats. Then she resigned herself to the fact that the count was unrealistic in insisting that his fiancée be fluent in Russian. In the circles in which Valentina would mix it was simply not needed. Elizabeth Fyodorovna thought affectionately of Miss Knatchbull's preparations for the journey, of the trunks full of clothing, winter boots, flyswatters, fumigating powder, handguns and medical potions bought by the boxful because she considered Russia the most primitive country in the world. The old lady nodded approvingly. At least Valentina would have one strong ally within the palace on the Nevsky Prospekt.

The clock chimed five and the maid appeared to inform her mistress that someone was asking to see Valentina. Puzzled, Elizabeth Fyodorovna walked to the hall to meet the caller.

"I understand you asked to see my granddaughter, sir?"

The stranger turned to face her and the old lady saw that this was the Prince of Wales. She curtsied, looking with chilling disdain toward the maid, who had not recognized the visitor. The prince glanced at his watch as Madame led him to the salon.

"I shall be leaving Paris at seven-thirty, ma'am. May I see your granddaughter for a few minutes?"

"Of course you may. I shall send for her at once."

It was some time before Valentina appeared and curtsied before the prince. Seeing that she had been crying, the prince smiled encouragingly.

"I am returning to England this evening and I did not wish to leave Paris until I had given you this small souvenir of your first ball. Open it when I'm gone, my dear."

He handed Valentina a small velvet-covered box.

"Thank you for your generosity, sir."

"That wasn't the only reason for visiting you, mademoiselle. This morning the Duchess of Chambercy informed me that you are to leave for St. Petersburg tomorrow morning."

Valentina's eyes filled with tears and she did not answer. The prince spoke gently.

"I know this will have come as a great shock to you. I kept remembering how you said you would never leave Paris and that you wanted to be a true Parisian."

Valentina pinched her wrist to keep from sobbing. The prince walked to the window and looked pensively out on the passing scene.

"St. Petersburg is a very Russian city, though it looks towards the West as Moscow looks towards the East. The people there are not at all like Parisians and you will have to make a stalwart effort to adapt yourself if you are not to be very unhappy."

"I know I shall, sir."

"I would like to give you a word of advice.

"Remember, whatever happens, that you are a beautiful woman and one who knows what she wants in life. Never lose sight of your goal and I promise that someday you will achieve it."

"I wish I could believe you, sir."

"My dear child, women as beautiful as you do exactly as they please in life. That I can tell you from experience."

Valentina fell silent as the Prince continued.

"I have not met Count Korolenko, who is to be your husband, but I am sure he will take good care of you because he is a very lucky man."

"I am grateful to you for coming to see me, sir."

"One more thing: when you reach St. Petersburg give this letter of introduction to my good friend Count Benckendorff. He is a charming fellow and the very kindest person in the city. If ever you should need help, I am sure he will be glad to assist you."

Valentina hid the letter in her skirt and curtsied, holding out her hand, which the prince kissed.

"I wish you bon voyage on your journey back to St. Petersburg, mademoiselle."

"I notice you do not say back home to St. Petersburg, sir."

The prince smiled wryly.

"For you, my dear, Paris will *always* be home."

The following morning Valentina and Miss Knatchbull rode in a carriage to the station. Looking out on the passing scene, they saw poodle clippers on the embankment and the stalls of a flower market gaudy with blossom. Young dandies were strolling along the boulevard, pausing here and there to tip their hats to ladies parading in the latest fashion. A military band was playing in a crowded square and children were marching back and forth in imitation of French grenadiers.

When Miss Knatchbull saw Valentina brushing tears from her cheeks, she felt furious that Elizabeth Fyodorovna had upset her granddaughter so cruelly. It was one thing to want the child launched on society but another to send her off to Russia, where even the aristocracy were barbarians. The Englishwoman clutched her Gladstone bag and pursed her lips fiercely, resolving to be Valentina's staunchest ally.

At the station, as porters hurried to collect her luggage, Valentina smelled the acrid smoke of the waiting locomotive. She walked reluctantly behind her governess through the crowded concourse, pausing to buy violets from a flower seller before stepping onto the train. For a moment she looked longingly back at the pink rooftops of Paris. Then, as the guard blew his whistle, she closed her eyes so she would not see the city disappear.

Soon the movement of the train made Valentina drowsy and when she opened her eyes again she could see nothing because it was dark. She inhaled the scent of the violets and touched the tiny diamond-studded watch the Prince of Wales had given her, going over and over what he had said: Remember, whatever happens, that you are a beautiful woman and one who knows what she wants in life. Never lose sight of your goal and I promise that someday you will achieve it. Valentina wondered if what the prince had said was true. Was Russia to be her destiny? Or would determination be enough to bring her home someday to Paris?

# BOOK I

## Russia, 1900-1918

*Love without slinking doubt and love your best;*
*And threaten, if you threaten, not in jest;*
*And if you lose your temper, lose it all,*
*And let your blow straight from the shoulder fall;*
*In altercation, boldly speak your view,*
*And punish but when punishment is due;*
*With both your hands forgiveness give away;*
*And if you feast, feast 'til the break of day.*

Rhyme on Russian sentiment by Alexei Tolstoy

# CHAPTER ONE

## St. Petersburg, October 1900

By the time she neared her destination, Valentina was exhausted. She had lost weight and her face was pale and drawn. An early snowfall in Warsaw, where she and Miss Knatchbull had left the first train, had delayed their arrival by two weeks. Now, after the final journey by diligence and train, she could see the terminus of St. Petersburg ahead. She listened to the wild song of the driver and thought of the times she and Miss Knatchbull had been dug out of snowdrifts, the storms they had encountered and the filthy inns where they had been obliged to rest. She looked curiously out at the city she had not seen since she was four years old and thought it was far more beautiful than she had remembered.

The buildings of St. Petersburg were so high and the boulevards so wide that the people were dwarfed by their surroundings. The men wore stout leather boots and heavy skin coats, fur-lined against the cold. The women wore scarves that hid their faces and members of the aristocracy were driven by at high speed in horse-drawn troikas, their bodies insulated against the cold with wrappings of lynx, fox and sable. The sky was clear and blue. There was a strong northerly wind and it was bitterly, icily cold. Valentina watched a fellow passenger wrapping her dog in ermine and a priest covering himself with layers of sheepskin. Shivering, she wished her grandmother had had enough money to equip her suitably for the Russian winter.

Valentina and Miss Knatchbull were standing outside the station when a tall young man appeared followed by a dozen servants. He was dressed in an overcoat of sealskin lined with sable and had a lavish lynx fur cloak over his arm. Valentina saw that his face was very pale, his eyes dark and languorous with blue shadows of sleeplessness underneath. He bowed formally and spoke in a deep, resonant voice.

"I am Gavrilo Vasilievich Korolenko. My brother, the count, is absent from St. Petersburg and I have come to meet you. I apologize for my late arrival."

Valentina curtsied, trying hard to conceal her disappointment. She had expected the count to meet her, not this diffident man who seemed amused by her uncertainty. Korolenko summoned servants to load her baggage onto a wagon. Then he inclined his head toward a carriage waiting on the other side of the street.

"My sister, Yekaterina Vasilievna, awaits you in that carriage. No doubt she will be surprised by your appearance, because you are not at all what we expected."

Offended by his familiarity, Valentina said icily, "I hope I disappoint you, sir, so I can be sent home at once to Paris."

"On the contrary, you are infinitely more beautiful than I imagined. The count expects a child who can be molded to his tastes. I fear he may be shocked to find you so mature."

"You are very familiar, sir."

"I am Russian, and as I shall soon be your brother-in-law, I feel I may be familiar."

Their eyes met and Gavrilo's showed the same sardonic smile with which he had welcomed her. Valentina looked questioningly at him, trying to decide what he really thought of her. She allowed him to wrap her in the voluminous cloak. Then, when she was comfortably buried in its folds, she turned again to her companion.

"Did you bring a cloak for my governess, Miss Knatchbull?"

"Miss Knatchbull is a servant, surely?"

Valentina's eyes flashed with anger.

"I saw a Russian lady in the diligence wrapping her dog in ermine. If that is the custom in St. Petersburg, surely you do not think it strange that I should consider Miss Knatchbull's comfort?"

For a moment a serious look replaced the mask of indifference and Valentina knew that the smile and the careless manner were a pose and that Gavrilo Vasilievich Korolenko liked her and was displeased by his own reaction. She was relieved that one member of the family might be disposed to be a friend. Her newfound confidence diminished when she met Yekaterina, her fiancé's elder sister, who looked disapprovingly at her because she had been brought from Paris without her approval.

"My brother is absent from the city, Valentina Ivanovna. That is why I came to bid you welcome and to show you our home."

"I am grateful to you, ma'am."

Valentina looked hard at the piercing black eyes and the thick plait of iron-gray hair framing Yekaterina's plump, pale face. Yekaterina's clothes were styled in the fashion of decades past and her podgy fingers were weighted down with large pearl and diamond rings. She conversed as though angry to have been made to meet Valentina.

"Was your journey pleasant, mademoiselle?"

"Until we left the train in Warsaw it was very pleasant. After that we traveled some distance by diligence and had to be dug out of the snow. The inns where we stayed were infested with vermin and the final part of the journey by train was very cold."

"All Russia is infested with vermin, dear child. We contrive not to let such things distract us from our duties."

Valentina sighed, hoping fervently that the palace would be clean and free from the rats and cockroaches that had plagued her on the journey. As neither Gavrilo nor his sister paid her any further attention, she looked out of the window at a vast cobbled square surrounded by exotic buildings. Some of the palaces were painted green and white, some yellow and Venetian red. All were domed in gold and pillared in the Grecian style. Enchanted by the strangeness of the scene, Valentina asked who owned the houses. Gavrilo explained.

"The buildings over there are the Winter Palace, the principal residence of the Tsar and his family. Adjoining the palace is the Hermitage and beyond that the River Neva. Farther along the bank, which is called the Bolshaya Millionnaya, are the British and French embassies. The other buildings around Palace Square are the ministries of War, Finance and Foreign Affairs."

"And who are the soldiers?"

"The Gardes à Cheval ride on black horses and are dressed in red. The Chevaliers Gardes wear white and ride on chestnut horses."

"I have never seen anything quite like St. Petersburg. I am most impressed."

"And this, Valentina Ivanovna, is our home. I fear it will take you weeks to learn your way around the palace."

Valentina looked up at a building that stretched along the Nevsky Prospekt from the Mayakovskaya to the Vosstanyaskaya. The exterior was painted peacock blue and there was a gold dome above that glittered in the winter sun. Awed by the size of her future home, Valentina questioned the count's brother.

"How many rooms are there in the palace?"

"We have three hundred bedrooms and seventy staircases, but I do not know how many rooms, perhaps six or seven hundred. Whoever would wish to count them?"

As she stepped down and was helped over the ice, Valentina saw Gavrilo motioning for her to give precedence to his sister. Yekaterina swept by, leaving her brother alone with the new arrival. Valentina looked up at the high-domed roof and around the hall, which was ill lit and damp. Miss Knatchbull hurried past her, muttering disapprovingly at everything she saw. Valentina turned uncertainly to Gavrilo.

"Where has Madame Yekaterina gone?"

"I imagine she has retired with a headache. My sister suffers terribly from headaches and can sometimes barely see for the pain. The doctors insist that there is nothing seriously wrong with her but I can assure you she is frequently debilitated. She rarely goes out and only came to meet you because the count insisted upon it."

"Will you show me to my rooms, sir?"

"Of course, I shall be delighted."

"When will Count Korolenko be returning to St. Petersburg?"

"Who knows? My brother is not given to predictable behavior. No one ever knows where he is."

"I had thought he would be curious about me."

They walked along a gallery lined with somber portraits. Valentina looked up at the stern ancestral faces and then back to Gavrilo.

"Is there a portrait of your brother in this gallery?"

"That is the count, Valentina Ivanovna. He is handsome, is he not?"

Valentina saw a portrait of a slim, tall, saturnine man with a pointed black beard and penetrating gray eyes. The man was surrounded by hunting hounds and carrying a gun. She was surprised to see Gavrilo watching her closely.

"Does the count often hunt?"

"My brother loves shooting anything on four legs or two."

"You do not like your brother, sir?"

"I do not, and he dislikes me with the same depth of feeling. It was always so, even when we were children. Now, here are your rooms."

Gavrilo opened two doors and led Valentina into a high-ceilinged salon decorated in faded pink and rust. The furniture was covered in dust, and there were cobwebs on the windowsills and mouse droppings on the bed. Valentina stared in alarm at this unexpected sight. Unaware of her concern, Gavrilo led her to a bathroom containing a copper-lined sink and tub. Then he passed on to a study, a servants' quarters with pantry and another bedroom where Miss Knatchbull would sleep. All the rooms were in the same musty condition, though the furniture was costly and the curtains made of the finest brocade. When they returned to the salon Valentina asked with chilling politeness, "Is this your idea of a joke, sir?"

"Do the rooms not please you?"

"They are not clean. They are covered in dust and vermin droppings and have not been touched by a servant for months."

"This wing of the palace is rarely used."

"You knew I was coming. Why were the rooms not prepared?"

Surprised by the vehemence of her tone, Gavrilo retreated toward the door.

"I am not in charge of the domestic arrangements in this house, mademoiselle. My sister is mistress here and as she is often ill the servants have become used to lying about the work they have accomplished. Yekaterina must not have checked the rooms. I apologize on her behalf."

"I will not sleep in such filth!"

"I assure you the other rooms are no better."

"How many servants are there in the palace?"

"Five, six, seven hundred—how the devil would I know? What a one you are for numbers."

"Send me three girls who will serve me exclusively and please send them at once."

"I must consult my sister."

"Then consult her or I shall leave within the hour."

Alone again, Valentina sat staring into space. She was so shocked and disappointed that she could barely marshal her thoughts. She had expected to be received with Russian formality by the man she was going to marry. She had known that she might not like the Korolenko Palace, but had not for a moment envisaged living in dirt and decay. When she was calmer she called her governess.

"Have we cleaning materials with us, Natty?"

"Of course we have, child. I brought half the house with me. You know I can't bear to leave anything behind."

"Get them out, please, in case these ignoramuses haven't the means with which to scour our rooms."

Miss Knatchbull hurried away and Valentina turned to meet three young women led into the room by the count's brother. She was shocked to see that their clothes were dirty and sweat-stained and their hair was matted and dirty. Could girls who were unable to keep themselves clean be expected to understand her own desire for cleanliness? She was struggling to decide how to explain her requirements when she saw Gavrilo smiling mockingly. Angry, she turned on him, her voice trembling with emotion.

"May I ask how often people in Russia bathe?"

"I bathe frequently because I love water. The count is also fond of immersing himself. The servants bathe once a year and my sister would not divulge such information to her mirror."

"I would like you to explain what I want to these young ladies. I am not sure I can find the words to say all that is necessary. First, all the upholstery must be taken away and beaten to remove the dust. Then the carpets must be cleaned. Thirdly, all bedding and pillows must be removed and put away. I have brought my own linen and do not wish to use what is here. Finally, all the ornaments must be washed and also the skirtings and cornices. Then, when the room is empty the floor must be scrubbed with carbolic."

Gavrilo explained to the servant girls what Valentina had ordered. Then he asked her if there was anything else he could do.

"If you will leave me alone with these girls I shall supervise what must be done. In the meantime, I would be obliged if you would order a ratcatcher and fumigator to be brought here, for I see there are fleas in the lace of that bedspread."

"There are fleas everywhere in St. Petersburg. Probably there are even fleas in the Tsar's palaces. Servants pick them up in the bazaars and return home with them."

"I cannot live in filth, sir, so I must do my best to overcome what I cannot abide. I am grateful to you for your kindness and I would be obliged if you would indulge me in this matter."

Gavrilo withdrew, shaking his head in confusion. Was it possible a fourteen-year-old virago could accomplish what Yekaterina had failed to do in twenty years of trying? He sent a servant to bring the best ratcatcher and fumigator in the city and then returned to the corridor outside Valentina's suite and listened to the raucous protests of the maids inside. As their voices rose in defiance of Valentina's orders, Gavrilo heard a loud slap followed by silence. Then Valentina's voice rang out clearly.

"I *will* have my way and you *will* clean these rooms. You are paid by the count to work and that is what you are going to do."

By nightfall it became clear that the rooms were not going to be ready for hours, perhaps for days. Leaving Miss Knatchbull in charge of the servants, Valentina hastened to dress for dinner. As the clock struck eight she left her suite and walked past the portraits in the gallery to the staircase. At the top of the stairs she came face to face with a portrait of a red-haired woman. The painting would not have caught her eye if it had not been for the vibrant colors used in its composition, which were at odds with the rest of the portraits in the gallery. She lingered awhile, noting the scarlet satin gown, the opulent black pearls around the woman's neck and the look of indolent pleasure in her green eyes. The woman's skin had an alabaster tone. Her nose was straight and thin, her hair dressed in an elaborate chignon threaded with cockatoo feathers. Valentina thought the lady forbidding and at the same time seductive. She looks like a person I should not like at all, she thought. At that moment, a voice broke into her deliberations and turning she saw Gavrilo watching her.

"Are you a curious woman, mademoiselle?"

"Usually I am not, but I was wondering which of your relatives this is, because her portrait is quite different from the others."

"She is not a relative, though she would like to be."

"Who is she?"

"Her name is Magda Simoniescu and she is a friend of my brother's."

"Is she also a friend of yours, sir?"

"I fear not. Magda likes me no more than my brother does."

Valentina blushed and taking pity on her uncertainty Gavrilo took her arm.

"Shall we go down to dinner together?"

"Thank you, sir."

"May I compliment you on your dress. Violet is my favorite color and it becomes you."

The dining room was thirty feet high and eighty feet long, its walls lined with antlers and mounted animal heads. Ebony clocks with painted faces chimed every quarter hour and the only light came from a massive moose-antler chandelier. Valentina was displeased to see that the room was as grubby as her own. She thought how strangely the ruby-studded pepper holders contrasted with the austere surroundings. Salt had been placed in mounds at various points along the table and Gavrilo explained that this was because superstition declared that to spill salt heralded calamity. Sadly, the food did not match the quality of the tableware and Valentina shuddered as servants appeared with fatty soup, undercooked venison and a selection of sweets covered in icing. Sensing her displeasure, Gavrilo commented wryly.

"Are you going to send for Chef Dubrovsky so you can slap him as well?"

Valentina smiled enigmatically and her companion felt suddenly uncertain. As they ate, she confided her thoughts.

"If I remain in St. Petersburg and become mistress of this house I shall send to Paris for a chef. Count Korolenko is a rich man yet he eats food fit only for animals and no doubt sleeps in a room as dirty as those he has given me. What is the explanation, sir?"

"In Russia this is how we live. Some of the palaces are cleaner and more stylish than others, but most are infested with vermin. When we are young we learn to tolerate such things and so we make no effort to rid ourselves of contamination. I suppose it is that we Russians lack the will to make changes."

"I hope that I can be allowed to change this house, for I cannot live in such circumstances."

"Have you enough money to return home to Paris if you cannot change everything?"

"I have no money at all, sir."

"Then how do you propose to leave St. Petersburg?"

Valentina remembered what the Prince of Wales had told her.

"One of my friends in Paris told me that a beautiful woman can have her way in all things."

"You will need more than beauty to get you back to Paris, Valentina Ivanovna."

"No doubt someone could be prevailed upon to help me in my distress, sir."

Gavrilo met her eyes and looked away, conscious that she was right. Already he felt sympathetic toward the girl. Already he was having to control the desire to dwell on the emotions she awoke in him. He was relieved when she asked permission to retire.

"I should like to return to my suite now so I can see how the work is progressing."

"Good night, I hope you sleep well."

Valentina paused on the landing by the portrait of Magda Simoniescu. For a moment she weighed the arrogant gaze. Then she hurried back to her suite, pondering the reason for the presence of the portrait in the gallery. Was Magda the count's mistress? She was a beautiful woman obviously experienced in the ways of the world. Valentina felt instinctively that she would be no match for such a creature and she resolved to plan with meticulous care how to present herself on her first meeting with her fiancé.

Inside the suite Miss Knatchbull was still busy supervising the cleaning. The three maids had been joined by a dozen odd-job men, the fumigator, the ratcatcher and some curious scullery maids who had been enlisted to help with the scrubbing. It was 4 A.M. before they were ready for the fumigator to commence his work. Then, Valentina dismissed the maids and withdrew with her governess to sleep for a few hours.

Throughout the night the peace of the Korolenko Palace was disturbed by the sound of men working. In the morning, when Valentina returned to her room, she found the fumigator and his men still at work. The man explained what he had done.

"I have completed your room, milady, and the corridors in this wing of the palace. Next I shall tackle the rooms above and below your suite and the servants' quarters in the attics."

"You have done well, sir."

"When shall I return, milady?"

"Call as often as is required to keep this wing free from vermin."

"I shall come every day, milady."

Valentina wandered through her rooms, looking with distaste at faded paintwork and gilding long darkened by neglect. At seven the three maids appeared, their faces puffy with sleep. Valentina asked if they had eaten. Surprised, they looked at each other and then back to her. Haltingly, she explained what she had in mind.

"You cannot work as hard as I intend you to work if you do not eat properly, especially in the morning, when women are at their weakest."

"But our first meal is the midday soup, ma'am."

Valentina thought about this for a moment. Then she rang the bell and ordered cold cuts to be brought with bread, wine and a salver of spiced rice. The girls nudged each other nervously, half afraid, half impressed by the newcomer's determination. While they waited for the food to arrive, Valentina asked the maids to fill the bath in the room at the end of the corridor. They obeyed and were soon en route to the bathroom to be scrubbed clean by Miss Knatchbull.

An hour later they returned, wrapped in blankets and with their teeth chattering. Miss Knatchbull reported.

"All bathed, hair deloused, clothes burned. Gad, what a task! They screamed as if I were cutting their throats. We shall have our work cut out training these three."

"Bring the dresses, Natty, and the hose and underthings."

While her governess was out of the room Valentina explained her plans to the three maids.

"From today you will sleep in the servants' quarters adjacent to my suite. There is sufficient room for all of you and a fireplace where you can heat water and food. There is also a large cupboard for your clothes."

"That woman burned our clothes, milady."

"You are to have new clothes today and from this moment will be my maids, answerable only to me. You will bathe once a week on a Friday, when your hair will also be washed. You will eat regularly and work very hard. You will accompany me on any journeys I may make because once I have trained you I shall have no one else to serve me."

Miss Knatchbull reappeared with an armful of Valentina's old summer cottons, some aprons of her own plus three starched white caps. She dressed the three girls and led them to the mirror, where they stared warily at their reflections. Blond, blue-eyed Nina began to cry. Bibi was delighted by her mirror image and twirled around and around in sheer delight at the change in herself. Zita, the eldest of the three and as dark as her twin sisters were fair, walked to Valentina's side and spoke shyly.

"My sisters and I are very happy to have been promoted, milady. We will try to please you, but we don't really know how to be lady's maids as we have only ever worked in the kitchens."

"I shall teach you, Zita."

When breakfast arrived, Valentina dismissed the waiters and motioned for her three maids to sit down. Miss Knatchbull served the food and Valentina looked closely at the three. Zita was the most intelligent of the three and quite different in looks from the twins. Zita's face was truly Slavic, with high cheekbones and dark-gray eyes that seemed sad even when she was merry. Her mouse-brown hair was pulled tight in a knot at the back of her head and Valentina noticed she had put a clean white ribbon over each ear. She addressed herself to Zita.

"Today you will eat here with me and Miss Knatchbull so you can copy our manners. Tomorrow, when your rooms have been cleaned, I intend to have a table put there so you can eat breakfast together each morning. It will be best if you ask for cooking pots to be brought to your own pantry so you can prepare any additional food you may require."

Outside the sky darkened and snowflakes settled on the window-panes. When her maids had started work, Valentina sat looking out at the garden, despondency replacing the violent burst of energy she had experienced on first seeing the state of her rooms. She felt very tired and her thoughts kept wandering from the inhospitable palace in St. Petersburg to the ball she had attended in Paris. She remembered how elegant the women had looked, how gallant the men who had flocked to her side. Smiling wistfully, she remembered the Prince of Wales praising her father and waltzing at her side, his hand on hers, his eyes searching her face. She touched the, watch he had given her, comforted by the magic its presence released in the depressing dimness all around.

Seeing her charge looking sad, Miss Knatchbull hurried to Valentina's side with a tray of hot chocolate.

"Here we are, my dear, this will cheer you."

"Where did you find French chocolate in St. Petersburg?"

"I brought it with me, of course, with the tray and the cups and everything else."

Miss Knatchbull sipped her chocolate, closing her eyes as the taste reminded her of pleasanter days in Paris.

"I would like to report what I have ascertained about this house, my dear, and to make suggestions as to our future comfort."

Valentina listened intently as her governess read from the list.

"At this moment the maids are cleaning their own quarters. By tonight your furniture will be ready to be returned to the drawing room and bedroom. Tomorrow the girls will clean the bathroom and the next day the study and my own bedroom. I have taken the liberty of ordering logs to be delivered to us so they don't get filthy in the cellars. I have also requested foodstuffs to be brought directly to the pantry near the maids' bedroom. Zita is the brightest of those three and she has agreed to check that everything is delivered in a clean condition."

"What did you learn about Madame Yekaterina?"

"Only that she retired to bed on the day of our arrival and is still ill. I have prepared a herbal draft for her and I think you should deliver it."

"Will it cure her headache?"

"It may; it will certainly cheer her."

"What does it contain?"

"Never mind what it contains, it will do her good and she will be anxious to have more. Without Madame Yekaterina we shall be hard pressed to take care of ourselves in this house, so we must do everything we can to win her over. Judging by her attitude yesterday we have far to go."

Miss Knatchbull poured two more cups of chocolate.

"If you feel well enough to be left alone, my dear, I propose to go out and look around the estate."

"I'm quite well, Natty. I'm just tired and I can't stop thinking of home."

"This is our home now."

"Does it feel like home to you, Natty?"

"Of course it doesn't. It feels like a big damp barn, but in time we shall change it and when we remember our first few days here I'll wager we shall split our stays laughing."

Miss Knatchbull disappeared to dress for the snow. Soon she was visible in the garden, marching like a guardsman toward the woods. Now and then Miss Knatchbull paused and looked up at the sky. Then the Englishwoman trudged on, steadying herself with a briar stick and swinging a yellow-silk umbrella.

Valentina went downstairs to the library to look at the count's books. She was surprised to find works on a wide range of subjects, most of them well thumbed and some marked in the margins in an impatient handwriting. She was about to return to her room with a chosen selection when she saw a list on the table: Prepare dacha for Magda . . . take Magda to Yelagin . . . ask Yakov to deliver rings . . . attend the hunt at Tsarskoye Selo . . . arrange opera seats . . . obtain permits for alterations . . . Valentina Ivanovna arrives on the third . . . depart for Yelagin on the second. . . .

Valentina read the list again, wondering if it had been left deliberately for her to see. Was this the count's way of letting her know she was a person of no importance in his life? Desperately unhappy, she put the list back where she had found it and walked to the window. Outside on the Nevsky Prospekt traders were calling their wares. Valentina found their voices strident when compared to the voices of the traders in Paris. She looked out at the curious skyline of St. Petersburg, noting factory chimneys, shimmering domes, stone mansions and the spire of the church near the Volkov Cemetery shining like a needle against an ice-pink sky. Everywhere there was an unearthly silence because a heavy snowfall had muffled the sounds of the city. Valentina thought how strange everything was in her eyes, how unreal. Would she ever feel at home in St. Petersburg? Or would she remain an outsider, neither French nor Russian? She hurried back to her suite and for a while tried to read, but she could not concentrate. Her mind kept returning to the list on the library table. . . . Valentina Ivanovna arrives on the

third . . . depart for Yelagin on the second. Determined not to succumb to depression, she put down her book and examined the bottle of medicine Miss Knatchbull had dispensed for the count's
sister. First she sniffed the contents. Then she tasted some on her
finger. Finally she asked Zita to take her to Yekaterina's quarters.
Valentina had decided to follow Miss Knatchbull's advice. In the
coming weeks she would make a determined effort to make friends
with the count's sister.

Miss Knatchbull reached a clearing in the woods and found her
way barred by a giant. She judged the man's height to be close to
seven feet. With all the command she could muster she explained
in Russian who she was.

"I am Letitia Knatchbull, newly arrived with my charge, Valentina Ivanovna Nikolayeva, who is to marry Count Korolenko. May
I ask your name, sir?"

The man stared at Miss Knatchbull's height, at her stern brown
eyes and long, narrow face with its overlarge teeth. He saw no fear
in her gaze, nothing but sureness of purpose and confidence of
command. He studied the powerful width of her shoulders and the
aggressive look in her eyes. Impatiently, Miss Knatchbull asked
him to step aside.

"I would be obliged if you would let me pass, sir. I cannot walk
through the water and the snow is too deep on the other side of the
path."

The man hesitated. Then he spoke in a gruff voice and Miss
Knatchbull felt sure he was unused to speaking with anyone but
the animals of the forest and the birds of the air.

"I am Pyotr. I guard the master's land."

"There is no need to guard it from me, sir. I am hardly likely to
abscond with a forest!"

"It is not permitted to pass, milady."

"Why not pray?"

"The master said not to let anyone pass."

Miss Knatchbull paused. Then she asked cunningly, "Have you
seen the count lately?"

A blush crept up the big man's face and he looked away. "I do
not remember."

"You are a liar, sir. I'll wager the count is somewhere in these woods hiding from that poor girl he has brought from Paris. Well, I shall not insist on continuing with my walk. I shall return to the house, but I intend to tell Mademoiselle what you have said."

Turning, Miss Knatchbull saw a thickset man with unruly blond hair standing directly in her path. The man's clothes revealed him to be wealthy. His gun was English and finely chased in gold. His manner was arrogant and he seemed intent on enjoying himself at Miss Knatchbull's expense.

"I heard you threatening to make trouble for my friend, Count Korolenko."

Miss Knatchbull gave the newcomer a withering glance.

"Let me pass, sir."

"Why are you in such a hurry?"

"Who are you, sir?"

"I am Konstantin Amarevich Pirogov, best friend of Madame Simoniescu. And who are you?"

"I do not intend to discuss my origins with you, sir. Let me pass at once."

Pirogov took out a flask and swigged some vodka. Then he cocked his gun and walked menacingly toward Miss Knatchbull. She wondered with sudden apprehension if he was deranged and stood to her full six feet as he challenged her.

"You intend to make trouble by telling that foolish child it has been Vladimir Vasilievich's whim to buy for breeding purposes that he has returned for a few days from the island of Yelagin. It will be my pleasure to dissuade you from your intentions, madame."

Out of the corner of her eye, Miss Knatchbull could see Pyotr watching uneasily. Pirogov walked toward her, his eyes glinting malevolently, and for a moment she thought he was going to shoot her. Instead, he raised his arm as though to strike her. Miss Knatchbull made haste to strike first, landing Pirogov a resounding blow with the lead-weighted handle of her umbrella. With a howl of pain he crumpled at her feet. With a polite nod to Pyotr, Valentina's governess stepped over the gasping man and marched swiftly back to the safety of the house. As she walked she congratulated herself on having had the foresight to have such a weapon made before her departure for Russia. There was no telling when one might need to defend oneself in a country full of barbarians. Miss Knatchbull decided to bring a rifle with her next time she walked in the woods.

A small group of men gathered around Pirogov. Only Pyotr stood apart, staring into the distance at Miss Knatchbull. He judged the Englishwoman to be about forty, but what strength she had had, what courage and nobility. He returned to kneel at the side of the injured man, relieved that Pirogov was alive but delighted that this detestable member of the count's circle had been unable to intimidate the Englishwoman.

Over dinner that evening, Valentina chatted amiably with Gavrilo. She told him about Paris, about her grandmother and how she had been informed about her departure for St. Petersburg only the day before she left home. Gavrilo seemed preoccupied and Valentina realized that he was worried.

"Why are you so silent, sir?"

"This afternoon Miss Knatchbull went out walking. Did she tell you anything of what happened to her?"

Valentina's eyes sparkled with pleasure.

"Natty said she met a man in the woods who barred her way and refused to let her pass. She stunned him with her lead-handled umbrella. Natty's fond of unusual weapons. She has three guns and a sword stick disguised as a cane that was once owned by King George III of England."

"She broke one of Pirogov's ribs."

"Who is he?"

"He is a close friend of Magda Simoniescu and therefore of my brother. He is a very unpleasant character."

"Is Pirogov the reason for your despondency, sir?"

"Did Miss Knatchbull say anything else to you?"

"What else was there to say? Is there some mystery about which I am unaware?"

Gavrilo seemed to relax on hearing this and soon he was doing his best to be entertaining. Still, Valentina could see he was uneasy and in the late evening, when servants had put logs on the fire, she asked what was really on his mind. For a moment he sat looking into the flames.

"Pirogov intends to ask that Miss Knatchbull be sent back to Paris."

"If Natty goes I shall go with her."

"I'm afraid that will not be possible, Valentina Ivanovna. This arrived for my brother a few days before you came to St. Petersburg. Your grandmother died two days after you left Paris."

Valentina burst into tears and sobbed as if her heart would break. Gavrilo paced the room, unable to comfort her. At last he took her upstairs to her room and called Miss Knatchbull to care for her. The two women talked until the early hours of the morning, each trying to comfort the other, each conscious of the fact that another tie to the old life in Paris had been severed.

At dawn Valentina rose and wandered down the hall to the gallery where the ancestral portraits were hung. One by one she viewed the Korolenkos past and present, conceding that they were a handsome group, if somewhat uncompromising and haughty. Then she walked to the top of the stairs and looked again at the portrait of Magda Simoniescu, noting every detail of the striking face with its startling red hair and challenging green eyes. She was daydreaming about banishing the count's mistress from her future when she heard voices, one husky and sensuous, the other deep like Gavrilo's.

"But, Vladi, I'm dying to meet this schoolgirl you've bought. Why do we have to hide from her? First you rush me off to Yelagin and now we're returned for a few days you refuse to let me see her."

"I don't wish you to meet Mademoiselle Nikolayeva just yet. I told you before, I wish Yekaterina to get to know the child first."

"But why?"

"I respect my sister's opinion."

"You didn't respect her opinion of me!"

"Yekaterina Vasilievna is not qualified to judge a woman like you, madame."

"Pirogov tells me the child is trying to take over the household. I don't like it, Vladi. She has called in an army of servants to clean the rooms and now she's ordering fumigations by the score and throwing out the furniture."

"She has the right to do so. She is arranging the rooms in which she will live."

"You're on her side, aren't you?"

"I'm in your bed, madame."

"I shall dislike her intensely!"

"Of course you will, my dear. You have always disliked competition, though you've never had a moment's worry about my fidelity."

"It won't work, you know. A schoolgirl cannot be expected to interest a man of your sophisticated tastes. Where are you going, Vladi?"

"The door is open, I must close it."

Valentina heard a door slam and looking up knew that it was one of those on the second floor of the building. She clutched the stair rail, her heart thundering with anger. So, the count was in the house with his mistress and not more than fifty meters from where she was standing. He had lied to her. Gavrilo had lied to her. Everyone had lied to her. And Magda was already grumbling about her presence. Valentina thought once more of returning to Paris and knew that if she did she would be giving up before she even began to fight for the affection of her fiancé. In Paris, her grandmother had died congratulating herself on a marriage well arranged. How then, could Valentina now return in shame? A small voice whispered that returning to Paris would also condemn her to a life of penury or worse. She had no trade and it would take years to learn one. In the meantime, how would she live? To stay in Russia would mean a secure future for the children she would someday have and a peaceful life for herself. The Korolenko Palace had impressed her and St. Petersburg had been a pleasant surprise. She had already made plans for the future. She asked herself if it was in her nature to abandon everything before she had even met the count. Would she be intimidated by his strumpet and run away before the battle commenced? Valentina remembered the words she had overheard and all thought of returning to Paris flew from her mind. She hastened back to her room, furious that the count's mistress should have the effrontery to try to dictate what *she* should do. She thought defiantly that she would do precisely what she wanted to do once she was mistress of the palace. In the meantime she would take more of the medicine to the count's sister and tell Yekaterina about the changes she was planning for the property, because she had found this to be a subject which delighted the lady. Obviously Korolenko was greatly influenced by his sister. Valentina resolved to make sure that Yekaterina gave her the very best recommendation. Having made her decision, she slept like a child and dreamed of a St. Petersburg that looked just like Paris, where every man was the Prince of Wales and every lady her friend.

## CHAPTER TWO

### St. Petersburg, December 1900

Valentina woke with a start on an icy winter morning. It was two months since she had arrived in St. Petersburg and she had already settled into a comfortable routine. Looking up, she saw Miss Knatchbull standing by the bed holding a dressing robe.

"Madame Yekaterina wishes to see you, child."

"It's very dark, what time is it?"

"It's eight-thirty and just like midnight."

"Did Madame say what she wanted?"

"She just asked for you to go to her room. Since you befriended her and my tonic cured her headaches, she can barely be an hour without one of us at her side."

"She was angry with me yesterday for arranging for the rest of the palace to be fumigated."

"Don't worry, my dear, half of her likes to know that the work is being done and the servants trained. The other half is annoyed that it is you and not she who has managed to accomplish the miracle. Always remember to ask her permission before you make the changes. That makes Madame think she is still in charge here."

Valentina hurried to the suite of rooms occupied by the count's sister. She was greeted warmly by Yekaterina.

"I have decided to take you shopping, my dear. You have barely seen anything of our city since you arrived because you have been constantly busy arranging things in the house. Now it is time to rectify my negligence."

Valentina wondered why she had been called so urgently, if all Yekaterina wanted was to go shopping. The older woman explained.

"My brother is to return in three days' time. He has invited us to lunch with him at midday on Thursday. He will be accompanied by his friend, Magda Simoniescu."

"I am ready to meet the count."

"No, my dear, you are not. With the greatest respect, you need new clothes and new jewels. I should have arranged all this weeks ago, but when you first arrived I was not feeling well enough. Now we shall have to do what we can at the last minute."

"Please don't trouble about me, Madame."

"I am very grateful to Miss Knatchbull for curing my headaches. I swear it is nothing short of magic. I had suffered from them for so long I barely remember the days when I felt as well as I do now. I am also delighted with the progress you are making with the house, and I hope very much that you will remain here in St. Petersburg. Let us hope that you can retain the confidence of your youth when faced with my brother's uncompromising nature. The count is a kind man but he is inclined to offend with his forthright comments. New clothes and jewels will give you confidence. Now hurry and get dressed. We shall leave within the hour. I have made an appointment with Madame Marinovskaya, the most original dressmaker in the city."

As the clock struck nine, the two women drove along the Fontanka, past the Sheremeteyev Palace, across the canal, continuing down the Dzerzhinskovo to the Moika. Valentina thought wryly that the streets of the city consisted almost entirely of palaces. She tried to compare St. Petersburg with Paris but it was impossible, like comparing an emerald with an opal. Yekaterina ordered the driver to stop while a servant collected parcels from the pastry cook's establishment. Then they drove to the shop of a Bukhara merchant in the shawl dealers' quarter and picked up another large box. At the corner of the Sadovaya they stepped down outside the Gostini Dvor, a shopping arcade containing two hundred luxurious establishments patronized by the aristocracy.

As they walked around the arcade, Valentina perceived with some amusement that her companion was thoroughly enjoying the outing. Since Yekaterina's headaches had vanished she had changed visibly. She ate well, slept well and was looking years younger. Valentina wondered what was giving her companion such obvious enjoyment. Was it the prospect of seeing her brother

again? Or was Madame looking forward to the confrontation with
Magda? Valentina sighed apprehensively. It was well known that
the count's mistress hated his sister. Could it be that Yekaterina
was pleased to have an ally against her old enemy?

First the two women called on Madame Marinovskaya, the dressmaker. Madame looked with interest at Valentina's violet eyes and
silver-blond hair. As she measured her new client, she thought of
the count's mistress and wondered how Magda would react to the
newcomer. Magda had once been a client of the establishment but
she had refused to settle her account and had often behaved offen-
sively toward the staff. When Madame Marinovskaya had insisted
on being paid Magda had flounced out, never to be seen again.
Madame recalled how the count's mistress liked heavily or-
namented gowns and how Korolenko was known to despise the vir-
ginal. It was necessary to make his fiancée alluring without being
coarse, titillating without seeming available. Soon she had chosen
styles suitable for Valentina and cutters were summoned to take
her instructions. She agreed to hurry through one dress for Valentina's first meeting with the count. The rest of the new wardrobe
would be delivered within the month.

From the scented atmosphere of the Marinovskaya atelier the
count's sister took Valentina to visit three jewelers, a fur merchant,
a furniture maker and an exclusive shop that sold nothing but
pearls. By the time they adjourned for refreshments to the Europa
Hotel, Valentina had begun to realize the importance Yekaterina
attached to her first meeting with the count. She sat pensively at
Yekaterina's side as waiters hovered attentively. Hot savories were
offered with lemon tea and feather-light pastries. Yekaterina ate
with relish, smiling at her companion's glances.

"You're wondering about my appetite, I imagine."

"I'm happy to see you looking so well, madame."

"I haven't been here for five years, my dear, but in the days before my headaches began I used to come to the Europa often. My
good friend Count Orlov used to meet me here on Tuesdays and
Thursdays and we used to eat until we could eat no more. Since he
died I lost my appetite for the place and the headaches made outings unthinkable."

"Now you are well we must come here often. The food is beau-
tifully presented. I wonder if the chef is French."

"He is and they have to pay him a king's ransom to stay because he is forever homesick for Paris."

Valentina looked at the stained-glass windows of the room and the walls of *faux marbre* painted with roses. The long Russian winters made those with sufficient money contrive to have flowers everywhere, in corridors, recesses, even growing along treillage attached to interior walls of their homes. She turned to Yekaterina and made a suggestion.

"Would you like to have a room like this at home?"

"I would, but my brother only likes hunting trophies. He doesn't care for flowers and anything else that reminds him of women."

"He has no objection to being reminded of Madame Simoniescu."

"What have you been told about Magda?"

"I have been told that she is the count's mistress."

"When I first met Magda she was charming and I believed she liked me. She came to the palace only three times in the first two years and I made the error of thinking her a person of little importance in my brother's life. Then I discovered that during his long absences the count had been living with her on the island of Yelagin."

"I am not looking forward to meeting Madame."

"Well I am! You see, for years I have been trying to take my brother's mind off that woman. Now I know I have a chance to succeed. I want the count to be happy, and though that creature stimulates him she has never made him content."

"Gavrilo told me she is dangerous."

"She *is* dangerous, but not as dangerous as you."

Valentina looked uncomprehendingly at her companion, wondering what she meant and why she was so optimistic about the future. Aware of her uncertainty, Yekaterina explained.

"Magda was thirty when my brother first met her. She was the most beautiful woman in St. Petersburg and wanted by every man who met her. Now she is forty and terrified of getting old. She has started to drink and when she has drunk too much she becomes violently jealous. In the past few women ever visited the palace so Magda had no reason to be afraid of losing the count. Now you are here at my brother's invitation and I am hoping that your freshness will help him see his mistress as she really is and not how she was ten years ago."

"Miss Knatchbull says I shall be too young to please the count."

"It's true my brother detests innocence, but he has never met a woman who is both innocent and spirited, beautiful and yet not vain. That, my dear Valentina, is why I am looking forward to his return. Now you are not to worry. You will have my support in your efforts to establish yourself in our home and together I am sure we can overcome any difficulties we may encounter. This is the only chance we Korolenkos have of being rid of that woman, and I for one am going to grasp it with both hands."

In the Fontanka, on the way home, Yekaterina's driver had to halt while a mounted regiment of the Preobrazhensky Guard rode by. Madame whispered to Valentina.

"I love to see those handsome young men. They are specially chosen, you know, to guard the Winter Palace along with men of the Gardes à Cheval and the Volynsky and Pavlovsky regiments. Ah, there is Ivan Grigorevich Yanin."

Yekaterina waved regally to a young captain at the rear of the troop.

"His mother owns the estate adjacent to our own in Tsarskoye Selo. The count envies them their magnificent horses and the extent of their land."

Valentina caught the gaze of the young man about whom Yekaterina was talking. She blushed as she looked into the challenging gold eyes. Ivan Grigorevich Yanin smiled down at her. Valentina stared as though hypnotized. Then, when he had passed, she found herself unable to recall anything about him except the desire in the catlike eyes and the ramrod-straight back in the dark-green uniform. Thoroughly disturbed by the experience, she sat quietly at Yekaterina's side, wondering why she felt so elated.

On the day before the count's arrival there was feverish activity in the palace. On Valentina's instructions brigades of servants were rushing back and forth cleaning the rooms. Long-idle gardeners were wheeling plants into the corridors, and in the kitchen Yekaterina was discussing the menu for the luncheon party with Chef Dubrovsky. At first the kitchen staff had been unanimous in their dislike of Valentina. During the first four weeks of her stay in the palace she had sent back all the food prepared for her, often with notes of a constructive nature for the chef. These notes enraged the chef until it was pointed out one night by a drunken scullery maid that the young lady's criticisms were valid because Dubrovsky had long forgotten the art for which he had once been renowned. As the food improved, Valentina expressed cautious approval, provoking the chef to unprecedented effort. Now it was with pride that he found his food accepted. While Yekaterina wrote the menu in her book, Valentina looked around the kitchen, noting the new paint, the bleached floors, the refuse bins she had ordered to be neatly stacked in rows. Turning to Dubrovsky, she was lavish in her praise.

"I hardly recognize these kitchens, Chef Dubrovsky. You have succeeded in moving them from the Middle Ages to the twentieth century, and I congratulate you, sir."

"I have remedied most of the problems, but I can do nothing with the oldest of the stoves."

"They should be thrown out and new ones purchased, if the count's finances permit it."

Yekaterina gulped at this affront to her brother's wealth and hastened to instruct the chef.

"Of course, throw out the old stoves at once. Mademoiselle and I will purchase new stoves next time we go out."

The chef smothered a laugh at Valentina's cunning. A hundred times he had asked for new stoves, but each time Yekaterina had found excuses not to buy them. Now everything had changed, even his staff and the kitchens. Dubrovsky finalized the menu and accompanied the two women from the kitchen, returning in time to hear one of the maids calling to another.

"That minx can clean us up but what's she going to do when she comes face to face with Magda? Madame won't crawl to a schoolgirl, you'll see."

Dubrovsky sighed, knowing the maid's derision to be well founded. At forty Magda was a woman set in her ways. Her will had been law in the palace for almost a decade, and no one really believed that things could change. The chef remembered what he had been told by gossiping members of the household staff, of parties thrown by the count's mistress at which she was the only woman present and available to all who wanted her, of young girls brought into the house for inspection and his mistress's amusement, girls whose bodies were used to satisfy the jaded appetites of those within the Korolenko circle. Dubrovsky thought of Valentina and rubbed his chin anxiously. She had charmed her way successfully into the affection of the count's brother and sister. It was years since Yekaterina had been out of the palace. Now she talked constantly of shopping trips and even visits to the country. Shaking his head pessimistically, Dubrovsky tried to concentrate on his plans for the luncheon party.

At noon the following day Magda walked like a queen down the main staircase of the palace. Her dress was scarlet and she wore a sweeping cloak of imperial sable. At her throat there was a diamond choker designed for her in the form of a dog collar by Pirogov. At her wrist she wore a pair of jeweled manacles studded with diamonds and pearls. Servants bowed as this bizarre creature passed by en route to the dining hall. Then they hurried back to the kitchen to report what they had seen to Dubrovsky.

The count was very pale. His beard had been neatly trimmed to a point that morning and he had elected to wear his new emerald tiepin. It had not escaped Magda's notice that Korolenko had taken particular care with his toilet, a fact that riled her, as did the eagerness in her lover's eyes and the nervous twitching of his hands. As they sat at opposite ends of the dining table Magda called to her lover.

"Don't tell me you're nervous, Vladi."

"Of course not, I'm simply impatient for this meeting to be over."

"What shall we do this afternoon?"

"Whatever will please you, my dear."

"You're not concentrating on what I'm saying, Vladi."

"Smile, madame, or this precocious child will think you disconcerted by her presence."

Magda glowered at the count as Yekaterina arrived with her oldest friend, Countess Volkova. The two women greeted the count and nodded politely to his mistress. Korolenko frowned, offended by the late arrival of his brother and the girl he had sent for as a bride. Every few seconds he looked toward the door, straining to hear the sound of Valentina's voice, but all he could hear was the drumming of Magda's fingers on the table. At last she roared angrily.

"Does Gavrilo Vasilievich not intend to lunch with us, sir?"

"My brother does as he pleases, madame. He is not a child to be given orders by me."

"And this little girl, is she not to be taught that we do not like to be kept waiting?"

"Patience, my dear. I have never seen you so agitated."

Delighted by Magda's unease, Yekaterina wondered fondly if this was all part of Valentina's plan to disconcert the count's mistress. Her deliberations were interrupted by the arrival of Gavrilo, who greeted everyone and announced Valentina. The count noticed with annoyance that his brother's face flushed with pleasure when he spoke the girl's name.

"May I present Mademoiselle Valentina Ivanovna Nikolayeva."

The count rose and bowed as Valentina took his hand.

"I am delighted to meet you, mademoiselle."

Valentina curtsied, pleased by the courtesy shown her by the count, but disappointed by the formality of his tone. Gavrilo introduced her to Countess Volkova. Then he led her to Magda. Valentina nodded formally barely touching the outstretched hand.

"I have heard so much about you, Madame Simoniescu."

Magda's eyes flickered and she forced a smile.

"Welcome to St. Petersburg, child."

The count looked at Magda in her scarlet satin and sable. He thought wryly that she was sporting enough diamonds to fill a jeweler's window and wondered why she always overdid things so. Then he turned to Valentina, taking in the pistache-green silk of her dress, the lily of the valley edging the bodice and running in a diagonal stripe to the hem. Her face was eager, her eyes enticing, her skin like peach down. The count looked at Valentina's nails and the tiny wrists, each one with a seed-pearl bracelet, her only jewelry. He sighed, suddenly weary. Comparing the two women was like comparing a rare orchid with a gaudy sunflower.

The door opened and a procession of waiters carried in silver salvers heaped with caviar. The count looked down at the spotless tableware and linen, looking wonderingly around the room at the new order of things. In the weeks since his departure the atmosphere of decay had vanished and everything had changed. From the moment of her arrival, the young girl from Paris had ordered fumigations by the score, incessant scrubbing and polishing and the removal of many old and depressing pieces of furniture. The count watched Valentina as she chattered happily with his brother. Then he gazed at Gavrilo, frowning because it was obvious that he was infatuated with the girl. After years of avoiding contact with women, was Gavrilo now intending to pursue one? The count pushed his plate away and sat staring moodily at the jasmine heaped in scented profusion on the table. The staff seemed suddenly so anxious to please. How had she taught them, when they had always been so unreceptive previously? What kind of woman was she, this schoolgirl he had bought? How had she managed to change so much in so short a time? The count looked again at his fiancée, catching Valentina's attention as she turned briefly to speak with his sister. For a moment she seemed to assess him. Then, with a shrug and a roguish smile, she continued her conversation with Yekaterina, ignoring the count and his mistress completely.

The main dish was saddle of beef garnished with stuffed red plums, fire-roasted potatoes and candied yams. The count recognized this as an exact copy of a meal he had enjoyed in Romania and about which he had frequently talked with longing. He looked at his sister, wondering how much she had told Valentina about his likes and dislikes. He ordered the meal to be served and complimented the waiter.

"My appreciation to Chef Dubrovsky on this elegant meal."

"Thank you, Excellency."

"The food in our home appears to have improved since your arrival, Valentina Ivanovna."

Valentina replied with her usual candor.

"Since Madame Yekaterina recovered from her illness she has worked miracles, sir. When I first arrived here the food looked like pig swill. Now it is almost Parisian."

The count glanced toward his mistress, who had barely spoken since arriving in the room. Magda was motioning for more wine. Her face was flushed, her neck blotchy with signs of approaching rage. Korolenko's eyes glowed at the thought of the outburst that was imminent. What would the young lady from Paris make of the derision of one as practiced in insult as Magda Simoniescu? As waiters served him more sweet potatoes, the count heard his mistress addressing Valentina.

"That dress is delightfully quaint, my dear, but you must allow me to take you to my own dressmaker in St. Petersburg."

Valentina looked up, her face a mask of puzzlement.

"I'm afraid I don't understand, madame."

"The line of that dress is passé and too old by far for you."

"The line of my dress was designed by the fashion house of Worth, madame. It is in the very latest French line. I brought the designs with me from Paris because I had been told that in Russia you receive the latest fashions one year later than the rest of Europe."

Yekaterina swallowed hard at the enormity of the lie and everyone fell silent. As though nothing were amiss, Valentina turned to the count and began to question him.

"May I ask you, sir, if Madame Yekaterina has told you of our plans for the banqueting hall and the other public rooms of the palace?"

"She has indeed."

"And you approved them, of course."

The count hesitated, unable to resist such a blatant assumption of his good taste.

"I did, mademoiselle."

Valentina thought how thin the count was, how precise his dress, how bony his body. She saw that his eyes were dark gray and not black like Gavrilo's and that there was sadness in them as well as uncertainty. She smiled encouragingly at her husband-to-be.

"When we are married, sir, will I be permitted to help Madame Yekaterina in her efforts to refurbish the entire ground floor of the property?"

"Of course you will. I must admit, the rooms are a trifle dull."

"I am looking forward to making this the most beautiful palace in St. Petersburg."

"You have great confidence in yourself, mademoiselle. I am astounded to find such savoir faire in a schoolgirl."

Stung by the caustic tone of the count's reply, Valentina made an effort to show nothing of her disappointment.

"My confidence stems from the fact that I have the backing of your distinguished name, sir. Your brother and sister are here to advise me when you are away and already I have learned a great deal from them. Gavrilo is going to take me to see your country homes when the weather is warm and I am looking forward to learning the Korolenko family history from him. Madame Yekaterina takes me to St. Petersburg and is teaching me all I need to know to make this house more welcoming. When I first arrived, I must say, I thought it a dowdy place, but now it begins to reflect Madame's recovery."

The count looked at the curls in the nape of Valentina's neck and examined again the curve of her breasts, the fragility of her wrists and the blush of excitement in her cheeks. The violet eyes appraised him and the count realized that this was no child to be manipulated at will. This was a woman used to having her way, unafraid and unwilling to be subjugated by anyone. He looked in wonder as servants appeared with a lemon soufflé. He was amazed that Dubrovsky had been prevailed upon to show the culinary expertise that had once made him the most sought-after chef in the city. For a moment he wished he had not complicated his life with Magda. Then he admitted that it was already too late to enjoy a young girl like Valentina or to hope for the peace of mind that would enable him to do so. He looked with brooding melancholy at his mistress, conscious that she was still beautiful and that he still longed for her. But Magda was drinking too much and of late wine had made her hostile instead of merry.

Valentina examined the count's hands, admiring the long fingers and the carefully manicured nails. Though he looked older than she had expected, he had the manners of a fine gentleman and this reassured her. She looked again at his face and saw wrinkles around the eyes and the mouth. She shook her head, shunning the thought that the count was old enough to be her father.

The count turned again to Valentina.

"I would like to have a private word with you, Valentina Ivanovna. Shall we say at two o'clock in my study?"

"I shall look forward to it, sir."

"And now, if you'll excuse me, I must go and see a friend who is leaving for Moscow."

The count rose and left the room. There was a brief, awkward silence. Then Yekaterina and her friend made their excuses and disappeared, leaving Valentina, Gavrilo and Magda alone. Waiters served fruit liqueurs and wedges of Turkish delight. Gavrilo turned the lightly sugared piece in his fingers, wondering how long it would be before Magda's fury erupted. Suddenly she shouted across the table.

"Have they told you that I am the count's mistress and that I have been the only woman in his life for more than a decade?"

Valentina's face was impassive.

"Of course they have, madame, and I know that while I am too young to be the count's wife he needs a woman of a certain age to satisfy his physical desires."

"And when you marry, what then?"

"Madame, it is not for you to question me about my plans or for me to speculate about the future. When I marry I hope to live happily with my husband in this property. I shall be the true mistress of the Korolenko Palace and any impediment to my happiness will, of course, be removed. You will be welcome to visit us at any time with your husband."

"You appear to know a great deal about me."

"Everyone in St. Petersburg talks about you, madame, and now I have met you I understand why."

Unsure if this was a compliment or an insult, Magda made an effort to control her anger.

"Vladimir Vasilievich loves me. You will never change that and it will haunt every day of your marriage."

Valentina walked to the door.

"You must excuse me, madame. I don't wish to keep the count waiting a second time."

With a mischievous smile, Valentina swept from the room, leaving behind her the lingering scent of jasmine and iris. Gavrilo hurried after her. He was barely out of the room when he heard plates being broken and the voice of the count's mistress calling for more wine. He looked down at Valentina, his eyes alight with amusement.

"Magda is breaking plates. Next she will break glasses and then, if she is not feeling better for having vented her spleen, she will start throwing heavy objects at the count's hunting trophies. You were superb, but I fear you have enraged the lady."

"Madame's face is as red as her hair."

"And her soul is as black as the pits of hell. Never underestimate her, Valentina Ivanovna."

The count's study smelled of kvass, tallow and leather polish. It was dark-walled and gloomy and Valentina entered with some trepidation. Korolenko was at his desk writing a letter. For a while he ignored her and she sat on the settee looking around. There were figures in bronze and ivory on the bureaus and pietra dura tables of fossils, rock quartz and malachite, examples of the count's interest in geology. When at last Korolenko rose to greet her Valentina saw that his eyes were lighter than she had thought, and something in their expression puzzled her. The count offered her a glass of Madeira. Then he sat at her side on the settee. When he spoke, Valentina smiled, because his attitude was that of a schoolmaster with a recalcitrant pupil.

"My reason for marrying you, Valentina Ivanovna, is to produce an heir to the title. I am sorry not to be more romantic about our engagement, but as you know I do not love you and I do not intend to pretend that I do. At this moment, I do not even know if I like you, though I must admit I admire your courage, which borders on the insane. When we are married I shall not live here in the palace; I shall reside instead in my dacha on the island of Yelagin in the River Neva. I shall visit you for three months of each year and will not see you during the other months. Have you any questions to ask me?"

Valentina stifled her angry protests.

"I should like to ask what you intend to do when we have children, sir. Will you also only see your sons for only three months of each year?"

Surprised that she had made no objection to his strange plan, Korolenko hesitated.

"To be honest, I had not thought so far ahead."

"Sons need their fathers, sir, especially sons who will have to be trained in the duties of their heritage. I must be honest and say that at no time will I permit my children to visit or stay with Madame Simoniescu. I understand from Madame Yekaterina that you have strong feelings on family loyalty and will agree with me on this point."

The count poured more wine, eyeing Valentina's expressionless face with increasing admiration.

"Magda is important to me. She understands my needs and caters to them as no wife could."

"I did not realize that there were things that a wife could or would not do to give her husband pleasure, sir."

"That is because you are too innocent to understand."

"I had thought you would teach me how to please you, sir. I should be greatly distressed if you found your marital obligations distressing."

The count's heart thundered with provocation on hearing such direct words. Suddenly ashamed of his unwelcoming attitude, he asked gently, "When is your birthday?"

"I shall be fifteen on the twentieth of May, sir."

"We shall marry next year on your birthday."

"Very well."

"You appear unhappy with the idea, if I may say?"

Valentina knew that her reply would be of the utmost importance and grasping this brief moment of empathy spoke the truth.

"I was very unhappy at being forced to leave Paris and come to Russia, sir. You know the financial situation of my family and no doubt that is one of the reasons why you chose me. When I arrived in this house it was filthy and vermin-ridden. The food was inedible and everything spoke of your absence from and indifference to your home. I was told you were with your mistress on the island of Yelagin. Then, one night when I could not sleep, I went for a walk in the corridor of the garden wing and heard you and Madame Simoniescu arguing about me. I have since learned that you stayed for three days before returning to your dacha. Gavrilo has explained to me that you are besotted with your mistress and that you cannot live without her. After lunch Madame also told me in the most forceful terms what my position here will be. Under the circumstances, sir, I hardly think you can expect me to be happy at the prospect of marrying you. I had hoped to love my husband and to be loved by him. I am not a breeding machine and am not at all happy to be treated as such. However, I have decided to accept my fate because now that my grandmother is dead, it would be very difficult for me to return to Paris. I shall therefore attempt to please you when we are married. I shall not humiliate you in front of your friends and I shall make sure that this house is well run and welcoming. But I shall *never* love you. I could only love a man I respected and I am quite sure I could never respect you."

Korolenko flinched at the defiance in his fiancée's tone. Valentina continued calmly, without hesitation.

"One more thing, sir. When we are married, I expect that you will keep Madame Simoniescu and *all* your mutual friends out of this house. That is my position. Now it is for you to decide whether you still wish to marry me or whether you would prefer to send me back to Paris with sufficient compensation for the inconveniences and expenses incurred in my journey."

The count drew Valentina toward him.

"I intend to keep you, Valentina, and I would like to seal our bargain with a kiss."

Before Valentina could protest, the count kissed her on the lips, thrusting into her mouth and holding her body so hard against his own she could barely breathe. She closed her eyes, trying not to succumb to the strange emotions the unexpected kiss provoked. Then, suddenly, the count rose and with a curt nod dismissed her.

"I invite you to dine with me tonight at eight, my dear. Be so kind as to come to my private suite on time."

Valentina struggled to be calm but her hands were trembling and she could not collect her thoughts. She kept reminding herself that the count detested innocence, but she could not conceal her inexperience from him. When she reached the door she felt his eyes on hers and she blushed with embarrassment.

"I will come at eight, sir. May I ask if we shall be alone?"

"Of course we shall."

"Then I look forward to it, sir."

For an hour the count sat at his desk fingering the samples of rock, ore and precious stones collected over the past decades. A piece of pink marble that looked warm and inviting was icy to the touch because its hardness could not absorb the heat of the hand. A large pearl, pale and lustrous, seemed cold and forbidding until held firmly. Then its glow increased and its coldness diminished. The marble reminded the count of Magda, whose heat was superficial and whose heart was like stone. The pearl was Valentina, warm and enticing when ignited by the touch. Longing to be alone with his thoughts, the count strode down a private stairway and out to the stables. Minutes later he was riding in the forest, relieved to have left his possessive mistress behind.

In her private suite Magda waited in vain for her lover to appear. By four o'clock she was screaming for information as to Korolenko's whereabouts. By five she had passed out from drinking too much vodka. By six her condition was known to Yekaterina, who ordered champagne to celebrate her enemy's distress. News of what had happened spread like wildfire through the palace and the staff gossiped feverishly, placing bets on the outcome of the affair. In the kitchen Dubrovsky was beaming with triumph. The end of the Simoniescu era was surely imminent.

At eight Valentina appeared in the count's private dining room. She was dressed in the pink ball gown she had worn in Paris, with two white doves of peace swooping from the shoulder. In her hair there were a dozen diamond stars, a gift from Yekaterina. The count bowed formally when she entered the room.

"You look very beautiful, mademoiselle."

"Thank you, sir."

"This afternoon I went to my hunting grounds. Are you interested in hunting?"

"No, sir."

"Tell me about your interests."

"I like arranging houses, visiting shops, riding horses, skating and visiting exhibitions of antiquity. I am also a very good bicyclist."

"Are you interested in geology?"

"I am interested in archaeology, which is not quite the same, I know. I went four times to the exhibition of Egyptology and five times to the chinoiserie display which was held in Paris last season."

As dinner was served, the count looked curiously at the servants, conscious that even the most rebellious glanced constantly at Valentina, as though anxious to please her. He was impressed by the gold-edged menu: soupe aux truffes, escalope de saumon à l'oseille, canard à l'orange, les petites salades, fromages, bombe-Valentina. A white burgundy was served with the salmon. Then, as the meal progressed, a Château-Margaux, a Morey-St.-Denis, a champagne Roederer and a Grand-Bas-Armagnac-Laberdolive. For the first time in months the count enjoyed his food and the luxury of being master of his own home. Raising an eyebrow, he looked across the table to his fiancée.

"I must admit, mademoiselle, that this is much more enjoyable than the pig swill that I usually eat. Also my cellar seems to have acquired some fine French wines."

"Most of the wines were already there, sir, but the cellar was badly arranged."

"So you rearranged it?"

"Madame Yekaterina and I suggested ways of making it easier to operate."

"Yekaterina Vasilievna couldn't organize a fly to settle on cream. She has been promising to train the servants for twenty years, but as she cannot concentrate on anything for more than an hour she has been eminently unsuccessful."

"I am aware of that, sir, but I prefer to give Madame credit for doing these things because without her I could do nothing."

"You are a very clever young woman, Valentina Ivanovna."

"If I were clever I should not be here, sir. I should be married with a beautiful house in the Bois de Boulogne in Paris, which has always been my ambition. I should be a fashionable lady with a salon of repute. Indeed, I am not at all clever."

The count listened as Valentina told him of her life. Then, in the firelight glow, they roasted chestnuts, burning their fingers as they tried to eat the smoky remains. Tasting the acrid flavor, the count remembered the summers of his youth, when he had visited the country at harvest time and eaten with peasant workers on his grandfather's estate.

"The last time I ate something like this was when I was twelve. It was in the country, where my father had inherited his father's house."

"Was it a farm?"

"No, it was a house with one hundred and fifty bedrooms, an ornamental lake, a stable for one hundred horses and many thousands of acres of land. When I was a child I preferred the house of the estate manager, where they lit a fire in the field and roasted rabbits and potatoes for dinner."

"Will Gavrilo take me there when he shows me your other houses?"

"I imagine so. The property is only fifteen versts from St. Petersburg. It has not been opened since my father died many years ago. I could not bear to go there and find it decayed."

Before leaving, Valentina played a lullaby on the count's piano and for a few moments he felt so tranquil he forgot everything. She rose and took her leave.

"I shall retire now, sir. I am grateful to you for allowing me to be alone with you. I have so enjoyed our evening together."

The count accompanied Valentina through the dark, drafty corridors to her suite. In the gallery they paused before the portrait of Magda and Valentina whispered irreverently.

"One day I intend to draw a large black mustache on that portrait."

The count looked enigmatically into her eyes.

"One day, mademoiselle, I may let you."

At the door of the salon, Korolenko withdrew. Valentina watched until he had disappeared. Then she ran inside and told Miss Knatchbull that the meal had been perfect and the count a perfect host. Miss Knatchbull went to bed exhausted by the tensions of the day. Valentina looked thoughtfully into the fire as the clock chimed twelve and the wind rose to a howling lament. Then, suddenly tired, she lit an extra candle and went to her bedroom. For a long time she lay awake, thinking of the events of the night, of the things the count had told her of his childhood, his parents, his travels around Europe. He had been polite, watchful and curious, but his real feelings were impossible to define. Everything about the count seemed mysterious and beyond her comprehension, and when Valentina tried to analyze her own feelings for the count, she could not. The truth was she neither liked nor disliked her fiancé. Only when he had told her that he might let her draw a mustache on Magda's portrait had she felt attuned to his inner longings.

In the small hours Valentina woke with the feeling that she was not alone. The lace curtains were fluttering and she realized that the windows were open. Near the door something gleamed silver. Struggling to focus her eyes, Valentina saw that an intruder was approaching the bed carrying a pair of shearing scissors. A smell of stale alcohol lingered in the air, making her think of the count's mistress. Then she found her hair grasped, the scissors were raised and she knew that this *was* Magda and that the jealous woman intended to cut off her hair. With one leap Valentina was out of bed, her agility surprising the count's mistress. She shivered as Magda whispered into the darkness.

"Everyone in the house is asleep. I am much stronger than you, so you will gain nothing by screaming. By the time your governess arouses herself your hair will be on the floor and I shall be far away from this accursed house."

Valentina took her wrap from the chair, stumbling in the darkness as she tried to elude the advancing figure. She pushed Magda away and ran to the door, but it was locked and she knew her attacker would have taken the key. She tried to reach the other door that led to the passageway and Miss Knatchbull's room, but Magda grasped her and threw her down on the bed. Valentina screamed as she felt Magda hacking at her hair and ringlets falling over her face. Then, with all the strength she could find, she hurled the enraged woman away and ran to the window, holding her breath briefly before leaping out into the snow.

When Miss Knatchbull entered the room with the three maids, Magda was still standing at the window, staring in disbelief at the moonlit emptiness beyond. Valentina's governess looked at the scissors in Magda's hand and the ringlets on the floor. Then she roared at the count's mistress.

"Where is Mademoiselle?"

"Find her if you can."

Miss Knatchbull turned to Zita.

"Go and find the count. Tell him to come at once; there has been a calamity."

Magda smiled derisively as Miss Knatchbull snatched the scissors from her hand and demanded to know about her charge.

"I will ask you once again, madame, where is Valentina?"

"Then what will you do, report me to my lover?"

Miss Knatchbull's mouth tightened into a hard line.

"Then I shall simply beat you senseless, madame, and I warn you, I am losing my patience."

Magda remained resolutely silent. With a sigh Miss Knatchbull told the two maids to wait for her in the salon. When they had gone, she slapped the count's mistress on one cheek and then the other, cutting her lip so blood trickled down her neck.

"Are you going to tell me what you have done to Valentina?"

Magda snatched the scissors and lunged at Miss Knatchbull, who stepped aside and smashed her fist into the courtesan's face. Blood poured from Magda's nose and she shouted defiantly.

"She's out there somewhere, and don't think I pushed her, because I didn't. She ran to the window and jumped. She's mad, like everyone else in this house."

Magda ran from the room and Miss Knatchbull ran to the window and stood looking in horror at the scene below. She was still at the window when the count appeared. His face paled when he saw the blood, the scissors and the strands of silver hair.

"What is the meaning of this, Miss Knatchbull?"

"Your strumpet has attacked Valentina. I do not know how Madame Simoniescu entered these rooms, but she brought with her some scissors with which to cut off the child's hair. To escape the attack, it seems that Valentina jumped from the window. You are responsible for all this, sir. You are totally and utterly responsible."

The count ordered Zita to bring the doctor. Then he urged Miss Knatchbull to follow him while he searched for the injured girl. Within minutes they found Valentina lying at the bottom of a snowdrift. With frozen hands they worked frantically to free her. With profound relief the count turned to Miss Knatchbull.

"I can feel no broken bones, unless her skull is shattered. Help me carry her inside or we shall all freeze to death."

Miss Knatchbull took Valentina's shoulders, the count her feet and together they hurried back to the house. Gavrilo was waiting in the drawing room as they put the unconscious girl down on the sofa. He threw logs on the fire and ran to bring blankets from a chest in the hall, returning to stand helplessly by as Miss Knatchbull rubbed Valentina's hands. The Englishwoman spoke as though no longer aware that she was not alone with her charge.

"Come, child, say something to Natty. Please say something. You can't stay unconscious forever. Do say *something*, anything, my dear."

Tears ran down the Englishwoman's face and she forgot about the count and his brother. Gavrilo turned furiously on Korolenko.

"What in God's name has happened?"

"Magda attacked Mademoiselle and tried to cut off her hair. In order to escape the child jumped from the window of her room."

"Now will you send Magda away?"

"She has already left the palace."

"No doubt she has fled to Yelagin, where you will join her within the week. I wish I could tell you how much I despise you."

"I am how I am. You are fortunate to be so virtuous."

The count looked down at the slim body in the nightdress soaked with water and thought how lovely his fiancée was. Then he examined the front of Valentina's head, where Magda had cut off the hair. He smiled. The wisps were curling as they dried, giving her a gamin look which pleased the count more than he wished to admit.

When the doctor arrived the two men stepped outside to the hall to wait impatiently for his verdict. After what seemed like an age, Petrovsky called them in.

"How did this young lady come to be injured?"

The count remained silent, so the doctor looked at Gavrilo, who replied guarding his words for fear of a scandal.

"This is my brother's fiancée. She was attacked in her room during the night and we think she leaped from her bedroom window to escape the attacker. We do not yet know who is responsible."

"Well, sir, the young lady has no broken bones but she has taken a serious blow to the head and a chill from which she may not recover. I have not yet been able to rouse her and it is impossible to say when she will recover her wits."

The count interrupted.

"What are the chances of Mademoiselle living?"

"I do not know, sir. For the moment she must be put to bed and kept warm. She must not be left alone at any time of the day or night. I will call again tomorrow and each day until there is some change in her condition."

Within the hour Valentina was lying in bed surrounded by pillows, blankets and hot stones. A crackling fire lit the room and Miss Knatchbull sat nearby guarding her. The three maids had been told to go back to bed, but they were stunned by the events of the night and unable to sleep. In the small hours they lingered in the salon, listening at the bedroom door and making tea for Miss Knatchbull to ease her distress. And all the while Valentina slept, unaware of what was going on around her.

In the drawing room Gavrilo was alone. He had decided to ask his brother to release Valentina from her engagement so *he* could propose to her, if she recovered. The count's only reason for bringing the girl from Paris had been to provide an heir to the Korolenko title. Gavrilo reasoned that it was best that he marry Valentina because he loved her. The count cared only for Magda. What difference would it make to him? An heir was what the count wanted, and an heir he would surely have.

Magda was in her carriage en route to the island of Yelagin. The events of the night had been exciting, but Miss Knatchbull had hurt her badly. Magda thought of Valentina Ivanovna and shrugged. If the girl was not already dead she soon would be. She had already decided what to do about her rival. All she needed was Pirogov's help. He would know how to make the death seem like an accident. She must leave the details of how the "accident" happened to him. As for the count, if by any chance he did not return with his usual speed she would show him the error of his ways. Over the previous decade Magda had learned many compromising details of her lover's political affairs and these she now considered, knowing she would not hesitate to use what she knew against him. Suddenly she felt confident. She would remain mistress of Vladimir Vasilievich Korolenko or know the reason why.

The count was pacing his study. On the wall above him a portrait of his father looked sternly down and he remembered how he had respected the tall bearded figure for his wisdom. Would *his* son respect him? Would there even be a son? Or would he live eternally in the underworld of his desire for Magda Simoniescu? As the pale-yellow light of dawn appeared on the horizon, the count hurried to Valentina's suite and walked through the salon to the bedroom. While Miss Knatchbull dozed in the chair he stood looking down at his fiancée's feverish face. A purple bruise had formed on Valentina's chin, another on her shoulder and her forehead was severely swollen from the fall. For a long time Korolenko stood watching as she slept. Then, gently, he touched her hand, entwining it in his own. When he had kissed each of her fingers he walked outside to the stable and rode swiftly away.

## CHAPTER THREE

### The Flower House, Spring 1901

———————————

The dark days of winter were over and spring, the shortest season of the year in Russia, had burst on the scene, melting the snow and causing floods. Blossoms brightened the tree branches and everywhere people were emerging from the winter confinement in their homes. Within two weeks spring would give way with dramatic swiftness to the hazy days of summer. Already birds were singing joyfully in the trees, bees buzzing in the cherry blossoms and sunlight filtering through the crusty lace curtains at every window.

Valentina had recovered from her fall and the pneumonia that followed it, but the illness had left her listless and unable to take an interest in anything. She spent her days walking in the garden of the palace with Miss Knatchbull or sipping beef tea under the sympathetic gaze of Yekaterina. Often she sat at her window, looking wistfully at the woods, trying not to dwell on the fact that her future husband was still on Yelagin with his mistress.

Miss Knatchbull had been certain that the advent of spring would bring about a change in Valentina's disposition. She was therefore distressed when her charge remained a shadow of her former self. Sometimes she tried to provoke the girl into anger. Sometimes she encouraged her to make plans for the future, plans that included an annual trip to Paris. Sadly, the accident and its aftermath had robbed Valentina of her spirit, and despite all her governess's efforts she remained subdued and silent. In desperation Miss Knatchbull consulted Yekaterina.

At Yekaterina's instigation new clothes were ordered and Valentina was taken to her favorite shops and given permission to commence work on the restoration of the ground floor of the palace.

She worked hard, but it was obvious to everyone that her heart was not in her task. Miss Knatchbull shook her head wearily. Was the child ever going to recover from the accumulation of shock and depression that the fall had released? Would Valentina's continuing debility prevent her from surmounting the obstacles ahead? Was she going to remain forever deep in thought, a phantom presence seemingly disinterested in everything around her?

It was Gavrilo who unwittingly brought Valentina back to life. On a late-spring morning he came to her room dressed in traveling clothes. His first question surprised her.

"Are you ready, my dear?"

"Where are we going, sir?"

"We are going to the country. I am taking you to our country house, the one that lies on the road to Tsarskoye Selo. If you remember, I promised to show you all the count's properties when you first came to St. Petersburg. Miss Knatchbull says you are well enough to travel so I insist that you accompany me. If we don't go at once you will not see the countryside in spring. You know how quickly our spring passes. Hurry and dress, Valentina Ivanovna, I will be waiting in the courtyard."

Valentina rang for Zita.

"Prepare my country clothes and pack a bag for me, please. And Zita, tell Natty I am going to the country with the count's brother."

"Miss Knatchbull already knows, ma'am. She told me to tell you she had packed everything you'll need and Chef Dubrovsky's made you a picnic."

Valentina opened the window and breathed in the heavy atmosphere of St. Petersburg. It would be lovely to visit the country and be free for a few hours. She chose a pink dress and bonnet covered in daisies. Pinching her cheeks to hide the paleness of her skin, she looked in the mirror at her reflection. Miss Knatchbull appeared as she was putting on her hat.

"My dear, if you like the house in the country, why don't you ask Gavrilo if you can remain there for a few days? He is taking you by carriage in order that you can see the countryside. If you should decide to, send the groom back to St. Petersburg on the train to fetch me and the girls. I shall come at once, have no fear. We won't need any other servants. I am sick to death of them being under my feet all the time."

Valentina sat in the carriage, looking out at the Russian country-side. The scene was unchanging, flat fields as far as the eye could see, the monotony broken only by an occasional church or wind-mill. The churches were built of wood and colored red and green and gold. The few houses she saw were dowdy, the villages pa-thetic, but the people seemed happy and were friendly toward strangers. Valentina turned to Gavrilo.

"How long will it be before we arrive at the count's house?"

"About one hour."

"I am so glad you remembered your promise, Gavrilo. It will be wonderful to be in the country. I've been so very tired since my ill-ness. I fear the air of St. Petersburg does not suit me."

"The climate of St. Petersburg suits no one. The site is one of the worst places in the world, well known for its inclement weather and humidity. For many the worst time of the year is the autumn, when damaging floods occur. For me the summer is as bad. Every ceiling will be black with flies and breathing will be a penance. Over the years I have come to dread it."

"I shall gauze the windows in my room to avoid the flies."

"I have no doubt you will arrange everything."

They paused on the banks of a river to eat the picnic lunch. Valentina felt increasingly happy to be away from the palace and the watchful gaze of the servants. When the coachman and grooms had disappeared with fishing rods, Gavrilo handed her a glass of champagne and one of the salmon patties Dubrovsky had made be-cause he knew they were her favorites. She looked through the branches of a willow tree to a stretch of river busy with mayflies. Now and then a fish surfaced to catch a fly. Then the water re-turned to its mirrorlike smoothness. In the distance a cuckoo called and everywhere there were the sounds of the countryside, farm-workers singing, pigeons cooing and the gentle ripple of water on pebbles. Valentina lay back on the grass and closed her eyes, think-ing of nothing but the beauty of the moment.

Gavrilo looked down at her, thinking how much he loved her and how he could barely resist blurting out his secret. He decided to confide what he had done.

"Yesterday I went to Yelagin and spoke with my brother about you."

Valentina sat up and looked questioningly at him.

"Why did you speak to the count? You told me you never communicated with him unless it was strictly necessary."

"It was strictly necessary. I asked my brother to release you from your engagement so you could marry me. I am in love with you, Valentina Ivanovna. I cannot bear to think of you being forced to marry the count."

Valentina bit her lip uncertainly. Until now Gavrilo had been her friend, a pillar of consideration between her and his brother. In proclaiming his love he had placed himself in the same category as the count, as an unwanted suitor and yet another man she did not love. Valentina sighed despondently.

"I had no idea of your intentions, sir."

"Vladimir refused me. He would give no reason other than that you were his and no one else's. I cannot imagine why he insists on carrying on with this charade. He lives on Yelagin with Magda for most of the year. He adores her and has known no other woman but her for many years. Why then would he not release you? I have never understood my brother!"

Valentina lay back on the bank and stared dreamily through the branches to the sun. She was pleased that the count had refused to relinquish her. If he was reluctant to let her go he must have some feeling for her, even if he was still bound to Magda. She wondered why she could not love Gavrilo, who had expressed his own admiration for her. He was good and kind and considerate, everything most women wanted in a husband. She shook her head. Marriage to Gavrilo would be boring, with each day the same as the day before and the day to come. Marriage with Korolenko would be uncertain but exciting, unnerving and perhaps heartbreaking. Unable to understand the perversity of her own inclinations, Valentina turned again to Gavrilo.

"I should like to visit Yelagin."

When he did not reply, she persisted.

"You said you would show me *all* the Korolenko properties. When we have visited this house and the hunting lodge in its grounds can we go to Yelagin? We will have to leave the property at Narva until the last because it is very far away."

"Do you plan to pay my brother a visit on Yelagin?"

"I have no wish to visit the count or his mistress. I shall content myself with seeing his house and visiting the island, which they say is very beautiful."

"Very well, I shall arrange it."

They walked back to the coach and Gavrilo rang a bell to summon the driver. The man appeared with a string of fish and they drove away along a dusty road, past rich brown fields worked by peasants in red-cotton smocks. The farther away from St. Petersburg she traveled the more relaxed Valentina became, and soon, to Gavrilo's relief, her cheeks turned pink and she began to chatter as she had done before her illness.

A few miles farther on they turned a sharp bend and came to a halt. The coachman stepped down and ran to open the iron gates of a country property hidden from the road by trees. The drive, screened by yew hedges, wound around and about like the path through a maze. Then, as they turned the final curve, Valentina saw ahead an ornamental lake surrounded by acacia and maple trees. Behind the lake there was an old house of faded pink and yellow, with bell towers and window shutters like mansions in the South of France. The paint was peeling and in one of the upstairs rooms a window rocked on its hinges. Gavrilo called the coachman to halt and Valentina smiled. She was thinking that the house was as neglected as she, just like all the other count's possessions. She gazed at a blue-winged bird perched on a yellow water lily and then at a flock of scarlet butterflies settling on the bushes at the edge of the lawn. How beautiful it was, how utterly, perfectly beautiful.

Watching her, Gavrilo thought resignedly, Valentina has fallen in love at last, but not with me, only with this house. At the entrance he took out an iron key and handed it to her, amused by her impatience as she turned the key and rushed inside.

The interior was unlike anything Valentina had seen before. The hall was primrose and gold, the floor amber-veined marble. The ceiling was painted with flowers, giving the impression of an interior garden. She walked to the receiving room, where flowers again predominated. Then she turned to Gavrilo and clasped his hand.

"This is a beautiful house, a house full of flowers, and I love it dearly."

"My grandfather designed the house to please his wife, who

loathed Russian formality. Madame was English and she insisted that every room in the house be given the theme of a flower growing on the estate. The hall has primroses, this room lilies, another has roses and the bedrooms have lilac, violets, jasmine and every plant, fern and shrub you could imagine. Sadly the property has fallen into disrepair and now no one ever comes here. My brother has not been since our father died, though once he adored the place. There is a woman living in the servants' quarters whose name is Clara. She is old now and deaf and has obviously neglected her tasks. Perhaps she has become senile, who can tell?"

"I should like to stay here for a few days. Will you instruct the coachman to return to the city to bring Miss Knatchbull and my maids?"

"But there are no servants in the house except the gardeners who come in daily from the village and the old woman I mentioned, who is useless."

"I don't need servants. At home in Paris we only had one."

"But what will you eat?"

"Natty will bring food and changes of clothing and bedding. You may return in the coach if you feel unhappy to stay here with me, Gavrilo."

"My brother would be furious if he thought I had stayed the night in this house with you. I had best return at once to St. Petersburg. Is there anything else you want Miss Knatchbull to bring?"

"I should like to have the count's permission to use this house as my own. He has his dacha on Yelagin. I intend to use this property. We can meet and carry out our official duties in St. Petersburg, but this will be my real home, the place where my children can live."

Gavrilo sighed wearily.

"You had best do as you wish without asking my brother's permission, for he will certainly refuse you."

"Then I shall ask Madame Yekaterina if I can come here in secret."

"It's true my sister likes secrets. I will ask her permission on your behalf when I return to the palace."

"And will you order the ratcatcher and fumigator to come here from St. Petersburg."

"Very well, my dear. Now I had best show you around and introduce you to Clara. First, though, come upstairs and choose a room for yourself and one for Miss Knatchbull."

Valentina chose a guest suite of eleven rooms for herself and Miss Knatchbull. The suite included a kitchen and pantry with maids' bedrooms, laundry rooms and a storeroom with walnut shelves. When Gavrilo had gone she opened the windows and listened to the sound of the birds singing. The quality of light was quite different from that in St. Petersburg and the scene had the golden glow of an old painting. The air was clean and invigorating, not enervating like the air of the capital. Valentina threw herself down on the bed and smiled at the ceiling that was painted with violets. The room was much smaller than was usual in stately Russian homes, and in the corner there was a stove in which a fire could be lit. Valentina began to look forward eagerly to seeing its glow warming the forlorn interior.

When she had rested Valentina wandered through the other rooms on the first floor of the house, frowning at the dust on every surface and the sun-faded brocade of the main suite. When she reached the tower room, she found she could see for miles in every direction over the chestnut trees to the farmlands beyond, all of them owned by the count. In the far distance peasant workers were walking behind a cart piled high with earth. Brown rivers flowed by brown fields and the sky was gold with the advent of summer. Valentina was about to return to her room when a glint of silver caught her eye and she realized that someone was riding on the road near the house. Craning to look out of the window, she saw a man on a fine black horse, his sword glinting in the sun. He was wearing a dark-green uniform. Curious, she waited until the rider drew nearer, but instead of riding past the property he disappeared around the periphery and was hidden by the trees. Shrugging, Valentina ran downstairs to wait for Miss Knatchbull's arrival.

By early evening she was hungry. It was colder inside the house than out, so Valentina took the picnic hamper to the lakeside and ate what remained of the food. She was drinking a glass of wine and watching the sun set when she heard the sound of horses' hooves. Believing it to be Miss Knatchbull arriving, she ran through the trees toward the drive in time to see two young men riding by. To her astonishment, they were talking about her.

"I don't see how this young lady can have had such an effect on you if you have not even met her. Anyone who is going to marry Count Korolenko is *quite* unlikely to suit you, Vanya."

"She's the most beautiful creature in the world, Grisha. I have been following her around like a lapdog ever since that first moment when I saw her."

"And what does she say about that?"

"She doesn't know, of course."

"You need a holiday, my friend. You've been working too hard."

"Dammit, my horse has gone lame."

Valentina watched from the cover of the trees as Yanin stepped down and examined his horse's foot. She weighed his appearance closely, trying not to faint from the violence of the excitement she was feeling. Yanin's face was nut-brown from the sun. His hair was black and curly like that of a gypsy. His teeth flashed white and there was laughter and challenge in his gaze. Valentina drew back, terrified of being discovered. Yanin's companion stepped down and together they argued over what should be done about the horse. Then, with a shrug, Yanin led his mount back in the direction from which he had come. Valentina saw distress in the amber-gold eyes and had a sudden desire to rush out and comfort the gallant young officer. Instead she watched as he retreated into the trees. How long his legs were, how wide the shoulders, how strong the line of the chin. She thought of his mustache and the boldness of his stride. Then she ran back to the terrace and poured herself another glass of wine. What effrontery Yanin and Dolgurov had had to trespass on the count's land. What style too, in their green, red and gold uniforms. Had Yanin really been following her everywhere since that first moment when their eyes had met? Ivan Grigorevich Yanin was handsome and bold, young and strong, with all the confidence of youth. Valentina thought him as unlike Korolenko as an eagle was a swan. She began to fan her face with a fern leaf, nonplussed by the heat of her body and the strange thoughts careering through her mind. Darkness fell and the air became noisy with the sound of crickets. Valentina thought the place as near to paradise as any in the world. She watched the swans on the lake, one following the other, as Yanin had been following her. How exciting it was! How suddenly, miraculously perfect!

An hour later Miss Knatchbull arrived with the maids and two odd-job men. She brought with her food, gauze for the windows, clothes, wine, cleaning materials and bed linen. As she looked down at Valentina, Miss Knatchbull wondered how the country air had done its work so quickly.

"Here we are, my dear, is anyone else here?"

"Only an old woman who was supposed to keep the house aired. She hasn't done a very good job from what I've seen."

"Well, I must prepare the rooms."

"They're dusty but clean. I haven't seen a mouse since I arrived."

The next morning Valentina woke to the sound of farm carts crunching along the lane. She jumped out of bed, ran to the window and looked out on the garden and the fields beyond. When she had admired the scene, she went to the kitchen and asked Zita for a cup of hot chocolate. Then she put on a wrap and ran out to the garden to pick all the flowers she could carry. Turning back toward the entrance of the house, she saw Miss Knatchbull watching.

"Whatever am I to do with you, child? Your lungs are only just recovered from the congestion and now you run around half dressed in the open air."

"I'm so happy, Natty. Everything seems quite different in the country, and I feel different, too."

"It's a pity we can't live here instead of in the city. I can't bear St. Petersburg. Until I arrived at this house I felt as if I hadn't smelled a breath of fresh air for months."

"I intend to restore the house and use it as the count uses his dacha on Yelagin."

Miss Knatchbull stared openmouthed at the statement.

"Count Korolenko will surely refuse to give his permission, so don't build up your hopes. Men of his age can be very jealous of their young wives. He won't agree to your coming here alone."

"I shall ask Madame Yekaterina and not him."

Miss Knatchbull pursed her lips and swung her parasol.

"Good idea, child. She's sure to agree to whatever will make you happy. We'll just have to keep our visits here a secret for as long as we can, though God knows there aren't many secrets in that barn of a house. You know, whenever I am in the Korolenko Palace I feel someone is watching me. I have never felt it before in all my forty years."

For breakfast they ate fresh eggs brought by Clara, the elderly caretaker. Delighted to have company, the old lady ordered the gardeners to go out and fish for trout to be cooked fresh from the lake and served in the garden under rose-silk umbrellas. Valentina ate as she had not eaten for months and slept as she had not slept for weeks. In the afternoons, while Miss Knatchbull was fishing, Valentina borrowed a horse and rode around the estate, learning all she could about it. On the second day she discovered a shooting lodge on the eastern boundary of the land. On the third day she examined the interior, a carved bed covered with patchwork, a writing table, some shelves of books and a locked cupboard full of rifles. On the fourth day Valentina found a group of workers' cottages near the fields where corn was planted. She paused to speak with the workers and was given a true Russian welcome.

On her final night in the country, Valentina returned to the workers' cottages and ate dinner with them in the field. The food was cooked on the fire, as it had been in the count's childhood. Baked potatoes swimming in butter, fire-roasted rabbit and wild duck were offered and enjoyed. Valentina listened as the estate workers told their stories of past times, smiling at their opinions and retaining every word because she felt instinctively that that new knowledge would bring her nearer the man she was going to marry. An old woman handed her more meat and spoke in a tremulous voice.

"Best not tell His Excellency that you came here. He believes that his title makes him different from other people and he would be displeased if he knew you had met us. It was not always so. Once, when the count was eight, he begged me to let him come and live in my cottage. The parents ignored those two boys, you know. Gavrilo had many friends, so the situation did not perturb him, but young Vladimir was always alone. It's different now, of course: when last the count visited the house he did not even ride in our direction."

In the dawn hours Valentina lay in bed, thinking of all she had been told. The count was an autocrat, who believed himself omnipotent in the eyes of his workers. The Tsar also considered himself omnipotent and was worshiped by many as a deity. Despite her elevated birth, Valentina had been raised in Paris in near-poverty. Her friends had been the children of neighbors, despite her grandmother's dismay at such lowly associations. Valentina knew in her heart that the past had made it possible for her to understand, in a way her fiancé never would, the people who would work for him all their lives. This ability would cause a rift, if it became known to the count, and she resolved to keep her opinions secret. During the count's visits to the capital she would be the perfect wife and hostess. In her own time, however, when the dampness of St. Petersburg weighed too heavily on her mind, she would come to the Flower House and be happy in her own way.

On her return to the palace Valentina was greeted by Yekaterina and hurried away to her private rooms.

"My dear, I'm half dead with curiosity to know what you plan for that house. When you have finished the restoration I shall accompany you there on a visit."

Yekaterina took out a tissue-wrapped package and handed it to Valentina.

"I bought you this during your absence, which seemed like five months and not five days. I had to occupy myself to make sure I should not miss you too much."

Opening the box, Valentina saw inside a necklace of sapphires. She kissed Yekaterina's cheek.

"Thank you for being my friend, madame."

"Now you are back and feeling better, I hope you and I can proceed with the restoration of the receiving rooms of this house."

"Of course we shall. After dinner I shall bring you the sketches I did while in the country. They show how the rooms will look when we finish them."

"Gavrilo tells me that he is taking you to Yelagin."

"Do you disapprove of my desire to go there?"

"Of course not. You will be chaperoned by my brother and you have as much right to go there as anyone."

For weeks the two women worked with scores of workmen and decorators on the receiving rooms of the palace. Valentina had decided that as these were the first rooms visitors would see they should look as one expected rooms of a palace to look. The flowery decor of the house in the country was perfect for its situation. The palace, however, was a massive stone edifice to money and power and she knew it must astound and impress. The receiving room, ballroom and formal dining room were stripped of their moose-antler chandeliers and paintings by Murillo, Canaletto and Rubens replaced the hunting prints and stuffed animal heads. The with-drawing room was fitted with cabinets designed to hold the count's jewel and gem collection. Rubies and emeralds were piled on shelves and the count's rare green diamond placed in a position of great prominence. Finally a bowl of pearls was displayed under glass. The pearls were lustrous and there were so many they overflowed the bowl onto the white velvet of the shelves. Valentina was satisfied that the snobbish society matrons of St. Petersburg would be impressed. She had been told that the rich who lived in the capital were interested only in money, gossip and adultery. Now they would have something new to discuss and that would be Vladimir Vasilievich Korolenko's wealth and the flair of his fiancée. She looked around at satin walls shimmering in the light of the new crystal chandeliers. It was well done. Even the count would think it perfection.

The staff gasped when they were shown the white receiving room, the all-gold ballroom and the reception hall walled in mir-rors. Some chattered excitedly as they crowded around the display cabinets, and everyone agreed that the transformation was nothing short of a miracle. Valentina and Yekaterina were content.

When Gavrilo called for Valentina in readiness for their trip to Yelagin, he found her dressed in white, with a bonnet of cornflowers and rosebuds.

"You look beautiful, as always. If Magda hears about your visit she will break every glass in the dacha so the count will have to drink from the wine bottles."

"I hope she does hear and that your brother will tire of her tan-trums. May I ask what your plans are for the day?"

"We shall leave at once and travel to the dockside. Instead of going by coach to Yelagin, crossing the bridge in the usual way, we shall travel by my cousin's yacht. Once there, we shall watch the sailing races. Then I will take you for a drive to show you some of the houses, including my brother's. We shall dine with my cousin Viktor and his wife. Everything has been arranged. You need not worry, Valentina."

The quayside of Yelagin was lined with yacht berths and expen-sive restaurants. Valentina thought the place charming, its atmo-sphere more akin to Paris than to St. Petersburg. When they had watched the yacht race and shared a glass of champagne with the winners, she stepped inside the coach and was driven away. The sun was shining brightly and she noticed that Gavrilo had ordered pink carnations to be threaded in the horses' bridles. She told him how much she was enjoying her visit to the island and how she admired its scenery. Pleased, Gavrilo began to point out some of the places of interest.

"That is the dacha of the Grand Duke Sergei and the one nearby belongs to Count Kokovtsov."

Valentina was disappointed by the formality of the houses. They continued toward a patch of woodland and she saw ahead a neoclassical villa surrounded by trees. Gavrilo urged the coachman to hurry.

"That, my dear Valya, is where the count and Magda live when they are not in St. Petersburg."

Valentina eyed the Doric columns and the stark grayness of the house. There were no flowers in the garden, only funereal Lombardy poplars that formed a path to the entrance. She looked back as the coachman urged the horses on and for a moment imagined she saw Magda watching from an upstairs window. Around the next bend, a forest of oak and aspen hid another group of villas. Seeing Gavrilo looking uneasy, Valentina began to question him.

"To whom do those houses belong?"

"They are owned by the rich and used as places of assignation."

"Why are they hidden from the road?"

"They are placed out of sight because the women who go there are strumpets and actresses from the theater. You should not ask about such things. You are too young to know about the darker side of life."

Amused by her companion's discomfort, Valentina thought that Gavrilo was as different from his brother as chalk from cheese. The count adored the corrupt, the bizarre, the decadent. Gavrilo despised all three but had no alternative interest in life. Looking at him, she thought how unkind she was being. He was a good friend. What more could she ask? Suddenly her mind turned again to Ivan Grigorevich Yanin and she recalled how he had talked of following her everywhere she went. She looked back to see if he was following her on the island but there was only an empty road. She shivered as she remembered Yanin's tawny eyes that were challenging in a way she had never seen before. She admired the memory of his muscular soldier's body and the determination in his manner. Blushing at her thoughts, she turned to Gavrilo and tried to take her mind off Yanin by discussing her surroundings.

Valentina and Gavrilo wandered around the island until sunset, enjoying the smell of the sea and the subtle scent of the wild flowers. At dusk lights were lit in the restaurants along the quayside and storm lanterns along the harbor's edge. She followed Gavrilo into his cousin's house and was introduced to Viktor's wife, Ducha.

"Welcome to Yelagin, my dear. We have all been longing to meet you. I shall go and fetch my husband at once."

Valentina looked around the room, which was full of objects collected by the couple on their travels. There was barely room to sit and hardly enough light to see. She wondered why electricity was still unusual in St. Petersburg when Parisians were already becoming blasé about it. At that moment Viktor entered the room and greeted her.

"I am enchanted to meet you, Valentina Ivanovna. Gavrilo, welcome to our home."

Pleased by the warmth of her welcome, Valentina was unperturbed when Viktor explained that they would have to eat out.

"Our servants disappeared yesterday and I have no idea where they have gone. They had the audacity to ask for more money. For decades I have fed them, clothed them, paid their bills with my doctor and buried them when they died. Now they demand higher wages. Servants are fast getting ideas beyond their stations. God only knows what will happen next. This morning I had to tie my own bootlaces."

Gavrilo sympathized.

"You will soon find better servants, Viktor. On this island they are reputed to be avaricious. You must go to the country and recruit people there."

"Well, as there is no one to cook for us, I have reserved a table at Marina's. I hope you are a good eater, Valentina Ivanovna: at Marina's they cater to appetites like mine."

The restaurant was a barge attached to the landing stage. Only twenty people could eat at one time, so the prices were exorbitant. After spicy soup there was swordfish, followed by shashlik served

on swords. Valentina watched Viktor and his wife piling food on
their plates. Already Gavrilo was sleepy. She nudged him gently to
keep him from dozing. Sweet courses followed savory ones until
even the cousins could eat no more. Then the toasts began in
vodka. Valentina laughed as the two men tried to outdo each other.

"To your brother, the count."

"To Valentina Ivanovna."

"To having a good time and one's own way."

"To future happiness."

"To the Tsar, God bless him."

"To Russia, may she be forever great."

"To hell with servants."

"To life and love."

When it was time to part, Viktor suggested that they might enjoy
a nightcap at the gypsy encampment. Gavrilo turned to Valentina
and asked if she was tired.

"Would you like to see the gypsies of Yelagin?"

"Is it safe to go to an encampment at this hour of the night?"

"Of course it is, everyone goes there for supper or breakfast or a
glass of champagne."

A dozen caravans were gathered around a clearing lit by a roaring wood fire. Orange sparks flew skyward and there was a smell of
spit-roast pig and spilled red wine. Valentina watched a woman
dancing to the tune of an accordion. The woman writhed ecstati-
cally, her beads jangling as her head switched back and forth like
an angry tiger. Fascinated by this tantalizing creature, she turned
to see what effect the houri was having on Gavrilo and saw he had
barely noticed the gypsy. Valentina smiled wryly as he ordered
champagne and explained what was happening like a schoolmaster.

"For the gypsies the evening has only just begun. By three A.M.
the place will be so crowded you will hardly be able to move. Over
there you can see some of the cream of our society. More will come
later, I can assure you."

Valentina looked at her watch. It was one-thirty. She turned uncertainly to Gavrilo. "Are we going to stay here all night?"

"The yacht crew will arrive at dawn. Don't worry about anything, I will look after you."

Two little girls replaced the gypsy dancer. Valentina watched as
they imitated the woman's movements, their tiny hands rattling

castanets, their bare feet churning the ground in mock passion. Gavrilo had chosen a spot near the fire. Gypsies spread blankets over the ground so they could sit. Another walked toward them, offering meat impaled on a silver dagger. Valentina took it. Gavrilo did not. Soon they were enjoying the sound of Romany violins and the pungent smell of meat cooking and chestnuts roasting on the fire.

By 3 A.M. the arena was packed, as Gavrilo had forecast. By four the violinists had been joined by a group of men with tambourines and gembris and a group of dancers. Valentina drank more champagne, laughing delightedly as gypsy men grabbed haughty society ladies from the audience and whirled them wildly around the fire in time to the music. A swarthy young man came and grasped her and whirled her around with the others, whispering ardent phrases in her ear as he pressed her body against him. When the music stopped, Valentina was relieved to be returned safely to Gavrilo. To his amusement, she took out a vial of orange flower water and spread it on her cheeks.

"I don't care for dancing with that fellow. His breath smelled so strongly of garlic I think he had eaten a whole fieldful."

"Have some more champagne and whatever you do don't look to the opposite side of the arena."

"Why not?"

"My brother is there with Magda. She has seen us. He has not."

Valentina continued to look into Gavrilo's eyes, her heart churning with apprehension at the news.

"What shall we do?"

"We shall do nothing, Valentina. We have as much right as they to be here."

Champagne flowed, dogs barked, men danced with their wives, gypsies danced with each other and ladies accustomed to the formal drawing rooms of St. Petersburg forgot themselves and danced like dervishes with everyone who asked them. Valentina danced with Gavrilo. Then, out of the corner of her eye, she saw the gypsy who had whirled her around the floor. He was eyeing her hungrily. She turned to Gavrilo.

"That surly fellow is watching me. Are you sure his intentions are honorable, sir?"

"They are here to entertain, Valentina. It is not the gypsies' business to be frightening."

As dawn streaked the night sky with pink and yellow the young gypsy grasped Valentina and led her to the clearing. First he whirled her around until she was dizzy. Then he ran his hands over her hair, excited by its silvery sheen. Valentina pushed him away and made to return to Gavrilo. The gypsy grasped her by the hair and pulling her toward him kissed her on the lips.

Gavrilo leaped up and threw the gypsy aside. Within seconds merriment turned to menace. Gavrilo lashed out at the gypsy but another crept up behind him and knocked him senseless with a wooden club. Crouching by the fire, Valentina was aghast at the ugliness of the situation. Then, as angry voices rose around the arena she ran to Gavrilo's side and tried to revive him. Gypsies appeared from the trees and closed in on the merrimakers. Valentina saw the count watching her, his face a mask of disdain.

Suddenly a shot echoed in the night. Valentina looked up and saw Yanin walking from the edge of the clearing. She almost cried with relief. Ignoring her, he stood with his back to the fire. Fellow officers of the Preobrazhensky Guard joined him, their swords drawn, their faces taut with anger. The gypsies retreated. The aristocratic ladies and their escorts drifted until only Valentina remained with Gavrilo and the young men who had saved her.

The count approached and she saw that his face was twitching with rage.

"You will never come to this island again, do you hear me, Valentina Ivanovna?"

She nodded, her face paling with distress at his tone. Korolenko continued.

"I will not have my fiancée behaving like a trollop and provoking these animals to maul her."

The count returned to his carriage. Valentina watched him, conscious of the gleam of triumph in Magda's malevolent eyes and aware that she had made her first irredeemable mistake in the eyes of her future husband. Tears of rage and humiliation fell down her cheeks and she wiped them impatiently.

Yanin handed her his handkerchief.

"The yacht you came on will be leaving at five. My fellow officers will carry the count's brother to the quayside. By that time he should have recovered his wits, though I must admit that gypsy hit him hard enough to have cracked his skull. Don't cry, dear lady, crying makes the eyes red."

Valentina glowered and Yanin laughed delightedly.

"That's better; my memory of you is of a haughty young lady with a bonnetful of roses sitting in a gilded carriage. I have no desire to dream of you bloated with tears. Forgive me, I forgot to introduce myself. I am Ivan Grigorevich Yanin."

"Valentina Ivanovna Nikolayeva, sir."

She watched as the young officers carried Gavrilo down the hill toward the quayside. Yanin held out his hand.

"Let me help you, dearest Valya."

"My name is Valentina Ivanovna Nikolayeva. Please do not address me so familiarly."

"You are Count Korolenko's fiancée and should be addressed as such. Or does the role not suit you?"

Valentina looked down, unwilling to meet the searching gaze. When she spoke, Yanin could barely hear her.

"You are a very insolent young man."

"And you, Valentina Ivanovna, are a mystery. Now I had best take you to join your escort or I may be tempted to forget myself like that gypsy."

Valentina smiled apologetically.

"You have been most kind, sir. Without you I fear there might have been a riot."

"Nonsense! Now and then one of the gypsies forgets his manners and makes advances to one of the visiting ladies. Most of the women enjoy it because passion is conspicuously absent from their lives. He was not to know that you were such a correct little madame, or that your fiancé was watching the entire proceedings."

Valentina mulled over his description of her and looked quizzically at Yanin.

"I should like to go to the quayside now, sir."

"Of course you would. There is nothing to keep you here."

She looked down as Yanin again held out his hand.

"You had best hold on to me, Valentina Ivanovna, or you may fall down and hurt yourself."

On the quayside, Valentina approached Gavrilo, who was struggling to get up from the ground.

"Are you feeling better, sir?"

"I have a lump on my head the size of an egg but I think I shall survive. I am so sorry you were placed in such an embarrassing position and I hope you will forgive me, Valentina."

"Gavrilo, this is Ivan Grigorevich Yanin, who rescued us."

Gavrilo shook hands with the young officer.

"I am obliged to you, sir."

"At your service, sir."

From the rail of the yacht in which she was to travel back to St. Petersburg, Valentina looked down at Yanin as he stood on the quayside with his colleagues. He was watching her as intently as she was watching him and his gaze was direct and disturbing. As the boat drew away Gavrilo went below to wash the dirt from his clothes. Valentina remained on deck, still staring into Yanin's eyes. The distance between them began to widen. She looked down at the surging foam and then back to Yanin. Then she took a yellow rose from the spray at her shoulder and threw it toward the quayside, watching as it floated slowly away.

Yanin grasped a fishing net from the railing and gently scooped the rose from the water and tucked it in his jacket, close to his heart. Then he blew a kiss and walked smartly away into the early-morning mist.

Valentina watched until the landing stage was no longer visible. Her mind was racing disjointedly and she felt oddly lightheaded. Yanin had said he remembered her as a haughty young lady in a gilded carriage. She recalled her own feelings on first seeing him that day in St. Petersburg and the pleasure she had felt when he had reappeared unexpectedly in the country. Yanin's defiant face and the command he had shown when danger threatened were fascinating and she wondered fearfully if she had fallen in love. To love a husband would be wonderful, but to love a man she might never see again would be a calamity. Valentina shook her head defiantly and told herself that love was something to which she must endeavor to make herself immune until the time was right.

Gavrilo emerged from the underdeck area and kissed her hand.

"My dear, thank you for being so forgiving. We were lucky Ivan Grigorevich was there, because the count would not have raised a finger to protect us."

"Do you know Yanin, sir?"

"I have never met him before but I have heard of him. They say his breeding and his bravery are so distinguished that he will some-day become the youngest-ever commander of the Preobrazhensky Regiment."

"What kind of man is he?"

"I know nothing of him, except that he is known to disdain the women who are forever chasing him. He is undoubtedly a most difficult man to know. Personally I envy him and wish I had half his abilities."

Blushing with pleasure, Valentina concentrated hard on control-ling her desire to ask questions about the young officer. Ivan Grigorevich Yanin was a most difficult man to know, an unavailable officer in a city of legendary womanizers. She told herself firmly that she must not think of him again. But as they traveled toward the palace she kept remembering the tan of his skin, the boldness of his amber eyes and the challenge in his manner. She decided that Yanin was like lung congestion, an obstacle to good health to be overcome with luck and fortitude. She touched the flowers at her shoulder and looked longingly into space, remembering how Yanin had scooped the solitary yellow rose from the water. Yanin was a brave and brilliant soldier and a fascinating man. It was going to be very hard to forget him.

# CHAPTER FOUR

## St. Petersburg, Late Summer 1901

Valentina was on her way to what she and Miss Knatchbull had christened the Flower House. She was alone but for Zita and the count's coach driver. She had hurried away from the palace because she wanted to think. A few days previously the count had returned from Yelagin and had viewed for the first time the changes in the palace. Delighted by the new rooms, he had invited Valentina to lunch with him on three successive days, first in his suite, then in the garden and finally in the new dining room. He had complimented her on her work in the palace and had then startled her with an announcement. As she traveled through the scorching heat of summer, Valentina remembered her fiancé's words: . . . I have decided that we shall be married earlier than previously planned. You are not a child, indeed you are far older than your years, as I realized during your escapade on Yelagin. Since then I have spent many hours considering what to do and I have decided to marry you on the twelfth day of September, which is my sister's birthday. Yekaterina and Countess Volkova will arrange everything so you have nothing to worry about. I shall return to this house one week before the ceremony. Now tell me you agree. . . .

Valentina looked toward the fields of corn, a gold, undulating sea that stretched to the horizon. The peace of the countryside contrasted oddly with the turmoil in her mind and she asked herself over and over again why she was suddenly so apprehensive. During her first few days in St. Petersburg she had resigned herself to marrying the count. Why then was she so depressed by the prospect of the ceremony? Her mind turned yet again to thoughts of Yanin and she had to pinch her wrists to avoid bursting into tears.

The truth was her feelings for the gallant young officer had weakened her resolve to go through with the marriage to the count. Valentina told herself that as Yanin was responsible for her distress she should shun his image and stop dwelling on the memory of his touch, his voice, his manner. She sighed. She was fifteen years old, too young to know how to prevent herself from falling in love, too inexperienced to find ways of avoiding Yanin's image as it danced before her eyes.

Throughout the afternoon Valentina wandered in the garden, picking flowers and watching the sun burning down on the lake. Within a month the restoration of the downstairs rooms would be complete. By the time spring came again the entire house would be in pristine condition. She ran upstairs to the tower room, her eyes searching the road for a glint of silver. But no handsome rider on a bold black horse rode by. For an hour Valentina sat watching the road, willing Yanin to appear, but as the sun set over the fields no one came, except a group of peasant workers singing a hymn. She went back to her bedroom and dressed for the journey to St. Petersburg.

The following week was taken up with fittings for the wedding dress. The bride-to-be had lost weight so the dress had to be altered twice, to Madame Marinovskaya's annoyance. On the third fitting she measured Valentina's waist again and exclaimed, "My dear child, you are growing so thin I swear the count will barely recognize you. Russian men favor sturdy girls. They are not at ease with skeletons."

Valentina glanced at Madame's enormous girth and the mahogany-dyed corkscrew curls around her face. She thought wryly that the dressmaker did indeed look as if she enjoyed all of life's excesses with the greatest pleasure. No doubt she had the right figure for the Russian gentlemen about whom she spoke. Valentina replied politely.

"When the cooler weather comes I am sure I shall feel better."

"Are you happy, my dear?"

Valentina hesitated and Madame Marinovskaya watched every flicker in the violet eyes. Valentina answered reluctantly.

"I suppose I am a little nervous about my wedding."

Madame Marinovskaya frowned. Rumor had it that the poor child was terrified of the count and even more terrified of his mistress. She wondered if she dare give Valentina a good piece of advice: to take a lover as soon as possible and have all the happiness a woman needed with or without the count.

The days passed quickly. Valentina's wedding dress was delivered, the trousseau wrapped in tissue paper and stored in trunks Yekaterina had bought. The guests had replied to their invitations and it was known that there would be two hundred relatives of the family in the private chapel and two thousand at a reception to be given within the palace. Valentina felt no excitement at the thought of the wedding. The count was due to arrive the following day, on the eve of the marriage and a week later than he had promised. He had stayed with Magda until the very last moment. Valentina knew it, Yekaterina knew it and so did every member of the household staff and every gossiping aristocrat in St. Petersburg.

Miss Knatchbull was knitting a silk vest to wear under her winter clothes. Valentina was pacing the room when her governess's voice broke into her thoughts.

"My dear, do you want to tell me what is making you so unhappy?"

"I am worried about my wedding."

"I know you are worried, but why? When we first came to Russia you seemed settled to the idea of marrying Count Korolenko. But from a few weeks ago you have become more and more upset at the idea. I hear you every night wandering up and down the corridor."

Valentina evaded Miss Knatchbull's eyes. The governess continued.

"How long have we been together, my dear?"

"For as long as I can remember."

"Do you trust me?"

"Of course I do."

"Then won't you tell me what is on your mind?"

Valentina hesitated. To speak of Yanin would shock Miss Knatchbull, to lie would be unthinkable. She was about to confide her innermost thoughts when the count entered the room.

"My dear! I have been looking everywhere for you. Must you spend all your time with Miss Knatchbull?"

"You spend all your time with Madame Simoniescu, sir. I am left alone much more than I had anticipated."

Korolenko dismissed Miss Knatchbull, who withdrew, controlling her desire to laugh out loud at the impertinence of her charge's reply. Valentina watched her fiancé, aware that her directness had taken him off guard. The count walked to the window and stood with his back to her. Finally he spoke.

"I am still not used to your manner, my dear. I fear your forthrightness will offend some of our friends."

"I shall do my best not to offend your friends, sir."

"They will be our friends once we are married."

"To whom are you referring?"

"To Pirogov, Kirkov, Vasilyev, you know them all."

"Those men are all mutual friends of yours and of Madame Simoniescu. You promised to keep them out of this house whenever I was here and I intend to hold you to that promise. No doubt you and I will have our own circle of friends and I shall enjoy entertaining *them*."

Korolenko sighed.

"You are something of a monster, Valentina Ivanovna. I am not at all sure I can learn to cope with you. But I shall try."

On the morning of the wedding, Valentina woke at dawn. The sun was rising over the horizon and the garden was noisy with the sound of workmen. She wandered to the kitchen nearby and found Zita and Bibi making breakfast.

"The sun is shining for your wedding, ma'am."

"Indeed it is, Zita."

"We couldn't sleep for the excitement, ma'am."

"Neither could I; I fear I shall look tired."

Miss Knatchbull appeared as Valentina was drinking a glass of lemon tea.

"Dear me, child, I'm as tired as a ninety-year-old and you're looking peaky. Did you not sleep?"

"Sleep is impossible on such hot nights, Natty."

"I'll ask Zita to bring breakfast at once. Without food you'll faint during the ceremony, so don't shake your head at me."

The clock chimed ten and Valentina went to her room to be dressed for the ceremony. First the blond-silk robe with its girdle of opals. Then the Korolenko pearls, which hung to her knees. A silk scarf trailed from the back of her head to the ground, held in place by a diamond clasp that had once belonged to the Empress Catherine. Valentina looked at herself in the mirror, still unable to believe the moment had come. Miss Knatchbull appeared with Gavrilo and Yekaterina, who had agreed to act as parents for the bride. Gavrilo admired the dress and paid Valentina pretty compliments on her beauty. Then, having wished her luck, he left with his sister for the chapel. Knowing that Miss Knatchbull would be her only loyal and true friend in the chapel, Valentina hugged her fiercely.

"Whatever would I do without you, Natty?"

For a moment Miss Knatchbull's face clouded. Then she spoke encouragingly.

"You're old enough to be independent of me now, my dear."

"I don't ever want to be without you."

"It's time we left for the chapel. God bless you and keep you safe and happy."

The chapel walls were covered with embossed leather that glowed mellow gold in the candlelight. The ceiling was so high and so dark it could barely be seen through the haze of incense. Choristers were singing a hymn of jubilation as the congregation waited for the bride to appear. The dark interior looked eery and as Valentina approached she had a sudden and urgent desire to run away. She told herself firmly that she had nowhere to go but still she looked over her shoulder with longing at the open window and the sunlit garden beyond. Reluctantly she entered the chapel and walked to stand beside the count in a spot where a priest and two deacons in bejeweled regalia were waiting. A lighted candle was placed in her hand and another in the bridegroom's, and the service commenced with prayers for the Holy Synod, the Tsar and the couple about to marry. Valentina listened disbelievingly as the priest intoned the words.

"Vouchsafe love perfect, peace and health, we beseech thee, O Lord . . ."

When the preliminaries were over the priest began the marriage prayers.

"Eternal God that joinest together them that were separate, bless thy servants Vladimir and Valentina and lead them in the path of goodness. Glory be to thee the Father, Son and Holy Ghost, now and ever shall be."

Valentina looked toward the count but his face was devoid of expression. The priest commenced the responses.

"Do you, Vladimir, desire to take Valentina as your wife with the authorization of the Tsar and the blessing of God?"

"I do."

Korolenko's voice was firm. The priest turned to the bride.

"Do you, Valentina, desire to take Vladimir as your husband with the authorization of the Tsar and the blessing of God?"

Valentina hesitated, knowing the moment had come when she would no longer be free to choose her future. She turned and met Miss Knatchbull's eyes. Then she answered in a whisper.

"I do."

The responses were repeated twice more, as was the custom. Then, in the silence of the chapel, Valentina felt her hand linked with Korolenko's. Tears fell down her cheeks as the count pushed the gold band on her finger impatiently, as though eager for the ceremony to be over. She slipped the gold ring on her husband's finger, slowly, as if to delay the pronouncement of marriage. The priest began to intone the blessing.

"O Lord bless thy servants, Vladimir and Valentina. Make their union fast in faith, a union of hearts and truth and love."

Valentina closed her eyes to control the panic she was feeling. It was done. She was married forever to a man she did not love. She looked down at the ring, then to the count, who was watching the priest bringing two diamond crowns from the sanctuary. Gavrilo and his cousin held the crowns for the bride and groom to kiss. Then they were raised over their heads. The choir burst into an anthem of celebration and two pages placed a pink-satin strip on the floor as the couple prepared to parade around the chapel with their retinue. Without thinking, Valentina stepped onto the satin. The count frowned. According to tradition the one to step first on the satin would rule the household. He thought furiously that no one would ever rule *his* house, not even Valentina Ivanovna. As choristers continued to sing, the couple walked three times around the chapel. A long sermon and hymns followed.

Valentina watched as women in the congregation prostrated themselves in melodramatic humiliation. She sighed wearily. In Paris devotion had never been so exaggerated. In Paris she had looked forward eagerly to marrying the man of her dreams, not an aging rake with an omnipotent mistress. At that moment she realized irrevocably that Russia would always be an alien country in her eyes. The thought was disturbing and she prayed that it was not so.

When Valentina had finished her prayers she was kissed by the count. Pulling gently away from him, she looked to the side of the chapel, where Yekaterina was sobbing and Miss Knatchbull looking strangely subdued. She wondered why her governess had been so depressed during the previous few weeks and resolved to speak with Miss Knatchbull as soon as she reached the reception hall.

The bride and groom appeared in the hall of mirrors and the assembly applauded. Valentina smiled dutifully and looked about her, dizzy from the reflection of two thousand people jostling, pushing and moving back and forth like a human kaleidoscope. The heat was oppressive, the noise deafening. Waiters rushed to and fro, champagne corks popped and the orchestra was playing a rousing mazurka. She saw the count talking with Countess Volkova and Gavrilo standing alone on the terrace. Of Miss Knatchbull there was no sign. Valentina walked from the reception hall to the dining room and then to the drawing room. When she could not find her governess she ran upstairs and found Miss Knatchbull packing.

"Natty, whatever are you doing?"

"The count asked me to leave as soon as you were married. I don't like the idea but I had to admit that you no longer need a governess."

"I don't want you to go!"

"Of course you don't, and I don't want to go, but Count Korolenko is master of this house and you don't wish to start your married life on a disagreement, now do you?"

"Why does he want you to leave?"

"He never wanted me to come to Russia in the first place, my dear. Your grandmother insisted, however, and he agreed on condition that I leave after your wedding."

"I do not want you to go."

Miss Knatchbull fastened her suitcase and walked to where Valentina was standing. For a moment she embraced the girl she had cared for for so long.

"My dear, you are a married woman now and a wife has a duty to her husband. You must do everything you can to wean the count away from his mistress, and I love you far too much to stand in your way."

"Promise me you won't leave until tomorrow."

"I am due to take the ten o'clock train in the morning."

Valentina went back to the reception hall and for hours concealed her feelings as she showed the count's friends around the newly decorated rooms. At dusk she revealed her secret and electric light flooded the reception rooms of the palace. The guests applauded, and the count was delighted by the adulation.

While his brother's attention was diverted, Gavrilo beckoned Valentina to the room by the library.

"I want to give you this to celebrate your marriage and to wish you luck in the future Valentina."

He handed her a ruby so large it almost filled her palm. She looked at the stone and then back to Gavrilo, conscious that he had been drinking too much champagne.

"I have never *seen* anything like this. Does the count know you have given it to me?"

"My brother would be furious if he did. Hide it, Valya, and use its value if ever you need to get away from Russia."

"Don't look so unhappy."

"I love you. God knows how I shall bear living near you when I cannot have you for my own."

"I need you, don't ever go away."

For a moment Valentina thought he was going to kiss her. Then Gavrilo hurried to the door and was gone. She looked into the wine-dark depths of the ruby and wondered where he had acquired it. It was not one of the Korolenko family jewels, because those belonged to the count. She put the gem in a satin purse hidden in the folds of her dress and returned to the reception.

Korolenko continued to ignore his wife and after dinner disappeared for a game of backgammon with an elderly relative. At ten he reemerged in an excellent humor and made his way back to the reception. Now and then he smiled across the room to Valentina and often he accepted compliments from friends about the changes made to his home and the exquisite food that had taken everyone by surprise. Korolenko became expansive. By midnight he had almost forgotten his annoyance over the fact that Valentina had stepped before him onto the satin rug in the bridal chapel.

By 2 A.M. the guests had gone and the air of the downstairs rooms was heavy with the scent of cigar smoke, perfume and crushed flowers. Valentina had retired to the honeymoon suite, leaving her husband alone in his study. The count smoked one last cigar. Then he walked slowly, thoughtfully, upstairs. He was feeling unaccountably nervous.

Valentina was sitting on the sofa in front of the fire. Zita had brushed her hair a hundred times so it fell like a silver cloud over the diaphanous silk of her negligee. She was afraid and to still the fear had ordered a pot of chocolate and some gilded opium pills. She had just swallowed one of the pills and poured a cup of steaming Parisian chocolate when the count appeared. Valentina remembered the Prince of Wales's advice and wondered if what he had said was really true. Would the count turn out to be a gallant husband or were the hard times only just beginning? Would she be able to overcome the count's feelings for his mistress, her own dissatisfaction with Russia and the fact that they did not love each other?

Seeing his wife's pale face and the trembling of her hands, Korolenko spoke gently.

"You look lovely, my dear, please don't be nervous. You are about to be loved, not executed."

"Would you like some hot chocolate, sir?"

"No, thank you, I do not have your Parisian tastes. I must try to make a good Russian out of you before I am through."

"Is that why you told Miss Knatchbull to go away? Did you feel she was one of my Parisian tastes?"

"Of course not. Miss Knatchbull is a governess and you are a married woman. You no longer need her. I shall teach you all you need to know from this moment on."

"Miss Knatchbull is my friend, sir. She is the only familiar person to me in all Russia."

"And I, what am I?"

"You are my husband. You are not yet familiar because I have only met you six times since I arrived in St. Petersburg. I am sure I shall soon feel more accustomed to you, but until I do I would be grateful to have Miss Knatchbull's company."

Korolenko took off his jacket and threw it down on the sofa.

"My dear, there is something you do not seem to understand. I am master of this house and of the other properties handed down to me by my ancestors. I own everything in these properties and can do with them as I wish. You are my wife and therefore also my property. You may not go out without my permission. You may do nothing unless I authorize it. Obviously, I shall be happy to give permission for whatever will make you happy and have no wish to play the despot. But from this moment on my word is law. You are no longer free to do as you wish, when you wish."

"I would like Miss Knatchbull to stay, sir. Will you indulge me?"

"You have not understood me, Valentina."

She pushed the tray of chocolate away and tried to still the bitter resentment in her heart. When she spoke her voice was gentle, but it was impossible to conceal her annoyance.

"I am not your property, sir, like a chair or a table or the flowers in the garden. I am Valentina Ivanovna Nikolayeva and I belong to myself and to God. You have no right to assume that you own me. How dare you use that word to me."

"But I *do* own you. By Russian law you are now mine to do with as I wish."

Furious at Korolenko's attitude, Valentina sprang to her feet.

"You are being unreasonable, sir. I have only one good friend in this city. You have scores of them. Why must you insist on depriving me of Miss Knatchbull?"

Korolenko picked up his jacket and put it on. He was pale with anger and his eyes seemed to burn though Valentina's uncertain confidence.

"I do not have to explain myself to you, madame. I am master of this house and intend to remain so. Because you are beautiful you have had your way, but you will not manipulate me. And now, good night to you, madame."

Valentina ran after her husband.

"Where are you going?"

"I am going to Yelagin, where Magda will know how to comfort my disappointment. She has always known how to please me and when to obey my wishes. You may keep Miss Knatchbull, but she has cost you dear, because I shall not return while she remains in this house."

Valentina grasped the count's arm as he opened the door.

"Please do not leave me, sir. This is our wedding night. Surely you will not run away."

"I shall do as I please. I always have and I always will."

Tearing himself away from his wife's grasp, the count ran down his private stairway. Within minutes Valentina heard horses' hooves on the cobblestones of the yard, and he was gone. The count had deserted her for his mistress on their wedding night. She shivered as though this were winter and not the gentle chill of a summer night. Then, for a long time, she stared out of the window as the night turned gray and then pink with the advent of dawn. In the meager light, she rose and took off her negligee. Looking at herself in the mirror, she wondered if she was so unattractive that the count fled to his mistress on any excuse. Her mind was in a turmoil of indecision. Had she been right or wrong? Obviously she had been wrong. How could she have been so foolish as to send Korolenko back to Magda? But was it unreasonable to want one familiar face in a city of strangers?

Valentina put on the dress she had worn for her visit to the country and ran all the way to Miss Knatchbull's room. It was empty. The Englishwoman had gone. Instead, the count's sister was asleep in the chair. Valentina roused her gently.

"Madame, what are you doing here?"

"My dear, Miss Knatchbull has left us. She was told of your disagreement with my brother and of his having left for Yelagin. She left at once, but not before she had given me this to give to you."

Valentina read the letter in tears.

*My dear child,*

Marriage is a serious business and you already have enough opposition. I would be lacking in consideration for you if I did not leave at once under the circumstances. I have taught you all I know, dear one, but please remember the following.

1. Be sure to get fresh air every day and always eat a hearty breakfast. You must look after your health if you are ever to achieve your ambition, to return to Paris. This is the most important advice I give you.

2. Do not allow any children you may have to have a Russian nurse, whatever the opposition.

3. The servants are becoming rebellious. I beg to suggest that you withdraw the jewels before someone absconds with them. In my opinion, some of the servants are bursting with resentment and envy. I have heard worrying rumors. Take care of yourself.

4. Visit the country often. That house will be your sanity.

5. Try to view the count's demands reasonably and remember he feels inadequate against your love of Paris. It is one thing to have a rival for the affection of one's wife. The count's rival is Paris. Imagine!

6. Remember your French and English by working at least one hour a day on your grammar.

7. I am enclosing the recipe for Madame Yekaterina's medicine.

I shall be going to Paris and you may contact me via my bank, which you know. I shall not say good-bye because we both know we shall meet again. God bless you, child.

*Letitia Knatchbull.*

Valentina began to sob uncontrollably. Alarmed, Yekaterina rang for coffee and smelling salts. Then she sat at Valentina's side stroking her hair, because she had seen Miss Knatchbull doing this to comfort her in times of stress. Yekaterina spoke gently.

"I know about your disagreement with the count and I know he has gone back to Magda. Don't cry, my dear, you will see Miss Knatchbull again, and my brother will return as contrite as ever. I believe he really loves you. He just cannot bear to think that you have such power over him."

"He called me his property."

"He spoke as he wished things were, and not as they really are."

"No. He believes I am his like his horse or his hounds or his carriage. I wish I were dead!"

"He will change his ways someday, my dear. On my word, you will change him completely."

Valentina went back to her room and sat in the armchair staring out of the window. Her husband had deserted her after barely half a day of marriage. The gossips of St. Petersburg would have a field day and Magda's power would be increased tenfold. Valentina was also aware that her own authority within the palace would be reduced to nothing from this moment on. She sobbed for all the unhappiness of the past year and for the impossibility of her situation. She was wiping her eyes when she noticed a yellow rose in a slim crystal glass on the table.

She picked up the rose and smelled its delicate perfume. Suddenly her heart began to pound with anticipation. Where had it come from? It was a rose almost identical to the one she had thrown on the water to Yanin. She wiped her eyes and sniffed the rose perfume again. Had it been there before? If it had not, where had it come from? She rang the bell for Zita, starting when she saw her maid's black eye.

"Whatever has happened to you, Zita? Have you been fighting?"

"Yes, ma'am, I have."

"*Why?*"

"One of the scullery maids said something rude about you so I pushed her into the fat fryer."

"What did she say?"

Zita looked down and did not answer. Valentina persisted.

"What did she say, Zita?"

"The staff had bets, ma'am. Rosa bet the count wouldn't even stay the night with you. She was the only one with so little confidence in your attractions, so she won fourteen rubles. I'm sorry, ma'am. The servants gossip all the time about you. Bibi's so upset she's gone to bed and Nina hurt her wrist punching the count's valet."

Valentina sat at the window, uncertain how to advise her maids. Then she remembered why she had called Zita.

"That yellow rose. Where did it come from?"

"I saw it this morning when I came in to clean. It wasn't there last night, I swear. It's a pretty rose but it's not one of ours. The count doesn't like yellow so the gardeners don't grow anything in that color."

"Very well, Zita, make my breakfast at once and serve it in the conservatory. I am grateful for your support, by the way, but I do not wish you to get hurt. You must learn to ignore what others say about me. You and your sisters are the most superior servants in this house and must always strive to remain above the rabble. We must not allow them to distress us."

Delighted by the "we," Zita hurried away to the kitchen. Valen-

tina looked again at the yellow rose. Zita had said it was not there
the previous night yet she had found it in the early morning. Was
it possible Yanin had delivered it personally? She shook her head;
of course it was not. But if he had not brought the rose, who had?
Valentina hurried down to the conservatory and ate her breakfast,
looking again and again at the rose that Zita had put before her.
Could Yanin have brought it? Could he have entered the palace
without being seen?

After breakfast Valentina sat in her room wondering what to do.
When would her husband return? Instinctively, she knew the count
would punish her by staying away for many days. She looked again
at the yellow rose and thought of the house in the country and the
harvest-gold fields of corn waving in the breeze. She told Zita to instruct the groom to bring her horse. Zita looked aghast.

"You're not going out riding alone, are you, ma'am? Whatever
will the count say if he finds out?"

"The count is with his mistress on the island of Yelagin. Why
should anyone tell him what I am doing?"

The sun was hot, the breeze playful as Valentina galloped along
the main road, turning into a lane running beside the cornfields. A
child passed by in the opposite direction, holding his dog on a
string. As Valentina rode by, the child raised his cap dutifully. She
smiled down at him and rode on, telling herself all the while that
as she was not in love with the count there was no reason to be
distressed by his disappearance. As for the gossips, she would ignore them. She bit her lip, knowing what they would be saying
about her marriage. She would follow Miss Knatchbull's advice to
the letter and visit the country often. Indeed, during her husband's
absence, Valentina had decided to make arrangements to move into
the Flower House.

On reaching the gate she leaped down and unlocked the pad-
lock. Then she walked up the drive, leading her horse and pausing, as she had that first time, to admire the lake and the water
lilies. A bird trilled in the branches of a cherry tree. Dragonflies
dived recklessly into the water and in the distance she could hear
the sound of men singing in the fields.

Clara was asleep in the kitchen. Relieved to be undetected,
Valentina tripped upstairs to her room and threw herself on her
bed. She had been there for a few moments when she heard a

sound in the nearby kitchen. Suddenly alert, she sat up. The sound
came again, a sharp crack like twigs being snapped for a fire. Hurrying to the kitchen, she was amazed to find the stove lit, coffee on
the hob and some delicate pastries from the finest pâtissier in St.
Petersburg on the table. She looked around uncertainly, half afraid,
half expecting the count to step out and surprise her. She was
sniffing the coffee when a voice startled her.

"I thought you would never arrive. Do you realize it's after two
o'clock?"

Valentina turned to face Yanin. She was so shocked she could
not reply. He took a cup from the dresser and poured coffee into it.

"I hope it's still hot."

Valentina stared as if she had seen a ghost.

"What are you doing here? How did you get into this house and
why did you come?"

"I came to see you, of course."

"But I only just decided to come here. How did you know I was
free to arrive?"

Yanin smiled patiently and spoke slowly, as though to a child.

"I left the yellow rose as a message. I knew you would understand."

Confusion made Valentina's mind dull and she kept asking herself how Yanin had entered the Korolenko Palace without detec-
tion. After a while, she spoke.

"The count left me in the middle of the night."

"I know."

"How did you know?"

"My dear, officers of the Preobrazhensky Regiment are well
trained in warfare."

"What do you mean?"

"I am at war with the count because he has married you. He is
unfit to be married to any decent woman."

"But how did you know the count had left me?"

"After the reception I hid in the count's dressing room. To be
truthful, I felt he might invite his degenerate friends to share his
wedding night."

Aghast at the statement, Valentina fell silent. When she had
recovered her composure she spoke sharply.

"You took a fearful risk, sir."

"Risk is food and drink to a soldier."

"You had no right to eavesdrop, even though I am grateful for your concern. Now, may I ask again, what are you doing in this house?"

"I am having my first assignation with you, Valentina Ivanovna."

Blushing with excitement, she tried to assess her situation. If the count was enjoying himself with his mistress, was it right to enjoy herself with Yanin? She knew it was not, but the forbidden was enticing and she looked up at him and then down at the cup of coffee he had poured for her. Uncertain how to answer, she decided to tell the truth.

"I have never had an assignation before, sir, and I do not know if I should permit myself the indulgence now I am married."

"You could wait in the palace, mooning over your husband until he deigns to return. Or you could show your independence by coming here to me. I plan to give you all my attention in the future, Valentina Ivanovna, and to make you happy. It is your decision. I would not be so ungallant as to make you do something you do not wish to do. I am offering you friendship, loyal friendship, at this moment and nothing more."

"Why did you do what you did last night?"

"You have asked enough questions for the moment. Let's go to the garden so you can pick some of the flowers and I shall eat some of those figs from the tree by the lake. Then we will ride to the hunting lodge and I shall show you something that will surprise you. In the evening I shall light a fire at the edge of the cornfield and make dinner for you. I am the best cook in the regiment, so you are in for a treat. We shall eat roasted potatoes, chicken and grouse which I shot earlier in the week. Do my plans please you?"

Valentina hesitated but Yanin took her hand and led her downstairs. She was about to speak when he read her thoughts.

"You are wondering about Clara. There is no need to worry. Clara is the sister of my mother's housekeeper. She dislikes the count intensely so she will never speak of our meeting."

"What if anyone else speaks of seeing us together?"

"If they tell the count, what can he do? He cannot challenge me to a duel because I am also the finest shot in the regiment. He cannot divorce you because he is longing for an heir to the title. He will therefore be obliged to mend his ways or lose you."

Valentina allowed Yanin to lead her to the garden.

"How long shall we stay here?"

"After dinner I shall accompany you back to St. Petersburg and from tomorrow I shall see you here whenever I can. Until the count returns, would it not be a good idea for you to move into this house?"

"I had already thought of doing so, sir."

"Arrange it tomorrow and I will be your guest at dinner."

Valentina looked again at Yanin's face.

"If I had not heard that you disdain the advances of the women who pursue you, I should believe you well practiced in deception, sir."

"My name is Ivan, do not call me sir. As for your comment, it's true I am well trained in deception. I was an intelligence officer before being seconded to my present regiment. I am not a philanderer and in truth this is the first time I have risked my life for a woman."

"Why did you choose me for your first escapade?"

"When I know you well, Valentina Ivanovna, I shall explain all my thoughts to you. Until then, you must be prepared to trust me as a friend, a good and true friend who will not allow you to suffer."

Valentina looked from the terrace to the lake and then back to Yanin. When he held out his hand she grasped it and they walked together toward the trees.

"Where are we going, Ivan?"

Yanin looked down at her, his face flushed with pleasure.

"We are at the start of a long and exciting journey of adventure. Today is the first day of your new life, Valya; hold my hand tightly, because I am your guide and partner in this journey."

Yanin's eyes were soft on hers. Valentina looked into them and saw affection and trust. She held Yanin's hand tightly, as he had asked, and walked with him through the forest toward the golden fields.

# CHAPTER FIVE

## St. Petersburg, January 1902

At the end of January the count returned to the palace from Yelagin. For some time he had been feeling contrite at the punishment he had inflicted on his young wife. From the night of the wedding he had remained resolutely with his mistress, on the wintery island. He had toyed with the idea of returning to the palace for Christmas but had hardened his heart and continued to stay away to show Valentina the extent of his anger at her independent attitude. Instead, he had sent his valet to St. Petersburg, to inquire what had happened in the palace. He had been surprised to hear of a Christmas feast his wife had arranged and served to two hundred of the most influential citizens of the capital and of the toasts she had made to her absent husband. After endless self-searching the count was still unsure if Valentina had made the toast mockingly. His valet had also told him that she had filled an ornate chest with presents for him, presents he had not yet seen, and this touched him despite everything.

In his private suite within the palace the count rang for his personal servant. Flushed with anticipation, he was looking forward with intense eagerness to seeing Valentina and to enjoying her penitence and her relief at his return. The punishment had been harsh but the count knew he could now expect subservience, like every other nobleman in Russia. When the servant appeared, the count spoke impatiently.

"Where is the countess? I had expected her to greet me on my arrival."

"The countess is not here, Excellency. She went away some time ago."

The count stared at the servant as though scrutiny would change his mind.

"She cannot be away. I sent word a week ago that I should be arriving today. Go at once and ask where my wife is and tell her to come to me."

"Madame is away, sir. I have already checked with the maids in the corridor of her suite. She left the palace immediately after the ball on Christmas night and took her three maids with her."

"And where did she go?"

"No one knows, sir. Madame has been in the palace very little since your departure for Yelagin."

The count's face paled and he controlled his anger with the greatest effort.

"Go at once and bring my sister, if you please."

"Madame Yekaterina is also away, sir."

"I *demand* to know what is going on."

"I do not know, Excellency; I am sorry I cannot be of further assistance."

Korolenko dismissed the servant and began to pace the room. So, Valentina was still defiant of him despite everything and had chosen to make him appear ridiculous in front of his servants by disappearing when she should have been welcoming him home. Wiping his brow, the count cursed his wife's bad nature and the fact that he had ever brought her to Russia. A few minutes later he rang the bell and ordered Gavrilo to be brought to him. After what seemed like an eternity, Gavrilo's aged servant appeared. Korolenko looked sternly down at the old man and began to question him.

"Where is my brother?"

"He went away to the country, sir."

"And where precisely did he go?"

"I do not know, sir. He said he was looking forward to the trip because he had always loved the country since the days of his childhood."

"How long will he stay away?"

"He and Madame Yekaterina will return late tonight or tomorrow morning."

Korolenko ordered his fur traveling coat to be brought and the head groom to be summoned. When the man arrived, he gave his instructions.

"I wish the troika to be made ready for a journey."

"Where shall we be going, Excellency?"

"*I* shall be going to the country."

"Alone, sir?"

"Alone, and I should like to leave within the hour."

The countryside, once golden with corn, shimmered like an opalescent fairyland under a pebble-gray sky. Holly berries were the only color in the landscape because the brightly painted churches and windmills were blanketed with snow. The count drove toward the Flower House without seeing the beauty of his surroundings. He was angry, confused and apprehensive to have been made a fool of by a young, innocent girl. A hungry bird settled for a moment beside him before flying away to watch the silent world through eager, inquisitive eyes. The count shrugged and drove on. The bird had not stayed with him despite its need for food. Would Valentina also desert him despite her poverty and the abyss of her future without his wealth? He had deserted her on their wedding night and had stayed with Magda, making a fool of Valentina in the corridors of splendor of St. Petersburg. If this had not tamed her, if she had chosen to vanish at the very time of his arrival home, what was to be done? Should he send her back to Paris in disgrace to be divorced ignominiously in her absence? Should he beg her forgiveness and try to cajole her? Should he beat her into submission? The count sighed. He was fast coming to the conclusion that all the beatings in the world would not force Valentina into submission. But what to do? How to retrieve authority eroded by her actions? She was clever. She had retaliated by humiliating him as much as he had ever humiliated her.

On reaching the entrance of the property, Korolenko stepped down and unlocked the gate. Then he drove slowly, almost reluctantly, toward the house. Girlish screams came to his ears and on reaching the final curve of the drive he saw Valentina, Gavrilo and Yekaterina skating arm in arm on the frozen lake. Nearby, a local man was playing a traditional tune on an elderly fiddle. The count weighed the scene. Valentina was dressed in red, with a scarf and hood of fluffy white fur. His sister seemed fifteen years younger than when he had last seen her, the smile on her face warming him despite the circumstances. Gavrilo's eyes were on Valentina and the count knew his brother was in love with her. The three merrymakers had not seen him so he continued to watch until they abandoned their skates and took to throwing snowballs at each other and at a massive snowman in the center of the lawn. The snowman was wearing one of the count's hats and when he looked more closely he thought the snowman looked uncannily like him. He gazed at Valentina's flushed face and listened to her joyful laughter. She was happy. She was undeniably happy and more beautiful than ever. At last he found the strength to drive to the entrance of the property and stood waiting for his wife to greet him.

Valentina dismissed the fiddler and threw a snowball, catching her husband full in the chest. She called out, as though nothing were amiss.

"Come and join us. We've built the biggest snowman in Russia and he looks just like you. We are going to have pigeon and turkey pie for dinner with marzipan men and pink champagne punch. Don't look so miserable, come and join us."

Korolenko swallowed the reprimands he had been preparing and joined his wife, surprised to find that he had not enjoyed himself as much since the days of his childhood. He could not keep his eyes off Valentina, who seemed to ignore him completely. He kept asking himself what kind of woman she was that she could treat him in such a cavalier fashion when he was the richest man in St. Petersburg.

Sunset turned the snowy wastes deep red. Valentina looked wistfully at the fading light. Then she whispered to Gavrilo and his sister and held out her hands to her husband.

"It's time to show you my house, sir."

Surprised, Korolenko took her hands, watching as his brother and sister disappeared discreetly.

"Surely, my dear, this is *my* house?"

"You are the owner of the property, sir but I am its guardian. Whenever you go to Yelagin I intend to come here. I have given this house all my love. As you well know, you have refused to allow me to give it to you."

Valentina led her husband inside, watching as he gazed in astonishment at the once-decayed interior. Hurrying from room to room, he spoke excitedly, as though to himself.

"How wonderful. This room looks exactly as it did when I was a boy. . . . Nothing has been changed, how lovely it all is. . . . I have always adored violets. . . . I cannot believe this, it is a miracle. You have restored the house without altering a single thing. I would like to thank you for what you have done to restore this property, my dear."

Valentina blushed with pleasure. "You once told me you loved this house and could not bear to see it decay."

Korolenko looked wonderingly at the wife he could neither control nor understand.

"I would also like to apologize for my behavior in leaving you for such a long time. I cannot explain why I go to Yelagin, but I fear it is a habit I am not man enough to break. Whenever life becomes too difficult for me to bear I go there; even extreme happiness is an emotion I cannot tolerate. It is as if I need Magda's hate as much as I need her love, her coldness to match my own."

"We will not talk of your mistress, sir. Tonight we are going to have a celebration dinner. Now I shall go to my room to change. Madame Marinovskaya has made me the very prettiest dress in St. Petersburg."

Dinner was cheering, with fine wine and amusing conversation. French pâté was followed by a magnificent pie of turkey and pigeon and then by a chestnut soufflé, which the count remembered was Valentina's favorite dessert, recalled with longing from her Parisian days.

"This meal is magnificent. The pâté is as good as a French one."

"Miss Knatchbull sent it from Paris in the English diplomatic train, sir. She also sent the liqueurs and the recipe for the soufflé."

Yekaterina said good night. Valentina poured herself a glass of framboise and sat by the fire. The count stood looking down at her, admiring the delicate pink of her dress and the rosebuds in her hair.

"I understand you have been living here during my absence."

"I have, sir."

"Do you bring servants from the palace to serve you and who cleans the house?"

"I bring only my three maids from the palace, and the house is cleaned by local women who come each morning. I need few servants."

"I could not live with them and cannot understand how you can."

"Will you be staying long, sir? Or shall we be returning to St. Petersburg tomorrow?"

"Yekaterina and Gavrilo will return. We shall stay on together and become better acquainted."

Valentina looked at the slack skin on her husband's face and the puckered lines around his eyes. She compared the count with Yanin, with whom she had had frequent meetings in the autumn of the previous year, before his regiment had gone away. Valentina looked at the count's hands, comparing the white skin and heavy blue veins with Yanin's bronzed hands as they held hers in the poppy fields of summer. A shudder ran through her body and, believing her to be nervous at the prospect of love, Korolenko explained what he wished to do.

"We will retire now. It is late and I have traveled a great distance today. Tonight you will sleep in your own room. Tomorrow, when Yekaterina and Gavrilo have gone, you will join me in mine."

Valentina could not sleep. Korolenko's absence and her meetings with Yanin had made her forget that her husband was a man prematurely old. For months she had enjoyed Yanin's company and the private jokes they shared. At night, when she was alone, she had mulled over the thrill she felt whenever she saw the young officer and the longing they tried to conceal from each other. As the golden days of summer had turned to the smoke-blue days of autumn, she had dreamed of Yanin's tawny eyes, of being held in his arms and of being his completely. She had almost forgotten her husband and had put to the back of her mind the inevitability of his return. Now, soon, she would lie at his side, an unwilling pupil being taught Korolenko's way of love.

The following morning, after breakfast, the count walked with Valentina on the snow covered terrace, pointing out things of interest in the garden.

"That great cedar was planted by one of my ancestors hundreds of years ago."

"There is another like it near the hunting lodge. Do you remember that one, sir?"

"I have never been to the hunting lodge, my dear."

The count shrugged uneasily. He did not wish to tell his wife that the hunting lodge had been occupied long ago by his father's mistress, who had been as fine a shot as any man in St. Petersburg. Valentina teased her husband.

"I was told that one of your father's mistresses lived in the hunting lodge. She was related to the Yanins who live nearby."

"Have you met the Yanins?"

"I heard the story from one of the workers who restored the house."

"My father loved his mistress more than his wife."

"History repeats itself a generation later, sir."

"Nonsense! I don't wish to discuss this any further."

In the hothouse Korolenko frowned at the yellow roses Valentina was growing.

"I dislike yellow intensely. Must you grow such things?"

"Yellow reminds me of all the happy things that ever happened to me, sir."

Puzzled by this strange statement the count inquired about Valentina's plans for the day.

"First I am going to feed my new horse. Then I shall ride to the hunting lodge and back."

"In the snow?"

"Of course, he and I love the snow."

"Who will chaperon you? A lady cannot go out without a chaperon."

"I need no chaperon, sir."

"I forbid you to go out."

Valentina looked her husband in the eye and spoke forcefully for the first time since his return from Yelagin.

"You married me in order to have an heir to your title, sir. You will never have an heir if you vanish constantly to Yelagin at the slightest provocation. I have no intention of quarreling with you again; however, I shall *not* obey your archaic orders either. If you wish to keep me as your wife, you will allow me the same freedom you yourself expect. I do not intend to live constantly surveyed by your spies, and don't think I am not aware that you sent your valet to find out what I was doing at Christmastime. The staff laughed at you for that, and so did I."

Korolenko made to speak but Valentina interrupted him.

"I once told you that I could never love you because I could only

ever love a man I respected. I will repeat that and tell you that
since the day of our marriage you have done nothing whatsoever to
make me change my mind about you in any way."

Valentina stormed away to the stables, leaving her husband on
the terrace. Anger, hurt, confusion and helplessness made the count
remain there, numb and defeated, on the old oak bench. It began
to snow. The count did not notice it. He was thinking of the first
time he had met Valentina, at the lunch party his sister had arranged. Even then she had defied him, and he had found himself
admiring her spirit. Now, she had stated her position. He could ask
her to leave or keep her on her own terms. He stared out at the estate he had loved since childhood, remembering the miraculous ref-
ormation she had wrought from the decay. His deliberations lasted
so long the lunch bell rang to summon him and he rose, covered in
snow and soaking wet, and hurried inside, still unable to make a
decision about the future.

That night, as a blizzard blew snowdrifts against the walls of the
house, Valentina entered the count's bedroom. He kissed her
cheeks and untied her negligee with eager hands, trying not to notice that she was looking bitterly unhappy. When she was naked
before him, the count made her turn around three times. Then he
led her to the bed, smiling as she leaped unceremoniously under
the covers.

"You are none too eager to love me, madame."

"I am afraid, sir. I know nothing of the ways of married people."

The count began to regret the traditional ignorance of Russian
brides. Then, conscious that his own body was unable to accomplish his desires, he tried to explain to Valentina.

"I'm sorry, my dear. It would appear that my body is disobedient
of my desires."

"Have I displeased you, sir?"

"Of course not. Go to sleep and try to forgive me. In the morning
I shall try to love you as you deserve."

The count rose at two and went to his study. There he sat staring
into the darkness. Would it always be this way? Was he capable of
making love only on bizarre provocation? What would Valentina
think of him if he could never accomplish his conjugal obligations?
Misery clouded his eyes and he sat for hours smoking nervously.

Over breakfast, the count made an effort to be amusing. Trying to seem untouched by the events of the night taxed him, and soon he could think of nothing but the failure of his body at the crucial moment of his wife's first love. He asked her what she would like to do during the day. Valentina answered without hesitation.

"At midday I must see some workmen who are going to reconstruct the outer farms when spring comes."

"Must they come today?"

"They are eager for the work."

"And what of us?"

"You will teach me to shoot after lunch. I have heard unpleasant rumors of men who band together in order to kill the rich of St. Petersburg. If anyone tries to kill me and my children I intend to shoot them."

"But you have no children. In any case, my staff would protect you."

"I trust no one except my three maids, so you must teach me to shoot. After all, I am married to the finest shot in St. Petersburg, who better to be my teacher?"

That night the count tried again to make love to Valentina. And soon the familiar cloud of depression settled on him and he knew why Magda had ruled his private life for so long. Only with her could he achieve the longed-for sunbursts of ecstasy. Only with her was he fearless to demand.

The next night the count told Valentina she could return to her own suite.

"Perhaps in the spring, when I am recovered from my exhaustion, I shall be able to show you my affection. I hope you are not angry with me."

"Of course not, sir. I am only sad that I have failed you in some way because of my ignorance."

That day Valentina and her husband returned to St. Petersburg. The count departed almost at once to go bear hunting with friends, having promised to bring his wife back a trophy. Valentina sighed. At least he had not run away to Magda. At least he would return in a few hours to keep his promise to stay near her. Despite Yekaterina's company she was lonely and every few hours she took a pen and wrote more of the long letter she was composing to Miss Knatchbull. In this she told her former governess everything of the recent past, in the most ladylike terms. Miss Knatchbull would reply, as always, sending advice and cuttings from the Parisian newspapers, especially those showing the latest fashions.

At dusk the count's men dragged a gigantic black bear into the courtyard of the palace. Once there, the count fired his rifle in the air to get Valentina's attention. He succeeded in this and she ran to the window and stared down at her triumphant husband. Korolenko called out delightedly.

"This is the biggest bear we have ever seen. I brought it for you to admire, my dear."

Valentina looked at the inert black body with its stiffening legs and forced a smile.

"What will you do with it, sir?"

"I shall have the skin made into a rug for your carriage."

When his wife had disappeared, the count looked down at his prize, beaming with pleasure as his men dragged the bear away. Whatever else he lacked, he was the best shot and the finest huntsman in the capital. He hurried inside and ran upstairs to Valentina's suite, frowning at the solitary yellow rose at her bedside.

"Where did that rose come from? We do not grow yellow roses in the palace and never under glass."

"I found it here when I returned from the country. Perhaps one of the girls put it there."

Korolenko glowered at the rose, and to take his mind off the mysterious flower Valentina asked about the hunt. While her husband was describing his bloody struggle with the bear, she looked wistfully toward the rose. Since Yanin's departure a yellow rose had been delivered each week, "for the countess," whenever she was in residence in the palace. It was as if Yanin's accomplice lived within the very walls of the palace, that he should know so accurately when she was in residence. The count's voice droned on and Valentina tried to look as if she were enjoying the story. She was thinking how strange it was that Yanin, who was more a man than any she had met, was not averse to picking flowers, writing poems and collecting paintings and other works of art. The count, on the other hand, was less a man than many she had encountered, yet he, like an actor, pursued masculine occupations and dressed in fanciful uniforms, as though to emphasize that which he did not possess. When her husband had finished speaking, Valentina asked what his plans were for the coming week.

"Shall we be staying in the city, sir? Shall we go to the Opera or to see the Tsar at the blessing of the waters ceremony?"

The count listened wearily, admitting to himself that Valentina's interests had little in common with his own. He loved hunting, shooting, collecting precious stones and being spoiled by his mistress. His wife was young and eager to experience the joys of adulthood. She loved visiting new places and meeting new people and had plans for years of travel all over Europe once she had had her "family." Realizing that she was waiting for him to reply, the count apologized for his lack of concentration.

"Forgive me, my dear, I was many miles away. Of course we must go to the blessing of the waters tomorrow. Wear your new sable cloak and the blue outfit I admired the other day. It will be very cold on the open river and sometimes the Tsar arrives late, so everyone is frozen."

Evening came and the count disappeared to his study. Left alone, Valentina thought of Yanin. Soon, she knew, he would return, expecting to find her a fully experienced woman and the count's true wife. He would be shocked to find her still inexperienced, still uncertain of her marital duties, despite Korolenko's virile reputation. Yanin was a good and dear friend, but would he understand the agony her ignorance had caused?

On their return from the ceremony of the blessing of the waters, the count and Valentina stepped down from their carriage in the inner courtyard of the palace and went their separate ways, he to his suite and she to hers. The count dressed impatiently. Valentina had been more affectionate than usual on the way back to the palace. If they had not arrived at that moment, she might have said something of her feelings for him. He was about to hurry to Valentina's suite when he heard a coach arriving in the courtyard. Looking down, he saw Magda stepping out. She was dressed in a dazzling orange-silk ball gown, with a cloak of yellow parrot feathers billowing out behind her in the breeze. Before Korolenko could step back from the window she had shouted up to him.

"Vladi, do hurry. You promised to take me to Konstantin Amarevich's party; I hope you have not forgotten!"

The count remembered that during the winter he had made such a promise. During the long nights on the island of Yelagin he had made many promises, none of which he now wanted to keep. He rang for his valet and told him to deliver a note to Madame Simoniescu. He was completing the note when Magda swept into the room.

"Now what are you doing?"

Snatching the note from Korolenko's hand, she read it.

"Ha! So now you write me letters telling me you cannot keep your promises. 'Dear Madame' indeed! For ten years you have accompanied me to the party at Pirogov's house and to the ball of the foreign diplomats that follows."

"Magda, I can no longer accompany you anywhere in St. Petersburg. I am married, and I have decided that if an heir is to be conceived, so that my title will be secure, I must mend my ways at once."

Magda threw back her head and laughed.

"And have you loved your baby bride yet? Tell me, Vladi, have you loved that wholesome little girl? Did she hire eastern dancers to perform lewd rites to excite you? Did she bring whores to your bed to revive your wilting masculinity? Did she let you watch as she was loved by half the hussars in St. Petersburg, so you could finally accomplish what you wanted to do? Answer me, damn you!"

Valentina paused outside her husband's room, her face paling as she heard his reply.

"My wife knows nothing of our depravity, madame. She is only a child, but she is a lively one and is ready for love, of that I am sure."

"Then who will you get to love her? Tell me, Vladi, who do you propose to use as the father of your children? Orlov, Pirogov, Mankowitz? You have surely not attempted to love her yourself?"

The count's silence gave Magda her answer and she walked to the door, pausing to deliver a final word before leaving.

"If you are not at the party within the hour you will regret it, sir. You are obviously not aware that this day two important ministers have been assassinated by one of the new revolutionary groups. Tomorrow they will kill more and someday they will murder every aristocrat in St. Petersburg and cause the revolution they so desire. You know, of course, who is their chief assassin? Do you remember those letters you wrote to Azanov? Say something, damn you, don't stand there with your mouth open like a codfish!"

"I recall my letters to Azanov, madame."

"The police are searching for him and the death penalty will be given to his friends and accomplices, if they can be found. Imagine, the loyal Count Korolenko hanging from a lamppost for his part as a revolutionary paymaster. I kept copies of all your letters. I wrote them for you, if you recall. I need only show them to the Okhrana. . . ."

Valentina called out as her husband hurried after Magda.

"Where are you going, sir?"

"I am going to Pirogov's party. Do not wait up for me."

But Valentina did wait up and when the staff had retired she sat alone in the hall, anxious to show her loyalty to her husband by welcoming him home. The clocks struck ten, eleven, midnight, one, two, three. Valentina thought they sounded like a death knell. The count did not return and as dawn was breaking a messenger arrived with a note: Forgive me, I have gone to Yelagin.

Valentina crushed the note in her hand and threw it on the floor. Then she ran upstairs and threw herself down on the bed, sobbing with shame and fury. She had been deserted yet again. Would it be for a day, a month, a year? And what had Magda meant— "Who do you propose to use as the father of your children?" Unpleasant thoughts buzzed like a thousand bees in Valentina's mind and she wished she had not listened to Magda's conversation with her husband.

When she had returned to her suite, a manservant picked up the crushed note, read it and sent a message via one of the grooms to Yanin. The servant shook his head wearily. The count had deserted his wife yet again. Where was it all going to end?

# CHAPTER SIX

## The Flower House, Spring 1903

Valentina was in the house she loved. She had hastened to the country after the count's departure for Yelagin, taking with her the three maids and a young girl she was training for work in the kitchen. The snows of winter had gone, leaving flooded fields and a countryside lit only by dark-gray clouds. Then, suddenly as always in Russia, the damp weather had vanished and on waking one morning Valentina had heard a cuckoo call and had seen sunshine shining through the spring-green leaves outside her bedroom window. At once the shame and sadness she had felt during the dark days vanished and she was full of energy and hope. Yanin had said he would return in the springtime and that meant he would be here soon. She rushed downstairs and ordered Clara to arrange for extra women to come each day from the estate to give the rooms their annual spring cleaning. Without actually realizing it, Valentina was preparing for Yanin's return. Each day she picked fresh flowers and arranged them in colorful profusion in her rooms. Each night she listened eagerly, hoping for the sound of hooves on the drive.

In the first week of spring farmworkers and gardeners from the estate brought gifts for the mistress of the house. This was an ancient custom and one that they had been unable to carry out in the years when the house had been empty. Valentina was ready for them and when she saw the procession of men and women, dressed in their Sunday best and laden with spring flowers and lilies of the valley, she ran from the tower room to the kitchen and bade them welcome. The men were rewarded with buckets of vodka, the women with gifts of money. The village priest asked permission to bless the house. Valentina nodded graciously and everyone kneeled while a prayer was said and holy water sprinkled. Having given their spring homage, the line of men and women left the house and passed slowly back down the path, through the yew-hedge arch to the estate cottages situated on the other side of the hill. Valentina thought how happy the workers had looked, how content that old customs could be revived because the once-forgotten property had a mistress again. In the autumn they would return, to pay another tribute with mushrooms and wild berries instead of flowers. They would lay the fruit down in wicker paniers for her to admire, and the stone floor of the kitchen would take on the colors of the hedge-row, rose, green, prune and yellow, a display of mellowness before the snows came.

The days passed swiftly because Valentina was busy. The mornings were spent supervising the cleaning and overseeing the training of a new maid in the kitchen. Nadya was fifteen, a buxom girl with bright-red hair, uneducated but ambitious. She had learned to write in order to beg Valentina for a post in the house, which was near her home in the village. Valentina smiled at the memory of the clumsy hand: I am a country girl, daughter of Chaim, the spice vendor. I want to work near my home and not leave for the city. Cities are full of evil folk. . . . Valentina paused by Nadya's side as she scrubbed the pine table.

"Are you happy now you are working here, Nadya?"

"I am, ma'am, and grateful to you."

"Is your room comfortable?"

"Oh, yes, ma'am, it's too lovely to use to sleep in so I walk home most nights, except when I have to work very late. I go to my bedroom each morning to sit at the window to enjoy the view. I intend to have a room just like it someday."

April passed and the summer came, hot and scented with the heady smells of heliotrope and acacia. Valentina felt restive. She had heard that the count had briefly visited St. Petersburg and then returned to Yelagin. Relief mingled with despair, confusing her. She had no desire to be loved by her husband and even less to be ignored in what she foolishly considered to be the prime years of her life. Suddenly she had begun to long for love and a husband who would be the knight in shining armor she had always dreamed about. Often at night, when she could not sleep, she would take her horse and ride around the count's land, stopping for a word with the workers before they retired. As Valentina lingered by the embers of their fire, the women shook their heads and muttered that Count Korolenko was a fool to neglect a wife so obviously lonely and eager for love.

Valentina was seventeen on the twentieth of May. She had told no one about her birthday and so did not expect presents to remind her that she was a year older. On waking, she found at her bedside three small gifts wrapped in red paper, a clove pomander from Nina, an embroidered handkerchief from Bibi and a patchwork cushion made by Zita during the long winter evenings. She rang the bell and thanked the maids for the gifts. Then Bibi burst out excitedly.

"There's a huge parcel for you in the hall, ma'am."

Valentina went to the landing and looked down to where a cumbersome parcel wrapped in silver paper stood looking strangely gaudy against the amber marble of the floor. She ran downstairs and began to tear at the wrappings. Zita and her sisters joined her, giggling excitedly. At last the present was revealed and Valentina stared at a solid-gold bicycle with elegant black tires and a bell that tinkled to warn the unwary of her approach. She stepped forward and took a card from the handle: "From Yekaterina and Gavrilo, a bicycle fit for a princess." Bursting into squeals of excitement, she sat on the floor, never taking her eyes from the amazing object before her. It occurred to her that she might have forgotten how to ride the bicycle, so she dismissed the maids, having asked them to prepare breakfast. When they had gone back to her suite, Valentina looked furtively from side to side before pedaling around and around and around the hall, ringing the bell loudly. She leaped off the bicycle when Gavrilo stepped through the door, applauding her enthusiastically.

"There are not many ladies in St. Petersburg who can boast of owning a solid-gold bicycle and still fewer who ride them in their negligees. Happy birthday, Valya."

She ran and kissed Gavrilo on both cheeks.

"My sister has gone to Paris; I came to tell you all about her visit."

Realizing that she was still in her negligee, Valentina ran ahead of him up the stairs. While she was dressing, Gavrilo took his place in her dining room and ordered Zita to prepare breakfast for two. Within minutes Valentina joined him. She was wearing a tight-waisted dress of yellow faille, with velvet roses around the hem. Gavrilo complimented her.

"Yellow is not a color my brother likes and, to be truthful, I am not overfond of it myself. On you, however, it looks splendid."

"This dress was sent as a gift from Natty, who lives in Paris. She is no longer a governess. Indeed, I believe she is quite wealthy. A relative of hers, a gentleman who had been trading in the East, left her money when he died. Natty had not seen him since she was small. Imagine what a shock it must have been."

"I have many things to tell you, Valentina. Firstly—I am to be married."

Valentina felt surprised and disappointed at the same time. She struggled to conceal her true feelings.

"May I ask the name of your intended?"

"She is a distant cousin of mine, Tanya Stepanovna Milenova. I have not seen her for many years but it has been arranged."

"How old is she?"

"Tanya will be twenty-six early in September. We shall be married in the new year."

"My congratulations, sir."

"You look disappointed. You are probably thinking that I shall not love you anymore and that I shall forget to guard your interests. You are quite wrong. I shall always love you, but I am not a fool and know that even if my brother died tomorrow you would not marry me. You would rush back to Paris at once."

"On my gold bicycle!"

They finished breakfast and walked arm in arm around the garden, looking at the new lily pond and the scented bower Valentina had designed. As they walked, Gavrilo explained.

"What I am about to say is treason. My life is therefore in your hands. Well, this is it. The Tsar is a weak man and not at all the ruler Russia needs at this moment because his ideas are still those of two centuries ago. He has stated his opinions about liberalization and they have alienated him from everyone, not only the peasants and members of the new revolutionary groups but also from members of the ruling classes. In addition to his autocracy, the Tsar has a great desire to rule the world. As you know, in nineteen hundred he occupied the whole of Manchuria. For a while, this satisfied his expansionist desires."

Valentina sat on a twirled iron bench, listening in shocked silence. Gavrilo continued, speaking slowly as if to a child.

"My sister also understands from one of her political contacts that if we were to lose the war, the revolutionaries, who number only a few thousand at this time, would increase greatly and become a true force in the running of our country. For this reason Yekaterina has placed most of her fortune in the vaults of a bank in Paris. I have also entrusted her with the transportation of the jewels I inherited from my grandmother. Yekaterina is not the only member of the aristocracy to do this. Dolgurov's mother has gone to England to deposit her jewels, and gold bars were sent by armed escort to the same location. Ulanov's mother has done likewise."

"I can scarcely believe all this, Gavrilo."

"The revolutionaries assassinated the Tsar's grandfather and were indirectly responsible for killing his father. Who can vouch for his safety in the future, or indeed for the safety of any of us? Yekaterina and I are pessimists. We feel it is better to be safe than sorry. The count is also a pessimist, but he loves Russia too much to consider leaving it. He would be enraged if he knew what my sister and I have done."

"May I invite you to stay for the day, Gavrilo?"

"I would like to but I cannot. That is why I came so early. Believe me, I rose before dawn. My fiancée is coming to lunch today with her parents. Thanks to you, Chef Dubrovsky will put on a fine show for them. I must leave almost at once."

Despite the beauty of her surroundings, Valentina was troubled. If Gavrilo and Yekaterina had taken such a drastic step they must consider the possibility of war or revolution likely. She remembered Gavrilo's words one night at the palace as they sat before the fire: Revolution has been brewing for hundreds of years. Pray God it will not boil over in our time, though the Tsar may do his best to provoke it.

She watched as Gavrilo left, then she continued to walk around the garden she loved, eyeing the yellow climbing roses invading her rooms from the new pergola. It was a beautiful, peaceful place. Surely nothing could ever change her feelings about Russia.

Valentina rode by the side of the cornfield to the fishing stream.

There she sat under the lime trees watching the sun make dappled patterns on the water. A frog leaped nearby, startling her. She lay back in the long grass, looking through the cow parsley to the lacy green cover of the leaves. After resting for a while and daydreaming about her future, she rose and led her horse toward the hunting lodge. As she drew near, she saw another horse tethered outside and smoke coming from the chimney. Remounting her horse, Valentina galloped forward. Then she jumped down and burst into the lodge, breathless with excitement.

Yanin looked up with a mocking smile.

"I thought you would never arrive."

"That's what you always say!"

Valentina hesitated when Yanin did not rise to greet her. She spoke breathlessly.

"When did you come back?"

"I came this morning, early."

"Why did you not come to the house to wish me . . ."

She paused uncertainly and Yanin filled in the unsaid words.

"Happy birthday? I am a gentleman and know the form of such things. I am aware that the count is on Yelagin with his mistress. I also know the count's brother visited you in the early morning and I imagine the estate workers also came to call to give their greetings. I was planning to come in the darkness to surprise you. It would hardly do for me to appear when you were not alone."

Valentina looked at Yanin's face and saw tension and unhappiness.

"You don't seem very pleased to see me, sir."

"I am not sir, I am Ivan, or have you forgotten?"

Valentina felt close to tears. How strange it was that Yanin remained apart, not leaping to his feet as he usually did when she appeared. She was even more distressed that he sat with his back to her, not even greeting her civilly. She sat on the edge of the bed and looked at her hands, waiting for him to say something. When he did, she winced.

"And how is married life, Valentina? You are more beautiful than ever but somewhat uncertain, if I may say. Tell me, what is happening between you and your dishonorable husband?"

For the first time Valentina saw fire in Yanin's eyes as he waited for her reply. Suddenly she felt elated. He is jealous, she thought, that is the cause of his reserve. He is jealous of the count and jealous of all the hours I have spent alone since his departure. She spoke softly, looking out of the window as she recalled the winter months.

"Since you left St. Petersburg I have been very lonely. The count returned in the new year and found me here with his brother and sister. When they returned to the capital I stayed on in this house with my husband, because it was his intention to love me. As you know, he desires an heir to the title more than anything."

Yanin looked away as she spoke. Valentina knew instinctively that Yanin was afraid to hear of her union with Korolenko. She continued calmly.

"After three days we returned to the city. The count was distressed because I was in the same condition as when I had left St. Petersburg. I too was extremely unhappy, because I had proved so unattractive to my husband that he could not love me. Later, his mistress came to call and I listened at the door as Magda argued with the count. She said, 'Surely you have not tried to love the child. Tell me, who do you plan to use as father of the children you so desire?'"

Tears began to stream down Valentina's cheeks at the memory of that unhappy day and she spoke in a whisper.

"I did not know what to do. I know nothing of my marital duties and my ignorance was surely the cause of the count's alarm. That day he left with Magda and went with her to Yelagin. She had threatened to send some incriminating letters to the secret police if he did not."

"So, the count is in trouble with the Okhrana? Thank God for that. They will keep him occupied for some time."

Valentina sat alone on the side of the bed, crying softly, because the dream of Yanin's return had turned into a nightmare.

"And I, sir, what shall I do? I am the laughingstock of St. Petersburg, forever deserted by my husband. The count cries out for an heir to the title but he cannot or will not love me and I continue to wallow in my ignorance. Will no one tell me what is expected of a wife?"

Yanin rose and pulled Valentina to his chest.

"My dearest love, I have thought of nothing but you in all these months and have ridden like a Tartar to be here on your birthday.

I did not come to the house because I was filthy. I have been bathing the dirt from my body these past hours and trying to rest awhile so I should not fall asleep on your shoulder."

"You greeted me as though you were sad to see me."

"I *was* sad to see you looking so lusty and eager and full of womanliness. I am ashamed to say I am fiercely jealous of the count and of anyone else who dares look in your direction. All these months the thought of you being in that degenerate's bed has tortured me."

"There is no need to be jealous, Ivan. I am still the virgin bride, untried and unloved by anyone. They tell stories about my wedding night in the bawdy houses of the Moika and laugh uproariously when they come to the part where the count left me and rode back to his mistress."

Yanin pulled her away from him and looked into Valentina's eyes.

"How do you know such a thing?"

"Zita told me. She boxed the ears of one of the footmen for speaking about it. What am I to do, Ivan? Tell me what you think I should do."

"Valentina, I am back at your side and I shall not be going away for some time. I shall cry too, kitten, if you do not give me a smile at once. Now let me find the presents I have brought for you."

Then she saw that Yanin walked with a limp, and she cried out. "What have you done to your leg?"

"I got shot in the knee while we were chasing some marauders. I had hoped it would have ceased troubling me by now but it has not."

He took out a velvet box and handed it to Valentina.

"This is the first present. I bought it in Odessa. It has a surprising history which I shall tell you someday."

Valentina looked down at a ring fashioned in the shape of a China rose, made of yellow diamonds and topaz. The leaves of the rose were emeralds, the band gold. It had a look of Tartar opulence and barbarian antiquity. She put it on and held it closely with her other hand.

"I shall never take this off."

"Your husband will make you."

"I shall refuse."

Yanin continued to rummage in the pack until he pulled out a yellow-silk scarf. From its folds he took a box studded with rubies and handed it to Valentina. Opening the box, she heard the strains of a traditional cossack song:

> *Say goodbye my own true lover*
> *As we sing a lovers' song*
> *How it breaks my heart to leave you*
> *Now the carnival is gone. . . .*
> *Now the harbor lights are fading*
> *This will be our last goodbye*
> *Though the carnival is over*
> *I will love you till I die*

Blushing with pleasure, Valentina sat at Yanin's feet, her ear to the box, her hand waving gently in front of her face as she took pleasure in the ring. She barely noticed Yanin carrying a large parcel from the corner of the room and depositing it at her feet. Then something in his face made her curious.

"What is it?"

"This is my most important present to you, kitten. I hope you like it and I hope it fits because you are certainly going to wear it."

Valentina darted to the box and pulled out a dress of aged beauty. She stood looking at it for several minutes. The dress was encrusted with beads and very heavy. It was made of coral and gold silk with a tiny waist and a high collar. Tight sleeves ended in bejeweled points over the hands and the skirt was so vast it filled half the small room. Petticoats rustled as she twirled the dress to and fro and there was a faint smell of musk and honeysuckle. Inside the box Valentina saw another tissue-wrapped parcel and putting the dress down on the bed she picked up the remaining gift. It was a circular coronet, old, as she could see from the cut of the rubies. Attached to the coronet was a veil of gold lace. She put on the diadem, admiring the veil and the warm glitter of the rubies. She took off the veil and looked questioningly at Yanin.

"This is the most beautiful dress I have ever seen, but how can I wear it? People would think I was about to be married."

"Exactly. That is a Tartar wedding dress which once belonged to a princess of the plains. I know you are already married Valentina, but I intend to marry you again in my own way. Of course, in some ways the ceremony can only be a masquerade, but I cannot wait much longer to love you."

"I do not understand what you mean, Ivan."

"I bought you the wedding dress, Valentina, because I want to have the benefit of making vows to you. Tell me you will wear it?"

"Where and how?"

"I will arrange everything. Come here at ten tomorrow morning and I will show you a new world. This will be the marriage of our hearts, Valentina. I love you more than anything in the world and will marry no one else but you."

Valentina lay at Yanin's side as he put his arms around her and kissed her cheeks. Looking at him she caught his eye and he tweaked her ear and kissed her cheek.

"What are you debating as you lie there looking like an angel?"

"I'm not debating."

Yanin rolled onto his back, put his hands behind his head and spoke as if to himself.

"She is wondering if she will have to fulfill the marital duties she found so puzzling with her husband. She is debating what she must say to me to make me teach her the facts of love. She treats love as if it were a schoolroom subject to be learned from a book. Shall I show her how simple it is and how splendid?"

Angry, Valentina pulled away from him and sat clutching her knees.

"I am seventeen years old and married, but a virgin. My governess told me the count would explain what I must do to please him when we were married. The count said only that to make children a seed must be planted. This was done by placing the masculinity in the femininity. When I asked how this was accomplished he did not answer. Now he has left me again and gone to his mistress, who has the skills I lack."

"You do not need skills except with a man like the count. Married people learn to please each other easily. The man teaches his wife by example and they tell each other secrets they would tell no one else. Obviously the count was unequal to the effort that was required, so he blamed you."

"No, he blamed his own body and was greatly distressed."

Yanin rose and held out his hands.

"Invite me to dine with you at eight and I shall polish my boots and make myself presentable."

"You are invited."

Yanin peered out into the night.

"It's dark. I had best accompany you to the house. I will return at eight. Leave the new dress here, it will be waiting for you in the morning."

Valentina returned to her suite in the house and lay on her bed staring at the violets on the ceiling. Was it really happening? At ten in the morning she was to be "married" to Yanin. Surely he was teasing. Had he something else in mind? Had she believed him? She knew she had and confusion made her agitated. After a while she called for Zita.

"I shall be having a guest for dinner, a very special guest. The chef will not be here this evening. Can you make something special? It is so long since I saw my friend, and I want him to be very happy."

"Chef called yesterday and left a special dish for your birthday, ma'am. He also brought a cake of strawberries and sugar with a garden on the top. I'll get some champagne from the cellar and some of those fancy glasses from the cabinet."

"And yellow roses too. See you don't prick your finger when you cut them, Zita."

Yanin arrived and was greeted by Zita, resplendent in dark-blue serge with a frilly white apron. She was proud of her new uniform and curtsied gracefully, as Valentina had taught her, before leading Yanin upstairs to where her mistress was waiting in a room full of yellow roses. Yanin clicked his heels and Valentina marveled at the transformation in his appearance. The tension was gone, the uncertainty too, replaced by a warm, strong, purposeful gaze. Yanin bent and kissed her cheek.

"Is this beautiful room of flowers all for me? It is wonderful. Throughout the winter I have been dreaming of dining with you and drinking champagne together. I sleep with one of your yellow roses pressed under my pillow."

"So do I, sir. I am pleased to know you are also a romantic."

"I am only a romantic with you, kitten. I have never suffered the pangs of the heart before."

They sat together by the fire, drinking champagne and growing hungrier by the minute, as delicious smells came from the kitchen. At last Zita announced dinner. They took their places and looked expectantly at the maids to know what they were going to eat. Valentina's favorite soup of sorrel and leek began the meal, followed by a chicken dish left by the chef. A salad of lettuce and endive followed and then a compote of apricots scented with absinthe. The cake was a revelation, an iced garden of yellow roses, daisies and bluebells in tiny whorls of the pâtissier's art. Yanin complimented his hostess on the food.

"I have spent the winter eating turnips and roast rabbit and am heartily sick of both. Until tonight I thought I had lost my appetite."

"I hope we shall have many, many enchanting meals together, Ivan."

"Have you entertained many people since you came to the house?"

"I have entertained no one but you. Are you still feeling jealous?"

"I swear I am the most jealous man in Russia. I shall have to learn to keep my imagination in check, but you are so beautiful I cannot imagine any man resisting you."

The champagne had gone to Valentina's head and she longed to go to bed to dream of the exciting happenings of the day. Instead, she sat at Yanin's side after dinner, listening as he talked of the winter campaign and then about his family estate nearby. He teased her about the surprises in store for her the following day and kissed her a dozen times, each time more fervently than the last.

Then, seeing that Valentina was tired, Yanin rose and lifted her to her feet.

"That was a most beautiful evening, but now you are falling asleep. Let me carry you to your room. Then I shall return to my temporary quarters in the hunting lodge and wait for your arrival. Are you still awake?"

"Of course I am."

"Shall I instruct Zita to wake you early?"

"She always wakes me at seven."

"I am afraid you may wish to sleep on tomorrow."

"I hardly think that likely."

Yanin carried Valentina to her room and put her gently down on her bed. He kissed her lightly on the forehead and left the house as silently as he had come.

Zita watched from an upstairs window until Yanin had disappeared into the woods. Then she ran to Valentina's room and pulled off her mistress's satin slippers. Valentina was already asleep, so Zita bathed her hands and cheeks with rose water and left her alone to her dreams. She was about to join her sisters when Nadya came bounding into the room.

"Who was that handsome young man?"

Zita looked imperiously down at the kitchen maid.

"He was a guest of the house."

"What is his name?"

"I don't ask the names of Madame's guests."

Nadya laughed out loud at Zita's scornful expression.

"Aren't you a stiff one!"

Zita hustled Nadya back into the hall, furious when the kitchen maid burst into peals of excited laughter.

"I was just going home to the village when I almost bumped into him. He's as handsome as a dream, isn't he? Is Madame in love with him? Is she cuckolding the count, do tell me, will you?"

Zita drew herself up haughtily and replied with all the force she had learned from Valentina.

"I have ambitions in this world, Nadya. I wish to become indispensable to the countess and to accompany her on all her travels. I want to earn a good wage and to have a comfortable retirement too. I do not wish to remain forever the ignoramus I once was, and one thing I have already learned is that I should be unwise to answer questions from nosy women like you."

"Just tell me one thing. Is the young officer Madame's lover?"

"I shall speak to Madame about you in the morning."

Bibi joined her sister as Zita began to clear the table.

"Zita, what did that horrid little Nadya want?"

"She's nosy, that one. She wanted to know if Major Yanin was Madame's lover."

Bibi's eyes widened in alarm.

"I'll give her a good slapping if she ever comes up here again."

Nadya wandered out of the house and flounced down the drive, still smarting from Zita's comments. She was weighing the details of Yanin's appearance. He was tall and handsome, with dark crinkly hair and melting, light-colored eyes and enough charm for an entire regiment. His dark-green, gold and scarlet uniform was the uniform of a real soldier, not one of those made up confections the rich of St. Petersburg were fond of wearing. Nadya decided to ask her father if he knew which regiment the uniform indicated.

At ten the following morning Valentina arrived at the hunting lodge. She found Yanin ready to leave, her wedding dress and other accessories slung over the back of his horse. She looked eagerly toward him.

"Where are we going, Ivan?"

"Follow me, we shall soon be there."

They rode away, he leading Valentina through the grounds of the count's estate to the main entrance and then across the road to an iron-studded gate in a high stone wall. Yanin unlocked the gate and led his horse through. Valentina dismounted and followed, entering a courtyard surrounded on all sides by a high wall of gray pebble. In one of the walls there was a door painted white that led to a wooden pavilion covered in clematis and wistaria. The building was small, not more than four rooms. The windows had latticed panes and Valentina noticed heavy lace curtains of a style more familiar in Paris than in St. Petersburg. She spoke excitedly.

"That little house looks like something out of a fairytale."

"For us it *will* be something out of a fairytale. I shall explain everything in a few moments, kitten."

On entering the pavilion, Valentina was enchanted to see that it was furnished in the style of a country farmhouse of the previous century. The furniture was carved pine and aloe wood. The walls, a deep gold color, were stenciled with primitive designs of peacocks and flowers. In the hearth a fire roared, taking away the chill of early morning. And through the open windows birdsong came like a joyous chorus to reassure. Valentina touched an intricate patchwork cover on the table and turned to Yanin, who said, "Go in there and change into the dress. If you need help with the fastenings I will come."

"Whose house is this?"

"This is a pavilion in the garden of my mother's home. Next door is Mama's private chapel. This pavilion was used by my aunt for her love trysts with the count's father when the hunting lodge was not available."

"Where is your mother?"

"At our house in St. Petersburg. She will be staying there for at least another month."

Valentina walked into a bedroom sweet with the scent of flowers. Bunches of dried corn stood next to bowls of oxeye daisies and lavender. The bedhead was carved in the shape of a pair of doves. The walls were painted with designs of lilies and pink cabbage roses. On the floor wolf-fur skins kept her feet from growing cold and in the corner there was an ancient icon lit by a glowing candle. She took off her dress and stepped into the other. The sleeves were very tight, the bodice impossible to fasten. She called for help.

"I cannot fasten this dress, Ivan."

Yanin appeared at the door and she shivered as his hands touched the bare skin of her back. He looked over her shoulder at her reflection in the mirror.

"You look sensational."

He placed the diadem of rubies on her head and lifted the veil over her shoulders.

"Now you really are a bride."

Alone again, Valentina stood at the window looking out at the garden. It was planted with flowers of the sweetest fragrance, all pink and yellow or white. Yanin reappeared in his dress uniform and held out his arm. Once outside the pavilion he took Valentina to the chapel and she could see that he was as excited as if this were his real wedding day. She kissed Yanin as he turned the key in the lock.

"Are you going to tell me exactly what you plan?"

"I plan a marriage of our minds, Valentina. This is enough and all I can expect under the circumstances. It will signify that our minds accept our partnership and all that that entails."

The chapel walls were white, the altar gold, the only color a Greek-blue line running around each of the Gothic windows. Valentina followed Yanin to the altar rail and stared uneasily at the crucifix above her. Would God think this a sacrilege? Yanin read her thoughts.

"You are already married, Valentina. This ceremony is for me, because I would dearly love to have been the man who knelt at your side in the wedding chapel. I intend to pray for a blessing on our union. You must pray for guidance, because before we are through we shall surely need it."

"You frighten me, Ivan."

"I mean no harm, but in truth you have not yet realized what I intend for us. When you do, you will understand."

Valentina knelt at Yanin's side, trying to find words to ask for guidance, but she could not concentrate. Her eyes kept taking in things of interest in the chapel, the heavy white lace of the altar cloth, the carved ivory crucifix, the smell of lemon and incense. She looked at Yanin, who was deep in prayer, admiring the sheen of his hair, the devotion in his manner. Impulsively, she kissed him and inclined her head against his. Yanin turned to face her.

"Here are my vows, Valentina. In a real marriage I should undertake to look after you, to honor you and to be true only to you. At least that is what would happen in a Parisian marriage, that is what I know you would have liked. As it is, I make all those vows of my own volition. I will always care for you alone. I will guard your interests and be true to you. I shall never cease loving you and will always be close at hand to do whatever I can to make you happy. That is my vow."

"And I shall always love you, Ivan, even when I am old and ugly. I shall be true to you and try in every way to make you happy."

"Then we are married in our fashion and may God have mercy on us."

Yanin kissed her cheek and touched the ring on her finger. Valentina felt a tear falling down her cheek when he spoke.

"The ring I bought you will have to serve as your wedding ring. It is hardly suitable."

She looked down at the Tartar ring Yanin had bought her.

"I love it dearly."

"And do you love me?"

Valentina could almost feel the silence as she looked down, overwhelmed by the moment.

"I love you as much as there are stars in the sky, Ivan."

They ran hand in hand to the pavilion and began to pick at the feast Yanin had put on the table. Valentina felt ravenously hungry when she saw the cold ham and chicken and suckling pig set out on lace napkins alongside fruit and pastries of the finest dimension.

"Where on earth did you buy this food?"

"Dolgurov brought it from St. Petersburg. He was overcome at what I planned and wanted to make sure you were content. I told him you were always hungry when you felt happy."

"Is Dolgurov discreet?"

"He has been my friend since I was three. We are in the same regiment and he is the only fellow I would die for."

"I hope you will not think of dying now that you are a married man, Ivan."

Valentina changed from the beaded gown to her own simple dress and for an hour they adventured together in the garden of the estate. The house was small but luxuriously appointed and she thought its informality as different from the normal stiffness of Russian country houses as any she had seen. She asked Yanin questions about the management of the estate and was thrilled to be shown the stables full of fine horses.

By midday the sun was burning down and Valentina was so hot Yanin decided to make an iced cordial to cool her. As she lounged on top of the bed, he appeared with a jug and two glasses.

"Here we are, this will stop your body from catching fire."

Valentina took the glass and held it to her throat. She was a little intoxicated by the excitement and the champagne. Yanin sat at her side and they talked and drank the icy liquid until it was almost gone. Then he rose and began to undress. Valentina leaped up in alarm.

"Whatever are you doing, Ivan?"

"I am going to love my wife."

Valentina sat stiffly down on the bed, fear sobering her in a moment. Yanin poured her more of the cold drink, weighing the trembling of her hands against the languorous look in her eyes. When he was naked, he lay at her side and began to unbutton her dress.

She tried not to stare at his body but she could not contain her curiosity. Yanin's body was different in every way from that of the count. One was a poppyhead withered at the end of summer, the other was a ripe gourd, ready to spew its seeds on the fertile ground. Her heart began to pound in her ears and she felt so unlike herself she almost burst into tears. Yanin's skin was brown from the sun, his muscles hard from the long winter campaign. He smelled of the fields and the ferns and the countryside and there was an increasing urgency about him that she had never seen before. Looking down at her breasts, as he exposed them, Valentina realized that this was the moment when she would make love for the first time. She struggled against Yanin as he slipped off her under petticoats and drawers. He smothered her protests with kisses. Valentina felt his body hard against her own and understood, at last, what her husband had meant about planting a seed within her. The thought shocked and she tried to resist, but as Yanin led her toward the moment of togetherness she became pliant in his arms and open to his body. Yanin devoured her breasts, her stomach and the inner core that was wet with longing. Valentina cried out because every nerve in her body seemed to be on fire. She wanted to show her own feelings but Yanin was firm. This time he would do all that had to be done to take her to the nirvana of ecstasy. At last she felt him part her legs and prepare to enter her body. Half conscious, half wandering from the violence of her desire, she opened her eyes and smiled up at him. A brief moment of hurt was followed by the oscillating heat of his body within hers. Valentina moaned and writhed on the bed but still the unrelenting pursuit continued until at last the moment of truth took all her strength and left her limp but elated at Yanin's side. Tears fell down her cheeks, her knees twitched and jerked as spasms of ecstasy robbed her of all control. Yanin cried out. Then he was silent and for a long time he did nothing but stroke her hair and whisper in her ear.

"I love you, Valya . . . I love you . . . you are the most beautiful lover in the world."

Yanin told her that in some parts of the world the moment of giving was known as the little death. Valentina blushed and said it was the opposite. It was the moment when a woman burst into life. As they lay together she held his hand tightly, as though afraid Yanin might vanish. He saw that she was happy and sighed with relief. The ordeal of first love was over, it had been a triumph of enjoyment. Impulsively he kissed her and told her all his most secret thoughts. He was thinking that from this moment they would build on the foundation of their love until they only need blink or smile to give each other their thoughts.

By nightfall, when they had loved again and again, they began to feel sleepy. Yanin brought Valentina a plate of food. Then, wrapping a towel around his waist, he raided his mother's ice pit again and made another jug of cooling cordial because her body was on fire with excitement. When they had eaten, she leaned upon one elbow and asked, "Am I now with child, Ivan?"

"Not necessarily. Only a few of the seeds form children, not all of them."

"If I am, how shall I tell my husband?"

"You will tell the count you are going to give him the heir he does not deserve."

"I must return home now, mustn't I?"

"I will accompany you in a while."

"Will we meet again tomorrow?"

"Of course we shall. I have taken my annual leave so we can be together every day. You are my wife, Valentina. You will come to me at the hunting lodge when you finish breakfast and we shall love the day away."

"What if we have been seen?"

"I don't care."

There was a brief pause before Valentina spoke.

"Neither do I."

She lay back, closing her eyes the better to recall the luxurious feelings of the day. As Yanin dressed, she spoke softly, as though talking to herself.

"Have you realized, Ivan, I needed no instruction? I only needed your body to show me the way."

Yanin smiled. At this moment everything was perfect. He uttered a silent prayer that the count would never try to destroy the beauty of their love for each other. He helped Valentina dress and rode back with her to the Flower House. As she passed inside, he waved and blew a kiss. Then, turning, he almost fell over Nadya. Yanin looked down, narrowing his eyes at the excited look on the maid's face. The girl had obviously been waiting for him and perhaps spying on him. Yanin spoke angrily.

"You are the same miss I collided with last night, are you not? Is it your intention to spy on me?"

Nadya stammered a reply.

"No, sir, indeed not, sir."

"I hope not, because that would be a very dangerous thing for you to do."

Nadya watched as Yanin strode back through the trees to his horse. Then, crying like a baby, she ran all the way home to tell her father what had happened.

## CHAPTER SEVEN

### St. Petersburg, 1904–1907

Summer passed slowly, with many thunderstorms but no welcome sound of horses' hooves that would signify Yanin's return. Yekaterina and Gavrilo went back to the city at the beginning of September, leaving Valentina to enjoy her home in its autumn mantle. Alone, she stood by the lake looking up at the façade of the property. The dusky-pink walls were covered with creeper, its leaves turning fiery gold and crimson as the days grew shorter. In the hothouse green grapes hung ready to be cut and in the fields estate workers were singing their harvest hymns. The winds of autumn had arrived, turning everything tinder dry with their warmth. As the wind moaned against the walls of the house, desire made Valentina's limbs feel torpid and she sat trailing her hands in the water of the lake. She was beginning to fear that Yanin had fallen ill. If not, why had he not returned?

Her loneliness came to an end in the middle of September, when Yanin came riding through the corn stubble. The sky was mustard-yellow, the air heavy with the smell of overripe fruit, bonfire smoke and fallen leaves decaying on the paths. Yanin's green jacket with its red facings was a welcome rush of color in the landscape. But his face was stiff with anger, and Valentina retreated anxiously as he leaped down from his horse.

"Is something wrong, Ivan?"

Yanin kissed her and held her to his chest. When he spoke it was obvious he was angry.

"I have just come from St. Petersburg. Your husband is flaunting his mistress all over the city. I hear he and Madame Simoniescu will sit together in the Korolenko family box at the ballet, as though she were his wife and accepted by his family. I fear he is deliberately trying to insult you."

"You're back and I'm happy. We'll talk of the count later."

As she walked with Yanin toward the house, Valentina sighed. For the count to take his mistress into the family box at the theater was an insult of the highest order. Had she been too willing to accept Korolenko's philandering? Did he take her passivity for lack of interest? She decided to think about her husband later. In the meantime she and Yanin retired to her suite for the rest of the day. He was full of questions about the count.

"Has he tried to love you?"

"He has not. He has barely spoken to me."

"Take off your clothes. I want to love you until dawn comes."

Yanin began to untie and unbutton. Within minutes they were in bed. Valentina thought with a start that this was the first time they had ever been together inside the house. Previous meetings had been in the pavilion or the hunting lodge. Was it wise to be so indiscreet? Yanin kissed her cheeks, her shoulders, her nipples, her feet. Then he threw back the bedclothes, parting her legs. Valentina's thoughts of discretion disappeared as she rolled over until she was sitting astride her lover. Then, throwing back her head, she enjoyed him with all the hunger of one who has been too long alone.

For two weeks Yanin stayed at Valentina's side. Zita and her sisters served the couple as though nothing were amiss. Nadya had been dismissed, so they were alone, without cause to fear her curiosity. Sometimes Valentina asked herself if she could trust the three girls. Then she shrugged. If she could not, it would mean discovery, not death. In any case, she trusted them implicitly and for their part they rose to every occasion on which she needed them.

Soon the frosts came. The mornings were chilly and full of the scent of woodsmoke. Fires were lit in the hall each day and Zita and her sisters put on their winter dresses. After Yanin's departure for the barracks in St. Petersburg, Valentina toured the estate, making lists of jobs to be completed by the time she returned. She walked alone through the garden, picking off poppyheads dried by the sun. Late autumn was a melancholy time of year, when the gold of summer turned to the icy blue of winter. She had decided to spend the coldest months in the country and was looking forward to the sense of isolation she always felt once the snow arrived. But first she would visit St. Petersburg to confront the count.

The Mariinsky Theater seated eighteen hundred people. The walls were turquoise and silver, the carpet cornflower blue. Crystal chandeliers shimmered spectacularly in the foyer and Valentina felt it was like entering a palace of light. She had waited some time before making her way to the auditorium, aware that all eyes would be on her as she entered the box of the French ambassador. She was dressed all in white, the chiffon of the dress appliquéd with satin tiger lilies. Only the ring Yanin had given her, matching a necklace of topaz and yellow diamonds, flashed color at the inquisitive assembly. Valentina was well pleased with the attention she received. Even the Tsar noticed her and nodded a regal greeting from the royal box. Valentina curtsied gracefully in reply, avoiding looking toward the Korolenko box on the opposite side of the theater, where the count and Magda were sitting. Magda was in scarlet satin and Valentina thought spitefully that the color of the dress matched madame's complexion.

At the interval, Magda disdained to withdraw to the foyer, in contravention of the established custom. Instead, she grasped her opera glasses and stared shamelessly at the group in the French ambassador's box. Footmen were busy pouring iced champagne for the diplomat's guests. Magda looked first at Yekaterina, fuming that her old enemy seemed so happy. Her glance darted past the ambassador to Gavrilo, who was raising his glass to Valentina. Magda's eyes widened when she saw the divinely handsome young officer of the Preobrazhensky Regiment, sitting at Valentina's side and watching her every move. The officer was a true storybook hero, his face tanned by wind and sun, his body strong and fearless. Magda wondered if the count would challenge the young man to a duel. Who was he, anyway, to sit like royalty with another man's wife, as if unaware that he was causing a scandal? She turned her glasses on Valentina. The girl looked so beautiful, and also bold. Her eyes were shining with excitement and every few moments she turned to the young officer and laughed merrily. Magda looked closely at Valentina's milky white skin and the blue lines under her eyes. From the way her body kept inclining toward the young officer so alluringly, the count's mistress decided that

Yanin was surely the girl's lover. She rose and hurried out to tell the count her suspicions. When she reached the foyer she burst out indignantly: "Vladi, I have something important to tell you."

"I don't wish to hear it if it concerns my wife."

"It does indeed."

"Then be silent, madame."

Korolenko's face was taut with anger. If he chose to shame his wife by appearing with Magda, that was his prerogative. After all, he had little choice but to indulge his mistress. But for Valentina to appear impeccably chaperoned by his sister and brother, and in the company of the French ambassador, while cavorting with a young officer of the Preobrazhensky Regiment, what could result but scandal? He would suddenly become the cuckold of the century, the middle-aged husband incapable of satisfying his young wife's desires. All the effort he had taken to preserve his potent reputation as a womanizer would be put to naught by a girl who had no idea of propriety. Inwardly the count fumed. He would break Valentina's pretty neck if she ever repeated this performance.

When the ballet was over and the applause ceased, Valentina thanked the ambassador for his cooperation in allowing her guests to use his box. Then she walked out to the foyer between Gavrilo and Yanin. Yekaterina followed on the arm of the Frenchman. On reaching the staircase that led to the entrance, Valentina came face to face with her husband and his mistress. She nodded to Korolenko as if he were a mere acquaintance. When his brother did not greet him Gavrilo walked ahead down the staircase, holding Valentina's hand to steady her as she stepped forward to follow. Magda put out her foot, intending to trip her rival. Realizing her intention, Yanin stepped hard on the foot, making Magda cry out. Yanin clicked his heels and apologized.

"I beg your pardon, madame, but naturally I did not expect your foot to be in front of mine at that moment."

He nodded curtly and walked smartly down the staircase after Valentina. The Frenchman followed, his face showing nothing of his desire to laugh at Yanin's audacity. Yekaterina stole a look at her brother as he tried to calm Magda's tears. Then she put her fan in front of her face so he would not know that she was laughing too.

Late that night, the count sat alone in his study trying to decide what course of action to take about Valentina's monstrous charade. He could forbid her to go anywhere without his permission. She would ignore him, and in any case Yekaterina would come to her defense. To go out to the ballet with friends and relations was hardly a serious offense. The offense was his own. The count cursed Magda for her stupidity and himself for fearing her. The first thing to be done was that he must tell Magda he was through with her. Then he must try to retrieve his marriage and his reputation. Was it too late? For a moment he thought of Yanin's defiant gaze and the admiration in Valentina's eyes. He comforted himself by thinking how virtuous his wife was. She would not have made love with the officer, as Magda would under the same circumstances. Valentina was the perennial virgin, of that he had no doubt. The count walked to the courtyard and took his horse from the groom. Within minutes he was riding around the dark city streets, trying to clear his mind.

Two nights later Valentina appeared again at the ballet. This time her host was the British ambassador, and though Yekaterina and Gavrilo were again in attendance, the young man at Valentina's side was Dolgurov, Yanin's best friend. Valentina smiled a secret smile when she saw the reaction of the audience. The French ambassador had arranged for his colleague's box to be used and the Englishman, amused by Valentina's nerve, had agreed to act as an additional chaperon. She herself had arranged with Yanin for Dolgurov's presence. The young man was six feet five inches tall and as blond as Yanin was dark. He was already half in love with Valentina and his adoration was obvious to everyone. The aristocrats of St. Petersburg gazed in astonishment and babbled excitedly at the audacity of Countess Korolenko, in appearing a second time without her husband and in the company of a young officer of the Guard.

For the rest of the week Valentina attended the ballet or the opera with Yekaterina, Gavrilo and a member of the diplomatic corps. In addition, a young man appeared at her side, either Yanin, Dolgurov or Ulanov, Gavrilo's best friend and a legendary womanizer. St. Petersburg buzzed with gossip about the supposedly chaste young bride of Count Korolenko. "If she cannot have her husband, she is going to have every other man in the city," an officer told his friend, in the hearing of Korolenko. Stunned by this ribald comment, the count rushed home to confront his wife, but she had left for the Flower House.

The country house smelled of burning logs, peppermint punch and yellow roses. Yanin had a month's leave and planned to spend it all with Valentina. Their days were spent tobogganing, skating, riding and shooting in the woods. The winter was ice-white and silver, a pure, unsullied world of troikas, open fires and glowing lamps. Valentina had never been happier. Each morning when she woke her heart welcomed the new day. Each night she slept deeply content that Russia, once the unwelcome unknown, was now home. This was the place where her friends were. This was the place where she knew how to arrange everything, no matter what. In Paris nothing would be familiar anymore. All the old landmarks would have gone or been forgotten. She finally convinced herself that she had no need for Paris. The initial nervousness Valentina had felt in moments of intimacy with Yanin had vanished and often he teased her that they were like an old married couple. Her favorite moments were those spent with her lover skating on the lake in front of the house. Not daring to engage the fiddler from the village, they made music with the aid of Zita and her pennywhistle, Bibi, who knew a dozen traditional tunes and sang them in a high clear voice, and Nina, who played the flute. Often, at night, after love, Valentina would lie at Yanin's side smiling with sheer pleasure as she thought of waltzing on the shimmering ice and watching the winter sun make patterns on the pink façade of the house. This was how she would always remember the early days of her love, coupled with memories of riding through the cornfields of summer with Yanin and gathering red poppies from among the corn, red poppies that faded too soon.

One morning, toward the end of her stay in the country, Valentina woke with a premonition. She took her journal from the bedside and counted the days, realizing at once that her monthly cycle was disturbed. She looked wonderingly at her reflection in the mirror, relieved to see her face looking no different from before, her figure neither. She dressed as quickly as she could and hurried to the breakfast room. She was eating ravenously when Yanin entered and kissed her. As he sat at her side, Zita served him a plate of eggs and kidneys with his favorite smoked ham. When Zita had gone Yanin began to question her.

"You're a trifle pale. Is anything wrong?"

"I think I may be with child."

Yanin's delight showed in his eyes.

"Don't say think, say you are sure."

"I am not sure but I believe I am. I have thought many times in the past few days that this would be the time that I would conceive."

Yanin kissed her gently.

"I shall be the proudest man in Russia. By the way, this came today. I am to report to the barracks on the fourth."

"We'll go the day after tomorrow. I can't resist another afternoon skating with you on the lake."

"You'll do no more skating! I intend to treat you like rare crystal."

One Sunday Valentina resolved to visit Yanin at his residence in St. Petersburg. After the humiliating defeat in the Russian war with Japan there had been another series of strikes and the roads were full of demonstrators and dissatisfied people of every political persuasion. Valentina hastened from her carriage to the Yanin house and was admitted by a servant. She was taken through to a drawing room, where a tall, stately woman introduced herself.

"I am Irina Alexandrovna, Vanya's mother."

"I am Valentina Ivanovna Korolenko."

"My son is on duty today, so he will not be home until nightfall. I have just arrived from the country and find the city crippled yet again by the strikers."

"May I ask why you came to St. Petersburg?"

"I came to try to persuade my son to relinquish his military ambitions. I do hope you will help me, Countess."

"I want Ivan to be safe above all else. I will therefore do my best to persuade him with whatever influence I have."

"He loves you dearly; you have all his attention."

"And he mine, Madame Yanina."

It was late afternoon when Valentina left the Yanin house. In the distance she could hear voices raised in song. Recalling the patriotic verses her grandmother had once taught her, she wondered who was singing the old anthems and hymns. The light was failing, the sky pale lemon yellow streaked with gray. The snow glowed under the light of the gas lamps and there was an air of expectancy that was almost tangible. As she drew near the Tsar's palace Valentina saw that a crowd of many thousands was assembled in the square before the railings of the vast building. The people were led by a priest carrying a scroll or petition. She ordered her driver to halt and sat at the edge of the crowd listening as Russian voices sang hymns of praise for their country. Men and women in the crowd were carrying images of the Tsar, icons, banners and patriotic flags. Valentina was touched by their hopeful faces and aware from the banners that they had come to petition the Tsar to bring peace to the troubled land.

She was about to instruct her driver to continue on when a shot rang out. Aghast, Valentina looked toward the palace and saw a line of guards advancing and firing point-blank into the crowd. Other men and women were coming from one of the bridges over the Neva to join the demonstration. The infantry fired furiously to hold them back and women fell dead by the side of their children.

Valentina sat like a statue, stunned into immobility by the horror of the spectacle before her. Bullets whistled in the air, the dying cried out in agony, women screamed hysterically and men stood with their banners proclaiming honor to the Tsar and were shot as they gazed in anguish at the tragic scene.

At last she came to life and ordered the driver to make haste to the Korolenko Palace. He did not move when she tapped his shoulder with her umbrella and when she nudged him to obey her command he fell forward, dead from a stray bullet.

Valentina climbed up on the box and took the reins, trying not to look toward the Winter Palace, where soldiers were still firing on the crowd. Everywhere around her she could see cossacks riding like dervishes among the people, lashing their swords and knouts indiscriminately. There were bodies in the snow, their blood staining the pristine brightness, their sightless eyes looking in mute appeal at the evening sky. The ground was awash with the remains of the fallen and the gates of the Tsar's residence were stained irrevocably with the slaughter. Valentina urged the horses forward and they moved briskly on, skirting the holocaust and proceeding toward the Nevsky Prospekt.

They were almost out of the square when a shot fired across the horses' backs made them bolt. Valentina clung to the reins, terrified as the carriage was dragged on past her home. For a mile she tried

everything she knew to bring the horses under control. She could
see the great houses flashing by and people looking aghast in her
direction. She wondered if she was going to die, ridiculously, need-
lessly, because of a shot intended for someone else. Her arms began
to tire and she felt her strength draining. Then, miraculously, a
rider galloping alongside her leaped on the back of the leading
horse and pulled the reins. The horses halted. Valentina began to
sob desperately as the rider guided the carriage back to the courtyard of the palace. Numb with exhaustion, Valentina sat on the box
waiting to be lifted down. Her eyes met the count's as he looked
questioningly up at her, and she tried to control her distress because
his bravery had touched a chord in her heart. She felt his arms
around her as he lifted her down and carried her inside the house.

For the first time since she had met Korolenko, she was grateful
for his bravery, and she thought how dignified and full of mysterious silences he was.

The count rang for coffee and aquavit. Then he knelt at
Valentina's feet and removed her boots, rubbing her frozen toes
until life returned to them. He tried not to notice that she was closing her eyes, as though praying for the strength to tell him some
bad news. The count wondered fearfully if she was going to leave
him.

Valentina found her voice at last and begged her husband's attention.

"I wish to speak with you, sir, on a matter of some urgency to us
both."

"I had a feeling you might, my dear."

This strange answer silenced Valentina and made her hesitant.
The count nodded for footmen and maids to enter with trays of
coffee and cream and hot muffins dripping butter. Valentina's face
lit with pleasure.

"Where did you buy muffins and butter, sir?"

"I purchased them from a villain who seems short of nothing, despite the present situation."

Valentina ate and the count poured cup after cup of steaming
coffee for them both. Then he began to speak.

"This is a momentous day, my dear. The Tsar gave orders for his
guard to fire on the crowd of unfortunates who had gone to peti-

tion him for help. He will rue this day forever, because their blood is on his doorstep and no one will ever erase it. I'm sorry, my dear, you said you had something important to tell me."

Valentina took a deep breath and tried to still the trembling of her body as the count looked intently down at her.

"I am with child, sir. You are going to have the heir to the title you so desire."

The count was silent for what seemed like an age. Then he walked to the window and stood with his back to his wife, looking down at the garden. Jealousy thundered at his brain and he fought to control his feelings. He had thought at first that Valentina was going to ask for a divorce. He had been unable to love her and give her the child of his dreams. With him there would certainly be no heir to the title. But who was the father of the child Valentina was carrying? Was it Yanin or Dolgurov or someone about whom he knew nothing? The count struggled to take his mind from vain speculation. Valentina was going to have a child! Despite everything he trusted her taste and judgment in the choice of a lover and felt a curious regret that he could not be the man who had shared her bed and given her a child. If the baby was a boy he could be recognized as his heir, at least if he so willed. Whatever his whim to the contrary, the count knew that this was a moment of immense importance. He collected his thoughts, ground his teeth on the jealousy that had for months been devouring him and thanked God he was not going to lose his wife. When he turned to her, Valentina thought his composure regal.

"I am happy for you, my dear. You will realize that I am most anxious to know who is the father of this child, but I will leave it to you to tell me when you are ready."

Valentina closed her eyes, unable to assimilate the shock and gratitude she felt. Korolenko rang for his valet and the overseer of the upstairs staff. When the two appeared, he made an announcement.

"My wife and I are to have a child. Tell the staff and give Dubrovsky permission to make a celebration supper."

"Congratulations, Excellency."

The valet beamed like a fool. The housekeeper scowled, "There's no food for parties, Excellency."

"There will be. It will be arriving within the hour."

Alone again with his wife, the count took her hand and kissed it.

"I hope I shall always be proud of you, my dear. I am sorry I cannot love you, though I live in hopes that someday I may. I will ask no questions about your feelings for your lover. I beg only that from this moment you become the soul of discretion. It would not be right for you to act in a manner that might provoke gossip that this child is not my rightful heir. The father of the child must see you only in the country and only before your three maids. I shall swear them to secrecy."

"That is not necessary, sir. I am sure they understand the gravity of the situation."

"I have not seen Magda for some time."

"Has she reported you to the Okhrana?"

"Indeed she has, and they have been investigating me."

Valentina held her husband's hand, her heart fluttering with fear.

"Are you going to be arrested, sir?"

The count looked sadly down at her anxious face.

"I doubt it. Bribery is still the most powerful force in our land. Now tell me, when is the child due?"

"Dr. Kaminov says he will come in August, toward the end, as far as can be told."

The count looked at his watch.

"It is time to tell Yekaterina the news. My sister will have finished her nap by now. Let us go together."

Yekaterina did not betray the slightest flicker of surprise at the news of Valentina's coming confinement. Instead she kissed her brother and congratulated him as if he were the happiest father-to-be in St. Petersburg. When the count had gone to his study to write letters informing his friends of the good news, Yekaterina motioned Valentina to sit by the fire.

"My brother will love your child, my dear, have no fear. He loves you more than life itself, though he would rather die than admit it. Sadly, the baby will come into the world at a troubled time. From today nothing will ever be the same. I fear I was right, you see. The bad times have arrived."

The demonstrators who did not die on Bloody Sunday were exiled from the capital. The result of this punishment was that they took with them their horrific tales and spread hatred of the Tsar all over Russia.

Valentina had returned to the country and foreseeing difficulties ahead was doing her best to make the estate self-sufficient. These changes did not go unnoticed by the people of the nearby village, and some openly opposed the spending of so much money on an estate already rich with every material advantage. Valentina remembered the stories she had heard of peasants attacking estates belonging to the rich and sacking them of their wealth. Could it happen here? She thought of Miss Knatchbull's advice: Get everything you can out of Russia before they take the bread from your mouth.

It was a hot summer and Yanin had returned. Together he and Valentina walked around the estate, inspecting the new workers' houses, the water plant, the mill and fields planted with rye, wheat and millet. The greenhouses were full of fruit and a new herb garden had been established at the rear of the house. Yanin picked a bunch of cornflowers and handed them to Valentina.

"You've done well to make yourself as secure as possible. I suggest you raise the wall surrounding the property and have it edged with glass splinters, just in case."

"Will revolutionaries come here?"

"Who knows. They are plundering as many houses as they can. But tell me your news."

"Miss Knatchbull arrives next week."

"I am looking forward to meeting her."

Valentina looked down at her hands and blushed.

"I cannot imagine what Natty is going to say when she learns that I have a lover."

"She will either spit fire or she will shake my hand. Don't worry, kitten, we shall face her together."

"She is my dearest friend, Ivan. I could not bear to lose her."

"She will be mine too, you'll see."

Miss Knatchbull arrived in St. Petersburg and stood surveying the scene. A line of demonstrators passed by chanting slogans against the Tsar. Men of the Volynsky Regiment chased them away, trampling any who fell down. Miss Knatchbull adjusted her wrap and looked around her. Nothing had changed in the gray streets of St. Petersburg: only the people were different and they had obviously changed for the worse. She wondered who would come to meet her and carried her luggage to a safe corner outside the station, calling a warning at a group of ragged boys who were waiting to steal something from her.

Yanin saw a tall, strongly built woman of middle age dressed in a dark-gray-silk traveling suit. Her face was pale with fatigue but her dark eyes were watchful. Every now and then she tapped the hand of one of the boys with the handle of her umbrella. Yanin wondered if this was the celebrated lead-handled umbrella that Valentina had told him about. He approached Miss Knatchbull and stood to attention, saluting her.

"I am Ivan Grigorevich Yanin, Miss Knatchbull. I am honored to meet you. Valentina bade me welcome you to Russia on her behalf. She is living in the count's house one hour's drive from St. Petersburg. I am to take you there at once."

"I am obliged to you, sir."

Miss Knatchbull looked into the tawny eyes and blushed—why, she did not know. Yanin handed her into the carriage and set off at a cracking pace from the city. Miss Knatchbull looked at her companion out of the corner of her eye. He was handsome, young, intelligent and with a sense of humor. He was a guardsman of the Preobrazhensky Regiment and born, therefore, from a family of the nobility. He called Valentina by her name, not referring to her as the countess. This puzzled Miss Knatchbull, who knew only too well the formality of the Russian aristocracy. She weighed the dark, silky hair, the arrogant tilt of the head and the amber eyes that seemed to look clean through her.

Yanin restrained a laugh at the expression on Miss Knatchbull's face. She is weighing me as if I were a bull in the market, he thought. She is puzzled and a little apprehensive. Can it be, she is thinking, that this young fellow is up to no good with Valentina? He pointed to the cornfields alongside the road, their golden ears dotted with poppies and cornflowers. The fields stretched to the horizon, their uniformity broken only by an occasional scarlet windmill or a bright-blue cottage or a station painted green. Half an hour later, he pulled the carriage to a halt. Miss Knatchbull wiped her face with a silk kerchief. It was stifling hot and she could see the horizon oscillating in the heat like a mirage in the desert. She watched as Yanin took a picnic basket from behind her seat, his informality still surprising her.

Yanin interrupted her deliberations with a cheerful invitation.

"I know your journey has been very tiring, Miss Knatchbull, and that Russia is much hotter than Paris, so I brought some iced cordial, champagne and savory pies for us to eat. Come, let me help you down the bank."

Yanin put a fur rug at the side of the stream and loosed the horses so they could drink. Thankful for the shade of the willow trees, Miss Knatchbull drank her cordial and tried not to stare too hard at her companion. Yanin put one of the pies on a lace napkin and handed it to her. Miss Knatchbull watched flies darting in the sunlight and otters on the far bank of the river sliding into the water. She was still astounded by Yanin's behavior and at last decided to settle her uncertainties.

"May I ask you a question, sir?"

"Of course you may, Miss Knatchbull."

"What is your relationship to Valentina?"

"I am her lover. Please forgive me for answering honestly and shocking you, but Valentina has always told me that you are not at all fond of liars."

Miss Knatchbull sank her teeth into the pie and looked with exaggerated attention at the water. Yanin continued gently.

"The count has never made love to his wife. The excesses of his early life made it impossible for him to appreciate Valentina's innocence and this caused him distress because he married to obtain an heir to the title. Until recently he continued to see his mistress, Madame Simoniescu. Lately, though, because of her fury at being ignored by the count, she has reported him to the Okhrana and for some months he has been under investigation."

"Will this affect Valentina?"

"I think not. She lives for most of the year in the country, while the count lives in the palace in St. Petersburg. His sister is sympathetic to Valentina and I am of the opinion that Yekaterina Vasilievna knows well enough that this child is mine and not her brother's."

Miss Knatchbull cleared her throat and drank some of the champagne Yanin offered. Thoughts were racing through her mind like a train through a tunnel and she looked at Yanin and asked with her usual candor, "Did Valentina tell you to say all this?"

"No, she did not. In fact, she absolutely forbade me to tell you anything. She said she would tell you and that it was her place to do so. I am sure that you agree that it is better to have a child by a young, healthy man than by a degenerate like Count Korolenko."

Miss Knatchbull was silent for a long time while she digested Yanin's statement. Then, again, she asked a question.

"Does the count know of all this?"

"Obviously he knows the child is not his because he has never loved Valentina. He does not yet know that I am his wife's lover, and as far as I am concerned, he never will."

"Will he recognize the child as his own?"

"He has agreed to do so, and Valentina has accepted that if the child is a boy he will inherit the Korolenko title."

When she had rested, Miss Knatchbull returned to the carriage; Yanin helped her inside and they proceeded along the dusty road in silence. Miss Knatchbull looked at the cornfields swaying in the warm, summer breeze. These were the fields the child would inherit and with them power and riches beyond comprehension. She thought of Yanin's nerve and of the truth of his statements. It was true, the child should have a healthy father and not a strange, secret man like Korolenko.

When they reached the gate of the Flower House, Yanin stepped down and looked up at Miss Knatchbull.

"I told you nothing about myself, Miss Knatchbull. I will say only this. For me, Valentina is the love of my life. I love her and I shall always love her. Indeed, she is my entire life. I come from a family of ancient Russian aristocracy and am proud to say that I honor my ancestors. There, on the other side of this road, is the beginning of *my* family estate, which is many times greater than the count's. I am not a philanderer and if I could I would marry Valentina. As it is, I treat her as I would treat my wife. That is all. Now you may decide the issue."

They drove under the overhanging trees and Miss Knatchbull smelled the heady smell of mock orange blossom. On reaching the final bend she saw the house and smiled with pleasure because since its restoration it had become everything she had hoped it would be. She saw Valentina sitting on the lawn under a pink-silk umbrella. On seeing the carriage, Valentina rose and ran to meet the new arrivals.

"Natty! It's truly wonderful! You're here!"

"You're looking lovely, my dear—if a little heavier than when we last met."

"Come inside, I want to show you your room. Ivan will bring in the luggage."

Miss Knatchbull's eyes showed her alarm.

"Have you no staff to carry baggage, child?"

"No, Natty, there are no permanent staff except my three girls. The other house workers come in during the morning and sleep in the cottages in the grounds at night."

Ten days later Valentina woke in the middle of the night with a curious feeling in the pit of her stomach. She reassured herself that it could not be the child arriving because it was not due for another week or more. The pain in her stomach passed through to her back and she felt suddenly sick and frightened. Rather than appear a fool by calling everyone prematurely, she resolved to try to sleep again. For an hour she lay restlessly dozing. Then the pushing feeling began again but more urgently than before. Valentina rang the bell for Zita, who appeared wiping the sleep from her eyes. Valentina spoke gently, trying to restrain Zita's fears and her own.

"There is nothing to worry about, but please send Bibi to bring Dr. Kaminov. And I should like you to go at once to bring Major Yanin from his home."

"Is it coming now, ma'am?"

"I think so, but I am not sure. I never had a child before!"

Zita ran from the room as if her life depended on it. Valentina lay for ten minutes, not daring to move. Then Miss Knatchbull arrived as the clock struck three. She was fully dressed in her nurse's outfit and as calm as a judge. She helped Valentina dress and fussed over her as she drank some raspberry-leaf cordial. All the while she encouraged her with reassuring words.

"I heard you ring for Zita. Let me help you, my dear, we'll go together to the room you've prepared for the confinement. I am an expert nurse, so you have nothing whatever to fear."

"I don't know if I can walk, Natty."

"Of course you can. Lean on me, everything is going perfectly, I assure you."

Yanin came running up the stairs as Valentina reached the land-

ing. Seeing her pale face and frightened eyes, he picked her up and
carried her to the rooms made ready for this moment. Miss Knatchbull was relieved to see Yanin calm and without fear. When he
spoke Valentina relaxed and Miss Knatchbull had to admit that he
was a good man to have around at such a moment. Yanin whispered to Valentina.

"Everything is ready, kitten. They have sent for Kaminov and he
will be here within the hour."

"I fear he may arrive too late."

Yanin looked at Miss Knatchbull.

"Do you know what must be done?"

"Of course I do, young man. Go and boil water and bring me
plenty of clean linen cloths. This child is going to arrive somewhat
prematurely. We shall all have to concentrate hard on keeping it
warm and well."

Valentina watched as the two hurried about their business. The
feeling of urgency within her had increased and the bearing down
began so swiftly it took all of them by storm. The clock struck the
half hour. Valentina smiled dreamily. She was with the two people
she adored and she was about to give birth to a child. She pushed
impatiently, with all her strength, obeying Miss Knatchbull's instructions and gripping Yanin's hand so hard he winced. The clock
struck the hour. Valentina felt Yanin wiping her forehead of sweat.
Then, suddenly, she felt the release for which she had been longing. Yanin kissed her eagerly. Miss Knatchbull took the child and
disappeared. Valentina heard her call out delightedly.

"You have a fine boy, my dear! He's small but he seems well
formed and he certainly has a mind of his own."

A slap was followed by a hearty cry of protest. Valentina
snuggled against Yanin's chest, her mind suddenly crystal-bright.

"What shall we call him, Ivan?"

"That is for you to say."

"Let's call him Nikolai."

Miss Knatchbull passed the child to its mother, who looked
down at the tiny figure wrapped in white. At that moment Zita
rushed in to announce that Dr. Kaminov was on his way upstairs.
Miss Knatchbull walked outside to speak with the doctor.

"If you arrive as late as this with all your patients it is no wonder
you rarely get paid, sir."

While Miss Knatchbull sat in her rocking chair, Valentina lay awake, elated beyond all measure. In the moonlight she could see the painted butterflies on the wall and she thought of the pleasure she had had preparing the room for her child. She looked down at the baby she already loved and thought of Yanin's face at the moment of birth. It was well done. She had a son with his father's haste and determination. It was summer, so there would be plenty of time for Nikolai to grow strong before the winter came. She kissed the tiny hand and held the child close to her heart.

The count and his sister arrived a week later. To Valentina's relief they were both charmed by the baby. Korolenko spent an hour staring in utter fascination at the sleeping child. Though he had once sworn to ignore the baby, he could not resist him. Yekaterina softened as she watched the helpless admiration in her brother's eyes. The count examined the infant and turned to his sister.

"He certainly resembles his mother. I believe I can see the makings of her blond hair. He is rather small, of course, but when he grows he will be the finest boy in St. Petersburg."

Yekaterina was happy to see Miss Knatchbull. The count was not and as they traveled back to St. Petersburg her presence rankled in his mind. Yekaterina chided him.

"Valentina loves Miss Knatchbull, how can you be so petty?"

"My wife loves everyone but me."

"Well, my dear, you have hardly made an effort to be lovable."

"I wish to see that governess at once. I intend to tell her to leave St. Petersburg as soon as possible."

The following morning Miss Knatchbull arrived at the palace and was ushered into the count's presence. The count scowled at her stylish green-silk dress and the bonnet loaded with petunias that seemed at odds with her severe features. When he spoke, Miss Knatchbull pursed her lips.

"You seem extravagantly dressed for a governess, if I may say."

"I am no longer a governess, sir. A distant uncle was kind enough to leave me his fortune, you see. I now live in Paris and own a charming row of houses there, as well as property in India and the East."

The count turned away, struggling to find words to express his dislike and his desire for her departure. Without warning, Miss Knatchbull spoke, putting into words the count's thoughts.

"You have always disliked me, sir, and I imagine you are wondering how to be rid of me. Have no fear, I shall be leaving on the tenth of October for Paris. I came here only after many, many invitations from Valentina, because I knew she needed me. She is young and inexperienced and giving birth for the first time is an occasion when a girl needs her mother. I am the nearest thing Valentina has ever had to a mother, sir, because unbeknown to you I have been with her since the day of her birth and have loved her like my own child. You were not told this for fear of jeopardizing my chances of accompanying the child to St. Petersburg in the first place. Should Valentina have more children, I shall return to stay with her until she is strong enough to cope, and you and your pettish dislikes will not stop me."

The count opened his mouth to speak but Miss Knatchbull continued.

"It is obvious that your country is set on destroying itself, sir. I would like to ask you, therefore, to think of depositing money in Valentina's name in Paris. You are a father now and will wish to do the same for your son and indeed for the rest of the family."

"I will not. I am Russian and intend to stay here, whatever the rabble may do. My fortune is here, my land and my houses. I will never leave Russia."

Miss Knatchbull rose and took her leave with as much grace as she could muster.

"Good-bye, sir. I trust your confidence in Russia will not be ill placed. With your permission I will now say good day to your sister."

On her return to the country Miss Knatchbull said nothing to Valentina of her conversation with the count. Instead they talked of Paris and a piece of property Miss Knatchbull was planning to buy there. She also promised to buy a house for Valentina so that she would always have a home if she chose to leave Russia unexpectedly. Valentina's eyes shone with pleasure as she described the kind of house she wanted.

"It must not be too large but with enough room for the children and my three maids and the count and myself. I should like it to have shutters, but perhaps there are not many houses with shutters in Paris."

"I shall do my best to find one."

"Whatever would I do without you, Natty?"

"You seem to be doing remarkably well on your own!"

At the end of October the Tsar issued a proclamation providing for the formation of a general assembly, or *duma*, to which delegates could be elected. Despite this concession, order did not return to Russia as quickly as the Tsar had hoped. Peasants continued to invade the estates of the nobility, plundering everything they could find. Dissatisfaction with their lot made villagers bold where once they had been servile, and they were resolved to show their new aggression to their masters. As winter came and the icy cold chilled everyone, the disturbances were exacerbated.

Valentina had not suffered in the way other rich people had. She was astonished, therefore, in the month of February 1906 to find Nadya, her former kitchen maid, heading a delegation of peasants from the nearby village. They were vociferous in their condemnation of the Tsar and eager to dispute their rights with Valentina. Nadya had elected herself spokesman for the group.

"Madame, we have come to demand our rights from the count, your husband."

"And what are you demanding?"

Valentina saw how changed Nadya was. The innocent girl had gone, to be replaced by a sullen, hard-faced woman. When her former kitchen maid spoke, Valentina controlled a desire to pull out the orange hair in handfuls.

"We villagers live in houses owned either by Count Korolenko or by the Yanin family. All the land in this area is owned by the count and the Yanins and we want an end to the situation. We must be able to be independent of the two estates and also of the village council, which owns the rest of the land in the area."

Valentina took her place at the head of the table. At the other end, Nadya and her fiancé, the butcher Gagurin, stood with twenty hostile men and women. Valentina spoke without obvious anger.

"What exactly is it you want?"

"We want to own some of the land near our homes and also our houses and shops."

"You wish to buy them?"

"No, we wish to be given them. You have no right to own so much. Your land must be divided among us."

"Why?"

Nadya turned to her fiancé for guidance. Gagurin replied for her.

"We don't have to answer your questions. We're going to take, not talk."

Valentina rose and walked to the end of the table. For a moment she gazed at the group. Then she took the red silk scarf from Nadya's neck, the antelope-skin bag from Gagurin's shoulder and embroidered shawls from three of the women in the group. When she had taken all she wished she returned to the end of the table and dismissed the men and women.

"You may go now. I shall inform the count of your visit."

Nadya burst out excitedly.

"Give me back my kerchief! It took me months to save to buy it."

The rest of the women joined in, furious at Valentina's action. She looked at them with disdain.

"Why should I return this scarf to you, Nadya?"

"Because it's *mine*."

"I give you the same answer about the land you wish to steal."

"It took me a year to buy that, a year of working twelve hours a day. Count Korolenko never worked for his land."

"It took the count's ancestors four hundred years to acquire all the land they eventually owned. They were not born rich. They became wealthy from their ingenuity and hard work or from what you call their villainy. There are rich and poor, Nadya. There always have been and always will be and any effort on your part to make us all alike, in contrariness to God's intent, which made us different, would be ridiculous. Now, you may take back what is yours and leave this house."

Nadya spoke furiously.

"There are a couple of thousand rich families in this vast country, madame. They own everything, all the land, all the stock, all the jewels and most of the food. They have all the power and rule the land in defiance of what most of the people want. A hundred million of us go hungry while *they* live like kings. Is it right? Tell me, is it right?"

Valentina watched her visitors leaving the house and trudging away through the snow. Anger made her head ache and her hands shake and for the first time she was afraid for herself, for her son and for Russia. As dusk fell she went to her room to rest before dinner. Nadya's words kept ringing in her ears and she asked herself if it was right for so few to own so much. Many times she tiptoed to her dressing room, where Nikolai slept in a lambswool-lined crib, and stood looking down at him. Then she returned to her room and looked out on the estate. Nothing moved in the woods encircling the house. Only a lonely bird swooped through the dark-blue sky to the lake. Valentina asked herself how much longer it would be like this. Would the revolution last? Would fear become a constant companion for the night?

To Valentina's relief things began to improve. The new chief minister of the Assembly, Pyotr Stolypin, applied himself to creating peace out of havoc and controlling both the Tsar and the people. The exhausted rich and the landowners around St. Petersburg began to breathe freely again and it was agreed that with Stolypin as head of the government there was a chance of retrieving peace and prosperity. The only cloud on the horizon was Gavrilo. At first letters came every few days praising the beauty of the Italian countryside and the magnificence of Rome. Then, after a few weeks, Valentina received a black-bordered card in Gavrilo's own hand: My dear wife Tanya died of the cholera last evening. I am returning home to St. Petersburg within the week.

The following Christmas, as Yanin was away, Valentina went to stay in the Korolenko Palace. The capital was agog with gossip about Magda Simoniescu, now seen openly on the arm of one of the leading womanizers of the city. When she was not with the womanizer she was entertaining a Georgian bandit and revolutionary, rumored to be the organizer of the bank robberies, bullion-train holdups and spectacular jewel thefts from the great houses of St. Petersburg. The count had bought himself out of the charges Magda had placed against him but was apprehensive as to what information she had given the bandit in her attempt to help him fill the coffers of revolution. Magda knew all the houses of the city and all the secrets of the rich. The count decided to talk to Valentina about his worry.

"I have been toying with the idea of putting my jewel collection into the bank vaults. I can no longer be certain it will be safe here in the palace."

Valentina remembered Miss Knatchbull's advice: Put nothing into the banks, because revolutionaries may open the vaults and wallow in the contents someday. She replied coolly, to the count's surprise, "It is your jewel collection, sir, you must do with it as you wish."

"I would like your opinion on this, my dear."

"I should not put anything of mine into the vaults. Whenever there has been a revolution in history everything belonging to the rich has been stolen, and raiding the banks has always been first."

"What then would you do?"

"I should send the jewels to Paris. You, however, are so determinedly Russian I am afraid you will entrust your family fortune to the bank and lose everything."

The count shook his head helplessly.

"How can I leave Russia with two trunks of jewels when every train is being held up?"

"We could send some of the stones with Zita and her sister. They could travel together in the hard class with other servants and members of the working classes. They could carry the jewels in their carpetbags. If the train were stopped by thieves or revolutionaries, they would not search servant girls."

"Ridiculous! The maids would run away with the jewels. The temptation would be too great."

"If Zita and her sister run away with your jewels you will lose a small part of the collection. If they do not you will have saved at least something. If you leave your collection here in St. Petersburg, you will lose everything, should revolution come."

A month later, in the coldest part of the year, Valentina saw Zita and Bibi off on the train. They would be met in Paris by Miss Knatchbull. Both girls had been tutored in every aspect of the journey and both were conscious of the heavy responsibility they were being entrusted with. Valentina pressed a gold coin into each girl's hand and gave them her parting advice.

"Do not allow any young men to accost you and cause your attention to wander. And remember, there are thieves everywhere— on trains and also in the streets and markets of Paris."

The Korolenko Ball was held on the day before Christmas, when five hundred aristocrats came together to eat a fifteen-course dinner and to attend a masquerade ball. The talk was of peace and the welcome return to order. If Stolypin was the hero of the conversation, Valentina was the sensation of the night. She wore a dress of silver tissue, the waist heavily boned, the bodice edged with pearls. The voluminous skirt was caught with bunches of flowers fashioned from rubies, emeralds and diamonds from the Korolenko treasure chests. When he saw her, the count embraced her.

"My dear, you look exquisite. Turn around, let me see you."

Valentina twirled obediently, fluttering a silver-lace fan. The count smiled.

"Every man will desire you and I shall revel in their longing."

They linked arms and bade their guests be seated. A hundred pages in turbans and silk tunics ran in with fresh lobsters, crayfish and every manner of seafood. Valentina watched her guests, wondering what they were thinking as they saw the count so attentive, Yekaterina animated and Gavrilo seemingly relieved to be back where he belonged. There had been gossip during the early days about the count and his mistress but since the birth of her son, Valentina and her husband had striven to seem united. The playacting had had an effect on their real relationship and they were fast becoming settled in each other's company.

After dinner Valentina led the company to the ballroom, where everyone donned a mask. Lights were lowered and scarlet candles replaced the electrified chandeliers. Valentina waltzed with her husband and led the first quadrille. Then, feeling hot, she walked outside to the terrace and stood fanning her burning cheeks.

At that moment a man climbed over the outer wall of the palace. Valentina stepped back into the shadows and watched him. The intruder stripped off his outer coverings, revealing a dark-haired man wearing an unkempt frock coat and the ribbon of an imaginary order over his breast. His manner was confident, and as he strolled past Valentina he bade her a hearty good evening. She knew this man must be a thief or a revolutionary and was torn between calling the count and following the intruder to find out his intentions. She decided to call her husband.

"A young man has just climbed over the wall. He took off the robe he was wearing and underneath had a shabby frock coat and a decoration I have never seen before, surely a fake. He went in the direction of the staff quarters. I fear he is a thief, sir."

The count summoned two footmen and went off in the direction of the kitchens. Valentina made her way to the jewel room to ascertain that nothing had been taken. She turned on the light in the

room and saw that the count's collection of rare rocks and stones
was intact. The shelves of uncut rubies and emeralds were also in
place but the bowl that normally held the Korolenko collection of
pearls was empty, and the famous green diamond was no longer on
its pedestal. She rang the bell and ordered a servant to bring the
count at once. Then, she saw a note on the table where the bowl of
pearls had been. The note said only "Koba." Valentina looked again
at the cabinet full of emeralds and rubies. The stones were uncut
and seemingly without value, at least to the untrained eye. This, she
knew, was why they had not been stolen. She rang the bell again
and ordered that all the stones from the cabinets be taken in boxes
to her personal suite.

That night the count removed the gold bars and jewels kept in
his bedroom safe and put them in one of the guest suites, where he
slept. If Magda had drawn Koba a map of the property it was best
to place himself well out of the felon's way. He slept peacefully
until Valentina's voice came to him from the garden.

"Good morning, Bibi. Have you seen Madame Yekaterina?"

"No, ma'am, I haven't. I saw her downstairs early yesterday
morning as she left the ballroom."

Having locked the contents of his safe in an armoire, the count
left the room, securing it behind him. On reaching his own suite he
was surprised to find everything intact. He could not fathom why
the bandit had left the safe unmolested, since Magda knew of it
and must have told him its location. He rang for breakfast to be
served at once. Then, as was his custom, he rang another bell to
summon his sister from her suite across the landing. There was no
reply.

Korolenko knocked on Yekaterina's door and went in. To his horror he saw that Yekaterina's wall safe was open and empty.
Drawers had been turned out, her wardrobe overturned, her mat-
tress cut to ribbons.

The count ran to the drawing room, where he found his sister
lying unconscious on the floor, a deep-purple bruise at her temple. Frantic, he called a servant and ordered the doctor to be summoned. Then he lifted Yekaterina on to the chaise longue, whispering.

"My dearest Yekaterina! Please say something. In God's name
make some sign that you understand."

Yekaterina's eyes were half open. Her breath came with a faint, ominous rattle. Her hands were icy cold and over her face faint blue marks were appearing under the surface of the skin. The count closed his eyes in agony. The intruder had obviously mistaken Yekaterina's suite for his own. Tears began to fall down the count's cheeks as he thought of the days of his childhood when Yekaterina had been his ally, the only one in his family who seemed to understand the torment within him.

When Valentina arrived with the doctor she found her husband holding his sister in his arms. Yekaterina was dead and, seeing the doctor's sign, Valentina did her best to persuade the count to withdraw.

As the count sat on the edge of his bed, numb with shock, Valentina sent for a calming draft and fed it to him. Then she sat at his side, silently mulling over the tragedy of the night. Yekaterina had been her friend, a worthy champion in the fight for acceptance and security. Now she was dead, sacrificed to a man who killed and robbed to fill the coffers of revolution.

# CHAPTER EIGHT

## The Flower House, Nikolai, 1910–1914

In August 1910, Nikolai was five, a child of deep perception who loved his mother above all else. His looks were typically Russian, his hair flaxen blond, his eyes blue, his skin given to turning red before brown in the sun. The days of his childhood had been peaceful and prosperous, though he had come into the world after the stirrings of the short revolution of 1905. Nikolai lacked only children to play with and constantly begged his mother for a brother. When no brother came he learned to play alone, adventuring in the woods, fishing in the stream near the hunting lodge and carving wood as he had been taught by Yanin. Nikolai loved Yanin with an intensity that was childlike and touching. If he could not have a brother he would pretend Yanin was his brother and during the summer he could be seen following the handsome guardsman like an ever-present shadow. Yanin returned this affection tenfold, to the boy's delight, and each time he returned to his duties in St. Petersburg it was with the greatest regret.

The count had long accepted the identity of Nikolai's father. Valentina kept her secret, but Nikolai fished with Yanin, carved spoons for his mother with Yanin and visited the house on the opposite side of the road to enjoy tea and cakes with Yanin's mother. Korolenko was grateful that his wife continued to be discreet, that no murmur of scandal had come to haunt Nikolai's future. Despite his original plan to avoid his heir as much as possible, the count had come to love Nikolai and often asked to have him stay at the palace, a request to which Valentina willingly agreed.

Nikolai's days with the count were spent examining stones, looking for fossils and learning about hunting. He respected this man he called Papa and did his best to act as was expected of the heir to the Korolenko title. In the absence of Yekaterina, her dear friend, Countess Volkova acted as aunt to the boy and it was his special treat to be taken by his parents to the old lady's home on the Kamenno-Ostrovsky Prospekt. Countess Volkova was a hoarder of everything, as if by keeping small fragments of the past she would retain a way of life that was fast slipping away. Her drawers and cupboards were full of miniatures, rings, souvenirs of visits to Baden-Baden and holidays in the Crimea. Pressed flowers mingled with lace gloves, train tickets, faded sepia photographs and love letters, a veritable treasure trove for Nikolai, who was given a drawerful of memories to enjoy each time he visited the house. For Valentina's son the world was an untroubled place, a wonderland of adventure. He was loved, taught, scolded and cajoled but never hated. Hate was a word Nikolai did not yet know as he waited eagerly for his guests to arrive for his birthday tea.

Valentina was in the drawing room, inspecting a brass samovar that shone like gold. The tables were full of chicken pies basted with honey, cakes, spice buns, fudge, savories and sweetmeats. Now and then she went to the window and looked out. Yanin had been away since the autumn of the previous year. Nikolai missed him dreadfully and so did she. She had been upset when Yanin did not return with the spring, and lonely in the house, despite her son and the presence of the maids. Zita and Bibi had returned from Paris, having safely deposited the count's jewels in a bank vault. They had made one further trip since, again successful, and now talked of nothing but Paris.

Valentina remained at the window, looking out on the estate she loved.

It was a warm day of bright sunshine and scented flowers. Valentina gazed at the cornfields and from them to the distant bridge. She was praying Yanin would come in answer to Nikolai's prayers. Then, impatiently, she told herself she must stop pining for Yanin. She was twenty-four and in the prime of her life, too young to spend her days longing for something she could not have.

She walked to the mirror and looked at her reflection. She had dressed her long hair in the latest style, high and curly on top of the head and full behind. Her dress was a present from Miss Knatchbull, a Poiret extravaganza of cyclamen silk, inspired by the

Ballets Russes. She looked at the bejeweled tunic and the harem trousers underneath. From the sideboard she took the silk turban that completed the outfit, but set it aside. She would wear the hat when she was with the count but not with Nikolai. She thought with pride of her son, who called to her each morning from the other side of her bedroom door: "Mama, if you will let me in I shall tell you a secret." On gaining access the secret was always the same: I love you, Mama, I love you a hundred times. Valentina found children a joy and a tribulation, because from the moment of Nikolai's birth she had feared for his safety, health and future happiness. She looked down at her hands, thankful that Nikolai was good and that his company was a pleasure. Worry about his future could be put at the back of her mind for the moment. It was a beautiful summer day and he was only five.

She glanced again at the window, her body aching with longing for Yanin. To her distress, he had been adamant about his military ambitions and neither she nor Madame Yanina had been able to persuade him to settle on the land. Valentina asked herself if it would always be like this—would Yanin forever go away, leaving her for months on end? Would she spend her days longing for his return when she should be enjoying herself?

The doorbell rang and she heard Bibi bringing the first guests upstairs. She hurried to join her son.

The count bowed to his wife and kissed Nikolai, hugging the child to his chest, pleased that he had grown and that his cheeks were flushed with pleasure.

"Papa, I was watching for you from the tower room but I did not see you arrive."

"I came from the opposite direction today, that is why. Happy birthday, Nikolai."

"Thank you, Papa."

Nikolai took a box from his father and looked to his mother for guidance. Valentina nodded for him to open it. Then the doorbell rang again and Countess Volkova appeared. Nikolai leaped up to greet her and received as his gift a silk-backed photograph album. Countess Volkova whispered to him, "Now you will be able to keep your photographs of Papa and Mama and all the important things in life in this album and not scattered everywhere, as I do."

Nikolai returned to opening his father's present, drawing out a book entitled *The Gentleman's Guide*. Inside the cumbersome volume he saw drawings of guns, fishing rods, horses and adult instructions on how to be the perfect gentleman. Valentina saw momentary disappointment in her son's face. Then Nikolai kissed the count and thanked him.

"When I am a man, Mama says I must try to be like you so I shall not really need the book."

The count's cheeks flushed with pleasure and Valentina thanked heaven for her son's ability to say the right thing at the right moment. Guests continued to arrive until there were eight, including Yanin's mother, Gavrilo and Dolgurov. Zita and her sisters served tea while Nikolai examined his gifts. Then, looking up, he saw his mother gazing out of the window. There was something akin to longing in her face and this troubled him. He worried when his mother was not smiling and of late he had noticed that she was not entirely happy. Impulsively, he ran over to her and kissed her, relieved when Valentina smiled at him.

"Would you like to see what I have bought you for your birthday?" Nikolai took his mother's hand and ran at her side out to the stables. There, looking over the door of its stall, was a new pony, all brown and white.

"Mama, I love you! When I am a man I shall marry you!"

"I love you too, darling, and I shall love you forever and ever and ever."

In the drawing room the guests were talking about Pyotr Stolypin, still chief minister of the Assembly. Stolypin was a man they all revered and depended upon for their lives and the prosperity he had done his best to secure since the days of dissidence. The count expressed the opinion that without Stolypin they would all have been lost to the madmen behind the turmoil. When Valentina returned with her son the guests changed the subject and spoke of lighter things, gossiping about people they knew though they avoided mention of the fact that Magda and the revolutionary, Koba, were now cohabiting openly in her house on the Moika.

At last the guests turned their cups upside down and placed a small piece of sugar on top of each. The signal that they had finished their tea marked the end of the party and one by one they took their leave until only Korolenko was left with Valentina and her son. The count sat on the settee at his wife's side.

"I would be obliged if I could take Nikolai to St. Petersburg with me. He has been invited to the Winter Palace for the Tsar's annual children's party on the twentieth. You may not wish to attend, my dear, but Nikolai should be allowed to make the acquaintance of the royal children."

Valentina agreed and Korolenko left with Nikolai for the capital.

An hour passed. The clocks chimed six. Valentina wondered if she should have accompanied the count to the party at the Winter Palace. Then her mind shifted once again to thoughts of Yanin and she went over their meetings from that first day when she had fallen in love with him. She had been so sure Yanin would come for Nikolai's party! Yanin was always there, always prompt to celebrate the child's day. Dusk fell and she went upstairs to her room. She was about to undress when she looked out the window and saw Yanin riding by the side of the cornfield.

Valentina thought of the count's eagerness to take Nikolai back with him to St. Petersburg. Had he known the boy's father was coming? Of course, he must have heard that Yanin's regiment was back in the city and he would know that nothing would keep Nikolai's true father from celebrating his son's birthday. Valentina thought then of her own longing for Yanin, and knew in her heart that her husband had taken Nikolai away to leave her in peace with her lover.

She ran downstairs and threw herself into Yanin's arms.

"Oh, my love! It's been so long, wherever have you been all these months?"

"Stationed in Irkutsk. Where's Nikolai?"

"He went with my husband to St. Petersburg, for the Tsar's children's party."

Yanin held her close, kissing her face.

"I'm so relieved to be here, kitten. I swear I am the tiredest man in Russia. We have been riding around the Empire for months and I have earned my treat, I can assure you."

Valentina looked into Yanin's eyes, inclining her head in puzzlement.

"What is your treat?"

"My regiment is to guard the Tsar's palace for the next two years. I shall not be going away again for a very, very long time."

Valentina clung to him, telling him about his son's birthday and everything that had happened in the months he had been away. He had bought Nikolai a saddle and a bugle that he apologized for in advance, because he knew it would soon be the boy's favorite toy. As they walked into the house, Yanin was greeted by Zita, who went at once to the kitchen to order food and her mistress's favorite champagne. Valentina smiled knowingly as she heard Zita calling to Bibi. "The master's home at last. Help me make something special for his supper." It is true, Valentina thought, Yanin is master here.

It was still light at ten when they rode to the hunting lodge to be sure of being alone. The romantic setting reminded them of the early days of their love and they lay side by side making plans for the future and holding each other close. As they made love a nightingale trilled its song and in the cornfields workers sat around fires singing hymns of praise for the magnificent harvests of the past three summers. Yanin whispered to Valentina, "I shall be in St. Petersburg for four days each week. When my work is done I shall come here to love you."

"And just now, what will you do?"

"Now I shall love you again, even though I am the tiredest man in Russia."

Valentina abandoned herself to the feeling of his body close to hers, his hand entwined in hers, his breath against her cheek. When they were one, she imagined there was nothing in the world she could not do. The delusion of omnipotence lasted only briefly; then she lay at Yanin's side, amused that only a few moments before she had thought herself capable of flying like a bird. With Yanin there was nothing she could not do. Alone, she had no idea of her capabilities and limitations, having been cosseted by the Korolenko family wealth ever since her arrival in Russia. It would always be the same unless revolution returned to change irrevocably the country and its traditions. As she closed her eyes, Valentina comforted herself with the thought that revolutionaries could have their way only when times were bad. In the abundant years, with success in Russian endeavors at every turn, no one wanted to listen to talk of rebellion. Thank God for our deliverance, thank God for Stolypin, Valentina thought as she snuggled against Yanin's shoulder and fell asleep.

Yanin held Valentina for a while, watching as she slept. He was too tired to settle down, his mind full of plans now that he knew he would be able to remain close to her for a long time. Each absence from her side had been a nightmare. Yanin had also known fear, because Valentina's beauty and her personality invited envy and a desire for revenge. He sat up in bed and stared at a crescent moon like a silver charm in the sky. The only sounds were the sounds of the countryside, the only intrusion on his thoughts a subtle scent of verbena wafting through the window. I am a lucky man, Yanin thought, one of the luckiest in the world, to be loved and to be here with my love.

The count walked stiffly into the Winter Palace behind a stoic-faced footman. Sounds of children laughing came to him from the garden and he looked briefly out to see what was happening. By his side Nikolai was fidgeting under a silk shirt with neck frill and velvet breeches too hot for such a day. The boy looked back at the entrance hall of the palace, frowning at a ceiling so high he could barely see the cupola. The walls were stark white, the balustrades richly decorated with gold, and a scarlet carpet wound down the stairs like a stream of blood on a snow-white arm. Nikolai wished he were back in the Flower House, in his room painted with butterflies and birds. Homesickness caught him like a blight of the soul and he drew nearer the count and looked appealingly up at him in search of a comforting word.

Korolenko was about to be introduced to the Tsar. He stood straight-backed at attention. Nikolai copied his stance as a major-domo announced them.

"Count Korolenko and his son Nikolai."

The count stepped forward, bowed and stepped aside for his son. Nikolai bowed to the Tsar and tsarina. Then he followed his father to a formal garden full of young people, English governesses, nurses, mothers, fathers and small boys. The tsarevich was six and always attended by a massive sailor whose job was to guard his health. Nikolai watched the small boy, who would someday be

Tsar of All the Russias, as he cycled to and fro, guarded by the ever-anxious sailor. He turned to the count and asked about the tsarevich's guard.

"Papa, that sailor looks frightened, doesn't he?"

The count thought of the rumors of the tsarevich's hemophilia and took care in his reply.

"I don't know, Nikolai. Perhaps he is afraid of the tsarevich hurting himself if he falls."

"Shall I be able to ride the bicycle?"

"If the tsarevich invites you, you may."

While their children played, mothers and fathers who had accompanied them to the party drank tea from a samovar on a table laden with extravagant cakes and savories. The count sat alone, conscious that he would never have been invited to the palace but for his son. The tsarina was puritanical in her choice of members of the imperial court. His behavior with Magda had placed him on her list of undesirables. Korolenko watched as Nikolai played with a twirling top, laughing in delight as the top rolled out of his control. The count thought proudly that Nikolai was the handsomest boy there. How natural and unassuming he is, the count thought, so European like his mother. Indeed, though he was born in Russia Nikolai was not at all Russian in his ways. The count was puzzling over this fact when the Tsar came to his side and began to speak.

"Your son is a fine boy, Count Korolenko."

"He is indeed, Your Imperial Majesty. I am very proud of him."

"I hear you are leading a quiet life these days. Children make us dull but happy in our dullness, do you agree?"

The count looked into the Tsar's lazy blue eyes and realized why so many people were charmed by him. But the Tsar was Russian to the core and oriental in the deviousness of his ways. Korolenko wondered what he really wanted to know. He prepared for further questions as the Tsar continued.

"And how are your estates, Count Korolenko?"

The tsarina appeared and stood behind her husband, looking at the count with her aloof blue eyes. He answered the Tsar's questions as truthfully as he could.

"My estates are flourishing, sir. Since the revolution of nineteen hundred and five prosperity has returned to us and as a result of our stable government everything goes well. The harvests have been record ones and my workers are happy as are those of all my friends. Thanks to Stolypin's devotion to Russia we are at peace and almost over the disasters of the recent past. Russia is now a wonderful place to live, as it was before."

"Indeed, indeed."

The Tsar nodded, his expression fathomless. Then he passed on to the guests at the next table. The count saw the tsarina's expression harden and an angry scarlet flush creep from her neck to her face. He looked at her without fear, his eyes unblinking. As though remembering her obligations, the tsarina turned and followed her husband. The count thought wryly that he had said the wrong thing. The tsarina disliked Stolypin because he had tried again and again to warn her husband about the influence of the healer Rasputin. Stolypin's spies had compiled reports on the healer's licentious behavior and these had been forwarded to the Tsar, thus far with no effect though alarming rumors of the tsarina's relations with Rasputin were legion and had been for some time. Korolenko shook his head despairingly. Stolypin might rule the country, but it was obvious who ruled the Tsar.

In the late afternoon, the count beckoned Nikolai and led him to take his leave of the royal couple. In his best English Nikolai spoke to the Tsar and tsarina.

"Thank you for inviting me to your party. I have rarely played with other children and I enjoyed it more than anything I can remember."

The count bowed and left the building. In his carriage Nikolai began to bombard him with questions.

"Papa, why do we not have an automobile like Ivan Grigorevich and those other people at the party?"

"I prefer the noble smell of horse manure to the stench of gasoline."

"Old gentlemen still love their carriages and have footmen in fancy coats on the back, but you aren't old, are you, Papa?"

The count hesitated and Nikolai looked up anxiously.

"Say you are not old, Papa. Mama told me that people go to heaven when they become old. I don't want to lose you."

"I am not yet old, Nikolai, I'm just in the middle years of life. I shall not die for a long time, not until you are old enough to look after Mama without me."

"Now it is summer, Papa, will you be coming to the country to fish?"

"No, I don't think so."

"Why do you not come to stay with us when the weather is fine? Mama told me you do not come in the winter because the weather is too cold in the countryside."

The count sighed, weary of the boy's questions.

"In the summer it is too hot for me. But I will take you fishing tomorrow morning; I know a secret place not far from here."

Autumn came, followed by the worst winter in twenty years. Valentina allowed herself to feel marooned in the country, a feeling she enjoyed because it cut her off from the gossip in St. Petersburg about Magda and her revolutionary ideas and her never-ending desire for revenge on the Korolenko family. Soon the routine of winter charmed and Valentina and Nikolai skated with Yanin on the frozen lake, roasted potatoes on wood-burning braziers in the garden and tobogganed down through the pine trees to the field near the hunting lodge.

For Christmas Yanin gave Valentina a cloak made from the pelts of foxes he had shot in her woods. For Easter he gave her a Fabergé egg. When she opened the egg she found inside a frozen lake made of opals and two skaters fashioned from malachite and diamonds. Watching her reaction to the gift Yanin sensed uncertainty.

"Do you not like it, kitten?"

"I love it and will treasure it forever."

"Is something wrong then? You look very pale. You're not feeling ill, are you?"

"I think I am going to have another child."

Yanin leaped up, grabbed roses from the vase on the table and handed them to her with a flourish.

"If you are, I shall buy you another egg with two horsemen riding together through a cornfield, for that is how I remember our earliest meetings. You are not to be apprehensive, kitten. You are to be radiant, like the last time."

Looking at the yellow roses in her hand, Valentina tried to put into words the fears that had haunted her mind for the past few weeks.

"The count has not visited me for some time. How can I pretend this child is his?"

"Invite him to the New Year luncheon and in a few weeks no one will remember exactly when he came."

"I will write to him today."

"Will Miss Knatchbull come again? When exactly is the child due?"

"In August, I believe, toward the end. I seem to conceive children who will be born in the summer."

Yanin held her and they talked of the child and the fun they would have together while they waited for its arrival. Valentina smiled at his dreams but was inwardly apprehensive. Perhaps all would not be well; she would die or perhaps the child would be ill. Try as she might she could not rid herself of the feeling of doom. To comfort herself she wrote a long letter to Miss Knatchbull and waited eagerly for the reply.

As usual the Englishwoman did not disappoint.

I shall come in the middle of August in case we have another young fellow in a hurry. I will bring with me photographs of the house I have bought in your name. In the meantime, I shall tell you absolutely nothing about the property. In that way you will be able to imagine it and be in a fever of longing by the time I appear. You will be pleased to hear that I have disposed of my properties in the East and have invested the money in property in Paris. It is very easy to make money. I wish I had realized it years ago. . . .

Valentina lay back on the chaise longue, dreaming of the house Miss Knatchbull had bought her. Would there be a garden? Would it have dark-green shutters like the houses of Provence or be one of those austere gray buildings that crowded the sixteenth arrondissement of the city? And where would it be? Days passed and during Yanin's brief absences she made a series of drawings of the property she owned but had never seen. When summer came she transferred the images of the house, as she imagined it, to linen and fashioned cushions of them. In the long months of waiting it was to be a constant delight to paint imaginary houses and to look forward someday to checking the original against her dreams.

On an August afternoon Valentina sat by the lakeside with her husband. The count had visited the Flower House a dozen times since he had learned of her pregnancy, because he understood only too well the need for such appearances, and anyway was always happy to see his wife. On this hot summer's day, he looked out at pink-and-yellow water lilies on the lake, tiny blue-and-green birds fluttering among the trees and scarlet butterflies settling on the wistaria. Whenever he visited his property the count marveled at the atmosphere Valentina brought with her, an air of enchantment that fascinated him. He held her hand and kissed it affectionately.

"The child is due at the end of this month?"

"Yes, as far as can be told."

"And Miss Knatchbull will attend you?"

"Natty should have arrived a week ago but she had an attack of the gout and was delayed. She told me she is tired of being wealthy, because she eats too many rich things and becomes ill."

"No doubt with your usual practicality the child will await her arrival!"

"What is happening in St. Petersburg?"

"I have no good news. New strikes are beginning and the Tsar has gone out of the way of the trouble. He is in Kiev unveiling a statue of his father. The Preobrazhensky Guard have accompanied him, as you know."

Valentina thought of Yanin's unwelcome absence and smiled when her husband spoke.

"You will have to make do with my company for a while, my dear."

"I shall make do very well, sir. You are a tower of strength whenever I am feeling uncertain."

On the first of September Miss Knatchbull arrived in St. Petersburg. Far away in Kiev, Pyotr Stolypin, prime minister of the Assembly and bane of the subversives, was shot while attending the opera. His assassin was a revolutionary who was also a police spy, so no one knew on whose orders he was acting. Unaware of the momentous happenings in Kiev, Valentina marked another day off her calendar and wondered when her child would arrive. Already he was two weeks late. She closed her eyes and said her prayers that everything would go smoothly.

On the fifth of September, at dawn, the pains began. This time Yanin was absent and Miss Knatchbull delivered the baby with Zita's help. Below, in the saffron drawing room, Korolenko leaped up on hearing the first wail of life. Then he ran upstairs and stood nervously outside Valentina's room, waiting for Miss Knatchbull to tell him the news. When she emerged she looked at the expression on the count's face with interest. He was in love with his wife! This was something that had never occurred to Miss Knatchbull. She announced the birth of another son.

"The countess has a boy, sir. He is a sturdy lad and was quite a long time coming, unlike the first. Would you care to see your wife?"

"Will Valentina permit it?"

"Of course she will. She is longing to boast about him to someone."

The count walked into the room where his wife lay with her baby. The bright sunlight of afternoon had been shunned and the curtains were drawn, giving the room the look of a pink cave. The count stood stiffly by the side of the bed, uncertain what to say. At last he coughed and found his voice.

"He is very dark, quite a contrast to Nikolai. Are you feeling better, my dear? May I offer my most sincere congratulations."

"I'm tired, nothing more. Thank you for being here."

"I must confess that giving birth has exhausted me."

Valentina laughed at her husband's pale face.

"What shall I call him?"

The count sat on the edge of the bed peering at the baby. Valentina continued dreamily.

"I think I shall name him Vasily, after your father."

The count started at this proposal.

"Surely you will wish to consult—"

"I have decided on Vasily. It is a noble name and he will be a very special boy, a fighter because he fought to come into the world."

The count looked down at his hands, trying to still his racing mind.

"I believe I love you, Valentina. I never knew how much until this moment. I am honored that the boy be called Vasily."

Far away in Kiev Pyotr Stolypin lost his fight for survival. Two trusted members of the Preobrazhensky Guard were delegated to take the news to St. Petersburg, to the Dowager Empress, to members of the Assembly and to members of the diplomatic corps. As Yanin rode at Dolgurov's side his mind was in a turmoil. The baby was due. Had he missed the birth? And what of the future now that Stolypin was dead? Nikolai had been born into a world of revolution that had settled mercifully to near calm under the guidance of Stolypin. The new child would come into a peaceful, prosperous Russia that could, now that Stolypin was dead, rush again toward revolution. Yanin felt anxiety and fear, emotions alien to his nature. He resolved to ride to the Flower House as soon as he had delivered the dispatches.

The count was walking around the garden thinking of the new baby. Here and there he picked a flower and a branch of blossoming creeper. He had never picked flowers before, except as a small boy for his mother, and thought it a somewhat undesirable pursuit for a gentleman. He looked frequently from side to side to make sure he was not being watched. Then, when he was satisfied by the splendor of the bouquet, he took it upstairs and delivered it to his wife.

Happy and relieved that her ordeal was over, Valentina kissed her husband's cheeks and thanked him for his kindness.

"I am so grateful you are here, sir. Whatever should I have done without you?"

"You would have had many willing workers to help you, not least Miss Knatchbull."

"I should, but I wanted you and you have been kind enough to overlook so many things by being here."

That moment, the count was to remember later, was one of the happiest in his life. Valentina had expressed a need for him. Somehow, someday, he would show her that he was worthy of that need and equal to any call she might choose to make on the endless resources of his wealth and experience.

A year later, after the christening of her second son, Vasily, Valentina was in St. Petersburg to attend a diplomatic ball at the French Embassy. Outside the hall crowds milled through the streets waving the red flag and singing revolutionary songs. Since Stolypin's death unrest had returned and now barricades had been erected in the streets and scarlet-clad officers rode among the workers, firing shots and bringing down their sabers. The cry was for shorter working days, for socialism and for the confiscation of private land. As she arrived at the banquet Valentina heard the cries and thought of the Flower House, the home she prayed each night never to leave.

At the count's table Valentina peered into a basket of rosebuds placed before her and drew out a small fob watch of gold encircled with pearls. This was a favor given to every lady by the French ambassador. Korolenko nodded approval.

"Delightful, a lesson to us all."

Valentina sat at her husband's side looking curiously around her at diplomats, famous writers, members of the aristocracy, all enjoying French hospitality at its best. The meal was perfect, with dishes, cheeses and wines from every region of France. Loire salmon, duck breasts and foie gras from Alsace mixed with Fourme D'ambert from the Auvergne, Mont d'Or from Lyon, in an ever-increasing display of perfection. The champagne was a Roederer grande fine, light and luxurious, that even the count, always jealous of things French, praised profusely. Valentina felt the atmosphere of Paris again and fell under its spell as she had long ago.

After dinner the ladies retired to a salon for coffee and crème de menthe. Instead of joining them, Valentina went to the garden of the ambassador's house and stood alone, savoring the smell of honeysuckle. She had enjoyed the dinner and had felt again the familiar and indefinable atmosphere of Paris. She shook her head, half angry with herself for dwelling on the past.

Magda was riding in her automobile past the French ambassador's residence. She was furious to have been excluded from the guest list of ninety-six chosen celebrities and their social and diplomatic counterparts. She could see nothing from the front of the building, so she ordered her chauffeur to drive around the back. It was then she glimpsed Valentina in the ambassador's garden, nuzzling the horses resting near her carriage and looking like a dream in a dress of white chiffon covered in daisies. Only Countess Korolenko would wear a dress like that, at twenty-seven and getting old, Magda fumed, and before she knew what she was doing she was marching toward the woman she hated, her face twisted with rage. Valentina had not noticed her; Magda cried out.

"Must you parade like a trollop for us poor citizens of St. Petersburg to admire?"

Valentina did not reply. Magda stood her ground, conscious that her rival was examining minutely the wrinkles under her eyes, the slack skin at her throat, the sharp green of her outfit. Aggravated by this scrutiny, she said, "Don't stare at me as if I were a horse at the fair. You have nothing to feel superior about. You have never loved your husband as I loved him. You have never excited him or made him want you, not even for a moment. You are only half a woman and everyone knows it. Where those two bastards of yours came from God only knows, though rumor has it you favor a soldier."

Valentina took the coachman's whip from the carriage rail and lashed it down on Magda's head. As the woman screamed, she rained blows on Magda's body until blood darkened the emerald bodice. Magda retreated, stumbling to her vehicle, mouthing curses and making threats on the boys' lives. Valentina whispered softly.

"You will not call my sons bastards, madame, not if you want skin left on your back."

She took a deep breath and turned to walk back to the house, halting, aghast, when she saw an elegant gentleman smoking a cigar and watching her from the window of the ambassador's study. Furious at his expression, Valentina marched into the room and confronted the stranger.

"Must you watch me as if I were in a circus, sir?"

"If you behave as if you're in the circus I feel at liberty to do so, ma'am."

Valentina's violet eyes met the brown of Alexander Masters, American diplomat and visitor to the French ambassador's residence. She weighed her companion.

"Who are you, sir?"

"My name is Alexander Masters. I'm an American."

"You are no gentleman, wherever you come from."

"And you, ma'am, are no lady!"

Masters walked from the room, letting the door slam unceremoniously behind him. Valentina picked up a heavy fire iron and battered the logs on the fire, pretending each time that she was beating the insolent foreigner's head.

Masters leaned against the door, listening until the logs had been battered into submission. Then, as he had expected, he heard Valentina sobbing. Someone had called the woman's sons bastards.

She had a right to cry. He took out his handkerchief and opened the door.

"It occurred to me that you might need this, ma'am."

"Go away!"

Valentina buried her head in the chiffon of her dress. Masters wiped her eyes.

"That's better. Now, ma'am, may I give you a word of advice?"

"You may not, sir."

"Well, here it is. In my experience a woman doesn't make that kind of comment, not even a woman like that one, if there's no ground for suspicion. If she has grounds others will too. If it's true, you must accept the gibes and not go thrashing everyone you meet. If it isn't true, you must get your husband to take that woman to court to obtain compensation for your discomfort."

"I don't need money!"

"Are you a fool?"

Valentina stared into the light, flickering eyes, weighing the wavy brown hair and the suntanned skin that smelled of tobacco and country fields. How impertinent he is, she thought, how detestable. She shook her head defiantly.

"I am not a fool, sir."

"Then make her pay. It's likely she hasn't the money you have."

Valentina hesitated, realizing the truth of his words. Masters nodded and took his leave. Valentina looked down at his handkerchief and traced the initials embroidered in white silk. Alexander Masters. She inclined her head disapprovingly. Only a foreigner would wipe a woman's eyes, only a hooligan would give advice when he had been told not to. She took out a compact and powdered her nose. Then, dissatisfied with her complexion, she pinched her cheeks and made her way back to the reception.

Korolenko looked closely at his wife, aware that she had been crying.

"Is something wrong, my dear?"

"Magda came into the ambassador's garden while I was taking some fresh air. She called Nikolai and Vasily bastards."

The count gasped.

"What did you do?"

"I hit her a few times with the coachman's whip."

The count looked into the distance without seeing his surroundings. Magda was right, of course, though she had no business creating trouble. Would she now spread the story all over St. Petersburg? The count knew she would and decided that he must try to buy her silence. He did his best to humor Valentina.

"I'm glad you did what you did, my dear."

"I have even worse news for you, sir. A man overheard everything Magda said. He is a foreigner from America. He is not at all like us. His manners were odd and I believe he could be indiscreet. There he is, the one in the brown-silk jacket. Everything about him is brown! God, how I despise him."

The count glanced at Masters, then back to his wife.

"It's true, he's an American diplomat visiting our city. I understand he will return to his own country after further visits to Italy, Bulgaria and France."

"How do you know all this, sir?"

"The French ambassador told me about the fellow. I asked about him and said he must be a cad to wear brown in contravention of our customs. The ambassador told me he is very clever and very American, that is the explanation. Those people know nothing of convention and even less about manners."

Valentina looked haughtily in Masters' direction; he inclined his head mockingly in reply. When she had turned her back on him Masters addressed his friend.

"Who is that woman with the blond hair in the white dress covered in daisies?"

"That is Countess Korolenko."

"And the man at her side?"

"Her husband, Vladimir Vasilievich Korolenko."

"Have they children?"

"A son aged nine and another boy about half his age."

The Frenchman looked uneasy and Masters wondered if everyone in St. Petersburg suspected Countess Korolenko of infidelity. He continued to question the friend who had invited him to the ball.

"Where do the Korolenkos live?"

"The count lives in his palace on the Nevsky Prospekt. The countess lives mainly in the country, though she joins her husband each year for the season. Don't waste your time, my friend. The countess has a lover, a man of the Preobrazhensky Regiment who

owns even more land than Count Korolenko does. I am sure Yanin
is the father of the two boys, though the count accepts them as his
own. You understand, Alex, nothing is *ever* said about this in public because the countess is very popular with the rich."

Valentina arrived back at the Korolenko Palace in a curious
mood. Instead of elation at her defeat of Magda, she was distressed
because she knew she had sunk to the level of her enemy. Instead
of a desire to return to the country she felt restless. She blamed this
on the American. She grimaced each time she thought of his suntanned face and challenging brown eyes. His suit had been quite
new in line and color. She admitted to herself that he had style,
even if he was the most ill-mannered man in St. Petersburg.

That night Valentina could not sleep. Her sons had been called
bastards and bastards they both were, so there was nothing to be
done. Tears fell down her cheeks as she remembered Masters'
words: If it's true, you must accept the gibes. . . . If it isn't true,
you must get your husband to take that woman to court. . . .
Russian law made no provision for slander actions, and in any case
the challenge would only draw more attention to the fact of her
sons' bastardy. Valentina thought how confident Masters had been;
indeed, he was well named. Then her mind turned to Yanin and
she asked herself if he too dominated. In her mind's eye she compared the two men, Yanin dark and slim, Masters aggressive, solid,
contained. Masters was slightly shorter than Yanin but more substantial physically. Valentina tossed and turned, her mind in a
turmoil. When she fell asleep at last she dreamed of forcing Alexander Masters into submission.

Magda continued to spread the rumor that Count Korolenko's
sons were not his own, but those of his neighbor Colonel Yanin.
The count had tried to buy off his former mistress but Magda
would hear none of it. Worse, she had paid two revolutionaries to
set off bombs in the Korolenko Palace and part of the pine wing
and most of the kitchens had been destroyed. To get away from
Magda's venom Valentina retired to the Flower House, where she
guarded her sons with the three maids. Talk of war was increasing
and in June 1914, after she had witnessed the summer ceremony of
the cutting of the lime trees, Valentina went to visit Madame

Yanina. She was led to a bedroom that smelled of ether. Madame Yanina held out her hand.

"My dear Valentina, how good it is to see you again. Tell me, is that dreadful woman still spreading her evil stories about you and Ivan?"

"Magda has taken a holiday, I am told, and is in the Crimea."

Madame Yanina wiped the sweat from her feverish brow with the back of her hand.

"I am dying, as you know, and slowly, I fear. Poor Ivan, he was aghast to hear he had been recalled to barracks."

"I came to see where Ivan was. We normally go to the ceremony of the cutting of the lime trees together."

"Have you not heard the news, my dear?"

"What news, madame?"

"War has been declared. Russia is now in a state of hostility with her neighbors. Forgive me for shocking you. I heard about it immediately because Ivan was summoned to go at once to St. Petersburg to join his regiment."

Unnerved by the news, Valentina led her horse back to the Flower House, pausing to watch some butterflies fluttering in the sunlight over the lake. Her sons were rolling down a green mound near the stables and shrieking excitedly all the while. Surely it was not possible that Russia was at war. Those who understood such matters said that another war like the one Russia had fought with Japan would bring with it the end of tsarism. Did that mean a Russian defeat would bring back the revolution? Or would the enemy invade Russia and take her beloved land from her? Panic filled Valentina's heart and she tried to decide what to do. She knew only that she would stay in the country to fight to preserve the house and the land and the safety of those she loved. She thought sadly of Yanin, praying silently for his safety and his speedy return.

# CHAPTER NINE

## St. Petersburg, The Storm, 1914–1915

The first reaction to war was a wave of patriotism and enthusiasm so buoyant that even the revolutionaries were swept up in it. Differences were temporarily put aside. Politicians formed coalitions with their enemies. Society ladies hurried to train as nurses and those with family obligations to prevent them from doing so held charity balls to raise money for the Red Cross. Rich merchants gave of their fortunes to endow hospitals and in the country peasant women manned the fields because many of their menfolk had been called to active service.

The Tsar was pleased. For the moment, at least, revolution was forgotten. All that mattered was that Russia be triumphant. This was his opinion and for once it was also the opinion of his people. The Tsar managed to overlook the fact that one million of his soldiers had no weapons and that his antiquated railway system would be hard pressed to supply them, even if manufacturers could be prevailed upon to produce arms and ammunitions in sufficient time. A triumphant Russia would be a Russia with a beloved Tsar. The Emperor also forgot Rasputin's warning that war would mean the end of the Romanov era. In a burst of patriotism he changed the name of the capital from the German St. Petersburg to the Russian Petrograd. From this moment on, he decreed, his people must be proud, above all else, to be Russian.

It was a burning-hot day in the country. Valentina was in the cornfields, encouraging her workers. The only men left were very old or very young and some of the women were pregnant. But everyone was anxious to show his worth and they sang as they labored in the suffocating heat. Thus far the war had only made small changes in their lives. They still had food and the security of believing Russia omnipotent. This gave them the impetus to work without complaint, all the while willing their country to conquer her enemies and be master of the world. As was the custom, the field workers brought the first sheaf of corn to Valentina. She bowed acknowledgment of their courage and praised the women, who stood watching her with cornflower garlands in their hair. She ordered everyone to be fed in the rear courtyard and mingled with her women workers, talking of her plans for the next year's harvest. As dusk fell, the women danced and sang to the sound of the balalaika. Upstairs in her room Valentina sat mouthing the words of her favorite cossack song as the women sang it. She took the music box Yanin had bought her and softly sang the old, familiar words:

> *"Now the harbor lights are fading*
> *This will be our last goodbye*
> *Though the carnival is over*
> *I will love you till I die"*

Tears came to her eyes and she tried to imagine where Yanin was and what he was doing.

Yanin was in an East Prussian field with a Russian force formed from many of the leading regiments. He was looking through a telescope at the battle area and wondering how it would be resolved. In command of operations was the elderly general Samsonov, who had won his reputation as a commander of cavalry in the Japanese war in 1905. Yanin felt a flutter of panic when he saw the old man parading about marking cavalry positions in the dust with his sword. Would the finest men of the Russian aristocracy, with all their courage and experience and patriotism, be enough to counteract the errors of an obsolete commander and regiments of raw recruits, many without guns? Yanin paced back and forth. Dolgurov called out to him.

"Are you afraid, Vanya?"

"More of our side than of the other."

"Me too. Kinsky says we'll all be cannon fodder by morning."

"To hell with Kinsky and his opinions."

"The trouble is he's always right. We'll stay together, won't we, Vanya?"

"As always, Grisha, as always."

Many of the Russian soldiers were tired. Some had marched one hundred and fifty miles in twelve days, over roads heavy with mud from summer thunderstorms. As he visited those on the right wing, the VI Corp of cavalry, Yanin heard the German guns and marveled at their power. No one in Russia had ever heard such volleys and they had never seen a howitzer.

On the twenty-sixth the Germans engaged, first on the left flank then on the right. The right fell back under fire, the left scattered because its men had no more ammunition. They were going home. They could see no reason to stay and be gunned into the ground. Officers who prided themselves on being descended from the oldest military aristocracy in Russia were ashamed of their companions and on the order to advance rode fearlessly forward to tackle the German howitzers. The guns sounded. The horsemen, arrested in full gallop, fell like stars from the sky, their bodies littering the dusty ground, their uniforms scarlet and gold under a deep-blue sky. As the flanks collapsed, the center was surrounded and the cream of Russian aristocracy annihilated. The German artillery fired on relentlessly until those brave enough to continue the unequal struggle were mown into the ground. General Samsonov, realizing that this almighty disaster had occurred because of his own lack of knowledge of modern warfare, rode into the nearby forest and shot himself. The survivors fled. Ninety-two thousand Russian prisoners were taken.

Dolgurov stood listening to the silence as he surveyed the scene of desecration. That morning he had been sent by the commander to tap out a telegraph appeal to the War Office in Petrograd for arms and ammunition to be sent immediately. On his return, he had found a field of dead bodies, of men in the familiar long white tunics of the Caucasian Regiment and the magenta shirts of the Rifle Brigade. He stepped over the bodies, mopping his brow as he flicked away black swarms of flies descending on the corpses. He bent and took the sword from his friend Kinsky, closing the dead man's eyes and picking up the bar of medals won in many campaigns. In a few days Dolgurov knew he would deliver these to Kinsky's widow in the capital. He shook his head wearily, uncertain if he could break the news to Kinsky's beautiful wife. They had nicknamed Kinsky the "immortal" because he had never even been wounded. Dolgurov walked on, cursing roundly. Damn war! Damn the Tsar! Damn every man who had sent men into battle so ill equipped.

At the forward periphery of the center section of the battlefield, Dolgurov found Yanin lying facedown covered in blood. He hauled a dead hussar off Yanin's back and looked intently into his friend's face, noting a blackening wound on the forehead. Dolgurov raised his eyes to the sky, thanking God when Yanin groaned. With one great effort he hauled the unconscious man onto his back and strode away, hoping no Germans had been left behind to act as a rear guard. Dolgurov decided to follow the railroad tracks back home. Looking up at an amber sky, he saw that it would be dark in an hour. Pray God he would have the strength to save Yanin's life. He thought of Valentina and knew he would die rather than fail her. In the middle of the night he stumbled into a barn and dumped Yanin on the ground. Then, having filled his hat with water from a nearby stream, he bathed the injured man's face. Yanin moaned again but did not open his eyes. Dolgurov placed him on a pile of straw and went to the door to gaze at the stars. It would be a long walk to Petrograd but he would make it. He would not leave Yanin behind to die in an area full of enemy troops.

Autumn had come and the harvest was in. The trees were crimson and gold, the wind dry and sultry. Each morning Valentina rose and took breakfast with her sons. Then she went to the Yanin estate to supervise the bringing of its harvest, the storing of apples, the bottling of beetroot and plums. Her own tasks in relation to the count's estate were done. The food had been locked in a pantry near her suite, the bottling completed a week previously. She had been lucky to have the support of very woman worker on the estate, though some were already growing discouraged by the distressing reports from the front. Valentina wrote her journal for the day and locked it in a cabinet in her bedroom. Then she sat thinking of her situation. In early September there had been a spate of Russian victories. Gala performances had been given in St. Petersburg in celebration of these. Then Russian guns and ammunition had run out and as the weather turned cold it was reported that the soldiers had no boots, no underwear, no socks or sheepskins to keep out the chill. Women in the cities began to knit but there was little hope of satisfying demand before the snows appeared. Valentina closed her eyes, trying to keep out the images of Yanin that kept coming to unnerve her. She had had no letters for many weeks. Was he still alive? Was he too freezing in the subzero temperatures?

That evening Valentina listened to her sons arguing. Nikolai was a patient boy, obedient to her wishes and given to daydreaming. Vasily was quite different. He was extremely disobedient, though he had charm and often softened her heart. He was rebellious, but given to small gestures that made people forgive him. Valentina knew that Vasily loved her dearly and tried to find reasons for his inability to settle in the staid atmosphere of the palace or even the flowery rooms of the country house. Vasily often wandered off to the estate workers' cottages to sit by their fires. Once he had stolen a gold vase and given it to a woman newly bereaved. On being reprimanded by his mother after the woman returned the vase, Vasily had answered, with the inalienable logic of a child, that the woman had nothing so pretty in *her* house. Valentina was perplexed by her younger son. Obviously Vasily was going to be something of a tribulation as he grew older. She told herself that she loved him and that love resolved everything but still she worried.

In December Dolgurov arrived with Yanin. After a spell in a hospital near the border Yanin had recovered enough to ride but he could not yet walk unaided. Both his legs had been fractured in the explosion. His neck had been dislocated and he had received a concussion. Yanin hobbled into the house and allowed Valentina to spoil him. Nikolai leaped up at him, unwilling to let go. Vasily regarded this exhibition of affection with suspicion. He barely remembered Yanin and was jealous of the attention the two officers were receiving. Sulking in a corner on his own, Vasily wondered if he could run away to the workers' cottages near the cornfield.

On seeing his son's surly face Yanin called out.

"And you, who are you? I don't seem to remember you."

"I am Vasily, sir, Nikolai's brother."

"Are you in the habit of sulking and upsetting your mama?"

Vasily looked down, ashamed of his behavior. Yanin patted the settee at his side and motioned Vasily to sit down. The child bounded over and eased himself against Yanin's side, pleased by the memory of the familiar smell of cigar smoke, metal polish and eau-de-cologne that clung to his father's body.

Dolgurov sat patiently by, admiring Valentina's new appearance. He said nothing of her suntanned face and limbs, though he was sure she had been working in the fields by the side of her peasant women. He saw that she had lost weight and indeed had become painfully thin. He loved her more than ever for the calluses on her hands and the lines of exhaustion under her eyes. He looked at his watch. Already it was five o'clock. He rose and took his leave of Yanin and Valentina.

"Thank you for your hospitality, Countess."

"Thank *you*, Grigory Pavlovich. I am in your debt forever."

"I am to rejoin my regiment in Petrograd tonight. Then, within the week, I shall return to the holocaust."

"May God walk with you."

By Christmas the Preobrazhensky Guard had lost forty-eight of its seventy officers. The Eighteenth Division had forty officers left out of three hundred and seventy. More than a million Russian soldiers were already dead, a quarter of those enlisted. Appeals for warm clothing became more frantic and a senior minister wrote to the Tsar:

Your Imperial Majesty,

The men have no winter boots and are suffering from frostbite. There are few of the original well-trained officers left so the ranks surrender whenever they encounter the enemy. In God's name, sir, what can be done? We cannot continue to send our men against the Hun without ammunition and the basic necessities of life.

The Tsar wrote in his diary: "I shall take up dominoes in my spare time."

By spring the army had been replenished. There were now six million men in uniform and nine million in reserve. Some said that Russia had only men to offer, men without training and often without rifles. The enlisted soldiers knew little of these rumors and continued doggedly trying to regain lost ground. In April there were Russian victories in Galicia and the fortress of Przemysl was captured. In Petrograd the Tsar held a celebration mass to express his gratitude. In June Przemysl was lost, then Lemberg and the whole of Galicia. Instead of the meticulously trained aristocrats who had commanded their regiments with pride, untrained men had been promoted, and these new leaders fled when the Germans introduced barrages of fire so rapid they burned everything before them. The Tsar issued a proclamation warning that those who surrendered too easily would be sent to Siberia on their return from the conflict. The new law had no effect and men began to desert in ever-increasing numbers.

Count Korolenko was in Petrograd. He was alone and lonely. He debated whether to join his wife in the country, but was reluctant to do this because he knew he could not bear to see Valentina working in the fields alongside what remained of her peasant workers. The land was everything to Valentina. The count knew she was willing to toil twenty hours a day, if need be, to sow the corn and reap the harvest and prepare the fields for new crops. She would allow her pale, delicate skin to become brown like that of the peasant women. The count frowned in perplexity. Where would it end? How could Valentina expect obedience when she was willing to demean herself by working like a slave? Despite his autocratic manner, the count admired his wife and was constantly trying to work out what *he* could do to keep her and the boys safe in the future. It was no longer enough to provide money for food, he must do something else to ensure their entire future. What to do? How to earn Valentina's admiration? Alone, it was easier to work out the present difficulties and how to contravene the laws and circumvent the regulations. After a few days of deliberation Korolenko made his decision and hurried out to the city he persisted in calling St. Petersburg to visit the manufacturer of a new type of private train. It was the first step of his master plan on how to get his family out of Russia, if the need arose.

Valentina was sitting in the cornfield reading Yanin's latest letter:

I love you dearly, forgive me for speaking of such ugly things but I must relieve my soul by telling someone my fears. We have no weapons to match the Germans, who can fire fifteen thousand guns and seventy thousand shells in four hours of a barrage against us. Men are being cut to ribbons by these barrages, sometimes before they can fire their own guns. Equipment is still in short supply and ammunition even scarcer. They tell the new recruits to be sure to pick up their neighbor's rifle when he is killed. Imagine being ordered forward in those circumstances, without a gun in your hand! No wonder the men are deserting. I fear what is now a trickle will soon become a torrent, if this needless slaughter continues. I dream of you in the hours of battle. I dream of you all the time. If I could have one wish it would be to ride through the cornfields with you and eat a picnic as we used to by the river. Think of me. Dolgurov sends his best regards. I send you all my love.

Your obedient and loving servant,

Yanin.

Valentina wiped tears from her eyes and walked wearily back to the house. She was exhausted, her limbs aching, her head whirling from weakness and tension. Why, when Russia had more men than any of her enemies and riches beyond compare, were her soldiers without rifles and boots? She began to hate the Tsar and everything Russian that came to mind, except her sons, Yanin and the land that was her life and her security. She thought of the estate workers' wives and daughters who were discouraged by the war and no longer willing to help by working at her side from dawn to dusk. Valentina shrugged defiantly. She would tend the fields alone and willingly die rather than neglect the estate she adored.

In Petrograd the count was gazing out of the window at the streets below. Lines of women were waiting for bread to appear in the shops. They had been there for eight hours but still no bread had been delivered. On the far side of the road demonstrators were smashing windows of the German Embassy and looters were ransacking two German-owned dwellings, destroyed by bombs the previous night. Korolenko frowned. Would the mob soon forget their indifference to the German-born tsarina and hate her with all the loathing building up in their souls? What then? Korolenko returned to his desk and sat reading a note his brother had sent him the previous day. The contents of the note had appalled him and he had barely slept for thinking of them. He rang for his valet. No one came. The count rang for the maid in his corridor. The girl appeared, her eyes wide with uncertainty. The count looked down at her.

"Where is Engel? When I ring for him he does not appear."

"He's vanished, sir. No one's seen him since last night. I assume he fled for his life. The staff were threatening to cut off his head because he is German."

"Kindly ask my brother to come here at once."

"Yes, Excellency."

Gavrilo appeared minutes later. The count looked with concern at his brother: Gavrilo's olive skin was now chalky white, his hair forming an unwelcome contrast to the pallid skin. He was so severely emaciated his clothes hung from his body in clown fashion. The count poured him a glass of brandy.

"This note you sent me last evening: I thank you for the effort you took to ascertain the facts. You say that out of our original staff of seven hundred only three hundred remain?"

"That is so. And of those, at least one hundred plan to leave within the next few weeks."

"Where will they go?"

"No one knows, or at least they will not say. I imagine they are working in the revolutionary print shops or the arms factories, where they can earn more money."

"I cannot believe it, though I am sure you must be right. Is this happening everywhere?"

"It's happening all over St. Petersburg. Countess Volkova has only ten servants left out of fifty. Princess Irina Yussupova has only three hundred out of eight hundred. Some enlisted into the armed forces, others have been killed. Many have simply gone away to the country or to the revolutionary offices."

"You also inform me that as soon as food is placed in the kitchen it vanishes and that ornaments in bronze, gold and lapis lazuli are missing from most of the rooms in the palace."

"It's true."

"Have you consulted Valentina about this?"

"I have. She suggested we close all but one wing of the palace and remove everything precious from the other rooms."

Korolenko put his fingers together and thought for a moment. He had no desire to change anything, but instinct told him that Pettrograd would be an ugly place if the present situation worsened.

He thought of moving to the country to the Flower House, but rejected this because he was more able to learn things to his advantage while in the capital. Finally he made a decision.

"I shall issue dismissal notices to the staff and will move all my most precious possessions to the pine wing."

"I will move my belongings too, Vladimir."

"I must persuade Valentina to join us. She insists on staying in that house because she believes her presence will deter wrongdoers and looters."

"She is wrong."

"I have ordered that the house at Narva be prepared in case we need to go there. I have asked the artist Bukharov to paint murals on the walls of the mistress's bedroom so Valentina will not feel homesick if we are forced to flee. I told him to paint yellow roses and daisies, though God only knows why she likes them so much."

In August 1915 the Tsar assumed control of the armies, relieving the Grand Duke Nikolai of his post, to the delight of the enemy. The army's failures would now be the Tsar's responsibility and he would be blamed for every lost life. The Tsar had rejected the advice of his ministers in this matter: he was willfully fulfilling his destiny of doom and approaching the black cloud of ill fortune he had sensed since childhood would someday engulf him. In September he took back some of the power he had lost in the formation of the Assembly and postponed any further meetings. The revolutionaries, underground for so long, took this as a direct challenge and began making plans for a Russia that no longer included the Tsar.

Food was increasingly scarce and Valentina was hungry. It was winter and she could see icicles hanging outside her bedroom window. Her sons came into the room and leaped onto her bed, one on either side of her. Nikolai said, "Mama, what would you like best for Christmas?"

"I should like a turkey with roast potatoes and chestnut stuffing, but I shall not be able to have them this year."

"Why not?"

"You know why not, Nikolai. There's very little food and even Papa cannot buy the essentials of life. We have sufficient flour to last the winter and plenty of pickles and bottled fruit, but that is all we have. Soon we shall have some potatoes to replace the ones that were stolen."

"I'm sick of bottled fruit and pickles."

"So am I, my dear."

Young Vasily listened to this conversation and decided to do something about his mother's hunger. He was still a difficult child but the suffering of the past months had brought him closer to his mother and the count. Whenever Korolenko called, he smiled a delighted welcome, because his father always brought food for the family.

Two hours later Vasily returned from the woods and looked up at his mother reading near the window of the drawing room. He called out to her. Valentina did not hear him. Vasily called again and this time Nikolai came to the window.

"What is it?"

"I have some Christmas food for Mama."

Valentina and Nikolai ran outside and stood under the holly tree, staring at the sledge Vasily had dragged up for their approval. Seeing the scratches on her son's face and hands, Valentina questioned him.

"Whatever have you been doing, Vasily? You're covered in mud and scratches. Has someone attacked you?"

"I brought you some food, Mama."

Valentina knelt to look under the tarpaulin covering the contents of the sledge, and gasped when she saw boxes of carefully wrapped peach liqueur and champagne, sides of ham, tins of tongue and a box that Vasily informed her contained a fruit cake. Picking her son up, she whirled him in the air. Ever practical, Nikolai ferried the food to the back of the house, where he unloaded it from the sledge and stored it in his mother's private pantry. He was sure Vasily had stolen the food and fearful that someone might discover the theft. His mouth watered as he thought of the ham and cake and he smiled joyfully as he envisaged the pleasure his mother would get from the unexpected bounty.

Inside the house Valentina was questioning Vasily.

"Why did you go out alone again, and where did you get the food?"

"I found it in the woods near Ivan Grigorevich's house."

"How did you know to look there?"

"My friend Duniasha told me a bad man hides food under the shed in the woods of Ivan's estate. Then he puts brambles outside the shed so no one can find the food."

"Stealing is wrong, Vasily, but I cannot scold you because to steal from a thief seems justified to me."

"Did that man steal the food, Mama?"

"I'm sure he did, and probably from people like us so he could sell it back for a fortune."

When her sons had gone out to play Valentina rode to the Yanin estate and found the shed Vasily had mentioned. She pushed the brambles aside with the stock of her rifle, then she went inside the hut and raised the floorboards. There, as the child had said, was food enough to feed them for a month. Valentina loaded a sledge with hams and cheeses, cakes and flour, boxes of dates, raisins, butter, sugar, lard and potatoes. Then she returned the brambles to their position and rode home in triumph. On reaching the house she packed up some of the food and sent it to her estate workers with her good wishes for Christmas. She offered her sons a glass of sherry and invited them to share a luxurious meal of smoked ham, pureed potatoes and candied peas. As they ate, she talked to them about the count's arrival.

"Tomorrow Papa will come. Imagine how thrilled he will be to know what lovely things we have found to eat. Thank you, Vasily, for your cleverness in bringing us such a wonderful gift, and thank you, Nikolai, for carrying everything inside."

The following morning the count appeared, his carriage laden with presents. He was not in the best humor and grumbled to his wife about his misfortune.

"I have brought you all some gifts and Gavrilo will bring more in the morning. I have managed to buy an excellent turkey, a brace of pigeons and four boxes of farm butter. The rest of the food I was to have bought from the black marketeer Sarinkov was stolen from his storeroom yesterday. I had hoped to be able to bring some smoked hams, cheeses, wine and a fruit cake for our tea party. . . ."

Valentina burst into peals of laughter at the thought of the money Vasily had saved her husband. The count joined in, though he had no idea why she was laughing. Vasily crept to his mother's side and looked imploringly up at her, as if to say "Don't tell Papa *I* stole the food." She told her husband she was laughing because she was happy. The lie pacified Vasily and satisfied the count and they went inside to talk of their Christmas plans. After lunch, as snow covered the pine trees and an icy wind swirled drifts against the walls of the house, the count and Valentina drank cherry brandy together by the fire. For a brief moment hunger had been kept at bay. She was profoundly grateful for this brief respite from the tension of the past.

Far away from Petrograd, Yanin and Dolgurov were eating plates of slimy leek stew heavy with grease and meat of uncertain origin. Yanin had begun to dread the evenings when he ate his meager meal and then counted the losses among his men from that day's conflict. He was now in command of the Preobrazhensky Regiment, not by the usual means of promotion, but because all his superiors were dead. Dolgurov was his second in command, a tower of strength in the worst moments of hell. After eating in the food hut, the two men walked back to their tents. The night sky was a mass of blue, red and yellow explosive flashes. The noise was deafening and never-ending. Yanin thought of the caviar and smoked sturgeon he had eaten on idyllic picnics with Valentina. His mouth watered uncomfortably because he was hungry and there had been little food for weeks. Potatoes and cabbages were rotting in the fields all around, because there were no peasants left to dig them. Bread bought locally was full of sawdust, cockroaches and gray dust. Yanin thought wryly that he had not eaten his fill since September. Dolgurov bade him good night and went to his tent.

"Pray God it will be a better day tomorrow, Vanya, though I am becoming ever more the pessimist."

"I too."

"Good night, Vanya, God bless you."

Knowing he would be unable to sleep, Yanin decided to take another turn around the camp. Gradually he had grown used to the smell of death, quicklime and cordite. He had even learned not to shudder as he stepped over the bodies of the fallen. But as he neared his tent and saw nearby a pair of shabby boots, the dead owner's bloody feet still inside them, he crossed himself fervently. It was hard not to sympathize with the thousands of enlisted men who were deserting each day and walking home through the ice white winter landscape.

Yanin stepped inside his tent and took a pen, intending to write to Valentina. A rat scuttered over his leg into the darkness. Outside he could hear rodents congregating near the bodies of the dead. He put down the pen and sighed. What was the point of writing to Valentina? What was there to say? My darling, I love you dearly. . . . I am covered in rat bites. My feet are rotting in these stagnant boots. Another million Russian soldiers are dead and more deserting. Happy Christmas. . . . Yanin covered his face with his hands and closed his eyes.

# CHAPTER TEN

## Petrograd, The Reckoning, 1916–1917

Exultation over General Brusilov's victories of mid-1916 paled in the autumn when it was realized that more than six million Russian soldiers were now dead. After the retreats of 1915 the victories should have heartened the exhausted men, but they had been undermined by persuasive leaflets distributed by revolutionaries with startling efficiency. The message on the leaflets read: "The war at home is where you are needed. It will be a war for the rights of your wives and children. They have no food. They need you. Fight for the revolution, which will give you all you desire."

In October 1916, troops of the Fourth Special Infantry refused orders to advance on the enemy. A few days later men of the Siberian Army Corps were ordered to take up the attack. Whispering and shouting revolutionary slogans, they put down their arms and refused to move. Despite courts-martial they still refused to attack and were persuaded to do so only when their general threatened to use his artillery against them.

The malaise spread, propelled by revolutionaries who papered the fields with leaflets and by men who had walked too long into battle against the howitzers, unarmed and inadequately fed. The legendary bravery of the Russian soldier still existed, but instead of being used against the forces of Germany and Austria-Hungary it sought to wipe out the very cause of its discomfort, a Tsar who played dominoes while his men rotted in the fields. During October the mutiny gained strength and troops of the Forty-seventh and Forty-eighth regiments refused orders. Executions were held after courts-martial in the field but the disobedience spread like wildfire. When the Tsar was informed of the problem he shrugged. He had been unable to control his people in peacetime. In time of war there was surely no hope.

By Christmas military censors were reporting that the armies wanted nothing but to go home. Where once "Mother Russia" had been their God, it now stood only for the agonies of the past, as did the Tsar, who *was* Russia. The soldiers had been indoctrinated over a long period by those who sought to be rid of the Tsar. The men's priority was to get back to their families and put an end to the restrictive black market that fed the rich and only the rich and even them infrequently.

On the thirtieth of December 1916, Sir George Buchanan, British Ambassador in Petrograd, visited the Tsar with a warning.

"Your Imperial Majesty, in the event of revolution our intelligence reports that only a small part of the Russian army will defend your dynasty."

The Tsar's impassive face did not change its expression as he nodded regal assent.

"It is kind of you to warn me, Sir George, but my life is now in the hands of God. I have always known that."

Defeated by this manifestation of eastern fatalism, Sir George hurried back to the embassy, exasperation mixing with admiration for the Tsar's courage. He was crossing the Petrovsky Bridge when a frozen body wrapped in a white-linen shroud was hauled from the icy water and then examined by military guards. Sir George heard the crowd murmuring that the body was that of Grigory Yefimovitch Rasputin, right hand of the tsarina and major cause of her intense unpopularity with the people. The Englishman ordered his driver to make haste to the embassy. On arrival he ordered a cable to be sent to England: "Rasputin found dead. Army on the verge of insurrection. Consider revolution now inevitable. Request orders in the light of immediate uprising. . . ."

Count Korolenko drove himself home from a party. Most of the leading aristocrats of Petrograd had been there and he had listened carefully to their conversations. The women had talked of the latest fashions and of hiding their jewels in holes dug in the gardens of their palaces. The men had talked about a new ballet star whose private life was more interesting by far than any of her performances onstage. Some of the less optimistic had already considered that the Tsar might abdicate, but they had been busy choosing new members of the Romanov family to succeed the Emperor and were not thinking that revolution was inevitable. The count entered his home, frowning because no groom met him. Out of the sixty-three staff kept on to run the pinewood wing, only forty remained, the others having disappeared with as many valuables as they could carry. The count ran upstairs to his suite, where Chef Dubrovsky was waiting for him.

"Excellency, there is no food left except flour, sugar and lentils. I know Milady is due to come to stay so I thought I should inform you."

Korolenko looked intently at the chef.

"I bought stocks of food last week. Where are they?"

"They have been stolen, sir. Some of the staff broke open the safe in which you had put the new stock."

"Broke open! I had that safe imported from England! It was made of solid iron and weighed three English tons. How, pray, did they open it?"

"With dynamite, Excellency, which they obtained from Madame Simoniescu like the last time. This explosion has destroyed part of the west wing, the kitchens and two bedrooms above it. I should have been killed if I had not gone to the woods to gather mushrooms for your breakfast, sir. I beg you to help me establish a new and smaller kitchen in this wing. It is better that I remain near you and your brother. I no longer wish to be isolated because of the danger."

"How many of the staff left after the explosion?"

"Ten, sir."

"So I am left with thirty?"

"No, sir, twenty. The others left a few minutes ago, because the villains who brought in the dynamite offered them a share of the food. Don't worry, sir. I shall cook without assistance until matters improve. Assistants are nothing but a liability at this time. I cannot trust them with a single thing when I turn my back."

"I shall try to buy more food, Dubrovsky, though heaven only knows where it can be found. My black market contact was shot dead two days ago, when he tried to steal stores from the Naval Yard."

"I will make inquiries, sir. Also I took the liberty of growing some herbs and winter vegetables in the hothouses earlier in the year. Milady said it would be in order."

"Thank you, Dubrovsky. You may go to the Gostini Dvor and buy whatever you wish. My name will be enough. You will not need a letter of credit."

The count went upstairs to where his brother lay ill. Gavrilo had taken to his bed after Christmas and the doctors had said he was dying. All differences forgotten, the count looked down as his brother slept. Korolenko shook his head in despair. Why, with all the money at his disposal, could he not save Gavrilo's life? He hurried from the sickroom and sat alone thinking of the future. He had resigned himself to leaving Russia for long enough to take Valentina and her sons to Paris. But would she agree to go? And how could she live there alone and unprotected? He went over and over the familiar conundrum, still uncertain how to resolve it to his satisfaction.

Valentina drove her new automobile into the courtyard of the palace. Her sons had been very quiet during the journey from the Flower House and she knew they were terrified that the vehicle might slip over the ice into the river. She turned to them.

"Please remember what I told you. Gavrilo is ill. He will enjoy our presents and small visits from each of us separately, but he cannot stand noise and must *not* be excited. Vasily, are you listening?"

"Yes, Mama. When will we be returning to the country? I hate Petrograd. I can't stand it."

"What you want is of no importance, Vasily, and I shall be very distressed if you choose to be difficult at this time."

When Valentina and Vasily had gone into the house the count spoke to Nikolai.

"How was the journey?"

"In truth, sir, my ears almost dropped off from the cold and I thought at least three times that we should end by sliding into a river. Mama is not yet very expert at turning corners."

"No doubt she will improve."

"Vasily has been whining again about wanting to go and live with the peasants. Mama's temper is somewhat uncertain as a result, sir."

"I used to want the same myself, so I cannot blame Vasily, but he must not trouble his mother now that she is in St. Petersburg."

While the Korolenko family was united in Petrograd, Yanin and Dolgurov were making their way back to the capital. The Preobrazhensky Regiment had been ordered to return to guard the Tsar with men of the Volynsky and Pavlovsky regiments. Such an order could only mean one thing—the possibility of rebellion—and both men were aware of this. Yanin looked ahead to where a cossack stood on his horse's back surveying the all-white, empty landscape. The cossack's scarlet coat was the only color in a shimmering sea of snow that stretched to the horizon under a storm-gray sky. Yanin and Dolgurov nodded as the cossack saluted them. An hour later he was a small dot in the distance and they were approaching the Neva. Yanin was thinking of Valentina and wondering if she would be in the city or home in the Flower House. Dolgurov was singing. Yanin teased him.

"You don't sound like a fellow who has been surrounded by corpses for three years."

"I don't feel like one either. I am on my way home, Vanya. I shall go and visit the gypsy ladies at the Villa Rode and perhaps come at your invitation to the palace to see Valentina and the boys. What more could I ask? Nothing could be worse than what I have been through in the war. I shall have nightmares about those rats forever."

"On the western front they are suffering from being gassed with mustard gas, which burns through the skin to the bone. Think of it, my friend, perhaps we were the lucky ones."

"Next time I meet the Commander of the Armies I shall suggest they use some of that gas you speak of on those damned revolutionaries."

Yanin remembered the snow and the puddles red with blood, the trench walls composed of yellowing corpses, the black rats hungry and fierce. Grisha is right, he thought, nothing could be worse than what has happened these past years. He thought again of Valentina and wondered if she had changed. For a moment he imagined he could smell her perfume and he smiled with pleasure as he thought of her lying by his side in bed. A nearby bell chimed ten. Yanin hastened on. They would be in St. Petersburg by midnight.

At noon the following day Yanin presented his compliments to the count, who led him to the study and spoke in a somber voice.

"You have suffered, young man. You are changed, as we all are."

Yanin thought that the count had always looked older than his years, and now looked little different. He tried to keep the eagerness from his voice.

"Is Valentina Ivanovna well, sir?"

"She is well but restless. The problems in our country since her arrival in nineteen hundred were at first a challenge. Now she is tired of all things Russian and every day I find her dreaming of Paris. I intend to deliver her to that city with her sons before the revolution returns. I shall then return alone to St. Petersburg."

Yanin was crestfallen. Was he never going to see Valentina and his sons again? Was she to pass out of his life irrevocably? The count's next words startled him.

"You had best sell your land to me, Yanin. A soldier cannot run an estate and my wife will not be here forever to toil in your fields like a peasant. After I have delivered her to Paris, I shall never leave Russia again. I could not live outside my own country and have no intention of doing so. Russia is my life and there is no changing me. You, on the other hand, must accompany your sons to France. I shall expect no refusal as you are an honorable man."

Yanin tried to find words to reply.

"But what of the title, sir? You longed for an heir to the Korolenko title for many years."

"I would not wish Nikolai to suffer as all men of substance will suffer someday if the Bolsheviks have their way."

Yanin fell silent and seeing the turmoil in him the count spoke gently.

"You chose your way, Yanin. You fell in love with Valentina when she was a mere child and have loved her ever since and I have no doubt always will. I love her too but she does not care for me in the same way. I shall therefore see her to safety and a new life. That is my duty as a husband. I should never have plucked her from her home in Paris in the first place. After that, I shall grow old in Russia and you will take over my responsibilities."

The count rose and continued sternly.

"We will say nothing of this to my wife. Come, she has been prettying herself all morning in preparation for your return."

Yanin entered the drawing room with eyes for no one but Valentina. She was dressed in dark claret silk, her lips rouged, her eyelids dusted with silver. Her hair, bleached from the sun, was drawn back in a tight chignon and decorated with diamonds. Her hands were hidden beneath lace mittens. Yanin took in the tanned skin and the anxious eyes. He clicked his heels and kissed her hand.

"I am truly happy to be in St. Petersburg and to see you again, Valentina Ivanovna."

Nikolai ran to Yanin's side and shook hands with him. Vasily, always out of step with the rest of the family, looked in awe at the scar on Yanin's cheek and then hid behind his mother, reluctant to express his feelings.

Valentina greeted Yanin, formally because the children were with her.

"How wonderful to have you back from the war, Ivan Grigorevich. After lunch I am planning to question you about what is happening at the front. Now do tell us your plans. Are you and your regiments to remain in Petrograd?"

"My regiment has been ordered back to guard the Tsar with men of the Volynsky and Pavlovsky regiments."

Korolenko spoke wearily at this news.

"Your tasks will be impossible. Things have changed beyond all recognition since you went away."

"The Preobrazhensky Guards are the most distinguished soldiers, sir. We have always had the responsibility of guarding the Tsar."

"Have the men remained loyal?"

Yanin remembered how the best men had fallen in the early days of the war.

"Our finest officers are dead, sir. The cream of our society fell in the earliest days of the war. However, now that I am in command I intend to show my men the ways of our regiment and to lead them to military perfection. Their loyalty is without question. They are members of the Preobrazhensky Guard. That will be enough."

The count had bought new stores of food and had ordered Dubrovsky to prepare the finest meal possible for their guest. He watched Yanin's eyes light with pleasure as favorite dishes were brought to the table. Yanin was full within minutes, but he continued to taste a few mouthfuls of each dish in deference to the count's hospitality and Dubrovsky's talent as a cook. The rest of the afternoon was spent regaling the boys with stories of Dolgurov's bravery in battle. Then, at dusk, Yanin walked with Valentina to the conservatory, amused to find cabbages, lettuce and tomatoes growing where once passion flowers had wafted exotically in the breeze. She seemed tense and unable to relax. Yanin took her hand and led her back to the house. Outside the cellar door he paused and looked into her eyes.

"Is something wrong, kitten? Has my long absence made you fall out of love with me?"

"No, Vanya, nothing like that has happened. I am relieved and delighted to see you back, but worried to distraction at the news you bring. There is surely going to be another revolution and then what will happen to us all, and to the Flower House?"

"A new house can always be built and new land can be bought. You cannot spend your life worrying about losing material things. Worry only lest you lose your sons or your limbs or your life."

"I know I am wrong to think so much about the house, but from the first moment of coming to Russia that house was my sanctuary, the breeding ground of our love and the birthplace of our sons. It means much more to me than mere bricks and stones. It is part of my life and I cannot and will not relinquish it."

"You may someday have to choose between your house and your life, Valentina. But I didn't come here to talk of sad things. I came here to tell you how much I love you and to ask you when I may visit you in the country. I am also happy to worship your new beauty. You have changed, like everyone else in this country, but only for the better."

Valentina knew he was trying to reassure her about the changes in her looks and was grateful. She held his hand as they walked through the dark cellar rooms to the hall and then to join the others in the salon. There they discussed the exorbitant prices in Petrograd. Yanin was surprised by her grasp of the practical things in life.

"Butter is now fifty times what it was before the war was declared and one cannot buy it anyway. Mutton and beef are treble in price and cheese is also unobtainable, even to the rich."

Yanin rose and brought the gifts he had purchased for the family, a snuff box for the count, a crucifix for Valentina studded with pearls and amethysts. For his sons he had brought a miniature theater with marionettes as performers. This he gave to Valentina with instructions to explain how it worked to the boys when they had eaten their evening meal. Then it was time to leave. Yanin rose reluctantly and made his way to the entrance with the count, leaving Valentina behind. Korolenko took him to one side as he neared his horse.

"My brother is very seriously ill and we have been told he will die within the next few days. If Gavrilo lives to confound his doctors, Valentina will return to the country by the middle of next week. You are welcome to visit this house while she is in St. Petersburg. I myself go to the yacht club each afternoon. You have no idea what a challenge learning to sail has been at my age. I can now sail anywhere in the world and I certainly consider it the achievement of my career."

That night Valentina lay awake, going over the events of the day. She was depressed because despite the excitement of Yanin's return and her love and admiration for him, she had felt none of the eruption of sensuality that usually affected her in his presence. He had appeared looking distinguished in what was obviously a new uniform and she had felt her heart fluttering with admiration but nothing more. She asked herself if all the days in the fields had robbed her of her femininity. Was she now unable to feel the intoxicating sensations that only women knew? Had something changed within her? She knew Yanin still adored her and that her own feelings for him were unchanged. She shook her head, half angry at her own thoughts. The fact was she had changed in every way since the war began. Dresses that had seemed thrilling years ago now seemed frivolous. Was it maturity or something else that had made her so different? Only the Flower House satisfied her now, assuaging her insecurities and making her feel peaceful and calm. Only Ivan, of all the men she had ever met, inspired her to want him and the dominating influence his body would have on hers. Why then had she not weakened with the old familiar longing? She sighed, certain that she had lost much more than youth in the years of work and hunger.

As Gavrilo clung to life, Valentina and her sons returned to the country. The weather was unusually cold and it was with some trepidation that they approached the empty house. Inside, to their surprise, they found fires lit and soup on the stove. When they ran from room to room they came upon Yanin asleep on a sofa in Valentina's suite. Looking down on him she felt her heart fill with love. She bent down to kiss his cheek, recalling the many times he had done this for her arrival home. Yanin slept on, exhausted. It was hours before he woke, looking up to see Valentina sitting by the fire telling Vasily a story. Yanin watched them, scrutinizing his son's face and accepting that for Vasily he was a person of little importance. It was different with Nikolai, who had always behaved like the perfect son. With Vasily, Yanin had the feeling that both he and Korolenko were outsiders, obstacles between the boy and his mother and also between his curious desire to live with the peasants. Yanin spoke softly.

"I hope you liked the soup I made."

Valentina turned and smiled.

"I've saved some for you so we can eat together."

Vasily ran from the room and joined his brother on the terrace. Nikolai was erecting a snowman with a black pipe in his mouth and one of Valentina's old hats on his head. Vasily looked speculatively at his brother. "What do you think of Ivan Grigorevich?"

Nikolai paused. "I've known him since I was small. I used to pretend he was my brother before you were born."

"Do you still treat him like a brother? Do you love him the way you love Mama and me?"

"I do love him but differently from you and Mama. Why so many questions, Vasily? Is something wrong?"

"Mama's always talking to Ivan Grigorevich. Now he's back she won't have time to play with me. If I lived with the estate workers I should have lots and lots of children to play with."

Nikolai put down his spade and looked into his brother's dark, turbulent eyes.

"The trouble with you, Vasily, is that you are never happy. Colonel Yanin has been away for years yet you complain he monopolizes Mama. You sleep in a comfortable bed in this nice house yet you want to go and live with the peasants. I think it would be best if you went to live with them for a while. I'm going to ask Mama if you can."

Surprised by his brother's vehemence, Vasily watched Nikolai returning to the house to ask their mother if he could go and live with the peasants. At first he felt defiant. Then he lapsed into uncertainty. He had never been inside one of the cottages on the estate. He had only been allowed to sit outside roasting potatoes on their harvest fires and listening to stories about running free and having no lessons at all. He always had wanted to go and live with the workers, why he did not know. Vasily trudged back to the house and went to his room to pack his belongings, a favorite stone, his train set, his kite shaped like a mushroom and five rubles the count had given him. Then, bag in hand, he waited for his mother to appear. He was surprised to be ignored for some time. Then Nikolai came with a message.

"Mama says Ivan Grigorevich will take you to live in the cottages. You don't want to have to wade through the snowdrifts, do you? And you cannot take your train set, Vasily. The peasants don't have electricity in their cottages so the set will not work."

Vasily put down the train set and followed his brother with a heavy heart. He was surprised when Nikolai turned to speak to him again.

"For a long time you have been asking to be allowed to go and live with the peasants and not with Mama and me. Remember that and don't come back here unless you are *quite* sure you can behave."

Vasily kissed his mother and was lifted behind Yanin on the horse. Valentina blew kisses as they rode away, her heart full of emotion when she saw the fear and uncertainty in Vasily's eyes. She looked at Nikolai and he at her.

"I hope we've done the right thing, Mama."

"Something had to be done. I'm truly sick of Vasily's longings. I suppose he was born to be malcontent."

"We'll see how he feels when he's spent a night with the Kubatovs."

Vasily entered the Kubatov cottage and was given a small corner of his own. He coughed repeatedly because the air was full of smoke. A damp sheet was put on a frame to form a partition behind which he could retreat into a private world, and this pleased him until he sniffed the air and smelled dirty bodies, cabbage stew and smoke from the fire.

Maria Dmitrevna Kubatova was an understanding woman. She left Vasily alone until he had settled to the room. Yanin had said only that Vasily would spend three days in her house. She had asked no further questions and was happy to obey Yanin's instructions to treat the boy as one of her own sons. As darkness fell, she lit a candle and called the five children to the table. Her husband would be fed later, when he returned from felling trees in the far reaches of the count's land. She ladled cabbage soup into a wooden bowl and handed it to Vasily, then a bowl each for the other four children.

Vasily wondered if he would be given a glass of wine to warm him but he was given only a glass of cold brackish water. He remembered his mother's instruction not to drink foul water and pushed the mug aside. Valentina's words kept tinkling like silver bells in his ear: Better champagne than water, champagne makes me feel as if I am glowing from head to toe. How pretty Mama is, he thought, with lovely skin, not black grimy hands like Maria Dmitrevna. He sighed and began to eat the cabbage stew that tasted of nothing but smoke. He wondered if soot had fallen in the pot and avoided retching only with the greatest effort. A plate of pickled beetroot followed. Then the children were hurried to bed. Vasily looked toward Maria, expecting to be called to his evening bath. When she saw him looking hopefully in her direction she leaned forward and asked what he wanted. Vasily was close to tears.

"I was wondering if you would bathe me before I go to bed. I always have a bath in front of the fire."

"Bathe you! Dear Lord, my children take a bath once a year and never more. Dirt stops the lice from biting. Come to think of it, I'd better rub some camphor around your ears. With your fine gentleman's skin you'll be bothered by them."

Vasily woke in the night, his body on fire. He leaped up out of bed, stumbling over two of the other children. A lamp was lit and his body inspected and found to be covered in flea bites. When he began to howl with distress Maria spoke sharply.

"Stop that noise at once and don't scratch the bites or they'll have the hide off you. In the morning you can go cutting logs with my husband. You used to fancy doing that, didn't you? Now stop crying or none of us will be able to sleep."

Vasily continued to wail and nothing could silence him. Maria lifted him back to bed and snuffed out the precious candle. Vasily watched the glow of the fire and thought of his mother. He had plagued her with requests to be allowed to live with the peasant workers on the estate. Now that he had been granted his wish, he loathed everything about the experience. How Nikolai would laugh when he returned home in the morning, but he *would* return home and beg his mother to get the lice off him. Then he would have a bath in warm scented water and eat some of his marzipan soldiers. Vasily dried his eyes and thought that life was a puzzle. Things one wanted greedily made one unhappy, yet discipline made one feel proud. He had imagined it would be fun to be a peasant running wild and free in the woods, eating by the fireside at night and never having to learn French, German and English. He began to cry again as he thought of his own stupidity, straining his eyes to watch for the sunrise. At dawn he would get up and go home. He blew his nose on the coarse smock Maria had given him and covered his head with it, wincing as the fleas feasted on his body.

At nine Maria arrived at Valentina's door. Her face was red from running through the snow and it was obvious that she was terrified.

"Is Vasily home, ma'am?"

"Of course not; he's with you."

"The boy left before any of us woke, ma'am. He must have decided to come back to you. He was covered in flea bites and I fear it upset him."

Pale but composed, Valentina dismissed Maria.

"Wait at your home in case Vasily returns. I will arrange a search for my son from this end."

Minutes later Yanin rode away, his saddlebags loaded with pigeon pie, blankets and flasks of beef tea. He had put some marzipan soldiers in a special pocket of his jacket because he knew they were Vasily's favorites. He was agitated beyond all measure, most of all because he had agreed with Nikolai's plan to allow the boy to go and stay in the workers' cottages for more than a single meal by the fire. Yanin rode one way from the house and then another, praying for guidance as he rode. But still he could see no sign of Vasily.

Remembering his brother's warning about walking through snowdrifts, Vasily kept to a narrow path leading into the woods. He was afraid, because he had expected to arrive home within minutes of leaving Maria's cottage. He looked up at the sky and thought it was going to snow again soon. Two hours later, exhausted from his long walk, Vasily sat on an abandoned cart and considered his position. He had been taught never to fall asleep in the snow, so he concentrated hard on staying awake. For what seemed like an age he heard nothing but the whine of the wind in the pine trees. He knew someone would come looking for him, either one of the workers or his mother. Yanin would not come because he had always been jealous of the guardsman and surly in his presence. Nikolai would not come because he was too young to be allowed out in such terrible conditions. Large flakes of snow began to fall. Vasily rose, terrified that he would die if he did not find shelter. He strode purposefully down a different path leading to a clearing full of felled trees. A fox slipped by, its coat of arctic white undistinguishable from its surroundings. Vasily was wondering how long it would be before he froze to death when he heard a bugle call. He leaped up and screamed to the emptiness all around.

"Ivan Grigorevich! This way! I am here . . . Ivan Grigorevich . . ."

The bugle sound came nearer and nearer. Vasily continued to shout until his throat was hoarse. Then Yanin rode into the clearing and jumped down from his horse. Vasily sobbed with relief when Yanin threw a blanket around his shoulders. Yanin ignored his son's tears.

"This is not the best day for a picnic, Vasily, but I brought you some consommé and a pigeon pie and a few of your marzipan soldiers because I was sure the food at Maria's house would have left you hungry. I also brought clean blankets, because Mama knew you would be cold."

They sat together on the trunk of a tree. Vasily sipped the soup and ate the pigeon pie. Then he ate all his marzipan soldiers, one by one, thinking hard as he enjoyed them.

"Is Mama very angry with me, Ivan Grigorevich?"

"She's not angry, only worried because she thinks you are lost. I told her you would never have upset her so terribly deliberately."

"Why did *you* come to find me?"

"Why not? I'm damned if I don't love you, Vasily, even though you are sometimes the most horrible boy in Russia. Also, I am well practiced at riding in these icy conditions. You wouldn't have wished your mama to come out to be frozen in the snow, would you?"

Vasily shook his head wearily. Then he looked at Yanin's hands and saw they were blue with cold. Suddenly he began to sob and without warning threw himself at Yanin and settled to warming himself on his father's shoulder.

"Can we go home now, Ivan Grigorevich, and will you get the fleas off me? I don't want to take them into the house, you know how Mama hates such things. Oh, it was horrible in that cottage. Don't tell Nikolai, but I cried all night."

Yanin kissed the boy's head and cradled him in his arms. Then he lifted Vasily on the horse and together they rode back through the pinewoods.

# CHAPTER ELEVEN

## Petrograd, Revolution, 1917

On the eighth of March there were riots in Petrograd. Hungry citizens wanted bread and were prepared to kill to get it. The Tsar had explained the food was on its way, stranded by snow on the railway. No one listened to him. The people had lost their respect for their ruler and no longer trusted anything he said. On the ninth there were more riots and the cossacks were called out to clear the crowds. Instead of bringing down their knouts, as was the custom, the cossacks sympathized with the demonstrators and joined the ranks of the revolution.

The count ordered his new private train to be taken at once to Pskov. Valentina was still at her house in the country. Korolenko sent a man to bring her back to the safety of his personal care. He was certain that this was the moment when they should escape and determined he must persuade his wife to leave the Flower House.

On the eleventh of March, another Black Sunday, the people of Petrograd were again on the streets. The Tsar had ordered posters to be attached to every wall, forbidding public meetings. The demonstrators tore them down and trampled them into the brown slush of the melting snow. The revolutionary who had robbed the Korolenko family of life and valuables looked with satisfaction at the scene. Across the city his best men were busy throwing grenades and bombs into the carriages of those rich enough and foolish enough to venture out. Koba looked toward the palace on the Nevsky Prospekt and thought of the favor Magda had begged of him. Later, he thought, later. There are more important things to be done than exterminating Magda's enemies.

The Preobrazhensky Guard was called out with men of the

Pavlovsky and Volynsky regiments. Yanin did not hesitate in his duty and with Dolgurov at his side forced the crowd to retreat from the gates of the Winter Palace. That same night men of the Pavlovsky Regiment mutinied and deserted their barracks to roam the streets, eager to join the revolution.

Yanin and his officers were given the order to disarm the men of the Pavlovsky Regiment. When the mission was accomplished they were allowed to take a few hours off duty. Anxious to see Valentina, Yanin rode from Petrograd to the country. As he rode he thought how urgent it was that she and her sons leave Russia. He would ask her to go with the count to his own house in the Crimea. Korolenko could then arrange for the family to travel to Paris and he would follow at the earliest opportunity. Yanin thought of the crowds jostling in the streets of Petrograd and knew that they were more dangerous in their fanatic zeal than any he had encountered on the battlefield.

Valentina was preparing a nutmeg punch when Yanin arrived. They shared this as they sat on a polar-bear rug in front of the fire in her bedroom. Yanin spoke of making plans to escape the coming holocaust, his voice shaking with emotion.

"Today the Pavlovsky Regiment mutinied. It is now only a matter of time before the revolution returns in full force. The Tsar will then have to abdicate and the Bolsheviks will make life impossible for you and me and for our kind. I have a house in the Crimea. Why do you not go there with your husband and our sons? I will join you as soon as I can."

"I shall not leave this house until I am forced to do so, Ivan. I pray every night that I shall never have to leave it."

"I love you, kitten, but you're too stubborn."

"Don't let's talk of revolution, Vanya. Tomorrow you must go back to your duties."

"Today: it's already one in the morning."

They loved tenderly, with the mellow joy of familiarity. Afterward, while Yanin slept, Valentina lay thinking of what he had said. On the one side Korolenko kept urging her to return to Petrograd. On the other Yanin talked of mutiny and revolution. She rose and stood at the window, looking out on the garden that had been her joy for seventeen years. Through the vanishing snow the green leaves of spring were peeping. Valentina knew that the cherry blossom would soon flower. Then spring would come with the sweet smell of damp earth and bluebells. She looked back at Yanin, loving him as she had always loved him, touched that he had ridden out to see her for a few precious hours. The clock chimed five. She woke Yanin, who rose and dressed.

"If you come to Petrograd during the next few days I will come to call. The count gave his permission."

"Then I shall come to Petrograd at once. My husband will be delighted. He has been sending a man every day to fetch me."

Yanin looked teasingly into her eyes.

"I love you dearly, kitten, but I had best not talk of love when I am about to leave. Is there any coffee?"

"I can hear Zita in the kitchen."

Hours later Valentina left the house with Nina and her sons. She had asked Zita and Bibi to stay behind locked doors and windows to guard the house against deserters, who were said to be roaming the area. The streets of Petrograd were in a turmoil and she took the quiet way to the house, driving the final distance through the count's garden. On arriving at the palace she went at once to see her husband. The count seemed preoccupied and grim.

"Did you see the crowds marching in the city? I have never seen demonstrations of such viciousness before."

"I heard a tumult of voices and people shouting revolutionary slogans so I took the way through the back streets and our garden."

The count beckoned her to the window and pointed to the street below. Valentina saw thousands of people marching like a human kaleidoscope in every street and square in the city. They were waving red flags and singing anthems of revolution. Among them she was horrified to see men of the Pavlovsky and Volynsky regiments. Tears of pride came to her eyes and fell down her cheeks as she thought of Yanin, whose regiment alone had remained loyal to the Tsar.

"So the revolution has arrived, sir?"

"It has, my dear. I'm sorry, I had hoped to have you and the boys out of the city before the worst trouble began."

After lunch they heard from Dubrovsky that the Law Courts were burning. The chef rushed to tell the count this news, his face streaming with tears because he too was facing the end of life as he had always known it.

"Mobs of people are looting the finest houses, Excellency. What are we to do?"

"To hell with the mob."

"Had you best send Milady and the children back to the country, sir? Surely it would be safer there, and they could drive a great part of the way on your own land."

The count rang for his new manservant and ordered Valentina to be brought to him. The servant bowed mockingly.

"Milady went out after her nap, Excellency. She told me to tell you she would be back in time for dinner. I believe she received a message to go at once to the stables of the Preobrazhensky Regiment. I happened to read the message before giving it to her."

The count stiffened with rage at this statement.

"Is it your habit to read notes before giving them to me also?"

Korolenko dismissed the servant and looked furiously at Dubrovsky.

"Women make it difficult for a man to keep them safe. Remind me to send that scoundrel away for his appalling nerve in reading our private correspondence."

Dubrovsky watched at the count put on his sable coat and took an ebony stick from the rack.

"You're not going out, are you, Excellency?"

"I am indeed."

"There are murderers all over the city. They are throwing bombs into carriages like yours. They hate the rich, sir. They will surely kill you."

"I will not be cowed by the rabble, Dubrovsky."

"Will you not change your mind, sir?"

The count looked loftily down at Dubrovsky's tear-stained face.

"A gentleman never changes his mind, Dubrovsky."

Valentina left her automobile in the courtyard of the palace and took instead one of the count's horses, a black stallion renowned for its ill temper. She rode at speed down the Nevsky Prospekt, avoiding Palace Square with its taunting masses and proceeding to the Bolshaya Millionnaya, where the Preobrazhensky Guard was quartered. She was wondering why Yanin had summoned her to journey alone through the streets on a day of such open hostility. The note had been signed "I," not his usual signature; had Yanin really sent for her? She knew she could not turn back until she had made certain of his wishes.

The count drove out of the palace at full gallop, scattering crowds chanting outside the gates. He did not slacken his pace until he turned right to avoid Palace Square and then only when a group of ruffians snatched the horses' reins from his hands. Above his head a sniper began to fire from the rooftops. The mob scattered to the shelter of the arcades on either side of the street. The count retrieved the reins and, with bullets whining around him, drove haughtily along the road, never ducking, never flinching, his steely gaze seemingly oblivious to the danger. It was the tradition of a Russian gentleman to ignore such trifles as imminent death. Even on the battlefield only a coward ducked bullets intended by fate for others. To the very end Korolenko knew he would disdain the rabble and those who sought to intimidate him. He was Vladimir Vasilievich Korolenko and no one would dictate his actions. He drove on, ignoring the bullets. On the rooftop above him the sniper gazed in awe at the count's sangfroid as he rode on to his destination.

Valentina stepped down from her horse and walked toward the barracks of the Preobrazhensky Regiment. From the stables, heated voices and shouts of derision came to her ears. She stood unnoticed in a deserted sentry box, listening fearfully to the men debating their future with Yanin and Dolgurov.

"Dammit, Dolgurov, must you always agree with Yanin? You're archaic, both of you. You speak of honor but the Tsar has no honor or he would not have sent his men into battle without guns. Who needs honor anyway, you cannot eat it. Face the facts, gentlemen, the Tsar is a weakling dominated by his German wife. Probably she has been in the pay of her country for years."

Yanin answered angrily.

"The tsarina has never worked for the Germans and you know it. You are seeking reasons to account for your ignominious intentions."

Valentina felt proud of the anger in Yanin's voice. He would have his way. He always had and always would. When the voices became more shrill she held her breath in sudden fear.

"Enough talk. We're going to join the revolution."

"You will not leave these stables!"

"Get out of the way, Dolgurov!"

Yanin's voice rose above the derision of his men.

"I ask you as gentlemen to continue to guard the Tsar. Our regiment has the most gallant history of all for guarding the Tsar of all Russia. Will you change that now? Will you allow your sons to know of your cowardice? Give me your answer to my questions!"

A shot rang out, then another and after a moment another. Valentina took a deep breath so she would not faint. Then a line of Preobrazhensky Guards rode out of the stables, their swords flashing in the sun, their traditional banners replaced by the scarlet banner of revolution. To her horror, Valentina saw that Yanin and Dolgurov were not with them. She tried to move but her legs felt like lead. She struggled to secure her horse and slowly, fearfully, walked toward the stables of the regiment.

At Yanin's side Dolgurov lay dead, one eye a mash of oozing red. Valentina cried out at the scene, the scarlet blood, the gray stone floor, the biblical ray of sunlight falling on Yanin's face from a high window. She ran and knelt at his side, touching the two bullet wounds in his chest. She clasped his hand and received a faint pressure in return. Tears began to pour down her cheeks and she felt cold, though the interior of the building was warm. She kept praying for strength to equal Yanin's and, lifting him against her breasts, looked down on the dying man and whispered her love to his pale face.

"I love you, Vanya. I loved you that first day when I saw you riding at the rear of the regiment. I loved you when we first rode together through the cornfield and every day since. Even when I was angry with you I loved you more than anything else in the world. . . ."

Yanin's face fell against her shoulder, his blood staining the cream silk of her jacket. Valentina knew he was dead. Loud noises buzzed in her ears and she felt numb and unable to move. She did not notice a man walking toward her from the darkness at the far end of the building and barely glanced at him when he spoke.

"I knew you'd come, Countess. A note in Yanin's hand was enough to bring you running."

The man cocked the gun and aimed it at Valentina's chest. She looked up at him disdainfully, still clutching Yanin's body as if she wanted to follow him in death as she had always followed him in life.

"You do me a favor, sir. I have no wish to live without Ivan."

The man hesitated. He had expected fear or pleading to escape the inevitable. Instead the woman seemed pleased she was going to die. He fired with all the hatred within him, exulting that one more aristocrat was dead. Then he took off his groom's jacket and put on the new red one, specially made to match his red revolutionary flag. Stepping over Valentina's body he repeated gleefully: "I *knew* you'd come if that arrogant young buck called you. I'll be remembered as one of the heroes of the revolution. . . ."

Minutes later the count stepped into the stables and took in the scene in a brief glance. On the ground Dolgurov and Yanin lay side by side. Near Yanin, her arms still clutching him, Valentina lay unconscious or dead. The count ran forward and seeing the two men were dead bent to listen to his wife's heartbeat, then he picked her up and ran with her back to his carriage. For a moment he looked down at her, pity, love and anguish passing on his face. He was pale with shock, and filled with hatred of the rabble who had murdered. He knew Yanin's death would affect Valentina, if she lived, for the rest of her life. His plans for her escape from Russia were ruined. The count looked again at his wife, praying she could be saved.

On reaching the palace Korolenko took Valentina to her bedroom and called Nina to run for the doctor. The girl stared down at her mistress, tears streaming down her cheeks.

"Whatever's happened, sir?"

"I don't know, but we shall presently find out. Perhaps it will be best if you make a calming tisane for all of us and send one of the footmen for the doctor."

"I'll do it at once, sir."

Alone with his wife, the count tore off the bloodstained dress, removing with it a solid-silver icon Valentina had been wearing at her breast. He turned the icon over, noting that it was now damaged, a large dent made by the bullet in the center of the madonna's face. Someone had tried to shoot Valentina! The count's face darkened with rage as he continued to undress her. When he realized that her body was unblemished, he broke down and cried with relief. Then, having covered Valentina with a blanket, he went to the window and looked down at the crowds below. Among them were men of the Preobrazhensky Regiment. Korolenko understood at once what had happened. Yanin and Dolgurov had surely been shot while trying to prevent their colleagues from joining the revolution. Had one of the Preobrazhenskys shot Valentina? Surely not. He returned to where she was lying and tucked the blanket more securely around her neck. He was about to leave when Valentina opened her eyes.

"Where am I?"

"You are home, my dear. I brought you home. These are no times for a lady to be out."

Valentina lay for a long time marshaling her thoughts and the count was alarmed to see tears flowing unashamedly down her cheeks. She spoke in a whisper.

"Ivan is dead. He was trying to rally his men's loyalty to the Tsar. Dolgurov was at his side, as always. One of the men from the regiment shot them both. I heard the shots and the sound of the men laughing."

"Where were you?"

"I was standing with your horse outside the stables. I had received a note purporting to come from Ivan, telling me to meet him there at once. It was not from Ivan at all. It was from a groom, who had written it to bring me there."

The count listened as his wife poured out her story.

"Ivan didn't speak as I held him. One moment he was still alive, then he was gone, like a flickering candle. He said *nothing*, not a word for me or for his sons. I was still sitting with him when the groom came forward from the darkness and shot me. I suppose it was his contribution to the revolution."

"You are not hurt, my dear. The icon you were wearing deflected the bullet. I imagine you merely fainted from the shock of the impact. Do you know the name of the man who shot you?"

Valentina shook her head.

"He was a groom, that is all I know. He had a red flag and was carrying a red jacket to wear when he went out on the streets. How I hate these revolutionaries. How I hate Russia!"

"He had good aim, my dear, he would certainly have killed you if you had not been wearing the icon."

"Your sister gave it to me the first Christmas after I arrived in St.

Petersburg. I have always treasured it because she gave it to me and said it would bring me luck."

"I must go out. I will not leave those two heroes to the damnation of the revolutionaries."

The count asked two of his oldest retainers to accompany him and returned to the barracks of the Preobrazhensky Regiment. It was raining hard so the streets were quieter than before, and he thanked God for his good fortune. On reaching the stables, he ordered Yanin and Dolgurov's bodies to be placed on the vehicle he had brought with him. For a moment he looked down on his rival, whose presence had ruined his chances of marital happiness. Then he closed the tawny eyes with two gold pieces and placed a spray of rosemary between the bloody fingers. The count knew he should hate Yanin but over the years he had come to treat the young officer like a brother. Yanin had been discreet, a Russian aristocrat of the highest order. The count stood rigidly at attention as the bodies were carried past him to the accompanying cart.

The count was taking a last look at the gloomy interior of the building when a drunken man appeared at the door. In his hand he carried a red flag that matched exactly the jacket he was wearing. The count recalled Valentina's words and hurried to close the gap between himself and the murderous groom. The drunken reveler narrowed his eyes.

"What is your business here, sir?"

"I have been removing the bodies of my good friends Yanin and Dolgurov, who were murdered earlier this day by accursed revolutionaries."

"And who are you?"

"My name is none of your concern."

The count drew abreast of the groom, who was fumbling in his coat for the gun with which he had shot Valentina. Korolenko inquired his intentions.

"Are you looking for something, sir?"

"I'm looking for my gun so I can be rid of you, you damned aristocrat."

As the groom dragged out the gun Korolenko hit him twice on the head with his ebony staff. The second blow fractured his skull and the groom fell like a sack of logs at the count's feet. Korolenko dusted his coat, wiped the blood from his staff on the groom's flag and stepped over the body and out of the stable to the waiting carriage. He looked down at the weighted staff and thought grimly of Miss Knatchbull, whose own penchant for such objects had inspired him to buy one of a like dimension. He smiled wanly. The groom would not be shooting any more aristocratic ladies.

Valentina was sitting in front of the fire talking with Gavrilo when a band of ragged, hostile citizens of Petrograd burst into the room. She leaped up and stood watching them, her heart thundering with fright. At that moment Vasily and his brother came charging into the room. Nikolai's voice trembled when he spoke.

"There are men everywhere in the house, Mama. They are taking the furniture out and removing all the gold pieces from Papa's safe. One of them has put his bayonet through your favorite painting and another is using the hall carpet as a lavatory."

A crash came from overhead as one of the count's precious stone cabinets was overturned. Valentina faced the intruders angrily.

"You are revolutionaries, not thieves and vandals. Why do you not get on with your business?"

"This is our business. From this moment all the homeless of the city will be lodged in the palaces, where there's plenty of room. They can also share the food you buy on the black market."

"You know very well we have been unable to get food for weeks. And are your friends going to live in the rooms full of the treasures they are so busy destroying?"

"There will be no treasures in the future, and when we are through there'll be no rich either. We shall all be equal and you will have to learn to work like any normal woman."

The count appeared, dragged in by four men. One of the revolutionaries screeched indignantly.

"This old fellow hit me with his cudgel."

"Shoot him."

"No!"

The vehemence of Valentina's tone startled the marauders and the leader swaggered over to her side.

"And why not?"

"Because this man is the father of the two boys. Even the revolution recognizes the right of a child to know his father. Would you dispute it?"

This piece of logic defeated the leader, who turned aside to supervise the rifling of a chest of Gavrilo's medicines.

"What's this?"

"That is the medicine chest used by the count's brother for his illness. Do *not* break the vials, they are of the greatest necessity to him."

The leader eyed Valentina with interest.

"You have too much spirit for an aristocrat. Join us and you'll be happy."

"I was perfectly happy before you appeared, sir."

The man grinned and made to drag her along with him as he left the room. Gavrilo stepped between them. Surprised, the intruder drew his revolver and shot the count's brother through the chest. Korolenko knelt at Gavrilo's side, cradling him in his arms. Vasily burst into tears and was comforted by Nikolai, who bit back his own distress because he knew his mother needed him. Valentina dropped to her knees, straining to hear what Gavrilo was saying.

"I am not at all averse to dying after this long wait. I was just trying to live long enough to see your beautiful garden in bloom again . . ."

Gavrilo's eyes closed and the count looked despairingly at his wife.

"He is dead and soon we shall all be dead. Dear God, what a fool I've been. Why did I not insist that you leave the Flower House months ago? Why was I negligent? I am just unable to face the thought of leaving Russia."

Valentina led her husband to the corner and called for Nina to make tea. There was no reply when she rang, so she went to the kitchen and found Nina struggling with an enormous cossack. Valentina hit the attacker on the head with a copper pan, but instead of falling unconscious at her feet he turned in puzzlement, as if she were merely tapping him on the shoulder. She called for help but none came, so she began to strike the cossack again. A blow to the chin stunned her and she fell to the ground. When she recovered consciousness she found Nina lying on the floor nearby, her skirts over her head. She was sobbing hysterically. Valentina dragged herself to the girl's side and tried to comfort her.

"The man has gone. He's gone and we are alone, Nina. Don't cry. Someday you will forget what happened and you'll be happy again. You're alive and we'll soon be returning to the country."

Nina stared into space as though unable to take in what was being said. The man had hurt her and had promised to return again that night. You will be my slave from now on, was what he had told her. When Valentina had gone, Nina walked to the uppermost floor of the building and opened the window. For a moment she looked down at men burning carriages in the count's coachhouse and other raiders carrying valuables outside to the waiting vans and carts. Wiping her eyes, she thought of Valentina and the Flower House. Her first days there had been wonderful and she had loved the house and its occupants dearly. There would be no more wonderful days now the revolution had returned. Nina hesitated. Then she crawled out on the ledge and stood gazing at the tumult below. Her mind went back to the cossack who had defiled her and she began to sob tears of bitter unhappiness. She looked to the sky and saw dark gray clouds overhead. They are the dark gray clouds of hell, she thought. Then she leaped to her death in the courtyard below.

Inside the palace the count appeared and called to his wife.

"These ruffians intend to stay the night. What on earth shall I do? One of them is sleeping in my bed."

"Let them have their way."

"And will you allow our sons to share quarters with this scum?"

"We have no choice, sir. However, I will put them to sleep in the gazebo and return to the country tonight to bring Zita and her sister back to join us."

"The men will not let you leave."

"Put your horse at the far end of the garden. I will leave when everyone is asleep."

At midnight, when the looters had fallen asleep in the corridors, reception rooms and kitchen of the palace, Valentina walked down a winding stairway concealed behind oak paneling. From here she reached the cellars and the garden. In the conservatory two men were arguing over the ownership of a bronze urn. Valentina ran past and made her way to the place where the count had tethered his horse. She galloped away to the far reaches of the garden and then on to the road for a mile before turning again onto the count's private land. As she rode through the fields that would soon be planted with corn she thought of Yanin and the golden days of their love. As she thought of him tears rolled down her cheeks and she realized that he was all she had ever wanted, the total of her ambitions, the sharer of every future plan. She had taken it for granted that they would remain together forever. Now the future seemed bleak and empty. Worse, she had no interest in it or in anything much at all. As she rode toward the house, even the thought of her sons did little to rouse Valentina from the depths of agonizing despair.

On reaching the edge of the field nearest to the Flower House, Valentina looked up at the outline of the property. Her eyes dwelled on the tower room and she remembered the times she had seen Yanin riding on the road, his epaulettes glittering in the sun. She rode on to the stables and fed and watered her horse. Then she let herself into the house, joyful to inhale the welcome smell of home. Again she remembered Yanin and frowned at what he had said: Someday you may have to choose between your home and your life. Her home *was* her life. Would anything ever be the same once she left it and became an exile?

Zita came to meet her with a wan smile.

"I made some cabbage soup, ma'am. We haven't anything else to eat except the bottled fruit. I daren't go out in case the villagers did something bad."

"What have they said?"

"They knew all about the revolution in Petrograd, ma'am. They tried to come inside the house to steal your belongings. Some of them are planning to live here, Nadya for one. She's the most vicious bitch I ever met, begging your pardon, ma'am. Bibi and I stayed inside so as to avoid the villagers. There must have been a hundred of them sitting like vultures on the lawn, waiting for us to open the door. I thought they would never go, ma'am. How shall we stop them from taking over your house?"

"I don't know."

"You always know what to do, ma'am."

Valentina thought of the image of invincibility she gave to those who depended on her. Then she remembered Yanin and sighed.

"I have very bad news for you, Zita. Our dear friends Yanin and Dolgurov are both dead."

Zita burst into tears as Valentina continued.

"Imagine, after all those years in the war they were shot by men of their own regiment."

"Are your sons safe, ma'am?"

"The boys are well but the count's brother was shot by revolutionaries when they occupied the palace. Come, Zita, let me give you a brandy."

Valentina gave Zita a brandy and made sure she was sitting down before she broke the worst news for the maid.

"I have even worse to tell you, Zita. Your sister is also dead. Nina was attacked by a cossack soldier when he entered the palace with the others. She leaped from the roof shortly afterward."

"God have mercy on her soul."

Throughout the night Valentina could hear Zita and Bibi sobbing. She herself could not cry. She could only lie there thinking of the past and steeling herself for the morning when the villagers would return. Lightheaded with exhaustion and shock, she could not even close her eyes, and as dawn filled the sky with the pink light of morning, Valentina asked herself if she would ever be happy again. Yanin was dead. Who would ride at her side through the cornfields of spring in some new, as yet unseen home? Who would make soup and light fires each time she returned to a cold house? Whose body would light fierce flames in her own? Whose eyes would glow on seeing her at the end of the day?

Valentina was eating breakfast when there was a loud hammering at the door. She rose and went to the balcony so she could see who was knocking. She was not surprised to see Gagurin and Nadya with a small group of people. Valentina called out to them.

"I am eating breakfast. Must you hammer at my door like barbarians?"

Gagurin replied.

"We are to take over this house in the name of revolution."

Valentina did not miss the gleam of triumph in Nadya's eyes. The former kitchen maid had once said she wanted a bedroom just like one of those on the upper floors of the house. Valentina spoke as forcefully as she could.

"You may take over my house if you have a document signed by the authorities giving you permission to requisition it."

Gagurin laughed derisively.

"If you don't come out of there by two this afternoon we shall take the house from you by force."

Valentina closed the window and returned to finish her breakfast. Zita and Bibi stood by, gazing in awe at their mistress as she poured herself more coffee and sat considering what to do. When she spoke Bibi ran forward to do her bidding.

"Pack a trunk of old clothes from the room in which we keep objects for charity. Then leave the house with your sister in the gig and take the trunk you have packed to Petrograd. Use the road through the count's land and private roads for as far as you can."

Bibi gazed in alarm at her mistress.

"But, ma'am, what will you do? We'll not leave without you."

"I shall stay here to deal with the villagers."

"No, ma'am!" Zita and her sister cried out in unison. Then they looked back at Valentina and for the first time Zita questioned an order.

"Why should we take useless clothes away, ma'am?"

"The villagers will stop you before you are out of the gate. They will not search your bodies because you are maids. However, I am sure they will take the trunk to satisfy their greedy hearts."

"We can take anything precious you want us to carry, ma'am."

"You are good and kind and I will be obliged if you will take these two objects back to Petrograd for me."

Bibi took a gold chain from which was suspended a gigantic diamond. Zita wrapped an emerald necklace in tissue paper and pushed it into her skirt pocket. Valentina explained her affection for the two pieces.

"Yekaterina Vasilievna bought me the diamond pendant as a wedding gift. The emerald necklace was a gift from Colonel Yanin."

Despite her self-control, Valentina felt tears falling down her cheeks when she mentioned the dead man. Zita and her sister left the room in silence. When they drove away from the house minutes later, a guard at the gate stopped them and confiscated the trunk, as Valentina had said he would. Alone, she made her plans. It was nine-fifteen. She hoped there was time to do what must be done.

First Valentina went to the stables and saddled the count's horse. In the saddlebags she put her jewelry and miniatures of herself and Yanin painted years previously by one of her favorite artists. Then she walked around the house taking photographs, as best she could, in the brilliant spring sunshine, of the lake, the stables and the façade of the house. These would be her memories when she was far away from Russia. When the photographs were complete she went upstairs to her private chapel and prayed for guidance, her mind dwelling on the image of Yanin. He had tried to preserve the old order against the revolutionaries' wishes. Valentina knew in her heart that nothing of the old order would survive the current conflict. They had all become museum-piece people, forced to drag themselves into the real twentieth century. She closed her eyes and prayed for Yanin's soul. Then she went to the kitchen and made herself some coffee.

Maria Dmitrevna Kubatova arrived with her husband at ten. Her eyes were bloated with tears and Kubatov's mouth was swollen from punches he had received from the raiding villagers. Valentina looked at his black eyes and Maria's distraught face and let them in. Maria burst out with her bad news.

"Milady, we came to tell you that we are leaving. Some of the estate men were shot in the night for trying to put a guard on your house. The mob has burned down our cottages because we would not leave them. All those lovely cottages you built of real bricks and all our belongings are gone and so are our friends. They have all fled to the south."

Valentina thought ruefully that Gagurin was carrying out his threat and enjoying the only power he would ever have in life. She knew then that the butcher and Nadya would occupy her house by force, if need be, and that the time had come to leave. Maria's next words confirmed Valentina's decision.

"The mob has burned down Count Meiren's lovely home and the Yanin residence too, even the chapel. Whatever will happen next, ma'am?"

"I don't know, Maria, no one can know."

"You've been so kind to us, ma'am; my husband and I want to do anything we can for you before we go away."

Valentina closed her eyes, unwilling to give Maria her final order. When she said what she wanted the couple gasped but did nothing to contradict her. Half an hour later, while Maria and her husband were working, Valentina sat alone in the chapel remembering the good times she had enjoyed in the Flower House; the nights of love with Yanin, the Christmas parties with the family, the games of hide-and-seek with her children, the moments of pure happiness with her lover on summer nights when darkness rarely came. Maria and her husband took their leave. Valentina walked around the house one last time, looking longingly at the swans on the lake and the water lilies budding in readiness for the spring. In the greenhouse she picked one last yellow rose, to be pressed between the pages of the family Bible. Then, as the clocks struck one, she went inside to make a snack of leftover soup and black bread. She was not hungry but knew she must preserve her strength. She drank some wine, enjoying the flavor of the imported French Burgundy and seeing, in her mind's eye, the vineyards from whence it came. At one-thirty she led the horse from the inner courtyard to the front of the property, nuzzling it lovingly and trying not to look at the hundreds of people lining the drive, all eager to witness the ignominious handing over of the countess's keys.

For a moment Valentina paused to ask herself if leaving her beloved home was really inevitable. She knew that it was and that Russia would never again be the country she had known in the early days. The mob had taken over. For good or ill they would now have their way and those who opposed them would be killed. She ran upstairs to her suite and took the music box given her by Yanin and hid it in the pocket of her riding breeches. Then she looked again around her bedroom with its violet-flowered walls and its view of the cornfields that had so recently seemed hers forever. Then she completed her plan and left the house, locking it securely behind her.

At two-thirty Gagurin saw Countess Korolenko riding away from the house on a coal-black stallion. As she approached him through the woods at the end of the drive, he shouted raucously: "Give me your keys, citizeness!"

Valentina threw them to the ground and galloped away, her horse leaping the fence at the end of the drive as she ignored the guards posted there to search her.

Gagurin hurried with his throng along the drive, nudging Nadya with sheer delight at the success of their mission. Someone screamed excitedly and soon everyone was shrieking. Gagurin ran ahead and stared aghast at the property he had coveted since childhood. There were flames coming from every end of the house and orange flickering light at every window. The kerosene-soaked rags placed in lines along every corridor by the Kubatovs had ignited at Valentina's instigation and the great house was doomed.

Nadya screamed shrilly and beat her husband's back. Gagurin stood in shocked silence, looking helplessly at the property. He was trying to comprehend how he had been tricked, how the Countess had found the strength to destroy the object of her greatest love. He ran toward the house, his hands outstretched, missing falling timber by inches and cursing Valentina Ivanovna and every other aristocrat in Russia.

In the dusk, many hours later, Valentina stood with her horse on the hill overlooking the property. The fire was still burning briskly. Maria Dmitrevna Kubatova and her husband had done well. Every room and corridor had been ignited. Tears fell down Valentina's face unnoticed and she cried for the life she had lost, the love that was gone forever. The villagers had gone home to commiserate over what might have been. The stone walls of the Flower House still stood strong, the tower room outlined like a twisted black bird against the rose of the evening sky. Valentina raised her hand in a last farewell and galloped away through the pinewoods to join her sons in Petrograd. It was over. Ivan was dead and the place of their passion devoured by a fire lit to protect it from being contaminated by the revolutionaries. Valentina took the music box from her pocket and listened to the old melody. . . .

*Say goodbye my own true lover*
*As we sing a lovers' song,*
*How it breaks my heart to leave you*
*Now the carnival is gone.* . . .

## CHAPTER TWELVE

### Petrograd, Winter 1917–1918

Valentina was sitting on a bench by the side of the Neva, looking with blank eyes at the frozen river. Everything was silent, only the bells of the cathedral booming now and then to remind her that this was the St. Petersburg to which she had come as a young girl to be given in marriage in the country of her birth. The ice reflected the dark gray of a leaden sky. No one walked or rode on it because the rich were cowering in their homes, the poor scavenging in nearly empty shops for food they could barely afford. Even the colorful Laplanders, who normally arrived at this time of year with herds of reindeer, had decided to stay away from the city without hope.

A burst of gunfire startled her. Valentina sighed apprehensively. Another firing squad had done away with another aristocratic family. Would she come across their bodies on her way back home? She had dressed in somber gray clothing, tying a scarf around her head to hide the cascade of silver hair that would instantly identify her. Her cloak was worn and darned, as befitted an ordinary citizen of Petrograd. Valentina frowned at the darns, ashamed to masquerade as a poor woman when her husband had so recently been one of the richest men in Russia. She asked herself if anyone was rich now that tsarist money had no value. All the great palaces were occupied by hundreds of poor people. The land had all been confiscated and diamonds deposited in bank vaults had gone the way of everything else, into the coffers of the revolution. Valentina was glad she had encouraged her husband to send away some of his best stones. The jewels smuggled to Paris were now all they legally owned. She looked toward the Winter Palace, that stretched

for a quarter of a mile along the river. No one had seen the Tsar
for months. Was he still alive? Or had he, like Yanin and Dolgurov,
been murdered in the name of revolution?

Valentina shivered, unable to face the bombardment of her own
grief. For months she had been silent and withdrawn, impotent
against the tide of reaction that had washed over her since her return to the capital. Ignoring her sons, her husband and the hordes
of people who now shared her home, she had gone over the events
of the past year, trying to resolve her own feelings so she could
begin a new life without Yanin. But nothing had been resolved and
she was resigned to feeling empty forever. She had also been unable to stop dwelling on the destruction of the Flower House, the
house she had loved and burned down. Many times she had
planned to make a journey to see the remains of what had once
been her paradise but each time the count had stopped her. And so
it was that she came to sit by the river, looking out on the ice and
the iridescent snow that muffled the sounds of the city. Cold and
hungry, she rose and made her way back toward the Nevsky Prospekt. She was thinking of her husband, whose days were now
spent plotting their escape from Russia, an escape Valentina had
despaired of long ago. Korolenko was getting old. How could he or
anyone else arrange for the family to get away from the iron grasp
of the military? Every exit to the city was blocked and patrols of
cossacks circled the landward edge of the city. Escape by sea was
unthinkable in winter, when the water was frozen, and in summer
because of naval patrols. Permits were refused even to visit relatives who lived in the country. How could they hope to get away
forever?

Valentina saw her reflection in the window of a shop and shook
her head resignedly. I am a skeleton, she thought. Her mind darted
to the picnics she had once enjoyed with Yanin on the banks of the
river and her mouth watered at the memory of the smoked sturgeon and the veal pies, the luscious roast beef charred on the outside and melting pink within. She shrugged, impatient with herself
for thinking so frequently and with such intensity of the past. A
company of soldiers galloped by. Valentina pressed her body into a
doorway, fearful of being arrested. When they were out of sight,
she walked quickly to the palace and upstairs to her sons.

Nikolai was in bed, recovering from the measles. Of Vasily there was no trace. Valentina ordered a peasant woman from her bedroom and sat down on the bed. Was all this a nightmare? Of course it was not. This was the new reality. From banquets extraordinary they were living on beetroot soup. From residing in the splendor of the palace with its six hundred rooms, they had been allocated two for themselves and their servants and had been forbidden to walk freely among the other residents. From life would they soon pass to an ignominious death? Valentina felt the first stirrings of rage she had known since Yanin's death. She called for Zita and asked where Vasily had gone. She knew she must keep him near the house. If she did not, he might be arrested for shouting rude things at the occupationary soldiers. He was still a small child, but recent events had made him street-wise, and cunning beyond his years.

Valentina knew she must find a way to leave Petrograd immediately. Anything would be better than waiting passively to be called before a firing squad. She wrapped a shawl around her shoulders and leaned against the cushions of the bed. Within minutes she had fallen into a fitful sleep.

Vasily walked along the Ligovsky Prospekt carrying a small tissue-wrapped parcel. Inside the parcel was a pearl, one of a whole trunkful he had found while adventuring in the deserted cellar with his brother. Vasily smiled at the stories of plague his mother had told the intruders in her house, to keep them from going in the cellar. Now no one would go there, not even for a bribe. Vasily had hidden the finest pearls from one of the trunks in the cellar in the compartment of his train set. Nikolai had put others into his writing box and together they had helped Valentina attach hundreds to her favorite black evening dress, because they could think of no other way of carrying them, if the moment came to escape. Vasily had heard the count talk of escape and was determined not to go to a strange country without valuables so his mother could have a new home. He thought of the way she cried in the night when she dreamed of the destruction of the Flower House. The count held her whenever she had nightmares and he and Nikolai sat watching the strange happening with awe. Vasily swore to himself that his mother would have the most beautiful house in the world when and if they ever got out of Russia.

Today Vasily's mission was quite different from his thoughts. He had decided to try to barter the pearl for some onions, chickens and potatoes. He had heard merchants in the market laughing at the ease with which they robbed the hungry aristocrats. He knew the value of the pearl and was determined to obtain at least a leg of lamb for it, with as many onions and potatoes as he could carry. Vasily smoothed his jacket, conscious that he had grown much taller since it was made. He bent to the ground and took some snow to wipe his hands and face so the merchants would not know that he no longer had access to a bath in which to wash himself. If the merchants knew how poor he now was they would not think of giving him a leg of lamb for his mother. He hurried toward the square where the half-empty stalls of the only remaining market were pitched. For a moment he stood taking in the miserable scene, six stalls covered with tarpaulin, which was in turn covered in snow. The spice counter was piled high with colorful saffron, pimiento, cardamom and cinnamon. Next to it stood a merchant with cabbage, beetroot and potatoes, most of them in varying stages of decay. A farmer with a stall piled high with root vegetables, apples and dried herbs stood next to a Tartar dealer, who had scrawny chickens, lamb and meat carcasses covered with bunches of rosemary to mask the smell. Next to the Tartar, his brother's stall displayed mint, cabbage, potatoes and the inevitable beetroot. Vasily continued to walk around, watching and waiting as he selected a man with enough produce on his stall to give value for the pearl. At last he made a move and approached the swarthy-faced Tartar.

"I have something to exchange for a leg of lamb and a boiling fowl and a sack of potatoes."

"Ha! If I had a leg of lamb and a boiling fowl I should have stayed home and eaten them. What have you to offer?"

Vasily took out the pearl and handed it to the merchant. The man turned it this way and that, admiring the lustrous object. Then, having put it in his pocket, he shooed Vasily away.

"Go away, you little villain!"

"Give me back my pearl, it belongs to Papa."

"It belongs to the revolution now."

Vasily screamed with rage and all the pale-faced, black-clad women turned to stare at him. Then, without warning, a tall young man upturned the merchant's stall, grabbed two scrawny legs of lamb, threw them to Vasily and made off with a sack of potatoes.

Vasily ran after his rescuer as fast as he could. A dozen merchants ran after the two boys and there was uproar in the quarter. A revolutionary policeman blew his whistle and suddenly more policemen with red armbands joined in the chase. Vasily was exhausted, his legs weak from hunger, when he felt his collar grasped as the older boy pulled him into a doorway. The crowd and the angry merchants ran by without seeing the two boys, who were standing in the dark shadow of the porch. Vasily turned to the young man and looked into his eyes, which were large and gray like the clouds of an autumn day. His face was pale, his hair worn long like a poet. His clothes were filthy, his hands begrimed with mud, his feet bare but there was something in the arrogance of his manner and the finesse of his features that made Vasily disobey his mother's advice and introduce himself by his real name.

"I am Vasily Vladimirovich, second son of Count Korolenko."

The older boy hesitated. Then he clicked the heels of his nonexistent boots and nodded.

"Dmitry Alexandrovich, only remaining son of the late Count Borshchov."

Vasily looked at the legs of lamb and the sack of potatoes on the ground.

"I'm lucky you were there, Dmitry. I tried to change a pearl for food but the merchant stole it from me."

"You chose badly. That fellow is nothing but a villain. Here, take the potatoes and my legs of lamb too, no doubt your family is starving like all the rest."

"What about you?"

Dmitry's eyes clouded.

"My parents were shot a week ago. My eldest brother died during the early days of the war and my other brother was killed in the first few weeks of this accursed revolution. Our home has been occupied for weeks by flea-ridden peasants so I left it. I live wherever I can."

"And you rob the market?"

"I rob everyone of everything. I dress like this to save my hide. As you know, the revolutionary police shoot anyone who looks clean enough to be rich."

Vasily tried to carry the heavy sack but he could not manage. Dmitry slung it over his shoulder and beckoned the younger boy.

"You had best hide in my new apartment until it is dark. Then I will help you carry these things to your home. If we move them in daylight someone will surely take them from us."

Dmitry led Vasily to a house only a few paces from where they were standing. The house had not been molested and smelled warm and inviting. There were wood-burning stoves in the hall and fresh flowers in every room. Vasily felt suddenly very tired. Dmitry handed him a glass of hot ginger and honey and he drank it eagerly. Then he lay on the sofa struggling to take in his surroundings. The room smelled of beeswax and was furnished with heavy mahogany pieces. Vasily thought of his mother's house in the country and felt hot tears in his eyes. The walls of this room were covered with sapphire velvet overlaid with Gobelin tapestries. There was a smell of iris, chypre and tallow. Vasily thought of Valentina's bedroom with the violet-painted walls and the unique scent that clung to her wherever she went. At that moment he loved her more than he had ever realized and his desire was to run all the way home with his presents of food to lay them at her feet. When he had examined everything in detail he asked Dmitry whose house it was.

"It belongs to the mistress of a revolutionary. She is very rich and he enjoys her money. When they are away I stay here. When they return I will find another vacant apartment."

"How can you tell when people will be away?"

"I have a friend who was once a general in the Tsar's army. He now works as caretaker in the building where the revolutionaries assemble for their meetings. He reports all he hears to me in return for an occasional basket of potatoes or some small acknowledgment of my gratitude."

"I hope you won't get caught, Dmitry."

"What will be will be."

"How old are you?"

"I am fifteen. I shall be sixteen in the autumn. At the time of the commencement of the revolution I was a student at the Imperial Alexander Lycee. Now, I fear I shall never finish my education. I have no future like all the other aristocrats of Petrograd."

That night Valentina and her family ate well for the first time in a year. Vasily was feted and congratulated by the count and questioned secretly by Zita, but he would not reveal where the food came from. The next morning he and Dmitry were to rob the revolutionary council's pastry shop of its finest spice loaves and yeast, that he knew Zita craved but could not buy. After that they would rob every shop in the neighborhood of everything they had. Vasily slept peacefully, untroubled by the nightmares that had previously troubled his rest.

The count lay awake wondering where Vasily had stolen the food and if anyone had followed him home. He tossed from side to side trying to work out plans for escape, conscious that they should go now, while winter was at its worst. If they waited until the spring everyone would try to escape and the guards would be vigilant. Korolenko looked toward Valentina and saw that she was talking again in her sleep. He walked to her side and sat rubbing her hands until she was calm.

The following day the count was at his desk writing in his journal when a young man was announced, a man he did not know but who wore the remains of the uniform of the Volynsky Regiment. The count looked closely at his visitor, noting his noble bearing and the fine hands that seemed at odds with the rough boots and armband of a revolutionary soldier.

"Do I know you, sir?"

"You do not, Count Korolenko."

Pleased that the visitor addressed him by his title and not as "citizen" Korolenko waited patiently for the man to speak. He was surprised when the man explained his visit.

"I am a former member of the Volynsky Regiment, Excellency. I owe a favor to a dead man from the Preobrazhensky Guard and I pay my obligations. I would not have him know I did not keep my word."

"Was this man a friend of mine?"

"I understand he was a friend of your family, sir."

The man looked uneasy and the count knew he was speaking of Yanin. He was as polite as he could be.

"May I ask what I can do for you, sir?"

"What I can do for *you* is the issue, Count Korolenko. I came across this at the head office of the Cheka."

"The secret police formed to replace the tsarist Okhrana?"

"That is correct, and twice as virulent as ever the Okhrana was."

The count put on his glasses and read a list of names. Some of the people at the top of the list had already been executed. Those below included Irina Borisovna Yanina, cousin of the dead man, Countess Volkova, Maria Sergeyevna Imeretinskaya and children (six), Boris Ivanovich Yelagov, former prince colonel in the Tsar's own regiment, Sergei Valerianovich Orlov, Vladimir Vasilievich Korolenko, Valentina Ivanovna Korolenko and children (two). The count scanned through the rest of the list and looked questioningly at the young man before him.

"What is this? I do not understand its significance."

"It is one of the lists, drawn up by the council, of people to be removed before the revolution can be truly successful. Lenin says all the aristocracy must die or they will survive to fight another day. Your name was not at the top of the list but now many of those who were are dead."

"What is going to happen?"

"Next week all servants will be sent away to do revolutionary work. None will be allowed to remain with their masters. Next the list will be completed and gradually each family will be executed."

The count eyed the list again, frowning at the brackets indicating the number of children in each of the condemned families. He looked up at his gentlemanly visitor.

"Do you agree with all this?"

"The revolution is a tidal wave. All who try to swim against the current will perish."

"So you condone the murder of members of your own social class in order to survive?"

The officer was silent. Korolenko continued.

"Do you have any idea when I shall be arrested?"

"I have heard that the people before you are all dead and that those in your section will die before the end of February."

"I have less than two weeks in which to escape?"

"That is so, most probably less than one week."

"May I ask what Yanin did to prompt this act of heroism in warning me of the danger?"

The officer hesitated and Korolenko thought he looked suddenly old and tired.

"At Tannenberg my regiment fought with the Preobrazhensky Guard and others classed as the finest in our land. When we charged the guns my horse was shot from under me. Yanin rode back in the midst of the barrage and hauled me up on his own horse. With guns on all sides of us he came back alone to rescue a man he barely knew. . . . I felt I owed him everything I could offer."

"I hope no one saw you come in here. If they did you will be arrested."

"To be truthful, sir, I am past caring. What I see all around me is a world I find unwelcome."

The count informed his family that they would be leaving shortly and in the greatest secrecy. They would each be able to carry one small case, nothing else. They must also find as much cash as they could to take with them, or, better still, gold. He repeated the need for secrecy, though he gave Vasily permission to find Dmitry and inform him of their imminent departure and the reason for it.

The following morning Valentina went with her sons to the Gostini Dvor, now a shadow of its former beehive activity. She made for the pearl dealer's shops and showed him three beautiful specimens. Over the years, since her early days in St. Petersburg, Valentina had been one of the dealer's finest clients, not for pearls but for antique and Tartar jewelry. Now she sat before him trying to sell, not to buy. The dealer gestured regretfully.

"Dear lady, everyone tries to sell me their pearls. As I am not the richest man in Petrograd I cannot buy everyone's pearls."

"I need money."

"So does everyone, Countess. Best if you go to the market and exchange your pearls for a leg of lamb, if such a thing exists in Petrograd. Otherwise I cannot advise you."

Valentina walked past the shops where once she had bought everything her heart desired. She smelled the enticing odor from the coffeehouse and longed for a glass of hot, dark chocolate sprinkled with nutmeg. Nikolai looked to her for guidance when the owner ran outside and called to them.

"Countess! Countess! Come inside, it's cold today and so very long since I saw you."

Valentina pushed her sons inside the shop. The owner, a fat Georgian woman who had once been mistress of a grand duke, looked with concern at the two boys as they hesitated to drink. Valentina explained her position.

"I have no money; at least the tsarist money I have no longer has any value."

"Be my guest, Countess. You and I are long acquainted and I have known your sons since they were so high."

Nikolai and Vasily drank the hot, filling liquid as their mother talked with the owner.

"I have pearls to sell but no one will buy them."

"I'll buy one of your pearls, Countess. I haven't as much money as the dealers, but will give you what gold I have."

"I'll take whatever you offer and I thank you for your kindness."

Gold changed hands and Valentina settled to drinking her chocolate, unaware that she was being watched from the other side of the arcade by Magda Simoniescu. She continued talking with the owner about the changes in the city.

"What is business like, now the revolution continues?"

"Good, good, but my clients are revolutionary guards with their red armbands and black marketeers who have not yet been sent to Siberia. I don't get any of my lovely ladies anymore. All the glamour has gone out of my life."

When they left the shop Nikolai and Vasily seated themselves in a horse cab, trying not to notice that both the driver and his horse were perilously close to starvation. Valentina was giving the man his directions when Magda stepped out of the arcade. Nikolai started, recognizing his mother's enemy at once, though it was years since he had seen her. Valentina turned as he tugged at her arm.

"Mama, look."

The cabby urged the horse to move and slowly it pulled away from the curb. Magda followed, walking by the side of the lamentably slow vehicle and shouting to Valentina.

"You think you got away with ruining my life, don't you? Well, it's not true. I've been waiting a long time for this moment, a very, very long time, but you rarely venture out of your precious palace these days. You don't have my powerful friends of the Revolutionary Council to guarantee your safety."

Valentina looked away as Magda continued.

"I followed you from the palace today. You didn't see me but I followed you to send you and your bastards to hell."

As she shrieked abuse, Magda threw something into the open carriage. Thinking she had thrown a stone at his mother, Vasily picked it up at once and threw it back at Magda. It caught her in the face. There was a scream and an explosion. The cab halted and Valentina told her sons to cover their eyes. Then, forcing herself to look, she saw that Magda had been killed by her own grenade. Stunned, she remembered the first time she and Magda had met and the fear the count's mistress had engendered. She frowned as she remembered Magda on the island of Yelagin and in the Korolenko box at the ballet, a triumph she had never forgotten. She had triumphed at last over Magda, but what would be the cost?

Realizing that she and her sons were in danger, Valentina ordered the cabby to move on. Minutes later they arrived at the palace and Nikolai ran inside to tell the count what had happened. Vasily said nothing at all. Even when his mother reassured him he found it impossible to reply. Realizing that her son was seriously shocked, Valentina took him inside and put him to bed.

At midday Dmitry arrived and staggered into the count's room. He was bleeding from a shotgun wound in the shoulder. Valentina introduced him to her husband, who, realizing that Dmitry was the son of an old friend, ordered him to be sheltered with the family. Dmitry lay on a makeshift bed while Valentina dressed his wound.

"I wondered where Vasily was and went to the market to find him. The Cheka were there, Countess. They were arresting some aristocrats and I got caught in the cross fire."

Valentina told him what had happened to Magda. Dmitry fell silent. Then he spoke of Magda's power.

"She had powerful friends among those who are in control of the revolution. They will ask questions and by evening will know of your son's involvement. You must leave at once, Countess. I will get you out of the city by some means. I know a way that will not be noticed."

After a hasty conference it was agreed that they would leave that night. Dmitry asked them to wait in the cellar of the palace while he went out to obtain all that was required. After nightfall he would return to collect them.

Valentina packed their rations of two potatoes each. With these meager supplies she put a small curl of salami, some liver and a hunk of cooked beef, all that had been bought with the proceeds of the sale of the pearl that morning. A knob of cheese and two cooked cabbages completed their supplies. The two boys asked to

take a small writing case and two dirty canvas bags, out of which
Valentina could see moldy bread protruding. She asked no questions and accepted her sons' strange baggage. The count had a
weighted stick and a small attaché case. With these they went to
the cellar, the only place where they knew they would be undis-
turbed by the occupants of the house.

In the small hours they heard the crunch of many feet in the
snow above their head. Outside the rear entrance of the palace a
revolutionary officer read out an order.

"Count and Countess Korolenko and their sons to report at once
to the offices of the Cheka."

A gruff voice replied that the family had gone out. The crunch of
feet disappeared from the house and there was silence but for the
dripping of a tap in the cellar. Valentina and the count exchanged
glances. Both were wondering if the officers would go next to the
home of Countess Volkova and others on the death list. Had the
moment of execution come earlier than expected? Or had someone
witnessed Vasily's defense of his mother that had caused Magda's
death? Valentina tried to conceal her fear but her face was as pale
as tallow. She was trying to work out how they could pass unnoticed through the streets of Petrograd during the curfew when
there were revolutionary guards on every corner. And how could
they leave the palace when there might well be arresting officers at
the gate? The count had done his best to relieve anxiety by
reminiscing about the lies she had told the occupants of the house.
Valentina thought of the day when she had told the unwelcome
squatters that the cellar was infected with the plague. Now none of
them would go down there, even for a bribe. The jewels hidden
there were safe, for the moment. . . .

At 3 A.M. Dmitry appeared and beckoned them to leave via the
count's garden, to a point overlooking the Moika Canal. Then,
having helped them over the wall, he handed them to a boatman
waiting below on the frozen water. Valentina marveled at Dmitry's
ingenuity. The boatmen of St. Petersburg operated flat-bottomed
crafts during the winter when the sea was frozen. They were a familiar sight on the waterways at night and would cause no curiosity among the guards. She watched as the count took Dmitry aside
and asked some questions.

"Has the boatman been paid?"

"He has, sir. It will be best if you and I go by different routes from the city, so I shall meet you at Narva; your house there could still be free. If it is not, Zita, Bibi and I will meet you at Pskov, in the coaching inn situated just before the town. You cannot mistake the place. It has the sign of a fox outside the door."

"I thank you for everything, Dmitry."

"Might I also suggest that you and your wife travel separately once you reach the coast. If the guards are looking for a family they will not take particular notice of a man or woman traveling with one son. Tell the countess to also meet us at your house at Narva. If, for any reason, we cannot meet there, she must come to the inn outside Pskov. Whoever arrives there first must wait for the others to come."

Dmitry watched as the family left. He glanced at Valentina's face and remembered her at a ball at his father's house long ago. She had been dancing a quadrille in a sugar-pink dress covered in diamond stars. Dmitry sighed, trying to shut out the memory of the family, who were all dead. Was it really only a few weeks ago that the soldiers had arrived and shot his parents in the sunlit garden? He had been in the attic, sorting through family papers in trunks stored for decades and rarely touched. He had seen everything. Dmitry looked again at the Korolenko family, smiling at the count's proud gaze and the regal manner of Valentina.

They passed along the canal, the boat's flat bottom sliding over the ice like a sledge. The boatman's spike made a hollow sound as it caught the ice and the bottom made a fearful din as it scraped slowly along. Valentina felt her heart thundering with fear. It was very late and though the boats were a familiar sight on the frozen river they were not usually seen making their deliveries of food and fish at this time of the night. She glanced fearfully at the bank of the river, terrified that they would be challenged by one of the guards. Then, as they reached the frozen sea, the boatman saw ahead a group of revolutionary guards on the bank and refused to go any further.

Korolenko stepped out and handed his family onto the ice.

"Well, my dear, we're clear of the city center but not yet of the periphery."

"There's a sentry box at the far edge of the city."

"Let's hope the men are asleep over their stove."

They walked on until they came to the sentry box that guarded the entrance to the outskirts of the city. It was 4 A.M. and they could see two soldiers dozing beside the fire inside the box. Valentina looked down at Vasily, normally such a chatterbox, and wished she could warn him to keep quiet. Slowly, fearfully, they crept forward. One of the guards sat up and threw a log on the fire. Then he fell back sound alseep. The count looked at his watch.

"Soon we must separate, my dear. You and Vasily will go on alone. Nikolai and I also. You will make for my house at Narva. I will be waiting for you there. If you cannot reach the house for any reason, you must make for Pskov, and the inn immediately outside the town. I will be waiting for you there and Dmitry also with the maids."

Valentina nodded. She must make for Narva and the safety of the count's house there. If it was no longer a safe place, she must meet her husband and Nikolai at the inn on the outskirts of Pskov. She repeated these instructions over and over again to herself, wondering fearfully if she would ever see the count and Nikolai again. She entered a small hamlet and went to the hostler's yard. The man sold her a mule and a ramshackle cart and she put Vasily into this and covered him with an old blanket the hostler sold her. She was so hungry her stomach kept rolling painfully, but she did not stop. It was necessary to put as much distance as possible between herself and the revolutionary guards in Petrograd. Despite her need, Valentina avoided inns and roadhouses in favor of a farmer's barn, where she and Vasily spent the night. They ate some of the meat she had brought with her and some apples stored in the barn. Then Vasily fell fitfully to sleep. Valentina lay on her back trying to reckon how far they had come and how far they still had to go to be reunited with the count at Narva. If they could not meet up at Narva she would have to travel alone to Pskov. She closed her eyes, unwilling to think of the endless snowy wastes between her present uncomfortable refuge and the end of the journey at Pskov.

The count and Nikolai bought skis from a man in a small village and traveled on these to a monastery on a hill. Here they were given food and a bed for the rest of the day. The count felt at ease, sure he could trust the monks, because they had the most to lose in the advent of the revolution. The word "God" was already being eradicated from every corner of the land and praying had been labeled bourgeois. The count looked around the cell-like room and wondered where Valentina was and if she was safe. Gogol's lament for Russia came into his mind: What is the inscrutable power which lies hidden in you? Why does your aching melancholy song echo forever in my ears? Russia, what do you want of me? He wondered desperately how he was going to survive the heartbreak of leaving his homeland. Nikolai's voice broke into his reverie.

"Why did we leave Mama and Vasily alone? Ladies are not supposed to travel unprotected. What if she encounters deserters or villains who support the revolution?"

"Better she encounter them alone than with me. Every revolutionary in St. Petersburg hates me for my breeding and my ancestors."

"Why do they hate us, Papa?"

"They hate us because we have what they have not and will have that indefinable quality even when they have stolen everything we own."

Nikolai looked out of the window at a still white world. Nothing moved except a tree as the wind blew the snow from its branches. He hoped his mother was warm enough, conscious that she normally smothered her body in sable in such weather. Tears of despair began to fall down his cheeks and he brushed them away impatiently. First he had lost Yanin and Dolgurov, then the Flower House and finally the palace in St. Petersburg. Nina and Gavrilo were dead and all the belongings of his family for generations past lost to the thieves and murderers who had come to take what was not theirs. The Tsar had vanished with his family and in the months since the revolution began most of Nikolai's contemporaries and their families too. Someday, he thought, I will return to Russia. If I cannot I shall settle in another country that has the same cornfields in summer and snow in winter. He would build himself a house just like the Flower House and stay there forever, dying rather than leave it. He would never retreat again. He knew Vasily felt the same way, though he was younger and less troubled by leaving Russia. The resolution satisfied Nikolai and soon he fell asleep from sheer exhaustion. The count sat by his bedside, listening for any sound alien to the monastery grounds. Would someone have sent guards to pursue them? He knew in his heart they would.

Valentina and Vasily arrived at an inn on the third night of their journey. Having abandoned the mule they had bought because it had become lame, they had been given a ride on a farm cart and were within walking distance of the count's house at Narva. However, Valentina did not wish to arrive there in the dark and to pass the night she asked for a room in a small inn nearby. The owner, an elderly Jew, led her upstairs to a small but clean room hung with bunches of rosemary and sage. Vasily fell on the bed and was asleep in a moment. Valentina lay at his side, wondering if her husband and Nicolai had already reached his property at Narva, and where Dmitry and her maids were. She looked at the icicles on the window frame and the small wooden table by the bed. She was glad of such a room. A year ago she would have disdained it but now she was relieved to be allowed to stay in it. How things had changed.

An hour later Valentina rose and sat at the window, thinking of the friends she had made in Russia. Madame Marinovskaya had retired to an elegant mansion on the outskirts of St. Petersburg. Would it have been requisitioned, like all the rest? Had a lifetime of work been rewarded with confiscation or death? And Countess Volkova, were she and her drawers of memories still intact? Or had she already been arrested with her daughter and the children? Maria Sergeyevna Imeretinskaya had talked of leaving the capital and traveling south with her family to the Crimea. Was the Crimea far enough away? Was there anywhere in the world that was safe for those whose names were undesirable? Valentina wondered if she and her family would be secure even in Paris and felt a shiver of fear running down her spine. She thought of Yanin, who had loved her and whose life had been dedicated to her and to his beloved Russia. Would there be men like Yanin and Dolgurov in the generations to come? Would there be love and honor or would that be forbidden, like religion and hope? Would the new code of equality be all it was vaunted to be? Would the leaders of the revolution really remain equal to those in the lowest ranks? Or would they and their Revolutionary Council members become the new elite, taking over the great houses, the fine horses, the elegant automobiles, they had so eagerly confiscated? Would they be able to resist gaining privileges unknown to the masses by exercising the fear their power would endow? Had they personal ambitions as well as their loudly proclaimed political aims? Would Lenin and

Stalin, who had once called himself Koba, become the new tsars of Russia?

Valentina heard a troop of cossacks approaching. She stepped back from the window, straining to hear the questions shouted to the owner of the inn.

"If you see such a family you are to report their presence at once. Do you understand?"

The Jew bowed respectfully to the leader of the troop.

"Of course, Excellency, of course."

The cossacks rode away. The owner spat after them, cursing the Tsar and the revolutionaries alike and their ancestors and their descendants for a dozen generations. It was obvious that the woman and the boy were hiding. Years of persecution by a Tsar who hated Jews had made him sympathetic to those who lived in fear. He closed the door and locked it. Then he called to his wife to prepare a tray of food for the guests. If the woman was the Countess Korolenko, he had best warn her that her husband's country house at Narva had been taken over and that revolutionary soldiers were hiding there, waiting to arrest the owners of the property if they were foolish enough to appear.

The count arrived at the inn with Nikolai in the hours after midnight. Unaware of his presence, Valentina asked the owner for a call at daybreak. Within minutes she was asleep, relieved to be safe for a few precious hours.

# CHAPTER THIRTEEN

## Pskov, Escape, February 1918

It was decided that Valentina and both her sons would wait for three days in the inn while the count went ahead to Pskov, to see if he could free his train from the sidings. They had seen nothing of Dmitry and the maids and were now seriously worried as to their fate. Each evening Valentina stationed herself at the window of her room, determined to watch for Dmitry's arrival. But no one came and by the third day she knew she must proceed for Pskov without them. That morning she spoke with the owner of the inn.

"Do you have any idea where I could buy horses, sir?"

"Where are you heading, milady?"

"We are going to Novgorod."

Valentina was shocked to hear herself lying, despite her gratitude to the owner. But she knew that if he were questioned after her departure and tortured to reveal what he knew, he would tell her destination. She regretted this when she saw his willingness to help.

"All the horses in this area have been requisitioned for the war, but I know a man who would drive you to Novgorod."

"I prefer to travel alone; forgive me for my caution."

"It is very dangerous for you, milady. This area is patrolled by cossacks, who are here to seek aristocrats heading for Warsaw and the private trains that will take them to Berlin and Paris."

"I must find some means of transport."

"I could make many suggestions but all of them would involve stealing. There are cossack horses stabled not far from here."

"Where?"

"On the road to Pskov. They use the horses for a month and then rest them for a week or more in the stables of a large estate confiscated at the beginning of the revolution."

"Does anyone have donkeys or asses for sale?"

"No, milady. This area has been stripped of all it has. We have nothing left to ride or drive. The revolutionaries left me only my inn, my wife and our lives."

Valentina went upstairs and explained what she had learned. Nikolai picked up his bag and made to leave the room.

"Vasily, I'm going to steal some horses. I don't care if I get shot. I just want to be out of this country. I feel every hour I stay here is an hour nearer to being arrested."

They walked from the inn on the road to Pskov, proceeding as quickly as they were able toward the gates of the estate the innkeeper had mentioned. Valentina cautioned her sons as they approached the gate.

"I had best go and see whether there are people about. Stay here and don't move from where you're standing or I may not find you on my return."

Nikolai held his mother back.

"I'll go, Mama. If someone sees me he'll think I'm a local boy wanting to ride a horse. If they see you they'll know you're an aristocrat and arrest you. Vasily, stay here with Mama."

Nikolai set off on the path toward the house. As he walked he thought of the Flower House and his mother's room with the violet-flowered walls and the scent of iris and lilac. Tears sprang to his eyes and he had difficulty preventing himself from sobbing at the agony he felt at the loss of his home. Nikolai and the count, of all the family, felt most keenly the pain that leaving Russia would herald. Every hour of the day Nikolai viewed the coming journey with dread. Every verst was a verst away from all that was familiar, but what else could they do? To stay would be to condemn themselves to death. He walked boldly to the stables and nuzzled the horses. There were saddles hung on the far side of the wall and he wondered if he dare saddle a couple of horses and take them back to his mother.

Vasily watched his brother with increasing admiration. He had disobeyed Nikolai's instruction and was sitting behind a rhododendron bush with a large stone in his hand, determined to defend his brother if necessary. When Nikolai went inside the stable Vasily's

heart beat like thunder with fear that someone might come out of
the house. After what seemed like an age Nikolai rode out on a fine
brown mare, leading another horse on a rope. Vasily ran from the
bushes and leaped up on the second horse. Nikolai called over his
shoulder.

"If you should ever obey one of my orders, Vasily, I swear I shall
faint with shock and probably expire at your feet."

Vasily rode behind his brother, well pleased by the theft. They
were approaching the spot where they had left their mother when
they heard the sound of approaching horses on the other side of
the wall. They rode at once into the trees and proceeded to the
densest part of the forest. Vasily's eyes scanned the undergrowth
for his mother but he could see no sign of her. He knew that if
they became separated she would be in danger and his hands trembled violently because he had never been so frightened. Nikolai
turned to him and spoke the same thoughts he had been thinking.

"We shall have to leave by another gate. In a while I had best go
back and find Mama."

Minutes passed; the two boys waited in increasing fear. Then
Vasily saw Valentina creeping cautiously through the undergrowth.

"Mama! We're here!"

Vasily's loud whisper made Valentina turn in his direction and
she ran to his side and smothered him with kisses.

"My darling, you can speak again."

Vasily began to cry. Valentina stroked his head and explained
what had happened.

"I came back from where I was waiting because there is a regiment of cossack soldiers halted outside the gates."

"What are they doing, Mama?"

"I don't know. They seem to be waiting for orders and listening
intently all the while. We had best wait here and be as quiet as we
can until we hear them ride away."

A hungry bird wheeled in the sky. Valentina watched it enviously. Hungry it might be, but a bird could fly to whichever
place it chose. She saw Vasily rubbing his feet and knew they were
frozen despite the boots he was wearing. Then, in the distance, she
heard a command called and the sound of horses passing on the
other side of the wall. She asked herself in which direction they
would be traveling. The snow made it impossible to judge direction

and Valentina feared that they might be riding ahead of her on the road to Pskov. For the hundredth time that day she wished herself a thousand miles away.

As dusk was falling they rode out of the drive in the direction of Pskov. Nikolai and his brother were riding together on the back of the second horse. While Nikolai held the reins, Vasily clutched both canvas bags. Each was thinking the same thing. Were the cossacks riding ahead of them? Would they encounter the troop before they went much further? And where were the count and Dmitry and the two maids? They should have met up in Narva but Dmitry and the girls had never appeared. Would they be waiting at the second meeting place, the inn outside Pskov? Or were they already dead?

In the white landscape, pink-shaded in the falling sun, coal-black wolves hovered near the road. Valentina watched as they ran away into the forest. Then she saw another rider traveling at a distance from them but in the same direction. She spoke to Nikolai.

"Have you any idea who that is?"

"He's been behind us for hours, Mama."

That night they huddled together in a disused warehouse, terrified that the man behind them might be an expert tracker sent from Petrograd to find them. The warehouse had been used in times past as a wine store and Valentina found some of the barrels still full. She refilled their water jugs and drank what she wanted. Then she slept by her sons' side until dawn filled the large interior with the gray light of a winter morning. By seven they were on their way, hungry and cold but still optimistic that they would reach Pskov and the train that would take them to freedom.

In Petrograd the former bandit Koba, now known as Josef Stalin, was in his office reading through a report on the escape of the Korolenko family. He looked down to the snowy square below and thought of Magda Simoniescu, who had been a good friend to the revolutionaries. Through her he had learned everything about the aristocrats of the city and had thus been able to make up a list of those to be eliminated. Stalin walked to the wall and looked thoughtfully at the map of the Narva area. He had sent cossacks to arrest the Korolenkos but the count had not been to his house there and the local innkeeper had told them that Valentina and her sons

were heading for Novgorod. The Jew had been brave, surviving everything they had done to him except the threat that they would
cut his wife's throat before his eyes. Stalin laughed. They had shot
the Jew and his wife anyway and good riddance to them. He
frowned distastefully at his thoughts about the Jewish race. Then
he looked back to the map. Where *was* the Korolenko family? They
could have gone west from Narva to Reval and thence by sea to
Germany. Surely they would not do that. They could have gone
south to Novgorod and then to Smolensk and Kiev, where many
aristocrats were hiding. Stalin debated this point. His cossacks had
gone as far as Novgorod but had found no trace of the family.
They must therefore be heading for Pskov, either to join the railway for Warsaw or to travel by other means to safety. Stalin called
a guard and gave instructions that the cossacks be ordered to wait
in Pskov.

Having left his sons with Valentina, the count proceeded alone
and unencumbered. Despite his dislike of disguise he bought old
clothes in a street market and covered his fine boots with mud. He
was lucky to obtain lifts from Narva to the outskirts of Pskov,
where he encountered a troop of cossacks riding by. The count
looked after them and wondered if they were here to seek out people like him, people who were making one last bid for freedom. He
made his way to the railway yard, where his private train was still
in the siding. His relief at this was so great he felt weak and for a
moment sat in the snow by the side of the track. A guard passed by
on the bridge above his head. Korolenko remained quite still. Then,
when the guard's back was turned he ran to the train, let himself
into the first carriage and locked the door behind him. He threw off
the dirty clothes and put them on one of the seats, to be used when
he went outside again. Then he walked up the train until he came
to the driver's section. Fuel would have to be found, but where?
The count puzzled this for a while. Then he put on his old clothes
again and left the train to walk to the coal yard outside the town.
Two hours later the fuel was on board and the count had paid
nothing for it. He had told the manager of the coal yard that the
train was to be sent to Petrograd to pick up Comrade Lenin. He
had been shocked to find the men as excited by the prospect of a
visit from Lenin as once they had been when told the Tsar might

pass through their station. The count thought of this as he slid down the snowy bank from where he had first entered the train.

In his youth Korolenko had watched the drivers of his father's private train with avid interest, never thinking that someday he might be required to drive his own train in order to save the lives of his family. He thought of the guards patrolling the station concourse. Obviously they had no idea that this was his train or there would have been a guard left on it. He knew the reason for this was that the train was comparatively new and that his previous one had been left on the siding in St. Petersburg. If there were guards anywhere they would be on that one. But for how long would they remain ignorant of his whereabouts? The count shook his head, praying the guards would spend the night scorching their hands over the brazier in the station concourse. He must do what had to be done and not think of the fear in the pit of his stomach.

That night the count arrived at the inn outside Pskov and took his place with Dmitry and Zita. The maid was ill and Dmitry kept pushing her back into an upright position so other occupants of the inn would not comment on her condition. The count spoke in a whisper.

"How are you, dear boy? Did you have much trouble getting here?"

"At Narva we found cossacks waiting at your house. Bibi was shot dead and Zita also injured. If she were not the bravest woman in Russia she would have been unable to get here. She has never complained once, though she must be in agony."

"Who are you watching, Dmitry?"

The count had noticed that his companion's eyes never left a stranger sitting in the far corner of the inn. Dmitry explained his fears.

"I swear that fellow is following me and has been for days. He is surely an informer and I cannot rid myself of the fear that he has already informed of our presence here."

"Damn his eyes. I shall shoot him if he moves."

"Do nothing of the kind, sir. I have no idea if he is alone or if there are others of his kind outside. God knows what will happen when the countess and her sons arrive. Then he will really know he has what he is searching for, the Korolenko family and all its remaining friends."

Valentina saw the light of the inn ahead and galloped forward, urging Nikolai to hide the horses in a group of trees in case a passing patrol should recognize the design on the saddles. She looked through the inn window and saw Dmitry and her husband sitting with an ashen-faced Zita. Valentina asked herself where Bibi was and why Dmitry kept watching a man sitting in the far corner of the inn. Valentina looked intently at the man, recognizing at once the full brown sealskin overcoat with the valance of frilled material on the shoulder. It was the man who had dogged their trail until they had lost him, that night when they slept in the wine warehouse. She resolved to stay apart from her husband until they had ascertained whether Korolenko also was perturbed about the man. If the count did not attempt to speak she would know that they were in danger and would leave the inn when they had eaten, to make her way to the station, where the count had said he kept his private train.

Having ordered food, Valentina sat with her sons drinking a hot rum punch and eating some stale nuts given her by the innkeeper. Now that she had time to look more closely at Zita, she saw that her maid was slumped at an odd angle on the bench and was obviously ill or injured. Valentina's face paled and she could barely control her desire to rush to her husband to ask him what was happening.

Korolenko looked down at heavy gray dumplings, beetroot and potatoes in a dark-brown sauce. He pushed the plate aside, unable to eat for tension and distaste at the unsavory smell of the food. He looked toward his wife and saw that she and her sons were eating hungrily. He shrugged. Valentina would probably have eaten mud if it had been put before her. He remembered her appetite with pleasure and wished he could give her something beautiful as a reward for her bravery.

Vasily whispered to his mother.

"Why is Zita so pale? She looks very ill to me. And why does Dmitry keep staring at that man in the corner?"

"I don't know, my darling, but I fear we are in a trap and Dmitry knows it."

"Shall we go back to our horses and escape, Mama?"

"We must wait and see what Papa advises. He knows better than we what is wrong."

It was not in Valentina's nature to wait without knowing what was amiss, but she curbed her nervousness and did her best to conceal her true feelings from the man, who was now staring curiously at her. She looked now and then in the direction of her husband, straining her ears to hear what he and Dmitry were saying.

At that moment the count heard the distant sound of approaching riders. He rose and called to Valentina, thrusting her with the children into the kitchen, despite the protests of the innkeeper. The man who had been watching them rose and drew a gun. Dmitry carried Zita to the kitchen, turning his back on the tracker and proceeding after the count because he knew there was nothing to be gained by remaining behind to fight. The man called shrilly after the escaping party.

"Stop, in the name of the revolution!"

Dmitry looked back in time to see a country man sitting near the watcher smashing a log down on the man's wrist and then on his head. The tracker fell to the ground unconscious or dead. Dmitry stared at the man, who waved him away.

"Get out while you can, friend, and remember me. Not all of us support these bastard revolutionaries."

The count and his family walked to the town. At the station he led them down the embankment and let them into the train. He was rushing forward to the driver's compartment to take them out of the station when he saw above him on the road a line of cossacks looking down. The cossacks fired, shattering windows and ruining the elegant silver paintwork of the exterior.

Zita slid to the ground. Vasily cried out, clasping his shoulder. Valentina crawled along the ground to where her maid was lying.

"We'll soon be away from here, Zita."

"My sisters are dead, ma'am, and I'll be with them before the night is out."

"Don't even think such a thing."

Nikolai shouted to his mother.

"Vasily's been shot!"

Valentina heard the welcome chugging of the train, the screech of the whistle and felt the motion as they speeded out of the station. She examined the wound on Vasily's neck, relieved that it was only a skin wound. She bound it with cotton and put him with Zita on blankets from one of the cupboards. As the train continued into

the night pursued by the cossacks, Valentina thought of the nightmares of her childhood and remembered how she had felt as she
longed for the light of dawn. Surely with the dawn the soldiers
would return to Petrograd. Surely the pursuit could not go on forever, until they were out of Russia and on their way to freedom.

It was light by eight the following morning. The count looked
from behind his iron screen and saw men riding alongside the
train. He had ordered everyone to arm and could hear his family
returning the cossacks' fire. He shoveled more coal into the fur-
nace, defying the bullets as he increased the train's speed. Would
they escape these persistent soldiers? Long ago he had felt safe to
be defended by cossacks working for the Tsar. Now he feared their
bravery and the tenacity for which they were renowned. He was
unaware that the troops had been given explicit orders not to let
the family leave Russia.

Valentina crouched at Dmitry's side shooting at any cossack who
tried to board the train. Still the pursuit continued and as noon
came she realized they were running out of ammunition. From that
moment she lay on the floor with her sons, leaving Dmitry to defend them. Her mind was very clear and she wondered if it was always like this and if the moment of their demise was approaching.
She thought of her husband, alone in the driver's cab and shoveling
coal like a twenty-year-old. The rear door opened and a man appeared. A shot rang out and Valentina felt blood pouring down her
neck. She raised her gun and heard herself firing. Then she lapsed
into semiconsciousness. The sound of gunfire faded. Valentina wondered if she was dying. She felt her head and realized that part of
her ear had been removed by a bullet. Blood was gushing onto her
clothes and down to her boots. She listened hard as the sound of
pounding hooves diminished. Then, suddenly, the gunfire ceased.
She sat up and looked questioningly at Dmitry.

"The cossacks stopped chasing us when we reached the border. I
don't know why because cossack patrols can go where they wish in
the Empire, as you know, Countess. I can only think they were instructed not to allow your family to leave Russia. Once you did
they had no further interest in you. Someone is going to be very
angry with them indeed."

Valentina felt tears rolling down her cheeks as the count

emerged from the driver's cab. His face was ashen, his hands and body black with coal dust. His voice trembled with emotion when he spoke.

"God only knows what has happened, but we are free. I never thought the day would come when I should pray to be free of Russia."

Valentina took the begrimed hands and kissed them.

"You are a hero, sir. Without you we should all be dead."

Korolenko sighed. His mind was already grappling with the agony of leaving the country he adored. He looked down at his wife, smiling at the jeweled evening dress peeping from under her somber black-wool skirts.

"I had not expected you to travel so elegantly, madame."

"All my remaining rubies are attached to this dress and the greatest number of diamonds and pearls I could carry. I would not ask you to live like a pauper, sir."

Nikolai opened the two dirty canvas bags he and Vasily had been carrying. Inside there were more pearls, diamonds and rubies. Tears of pride ran down the count's cheeks.

"If I have succeeded in bringing us safely out of Russia you have ensured our future with your bravery in bringing out those jewels. We shall never again be as wealthy as we once were. Indeed, what we have will not last for very long because there will be others whose desperation will force them to sell below the value of their jewels, thus decreasing the value of our own. But we shall be together and we shall do our best to settle in the new country in a new home. From this day we shall all have to learn new ways. We shall not have servants to do everything for us and will have to undergo the ordeal of learning to earn our own living. Pray God we shall not fail."

Two days later Valentina boarded the count's yacht, noting with pleasure that it had been named after her. The count joined her when he had cast off and together they watched the snow-covered countryside of the coast disappearing into the distance. Valentina held her husband's hand.

"We have both lost so much in the last year. I have been so sad, even when I should have been happy. But when I realized that you had brought your yacht here to aid our escape my heart almost burst with pride. I knew nothing at all of your plans. How did you learn to sail? And why did you not leave the yacht in St. Petersburg to save us this terrible journey?"

"The sea freezes in St. Petersburg. Here it remains open. As for my new abilities, I learned them in the months before the revolution. While you were living in the country I was occupying myself at the yacht club. You told me you needed me, my dear, and I wanted to be equal to protecting you. I love you, you see. I shall always love you and want you and need you. Don't ever leave me. I could not live if you did."

"I shall never leave you, sir."

Below, in the cabin, Dmitry was unpacking the mysterious single bundle he had carried with him on the journey. Nikolai and Vasily were watching, overcome by curiosity to know what it was that Dmitry valued above all else. Minutes later he emerged from his dressing room and turned in a full circle so they could admire him in his uniform of the Imperial Lycée, with its dark-green jacket, red facings and gold braid.

"When the revolution began I was a cadet at the Imperial Lycée, destined to go into the Preobrazhensky Guard. I brought my uniform so I could show it to my children someday."

That night the ship sailed on, a sleek white arrow in a sea of turmoil. Looking back, Valentina thought of Yanin and wondered if the exciting days of her life were over.

# BOOK II

# Paris, Kentucky, Spain, 1920-1936

There can be no peace of mind in love, since the advantage one has secured is never anything but a fresh starting point for further desires . . .

Proust, *A la Recherche du Temps Perdu*

Life was a damned muddle . . . a football game with everyone offside and the referee gotten rid of. . . .

Scott Fitzgerald, *This Side of Paradise*

## CHAPTER FOURTEEN

### Paris, Spring 1920

———————

For an hour Valentina paced the pavement outside the salon, changing her mind and losing her nerve every few moments. At last she decided to have her hair cut and went inside to sit in a private room, watching wide-eyed as the hairdresser snipped and patted and shaped and pulled, studying the effect of his efforts in an amber mirror. She was so surprised at herself for allowing the most beautiful part of her appearance to lie slaughtered on the ground that she could only gaze in awe at the coiffeur's skill.

To calm herself, Valentina allowed her mind to wander back over the happenings of the past three years. She frowned as she thought of the escape from Petrograd after the revolution. For weeks there had been no food and they would have starved if it had not been for the ingenuity of Vasily and his friend Dmitry Alexandrovich Borshchov. Then firing squads had been set up and aristocratic families had begun to disappear. Only the count's forethought and courage had saved them. Valentina thought how her husband had put his yacht and private train well away from the scrutiny of the revolutionaries. They had had to travel on foot, on mules and even in farm carts for three hundred miles through freezing conditions to reach the train that had brought them to freedom and had been pursued by cossacks for most of the way. Vasily still had nightmares about the escape, and only time would heal his anguish.

Valentina smiled as she thought of the day they had arrived in Paris. For her it had been a homecoming. For the count it had been a physical and intellectual shock so great he had withdrawn from reality during the first months. At home in Russia he had been powerful, one of the richest men in St. Petersburg and an aristocrat of the finest order. In Paris he was just another Russian émigré who had left all his riches behind and was living on the few jewels his family managed to smuggle out. Like every other Russian in Paris, he longed constantly for home. Like all Russians he was subject to wild swings in mood, from depression to elation. Neighbors viewed the count with curiosity but without respect and, sensing this, he tried to avoid them.

Vasily and Nikolai had reacted in different ways to the new environment. Nikolai had cured his homesickness by finding places in Paris that reminded him of the villages near the Flower House. He had wandered through Belleville, Menilmontant and Charonne until he knew them like a native, growing more used to the new city every week. Vasily remained close to his home, going out only into the Bois de Boulogne, or to stand shyly watching rich Parisians lunching at the Orangerie. Valentina had tried to reassure her younger son but he remained withdrawn, guarding his thoughts as though fearful of revealing his innermost self. She asked herself if Vasily was afraid of Bolsheviks coming to arrest him and his family. She had told him there were no Bolsheviks in Paris, but still he sat at the window, looking longingly out at the green forest all around and thinking of the days when he was a child playing in the fields his father owned, the cornfields that had stretched to the horizon.

The hairdresser raised his hands in a theatrical bow.

"*Voilà, madame la comtesse, c'est fini.*"

Valentina looked at her reflection, at the fronds of the boyish hairstyle so short it would barely need a comb. She liked it—she thought. She was almost sure she liked it. She tried not to dwell on the count's reaction. He had gone to the south of Paris to take Nikolai to a new school. He would not return until after she had retired. She touched her head lightly, attentive when the hairdresser began to advise her on the transformation.

"Naturally you will need new clothes to go with the new hairstyle, Countess. You cannot cling any longer to the quaint things you brought with you from Russia. I know you are no longer as wealthy as you were, but now you have a chic Parisian hairdo. No other woman in the city would or could wear it. They are beginning to bob their hair, of course, but this is pure style."

"Shall I buy the clothes here in Paris?"

"Of course, I have called my friend Chanel. She has invited you to her salon."

"She was a cocotte wasn't she, in former times?"

The hairdresser's eyes rolled in panic.

"Madame la Comtesse, never even *think* such a thing. Mademoiselle Chanel established her first salon of designs a few years ago. Since then she has gained a reputation for style, and in nineteen twenty *style* is what counts. She represents the voice of the future and that is what women of this age wish to hear. She will give you a special price for the clothes. You are just the model she has been looking for. When other women see you in her outfits they will want to buy things exactly like yours."

The designer's dark eyes weighed the woman before her. The Russian countess was tall and slim, with an angular face, high cheekbones, startling violet eyes and a full, sensual mouth. Chanel smiled. It would be a pleasure to dress the lady. But would the Russian accept what was best for her? Past experience had taught her that Russian clients clung to the past and the clothes and ways and emotions of the past. She spoke in a gravelly voice.

"I suggest day outfits with jodhpurs, jackets and a collection of silk shirts and suits. Evening wear in the style of *le smoking* with trousers. That is what I think will suit you best."

Valentina looked into the suntanned face and nodded.

"Make whatever you think will be right."

"I'm glad you're thin. Women are only just beginning to learn the value of dieting. I eat only one meal a day and if I put on a single kilo I don't eat until it is gone."

"I eat three meals a day and could not be without them. Russians are not very dedicated when it comes to dieting."

Chanel's dark eyes took in the statement and she scrutinized her new client. She was a tough one, this Russian lady. Chanel remembered the stories told by other Russian émigrés, of the atrocities that had taken place in the capital during the revolution. Had the countess suffered with the rest? If so, there was little to tell that she had, except for a wariness in the expression and a determination of manner that was not entirely feminine. She resolved to do her best to impress the lady and made arrangements for a fitting the following week.

Valentina left the salon and walked through the sunlight of an April morning. She no longer had a chauffeur and was used to walking or cycling everywhere. She bought camellias from a flower seller in the Champs-Elysées. Then she entered a pastry shop to choose some petits-fours. As she watched the assistant putting the small cakes into a box she thought of Chef Dubrovsky, who had just arrived in Paris, wailing that he had walked halfway across Europe to join the family. Thinking of him made her remember the palace and the six hundred servants who had attended the family in the days before the revolution. In those days she had never had to shop or worry about the necessities of life. Until he arrived in Paris her husband had never even fastened his own boots or his buttons and had had to learn how to dress himself as if he were a child. The truth was they had been cosseted like children in the days of Russian splendor. Nothing had been too much for the servants and nothing too little. It had not been easy to adjust to self-sufficiency and even now the independent life did not come easily. Since the war servants were at a premium and Valentina was perennially grateful to have Dubrovsky, his new French wife and Zita, the invaluable maid, who had fallen in love with Paris.

The American looked down from the terrace of his hotel and enjoyed the scene below. There were ice-cream and gingerbread vendors at the edge of the tree-lined boulevard, children selling baskets of rosebuds and a barrel organ grinder. A party celebrating the birthday of a rich young man was only now leaving Fouquets. The American leaned from his balcony and watched rich men and women getting into automobiles, exiled Russian princes alongside suntanned Argentinian millionaires, all members of the upper crust of French international society. He saw members of the Bourse hurrying to the stock exchange, their taxis passing through crowds of buses, tourists, actors, writers, tango teachers, royalty, all part of the milling scene in the most cosmopolitan thoroughfare in Europe. He was about to withdraw when his eyes lighted on a tall woman walking swiftly by on ludicrously high heels. Her hair was silver and clipped like a gamin's, her dress pleated and longer than was fashionable, its pink color matching a bunch of camellias in her hand. He watched as she turned into a street leading to the Avenue Victor Hugo, where she hailed a fiacre. The man's face lit with joy as he recognized Countess Korolenko.

Masters ran from the room, along the landing and downstairs two at a time. He reached the street and called out as Valentina was instructing the taxi driver where to go. She did not hear him. He shouted again, dashing across the road, dodging traffic without caution. The taxicab joined the traffic on its way to the Bois de Boulogne. Masters wiped his forehead and swore. God damn it, was he always going to arrive too late to get to know her? For months he had been making inquiries about the countess's fate after her family left Russia in nineteen eighteen. The last train of British and foreign diplomats and resident families had left at the end of nineteen eighteen. After that no one knew what had happened to the Russians who had stayed behind or those who had fled. He had been unable to find anything of the countess's whereabouts until this moment when she had passed by his window, a fleeting glimpse of the unattainable that would tantalize him for the rest of the day. Masters walked back to the hotel. It was a sunny morning full of the smell of lily of the valley, lime trees and coffee. He noticed nothing of his surroundings. He was planning to use every means at his disposal to trace the elusive lady of his dreams. He would take on a private detective, go to the Sûreté, call even the President, if need be, anything to find her. Preoccupied, he disappeared into the hotel.

The count returned from the country at ten the following morning. Valentina was eating breakfast in her bedroom. She was dressed in a blond-satin housecoat and sitting at a table laden with marguerites. Korolenko sat opposite her and looked gravely at the new haircut.

"You look outrageous, madame."

"I hoped you'd like the new style, sir."

"Your hair was exquisite as it was. I have always admired the beauty of it."

"I can't wear my old clothes forever. Women no longer wear long dresses with dozens of undergarments. Apart from anything else, we no longer have the staff to look after such clothes. My hair has been cut to match my new clothes."

"You must not go out in those obscene short skirts, exposing your knees. It is humiliating and I forbid it."

"Mademoiselle Chanel is designing a beautiful wardrobe for me. I shall wear trousers instead of the short skirts you dislike."

"Trousers! You should have been a man. Your will power is the most unfeminine thing about you. I no longer feel master of my own home."

Valentina sighed. She had had the same discussion with her husband a dozen times since their arrival in Paris. The count still drove his carriage, a replica of one he had used in St. Petersburg since the turn of the century. He still wore the same clothes, having them duplicated by his French tailor whenever he considered them shabby. Valentina glanced at Korolenko's face and saw it was pale with annoyance. She weighed the jeweled tiepin at his cravat, the silver-topped stick he now used. The count was sixty and becoming a walking, living antique and replica of every aristocratic Russian gentleman of two decades previously. She wondered if he was going to try to force her to remain suspended in time with him, a constant reminder of the Russia he would never see again. She poured herself another cup of coffee and offered the count one. He apologized with downcast eyes as she continued cheerfully to enjoy the croissants and scented apricot jam.

"Forgive me, my dear, I keep telling myself I must come to terms with the loss of my country but I cannot. I look at myself in the mirror and see a caricature of myself as I was twenty years ago. Now I have criticized the changes in your appearance. The truth is I long for you to remain the same as you were when I first met you. You are the only constant thing in my life, my dear. Without you I would not think life worth living."

The count paused and looked again at the silver hair cut in eel-like ripples to catch the light.

"The hair suits you, and God knows I shall endeavor to accustom myself to your new clothes."

"Did Nikolai like the school?"

"I don't know. I can never tell what he is thinking these days. He said I should tell you he will come home each weekend."

"Vasily said yesterday that he is going to become a soldier so he can fight revolutionaries."

"Nonsense! We've had enough of fighting and revolution in this family to last a lifetime."

"No doubt he'll change his mind again next week."

"I am going to my study to put the new stones in their cases. I shall take you to dinner at Maxim's tonight to celebrate your new look."

Valentina sighed wearily as her husband left the room. The count's idea of an outing never varied. He loved Maxim's not for the atmosphere or the food but because he liked sitting there surveying his fellow diners and pointing out the occasional Russian émigré wealthy enough to afford the prices. He would then recount the entire history of the diner's family, his eyes growing misty as he thought of the country he had lost, the friends who had been executed, the memories that were all that was left of a life lived to the full in the Russia of his prime.

Valentina brushed her hair fiercely. For months she had been trying to avoid admitting to herself that she was bored. Activity, she knew, was the antidote for boredom, but what was there to do? She knew few people. The count rarely went out, except to ride in the Bois in the early dawn hours, avoiding his neighbors and anyone who might express curiosity about him. She was free to go out but when she did the count sulked for days. She took off the housecoat and looked in the mirror at her body. It was still young although she was thirty-four. These, she knew, were the years of her prime and she was wasting them in a house of memories, a house she had never really liked. She wandered to the dressing room and looked down at the garden with its geometric beds in the latest formal style. She liked wild gardens full of flowering shrubs and flowering weeds and had little time for the home Miss Knatchbull had chosen for her. When she thought of the Englishwoman Valentina smiled wryly. Natty had just gone to London for the first time since before the war. She was being shown around the city by her two nephews and excited letters arrived in every post:

You cannot imagine how the women here dress. They are not just fast they are positively *rapide*. Also they smoke furiously and discuss unmentionable things such as free love and the prevention of conception. I shall be glad to be back in Paris. Once I thought it decadent but no longer. You will never hear me complain again. My good wishes to you and your husband and my love to the boys. I will be back at the beginning of September. Then I will tell you all my news. . . .

At the end of the month Valentina went to collect her clothes from the Chanel salon. She was well pleased with the items, all in silk, linen and velvet. She wore a pair of the claret-colored jodhpurs and matching jacket when she left the shop. At first she blushed at the curious glances of the women and the admiring looks of the men. Then she told herself that she was a new woman and that she must get used to attention now that Chanel had made her a fashion trend setter. She paused every few yards to gaze in shock at her reflection in the shopwindows, chastising herself for her vanity each time. She walked by an expensive restaurant, lingering to enjoy the succulent smell of food and the expensive odor of chypre, lilac and cigar smoke wafting through the door. In the Place Vendôme she looked into each of the jewelers' windows, admiring the precious stones and the haughty Frenchwomen passing by. Then, having patted her hair and adjusted her collar, she walked on, almost content in the sunlight of a spring day. In the distance an accordionist was playing a lilting love song. Valentina smiled wistfully. She was trying hard to be a new woman, a woman in charge of her own future. But did she know how? The new women had jobs and were independent of their husbands. She had tried to get a job but had failed dismally to impress because of her lack of experience of modern living, let alone business. It was obvious from her every move and word and thought that she belonged to a bygone age, the age of tsarist splendor in Russia and not of present-day Paris. She paused to look in another window. This time, in addition to her own reflection she saw that of a man in a fine tweed jacket of English cut. She inclined her head, weighing the brown hair and mocking gaze that seemed strangely familiar. When Masters spoke she whirled around.

"Still busy admiring your reflection, Contessa?"

"Do I know you, sir?"

"You know damned well you do."

"Of course I do. You are Alexander Masters and we met once before in St. Petersburg. I thought you were the rudest man in Russia, which at the time was something of a distinction. Obviously I've had no reason to change my mind."

Masters looked at her in such a way that Valentina felt herself blushing furiously. When he spoke she turned away.

"I thought you were the most beautiful creature I'd ever seen, Contessa. I shall never forget your dress or your anger or your tears or the look of devilment in your eyes."

Valentina turned to face him, conscious of the changes in her appearances since that first meeting. Masters took her hand and led her into a street off the square.

"I'll buy you lunch in one of the private rooms of your favorite restaurant."

"I must go home, Mr. Masters."

"You can go home after lunch. You don't have any really pressing engagements, do you, Contessa?"

When she did not answer, Masters taunted her with an accurate account of her current existence.

"You get up around eight. You bathe and breakfast in the conservatory of the house Miss Knatchbull bought you. Your husband rarely goes out, except in the early morning when he rides in the Bois de Boulogne. As for you, you're bored. You've had your hair cut and you've got new clothes from the Chanel salon and still you're bored. You tried to get a job but they didn't think you were suitable. You tried a couple of times, I understand, and didn't get a chance at either job. So you sit at home or walk in the woods near your home and complain to yourself that you're bored. I can't stand women who let themselves get into that state. Your trouble is you were born rich and though your childhood was spent in poverty you've forgotten what it taught you."

"And you, Mr. Masters, are you not rich?"

"I was born poor and I stayed poor until I was thirty. Now I have a ranch in Missouri and a small interest in my brother's stud in Kentucky. I have some money in the bank but not too much. Compared to your husband I'm chicken feed."

"The count lost everything after the revolution."

"He didn't lose you."

Valentina glowered as Masters led her upstairs to a pink-lined *salle privée*. She knew she could run away but that if she did she would attract attention. A small voice pointed out that she had no desire whatsoever to run away, but she avoided admitting her feelings and sat down looking fixedly at her hands. Masters left for a moment to speak with the headwaiter, ordering food and champagne without consulting her. Returning, he looked into her rebellious eyes.

"I bet you're wondering how I know all about you. I'll be honest and tell you I employed a private detective to find out everything he could buy or pry about your present life. You once told me I was no gentleman so I'm behaving like the cad you think I am. Now are you going to rage at me?"

Valentina looked at him with chilling venom.

"You may be a diplomat, as you say, sir, but you are not at all diplomatic. You're an American and therefore a barbarian and I could *never* waste my anger on you. Now I should like to go home. My husband will be wondering where I am."

"Let him wonder. I have a story to tell you."

Valentina found it hard to meet the searching brown eyes. She looked at the rolls and began to shred one into small pieces as Masters spoke.

"Last time we met it wasn't convenient to tell you what I'll say today. You were married and in love with a man who wasn't your husband. There was no room for me."

"Don't talk of such things. Don't say a single word more."

"I fell in love with you that day in St. Petersburg. I'm a married man so I did my best to forget you. I really worked hard at forgetting you but I didn't succeed. Now I know I can't forget you and I want to put a proposal to you."

"You waste your time, sir."

"We're both married and therefore not free. You need someone to love. I need someone to love. You're wasting the best years of your life with a man who doesn't know how to make you happy. I'm doing the same with my wife. During the next two years I'll be in Paris often. We could meet and live a little. I'm in love with you, Contessa. I don't have any other women stashed away. I'm not a playboy or a philanderer. When I married Davina I thought it was forever."

"And now you've decided that it isn't?"

"No, I'll never divorce Davina, but she has her life and I have mine and I'd like you to be part of it."

The food came and Valentina saw that Masters had ordered all her favorite dishes. She smiled despite herself.

"Did your private detective also tell you what I like to eat?"

"No, that came from the chef at the Italian Embassy. He told me you love food and can't resist chicken in the style of Kiev. The crêpes Suzette I figured myself. I thought you'd have those when you went to dinner at Maxim's."

"I'm not very fond of Maxim's, Mr. Masters. My husband likes it because he sees his fellow Russians dining there."

"I'll never take you to Maxim's. We'll have our own secret places, you and I."

Without warning, tears began to fall down Valentina's cheeks. She wiped them away with Masters' handkerchief, furious with herself for being so unnerved. He softened a little.

"I'm sorry, Contessa. I should have waited months and then told you how I feel, but these are the best years of *my* life too. I want you and love you and have been looking everywhere for you for three years. Don't cry, dammit. We're going to share this meal and you'll go home and you need never see me again. You've lost nothing coming here today. I'm the loser if you don't want to see me again."

When she cried harder than ever Masters held her by the shoulders and looked into her eyes.

"What's really wrong?"

"I'm crying because I hate to hear the truth. You are a man I could never understand but you speak the truth and make me sad. I do live an empty life. I am wasting the precious years of my life; but what would you have me do, meet you in a hotel or an apartment to make love and creep away afterward like a thief? Would that make me feel more useful, more successful as a woman? I'm nothing but a decoration. I've never done anything useful in my life except during the war, when I worked in the fields of my husband's estate in order to keep it safe from those who might take it away."

"The house you burned down?"

Valentina was silent, her eyes the only meter of the thoughts that came leaping through her mind. In a montage of bitter memories she saw Nadya and Gagurin braying their demands and Maria

Kubatova and her husband soaking the corridors of the Flower House with kerosene so they would burn more easily, thus eluding the people who came to plunder. Masters poured champagne and handed her a glass.

"You can't dream forever of the house you lost. I'll buy you another house. I hear you don't much care for that graystone box of yours."

"It's a fine property, but it's true, I don't like it very much."

"I'll buy you whatever will make you happy, Contessa. I'll help you plan your life. Make use of me, will you? What I won't do is give you the house so you can live the kind of life you live now. You have to have a purpose in life. You need to care for something or someone more than anything in the world. That's a deal, then. I'll buy the house and get it restored and decorated. You decide what use to make of it."

When they left the restaurant Masters led Valentina back to the Place Vendôme and walked with her to the spot in which his automobile was parked. He pointed across the street to a tall *maison particulière* with closed shutters and a mansard roof of forbidding black slate.

"Do you know who used to live there?"

"I've no idea, Mr. Masters."

"A woman called Virginia Oldoini."

"The Contessa di Castiglione?"

"The same. She lived her whole life gazing at her reflection in the mirrors. She was beautiful and astonishing in the days of her youth. Everyone worshiped her and she dedicated herself to the frivolous life and enjoyed robbing men of their wealth with her demands. When she was old she got fat and her teeth turned black. She draped all the mirrors with cloth to keep from seeing her reflection; then she went quietly mad."

"I don't wish to hear anymore, thank you."

Paris was in the grip of spring fever. A fresh breeze was rippling the chestnut trees in the boulevards and the cherry blossom in the parks was already casting its pink glow on the pathways. Valentina was thinking of the legendary beauty whose teeth had gone black and whose body had grown fat. Out of the corner of her eye she watched Masters' brown suntanned face with its straight nose and jutting chin. She wondered if it were possible to like and dislike someone at the same time, deciding that it was and that she did. But whatever her feelings, Masters was right. She was wasting the finest years of her life and still had nothing of interest to occupy her.

They were passing long the Avenue Kléber when Valentina noticed a large white notice on the door of her bank. She asked Masters to stop and ran to see what the notice said.

WE REGRET TO INFORM OUR ILLUSTRIOUS CLIENTS THAT AS OF THIS DAY, 30TH APRIL 1920, THIS BANK HAS CEASED TRADING, PENDING INVESTIGATIONS. SAFETY-DEPOSIT CLIENTS MAY BE ABLE TO RETRIEVE THEIR BELONGINGS BY APPLYING IN PERSON TO THE HEAD OFFICE IN THE BOULEVARD MADELEINE.

Masters saw her face go chalk-white. He held out his hand to support her but Valentina turned away and asked in a trembling voice what the notice meant.

"It means the bank's gone bankrupt. Any cash you had there is lost. The safety-deposit box contents might be safe but there seems to be some doubt of that."

Valentina leaned on the railings for support. The Korolenko jewels and her own few remaining pieces might, only might, be safe. The money in her account, with which she had planned to pay for the future of her family, was gone. On arriving in Paris she had sold most of her jewelry and precious stones and had added this to the cash already in the vault, the proceeds of previous sales of jewels taken out of Russia. It was all gone. It was all gone! The message echoed in her head and she could barely take in what was going on around her. Unaccustomed to handling the complicated financial affairs of his many homes in Russia, the count had handed over this responsibility to Gavrilo. Since coming to Paris he had refused adamantly to pay bills and had left all financial matters to his wife. Valentina tried desperately to assess what was left.

Masters spoke sharply to gain her attention.

"What does this mean to you, Contessa?"

"It means we are ruined and unable to pay any of our bills, sir. My husband's family jewels may be safe. They must be handed down to our sons. They will be Nikolai and Vasily's only heritage as everything else is gone. My own remaining jewels may also be safe; on the other hand, they may not. Everything else is gone. All the jewels I brought with me from Russia, all those which were brought before the revolution by my brother and sister-in-law, all were sold and the proceeds put into the current account. We have no cash at all left."

Masters pulled her into an alleyway alongside the bank and held her close to his chest. Valentina did not struggle when he spoke.

"Someday you'll think this is the best thing that ever happened to you, Contessa."

"Why do you call me Contessa? Everyone else calls me Countess."

"Countess has the cow sound. Contessa rhymes with musetta, much prettier in my ears."

Valentina looked wearily up to see if he was joking.

"I don't understand you, sir."

"Don't call me sir, my name's Alex."

"I prefer to call you Mr. Masters."

"I prefer to call you Valentina. Seriously, if you're really not as rich as you thought you were, you can either sell what jewels you have left or you can find some other way to live."

"What do you suggest?"

"You don't have the personality or the experience of Parisian life to get a job. You must find out what's needed and supply a demand."

"Are you being facetious, Mr. Masters?"

"Of course not. Something will strike you. There'll be a sign so you'll know which direction you have to take. You'll find yourself needed then and you'll be happier than you've been in years."

Valentina looked at her hands and saw that they were trembling. She looked into Masters' eyes and tried to assess the expression.

"I'm suddenly very tired, Mr. Masters. I would be obliged if you'd call me a taxi. I don't wish to arrive home with you, for obvious reasons."

"Thank you for everything, Valentina. I'll be seeing you soon."

"I doubt it, Mr. Masters."

"Doubt nothing. Doubt isn't on your agenda anymore."

Valentina let herself into the house and found Vasily waiting for her in the hall. He put his fingers to his lips and motioned for silence.

"Papa's terribly upset, Mama."

"Why is he upset?"

"He received a letter from the bank."

Vasily brought the crumpled letter from his pocket.

"I thought you'd want to read it, Mama."

Valentina read through the letter and put it down on the hall table. Zita came out of the kitchen and looked questioningly at her.

"Can I do anything, ma'am. What's happening?"

"We have lost all our money in the collapse of our bank, Zita. That means we have no cash. The box containing the family jewels is intact. However, the one containing my own remaining pieces has been stolen. We have nothing left but the Korolenko family heirlooms."

"I don't believe a word of it, ma'am. Who'd rob a bank like that one when there are banks twice as big and rich in the center of the city?"

"They say it was revolutionaries from our own country, seeking to fill the empty banks in Petrograd. They chose our bank because of its name, La Banque Impériale Russe. I've no idea if all this is true."

"What about the diamond pendant Yekaterina Vasilievna bought you and the emerald necklace that—"

"I keep those in my wall safe. They are still there with the rings I've been wearing this week."

Valentina walked upstairs to her room, leaving Vasily in the hall. Zita took the boy to the kitchen and kept him busy helping Chef Dubrovsky make gingerbread soldiers with currant eyes. Now and then Zita looked toward the chef and sighed wearily. Then she thought of Yanin and of Valentina's vow never to sell the gifts her lover had given her. What was going to happen? Would they be obliged to move to one of the tiny cottages normally occupied by road workers and gravediggers in the poverty ridden suburbs of Paris? Zita saw Vasily looking despondent. She decided to take him out for a walk in the park.

Valentina was still deliberating what to do when there was a hammering on the door at the rear of the house. No one answered it and the hammering continued. She rose and lifted up the window. Below stood three young children, a girl and two boys, each dressed in what had once been elegant traveling clothes. She called down to them.

"What do you want? Who are you?"

"May we speak with Countess Korolenko, milady?"

"I am the countess."

"I am Anatoly Alexeyevich Imeretinsky, and here are my sister, Natasha, and my bother Alexei."

Valentina ran downstairs and opened the door.

"You're Marya Sergeyevna Imeretinskaya's children?"

"We are."

"Where are your parents?"

The girl began to cry. Valentina poured them glasses of milk and asked Dubrovsky to make food for them. Then she knelt before the children, wiping Natasha's eyes and trying to calm her fears.

"Now tell me slowly, what are you doing here in Paris on your own?"

"We left Russia two months ago, milady. The Bolsheviks shot Mama and Papa and Grandmama outside our house. We were hiding in the gazebo at the end of the garden. Grandmama had always told us to hide in the gazebo if the Bolsheviks came. When the soldiers had gone and we had kissed our parents good-bye we decided to walk to Paris. Then Anatoly said we might be able to travel on the train instead of walking."

"And you, Anatoly, were you the leader of the expedition?"

"Yes, milady. I'm ten, Alexei is only eight and Natasha is barely six, so she couldn't make a plan. We hid in one of the trains that were about to leave for Warsaw. When we got there we asked an old gentleman to take us with him onto the Paris train. He was most kind and paid our fares. I knew all about the journey to Paris because Mama went there three times and told me all about it."

"And when you arrived in Paris, what then?"

"We couldn't find our relatives, Countess. I had not realized what a large city Paris is. We've been sleeping in an old bakery since last week. Today a policeman found us. Natasha was sure he was a Bolshevik so we ran away from him and hid."

"And how did you come to find me?"

"We were hiding near a bank in the Avenue Kléber when I saw you walking with a gentleman. I remembered you from the party you gave me and my brother and sister not long before you left Russia."

"When the palace was full of revolutionaries?"

"Yes, Countess. When you had driven away in the fiacre I took the liberty of asking the gentleman your address and he was kind enough to bring us here. He was sure you'd take us in. He said we must tell you we were the sign you've been looking for and we were very glad."

Valentina looked at Natasha, whose black curls were wilting in the heat of the kitchen. Then she turned to Anatoly and saw his boots were so worn his toes were sticking out of the leather. Alexei craned his neck to hear her reply, his pale face twitching with tension. Valentina feigned a carefree attitude she did not in reality feel and led the children upstairs to the guest quarters.

"These two rooms will be yours for the moment."

The children looked at the toile de jouy wallpaper and fresh-cut flowers on the table. Natasha began to cry again, joined within seconds by her brothers. Knowing how they had suffered, Valentina knelt and stroked their heads.

"You have a new home now. I'm going to look after you and feed you and see you have an education, if we cannot find your mama's family. But I am sure we will. Now stop crying. We have dinner at seven-thirty. You must all wash and change your clothes. I can find something of my sons' clothes for you two boys and tomorrow I'll buy you new dresses, Natasha. For now you'll have to wear one of these flannel nightshirts. We'll all pretend you're in fancy dress so you don't feel shy."

Valentina called Zita to supervise the children and went quickly to her own room to think. The count might be displeased but he would not turn the children away. Marya Sergeyevna Imeretinskaya was his friend's daughter and her three children were all that was left of the Russian part of the family. Valentina's head began to ache as she lay thinking of the future. Masters had said the children came as a sign. There would obviously be other Russian fugitives in Paris, small children who had seen their parents die. But how could she look after them? She had not enough money to look after her own family and the financial aspect of life had taken a turn for the worse. She lay on her back looking at the ceiling and trying to think what Miss Knatchbull would do.

The following morning in the post Valentina received a gold card on which was written "Payment in full received with thanks." It was from the Chanel salon. She leaped out of bed and danced with relief. The receipt was followed minutes later by a petit-bleu telegram from Masters: "Meet me at noon in front of Cooks Wagon Lits in the Madeleine." She sat at the window of her room looking out on the green woodland of the Bois de Boulogne. She was wondering how many Russian children there were in Paris and who would love them and teach them and care for them for the rest of their lives. It was a question that had hammered at her mind all night. The only conclusion she had drawn from her deliberations was that the children would be put in the Municipal Orphanage, to spend the rest of their days in dormitories smelling of disinfectant and urine. In such places children became institutionalized and numb. Valentina shook her head. The children who had escaped the Bolsheviks were not going to end their days without the love and security of family ties, not if she could do anything to prevent it.

The count joined his wife for breakfast. He was startled to find Valentina glowing with happiness. He wrinkled his nose at the strong smell of the coffee she drank and the elusive fragrance of the quince jelly she had chosen to eat with breakfast this fine morning. He wondered if anything would ever diminish her composure and the aggression with which she met every new setback. When he spoke, Valentina almost laughed at his sentiments.

"My dear, this is no time for merriment. We are bankrupt. We cannot pay our debts and I have bills which run into many thousands of francs. I may end by having to kill myself to save the honor of the family."

"We still have the family jewels. We must use them to guarantee our future."

"I shall never sell the Korolenko jewels."

"Then I shall have to raise money for my family elsewhere. We have two sons who must be educated and the Imeretinsky children too. I don't intend to let anyone starve."

The count watched as Valentina donned an elegant black dress and pinned a spray of violets at her neck that matched the velvet birds on her small black hat.

"Where are you going, my dear?"

Valentina's reply was so flippant the count mistook it for a joke.

"I'm going house hunting. In the years to come, we shall need a much larger home."

Korolenko gazed in awe at the speed with which his wife made ready to leave. He was taken aback by the change in her from the previous day, when she had seemed so depressed and uncertain of the future. What had happened to change her mind? What decision or news had altered her so noticeably? When she had gone, he looked at the letters on the table and saw among them the receipt from Chanel. He frowned. He had not signed any check for payment of the account and Valentina's money had been lost in the bank failure. He walked wearily back to his room, his head aching from confusion. He had lost his country, his homes and his wealth. Was he now going to suffer the loss of his wife? His face hardened and he thought defiantly that no one would ever take Valentina from him again.

# CHAPTER FIFTEEN

## Paris, Spring 1921

———————
———————
———————

Valentina was with her sons in the Bois de Boulogne, near the house she owned and was determined to sell. Since the count found the Chanel account marked PAID she had been confined to outings with her sons in the park. He had questioned her for days, watching like a hawk to see if she altered her story that she had paid Chanel in advance from her account in order to have the clothes delivered speedily. As she sat by the lake Valentina was thinking of Masters. They had lunched twice in May of the previous year and four times in June and July. Then he had returned to America and had not been back to Paris. She thought how Yanin had come back to the country each year with the spring and wondered impulsively if Masters would do the same. She blushed as she thought of her last assignation with him. They had gone a small distance along the Seine to Bas Meudon, to eat at La Pêche Miraculeuse, among writers and artists and old gentlemen in black berets busy reminiscing about Paris in the days when they were young and fit and given to chasing women. The day had been hot, the wine strong, and she had imagined herself able to forget the past and begin anew with a man whose eyes constantly searched her own for a signal to advance the relationship one step more and another and another until they were no longer mere friends. She had wanted Masters to kiss her, to touch her, to whisper inconsequential things in her ear, but he had only teased her about her flushed cheeks. When she had returned home the count had been busy in his study. She had hurried upstairs to her room, anxious to hide the telltale signs of tipsiness from him.

Nikolai watched his mother and asked himself what she was thinking of. Lately she had been acting strangely, always rushing to take the post from Zita and then being happier or sadder than usual as a result of the letters she received. He knew Valentina had recently taken a *poste restante* box at the local office. She had received no letters there and had been withdrawn and absentminded as a result. Nikolai wondered if his mother had a lover. He would not blame her if she had. In the past few months the count had become grumpy and given to quibbling over everything in a childish fashion. Nikolai remembered Yanin and debated whether the gallant colonel had been his mother's lover. Since going to school in Paris he had learned many things he had not known before. He was sixteen and attractive to women. He had had an escapade with one of the young women who worked as a stenographer in the school and another with a young society girl, the sister of his best friend. He continued to gaze at his mother as she looked down at the water lilies on the lake. Was she thinking of the water lilies outside the Flower House in Russia? Or was she thinking of a new lover who had all her attention? Ignoring Vasily, who kept calling for him to come to the lake, Nikolai took hold of his mother's hand.

"Mama, I should like to talk with you about my education. I like my school well enough but I have never thought my future lies in Paris. French society is chauvinistic. They admire what is French and everything else seems odd to them. I want to live somewhere where the fact that I am Russian will not impede me."

"I shall think about the future, Nikolai. Would you like to go to England or America?"

"The English have many of the same characteristics as the French. They prefer their own society and I could never be part of it."

Nikolai became aware of a handsome man sitting on an iron bench across the lake. The man was watching them intently. Turning to his mother, he saw that she too had seen the stranger, and that she was smiling an enigmatic smile. He noted the blush in her cheeks and knew his suspicions about an affair had been right. The stranger walked around the periphery of the lake toward them. Nikolai judged him to be about the same age as his mother. He was strongly built and dressed in the latest fashion, with a finely

cut gray suit and curved hat that resembled the hats worn by riverboat gamblers in picture books. Impressed, Nikolai waited for the
stranger to come near.

Masters noted the expectant look on Nikolai's face, and the pleasure in Valentina's. He inclined his head.

"Good day to you, Countess."

"Good day, Mr. Masters. May I introduce my son, Nikolai. Vasily
is here too, playing by the lake."

Nikolai smiled openly and shook hands. Masters looked at his
watch.

"I'm late for an appointment. This park charms me every time I
come to my house across the lake, and I find myself unwilling to
leave it. I hope to see you and your family again soon, Contessa."

Valentina's heart quickened as she looked at the house across the
lake. Had Masters rented the place to be near her? It was easily
accessible. She realized that Nikolai was watching her.

"Are you in love with that man, Mama? You blushed quite crimson when he appeared."

"Of course not. I barely know Mr. Masters."

"Were you in love with Colonel Yanin? Forgive me for asking
such impertinent questions, Mama, but I am a man now and I keep
thinking of the past and trying to work out why my family isn't like
the families of the other fellows at school."

"I was very fond of Colonel Yanin. If I had not already been
married to the count I should certainly have married Ivan. I suppose I was in love with him. I cannot lie to you about it."

"I'm sorry, Mama."

"Don't be sorry. We had some wonderful times together. I have
enough memories to last forever."

Nikolai understood more than his mother realized and longed to
ask her more questions about Yanin. He decided to keep these for
another day, perhaps some evening when they were sitting by the
fire together. He thought of the searching look Masters had given
him and tried in the politest fashion to inquire about the American.

"I think that man is in love with you, Mama."

Valentina tried to control the panic she felt at being asked such
questions by her son. Nikolai continued calmly.

"Why is Mr. Masters in Paris, Mama?"

"I don't know, my dear. He's a diplomat and forever traveling. I know nothing more than that."

"I liked him. If we meet again I shall ask him about the colleges in America. Oh, Mama! Vasily has fallen in the water again."

They ran to the side of the lake and pulled Vasily out of the weeds. Valentina put her stole around his shoulders and together they ran with him back to the house. The count met them in the hall.

"That boy will drown one day if he keeps meddling among the weeds. What does he think he is, a common fisherman?"

Valentina looked in surprise at her husband.

"How did you know Vasily had fallen into the lake?"

"I had just started watching him through my new binoculars. With these I can see almost the entire park around our home."

Valentina hurried to her son's room, unwilling to answer further questions. When she had handed Vasily over to Zita she went to her own bedroom and sat looking across the lake to the roof of the house Masters had taken. Even with the new binoculars, the count could not see through trees. She smiled mischievously, certain that Masters had taken the house so he could see her more frequently than before. She thought how they had always met in the Madeleine near Cooks Wagon Lits. Would he be there this morning, tomorrow? Would they be able to meet for a luxurious and secret lunch in the countryside outside Paris? She rushed to her wardrobe and took out a new outfit bought from a young designer who was trying to make her name. The outfit was in gray with a small hat to match and a seagull swooping down one side of the brim. She tried the hat, frowning because she knew she should not have bought it. They were now facing the worst financial year of their lives. But the desire to look beautiful for Masters was irresistible. Valentina chastised herself but could not help smiling at her reflection in the mirror. Masters was back. Everything would be all right. The money she had gained from the sale of her remaining jewels had lasted all winter. Now it was almost gone. She had left only Yanin's gifts and the diamond pendant given her by Yekaterina. She would have to sell them. She thought of the Korolenko jewels languishing unseen in the count's safe and was furious at his continuing refusal to dispose of a single item. Then she remembered her husband's courage in bringing her and her sons out of Russia. Why should he not cling to the vestiges of his former glory? Why should he not preserve the remains of his fortune to hand down to his sons in the traditional manner of the Russian aristocracy? She would have to sell the diamond pendant. She thought fearfully of the Paris jewelry market and knew she would get only a fraction of its value. Russian émigrés had sold everything they owned to pay for the establishment of new homes, thus lowering the value of jewelry offered by others. Valentina decided to ask Masters' advice. Immediately she was angry with herself for allowing her mind to turn constantly in his direction. Yanin had been dead for only four years. At first she had been numb and listless, so much so that even Paris had not revived her. Now the blood was coursing through her veins and she wanted to be in love and loved by the man of her choice.

The following morning Valentina rose like a tornado, opened the curtains and rushed out to the balcony to water the verbena. In the bathroom as she bathed she saw her cheeks were flushed and wondered if she had developed a fever during the sleepless hours of the night. Shaking her head defiantly, she thought that fever or no she would be in front of Cooks at twelve to meet Masters, if he was there. She dressed, annoyed to feel her fingers trembling with excitement. She found herself looking constantly at the clock, afraid of being late. It was 10 A.M. She had refused breakfast in favor of a large cup of milky coffee. She had told the count she was going house hunting and had made regular day-long expeditions during the winter months so he would not suspect her once Masters returned to Paris. Then, the previous day, the count had told her that the house-hunting expeditions must cease. Valentina wondered if he would try to stop her as she left the house and what she would do if he did. She pushed her hair into place and put on the hat. On reaching the hall she found a letter in a strange hand waiting for her:

*Madame la Comtesse,*
You kindly gave me back my three grandchildren Natasha, Anatoly and Alexei, almost one year ago. I now find that some of their young friends are about to arrive in my home from a refugee station in the suburb of Belleville. I can take three of the children but another hundred remain without homes and hope for the future. In view of my present poor health

and the news I have recently learned from my physician, I am writing to ask you to visit me to discuss the future of my grandchildren and those who will shortly be arriving in my house. Dear lady, do come as quickly as you can. You are the only person on whom I know I can rely.
Sincerely,
   *Annaliese Vadimovna Volkova*

Valentina read the letter through again and knew she had now received the sign Masters had spoken of in the past. She had led a life that seemed thus far to neglect the many talents she possessed. If she could help the Russian children who had come to Paris she would fulfill her early promise and make their future secure. She did not yet know how to accomplish her plan, but she knew that whatever was required she would try to accomplish it.

Masters was waiting under the chestnut trees outside Cooks in the Boulevard de la Madeleine. He had the day planned meticulously: lunch in a private room at the Ritz, a trip on a *bateau hirondelle* upriver to Bercy and then an idyllic hour in the house he had rented in the Bois. He looked at his watch. It was five minutes to twelve. He began to pace up and down. Then he bought some sprigs of lily of the valley from an old flower seller on the corner and sniffing it thought of the scent Valentina used, a perfume that lingered long after she had disappeared. At noon he heard the grinding of a taxi on the cobblestones and saw Valentina stepping down. She was wearing a dress of pale dove gray, her hair tucked into a small cloche hat that had a seagull in flight down one side of the brim. Masters handed her the flowers and helped her put them in her corsage. He was immediately aware that she had changed in some indefinable way. His long absence might have made her reject him. Instead, he was conscious it had made him more acceptable in her eyes. He wondered how she was and what she had been doing with her life. Then, as she looked up into his eyes, he saw that her face was alight with pleasure and purpose. Forgetting himself, he swung her around like a child.

"I am so glad to see you. I've been trying not to yell with impatience for an hour."

"You said between twelve and one in your note."

"I've been here since eleven. We Masterses are an impatient family. I've planned our day to the hour."

"I imagined you would have, Mr. Masters."

"Let's get out of here. I've taken a suite so we can lunch together at the Ritz."

They ran together through the streets and across a road full of cabs, automobiles and handcarts full of flowers. The smell of expensive chocolate came to them as they passed a deluxe bonbonnerie. Valentina heard the sound of a gypsy orchestra thumping out from the tango parlor, where ladies past their best hired partners to dance with them for a few hours. She wrinkled her nose, hoping fervently that she would never be obliged to hire partners for the dance. As they made their way toward the Ritz, cherry-blossom petals fell in the breeze, covering their heads with confetti. Valentina whispered to Masters and he laughed out loud.

"I hope they do think we're just married. Then the manager will send up a magnum of champagne and I'll forget all about my plans and not let you leave the hotel for a week."

She ate a light lunch of coquilles, salade de céleri and a baba au rhum. Masters ordered Ostende oysters, sole and a small orchestra to play in the salon. They talked of Valentina's plans for the Russian children and she was delighted to receive Masters' approval for the first time.

"It's a great idea, Valentina. I knew you'd think in that direction, but I didn't think you'd decide to adopt *all* the stray Russian children in Paris. There must be a hundred of them in the refugee house in Belleville. I'd better scrap my plans for the day and take you out there to see them."

"I was going to ask if you would."

"You'll need a property that'll house that number of children. We'll go look at one after we've been to Belleville. I was going to show it to you later anyway. Have you thought of the money you're going to need to keep the children?"

"I have a very fine large diamond and also an emerald necklace and two Fabergé eggs. I'm afraid I shall have to sell everything to buy a house large enough to house all the children. I've been seaching for months for a property I can afford. My husband won't sell his family jewels and I can't really blame him."

"You'll need money to keep the orphanage going forever. It's not something you can just put down and forget."

"It won't be an orphanage, Mr. Masters. I intend to live there with my family. The children will be educated and taught to remember their own language, manners and customs as well as those of the country which has accepted them. It is going to be a home for us all. I shall never allow anyone to call my children orphans."

Masters assessed the color in Valentina's cheeks and thought that she would make a success of the venture or die in the attempt. He tried to explain what he meant.

"You'll have to try to get bequests from the rich so the place can never fall in debt. Have you any idea how to do that? Do you have a good lawyer here in Paris?"

"I shall find one with your help. Then I will ask every Russian émigré in Paris for money."

"Some of them have no money."

"I shall ask the ones who still have their fortunes."

"Cheers, Contessa, I'll be the first to help in any way I can."

Valentina raised her glass and clinked it with his.

"I shall expect a donation from you, Mr. Masters."

That afternoon they went north of the city, to the suburb of Belleville, to visit the Russian children, who were housed in an old property near the main square. Valentina tried to cheer them, noting that their names were a roll call of the Russian aristocracy as it once had been. When she talked about their families, some of the smaller children cried desperately, others remained frozen in shocked immobility. Before she left Valentina heard the children sing the songs their mothers had taught them: "Kalinka" . . . "Stienka Rezin" . . . She hummed along with the old cossack melody learned from the music box Yanin had bought her. For a moment the children's faces lit with pleasure at the sound of the familiar song. Then, as Valentina made ready to leave, they began to cry again.

Valentina was thoughtful as Masters led her to his car. It occurred to her that this was her fate, the path she had always felt she must follow, despite her initial failure to find the right direction. The Bolsheviks had killed every aristocrat they could find. Some of the children had been shot, others, including the babies, suffocated or bayonetted to make sure the Russian dynasties of the past could not survive into the future. The ninety children she had just seen were the lucky ones, those who by chance or will to survive had made their way out of Russia to Paris. Valentina wondered how many more children there were in Italy, Germany and the countries bordering Russia. How many little ones whose empty eyes mirrored the emptiness in their souls?

Masters stepped out of his car in Rambouillet. Valentina looked around her at a typical French town with stone houses, a charcuterie, an old-fashioned shop and a hotel with a beautiful garden. Masters bought her a glass of red wine at the zinc counter of the local bar, surprising her with French spoken like a native.

"I didn't know you were so fluent, Alex."

"Thank you, ma'am."

He kissed her cheek and the old people in the bar grinned knowingly.

"I've been waiting for you to call me Alex. I'm sick of being Mr. Masters."

"Where did you learn your French?"

"I was taught by a Frenchman who worked for my father."

"Why did we come here, Alex?"

"I want to show you something."

"Here, in the town?"

"No, in the countryside between this town and the château; it's only a few hundred yards from here."

"I can't wait to see your surprise."

Masters drove to the edge of a field bright yellow with mustard flowers. Valentina stepped down at his side, following the direction in which he was looking. Before her, to the right, she saw the château with its solid French walls, picturesque towers and forest of centuries-old oaks. She scanned the horizon, but nothing else of interest attracted her until she was facing the opposite direction from which she had started. Then she saw a massive house with outbuildings that stretched to the edge of the mustard field from behind a high castellated wall. She felt as eager as a child and tapped Masters on the shoulder.

"What are you looking at?"

"I'm looking at that house. I found it a year ago, last time I was over in France. I almost talked to you about it then but I thought you were too busy worrying about your appearance to be interested in what I had to propose."

"Tell me about the house."

"It's been empty for twenty years. It's in a God-awful condition, though it was once one of the most beautiful houses in the area. These days I reckon it's one of the shabbiest."

"It's very large; how many rooms are there?"

"Originally it had forty bedrooms and the outbuildings included stables, barns, dairies, wash-houses and a cheese-making room. Within the walls there's also a small herb garden, or was. Then there are five hundred acres outside. I went over the place with the head of the family last time I was here but he wasn't sure he wanted to sell. It's been in his family for generations and he's stuck with it. He can't afford to restore it or live in it as it is, so it's going to ruin."

"And now, what do you plan?"

"Come and look, Valentina. Let me help you across the field. Those shoes weren't made for country walking."

In the courtyard, safe inside the massive walls, Valentina looked up at a house of pale-cream stone with dark-green shutters and shiny green ivy climbing over the façade. In a spot by the stables a venerable walnut tree was newly in leaf. The main stable door rocked on its hinges in the breeze. She closed it, already concerned that nothing more deteriorate now she had found the place of her dreams.

Masters watched her closely, knowing immediately that he had been right and that this was the key to the elusive woman he loved. She moved like a sleepwalker to the entrance, pushing impatiently as he put the iron key into the lock. When she saw the hall she sat down on the inlaid wood floor and sobbed. Masters looked up at the ancient French-leather wallcovering printed with peacocks, wild birds and violets. Some of the leather had become detached from the wall and was hanging forlornly in strips down the mildewed wall. He knelt at Valentina's side and let her wipe her eyes on his handkerchief.

"I seem to have a talent for making you cry."

"I was surprised because the butterflies and flowers reminded me of my country house near St. Petersburg."

Masters helped her up and together they wandered from room to room, admiring the ancient architraves and the doors of solid yew. The kitchens were archaic, with black-iron ovens and hanging rails for hams, herbs and knives. Valentina said she loved it all, however old and dusty, however musty its condition. In the master bedroom she found walls covered with silk patterned with cabbage roses. She turned to Masters in surprise.

"This paper looks new. It's like the wallpaper I keep admiring every time I pass Déschamps in the rue de la Paix. And the wiring looks new in the upstairs rooms. Isn't that strange."

Masters opened the window and Valentina saw before her a terrace overlooking the fields that stretched to the horizon. She spoke in a whisper.

"It was kind of you to bring me here, Alex, but I wish I hadn't seen the house."

"Nonsense, you've got to rid yourself of that Slavic depression of yours. Say ten times a day I can, I will, I am."

Valentina touched his hand, conscious that she no longer merely liked him. She was unwilling to think of love but more and more wanted to feel his body close to hers, his hand on hers, his voice asking questions she had tried for so long to ignore. Masters came nearer and she smelled the fragrance of his skin. Impulsively she put her arms around his neck and looked up at him.

"You have some fine dreams for me, Alex, and I shall try not to disappoint you. Tomorrow I'm going to see Mr. Cartier to offer him my remaining jewels, even the ones my lover bought me that I swore I would never sell."

"You want the house that badly?"

"I do. It's my intention to bring my children here, all the ones who aren't claimed from the home. Nikolai misses his home in Russia and so does my husband. Perhaps this house will make them feel as if they can preserve a small part of their former existence. I shall call it Le Domaine Russe."

"I'm glad you fell in love with the house, but what about me, Valentina?"

Her arms tightened around his neck and Masters bent and kissed her on the mouth, pulling her toward him and holding her so tightly she could not move away. Her lips felt cool against the heat of his own and he felt her body stirring with longing. He recognized the look of intense desire in her eyes and struggled to control the excitement he was feeling.

"You haven't answered my question."

"I seem to have changed my mind about you, Alex. You're still the rudest man I ever met but now I love you a very tiny bit."

"Only a tiny bit."

"It's growing, be patient."

Valentina caught his mouth before he could reply and Masters felt her body tauten as he held her, pulling her insistently against him so she could feel the response within him. She pulled away at last and walked to the window, crouching down to peer through the iron lace railings to the fields beyond.

"I'm afraid you'll think me shameless. I can assure you that until today Colonel Yanin was the only man who ever kissed me."

"I don't give a damn if the entire Preobrazhensky Regiment loved you. You're here with me and I don't intend to lose you."

"A man should be jealous of the woman he loves."

"I've never been a jealous man. The woman doesn't exist who can make me jealous."

Disappointed, Valentina looked into his eyes, wondering if he was right.

"We had better go back to Paris, Alex. You've shown me this lovely house and made me want it, but my trouble is I still have expensive tastes without the means to accommodate them. I have no idea if the owner will accept my offer for his house."

"We'll have dinner on the way back."

"If I have dinner with you I shan't be home until after midnight."

"You may not be home until dawn, my dear."

Valentina tried to change the subject, aware that the moment of decision had come. She thought of the count, berating herself as she thought of his kindness and sympathy during the years of her affair with Yanin. It was not right to torment him with yet another lover. But what was the alternative, life in Paris alone and lonely, with a husband who longed for Russia and for nothing else? Thoughts kept bubbling through her mind but still she could not define her position. She inclined her head and looked speculatively at Masters.

"May I ask you for the address and telephone number of the owners of the property? Better still, will you act for me and ask them what price they require?"

"I already have."

"And what did they say?"

"I bought the property and five hundred acres last week. That's why I'm so relieved you like it. I was on edge in case you didn't. I bought it for you because I know you hate that gray house of yours in Paris. I didn't know at the time that you'd decide to adopt some of the kids from the orphanage. If you bring them here all the better. This is a house that needs children."

Valentina clutched the rail of the terrace, whooping her exultation to the birds and the bees and the fields all around. Masters stood behind her, kissing her ears and the back of her neck. He spoke slowly, deliberately, as though choosing his words with deliberate caution.

"This is my gift to you, Valentina. I'm giving you the Domaine Russe as a present to make you happy. It's not a bribe. I want you to love me but I'm resigned to the fact that you've a mind of your own and that nothing is going to change it. From the end of the year this house will be the home for your children and I'm going to help you get it ready for them. By my architect's reckoning the outbuildings can be turned into another twenty bedrooms. The stables can still hold about a dozen horses when all that is done. If you use the house for the children you'll need enough room for them and for your family and the teachers who'll come to live here. The estate isn't productive right now but perhaps it will be someday. The wine's good, though the vineyards and cellars need modernization, like everything else. You're going to have to figure out how to make it all pay its way once I've helped you with the restoration. The truth is, Valentina, I'll have to mortgage my property in the States to pay for the restoration. That'll leave me my stocks and shares and my cash in the New York account. I won't be able to keep the place going for you."

"You've worked out my entire future."

"That's just what I haven't done, and I don't intend to. I'll help you get the place in order. My money's bought it for you in your name. My money can pay for all the work and that's it. Once the children get here it's up to you. You've relied on other people for too long. This house and what goes on inside it is all up to you; no one is going to tell you how to run it or how to keep it from falling into debt."

On the way back to Paris Valentina sat silently at Masters' side as he drove away past the fields of early summer. She was thinking of the girl she had been before she went to Russia. In those days of innocence she had thought herself capable of anything and everything. Now, at thirty-five, she was not so sure. They reached the Valley of Chevreuse and she looked out at green fields full of wild daisies and mallow. The village names imprinted themselves on her mind and she knew this was a day she would never forget. She watched them pass by, St. Robert, Cernay-la-Ville, la Ferte-Choisel, St. Remy-les-Chevreuse. A village clock struck seven and the setting sun turned the stone houses deep rose. Valentina saw Masters was turning in to an ancient inn. She held her breath, uncertain what he was going to do next.

The patronne rushed out to greet the couple and led them to the bar, where Valentina sat by a glowing fire. She looked around the wood beamed interior and remembered the pavilion where she and Yanin had made love for the first time. She listened as Masters ordered dinner to be served under the apple tree in the garden and watched as the patronne rushed outside to pile wood in readiness for the exterior fire. Masters' voice nudged her to consciousness.

"What are you thinking?"

"I was remembering a pavilion next to the chapel of a neighbor's estate in Russia."

"Yanin's estate?"

"Yes, a long time ago."

Masters showed nothing of the resentment he felt for the ever-present Yanin. Someday, he thought, someday I'll banish all thought of him from her head. He replied casually, shocked by the realization that he was jealous of Valentina's former lover.

"I love you. We both have pasts that can't be forgotten. I just want to be the man in your present and your future. I hope you've enough love left for me because I want everything you ever thought of giving."

They ate under the apple tree, kept warm by the open fire. Masters ordered fresh liver pâté, wild goose and soufflé framboise. They drank wine from the local vineyard, wine that was a little green and highly intoxicating. Valentina remembered becoming drunk on mare's milk long ago when she went to a village market in Russia. She shook her head impatiently, trying in vain not to keep going back to the past. In the distance a cuckoo called. She looked at Masters, admiring his handsome looks in the firelight glow. His face was burnished copper, like an ancient statue, and she thought he had the looks of an adventurer. The church bell struck nine. Valentina thought of going home and then forgot about her home. Intoxicated with happiness and wine, she barely felt guilty.

Masters led her from the garden to a room above the bar. Valentina wondered if she should protest but she said nothing as the patronne turned down the bed and closed the curtains. She looked down at an olive-wood floor that smelled of beeswax polish and then at the bedspread embroidered with lovers' knots in white silk. She watched as Masters lit the candles and a pink-shaded lamp by the bed. She sat at his side, unwilling to undress and suddenly afraid of being disappointed or, worse, of disappointing him. She could not remember the moment when Masters had become important to her, but it had happened, perhaps a long time ago. She thought of their first meeting in St. Petersburg and the dislike she had told herself she felt. There had followed endless nights of sleeplessness when his image had passed before her eyes like an ever-present phantom. Had she really disliked him so? Or had she fallen in love in a different way from what she had thought possible and rejected him because it was not the time and the place? She ran her hand over the coverlet and thought wryly that this was the time and the place.

Masters undressed her, unbuttoning her jacket, slipping down the skirt and smiling at the fanciful French knickers edged with lace. Valentina stretched out her arms to stop him joining her in the bed but he pushed her aside and silenced the chattering of her teeth with kisses. Finally he entered her and she felt the familiar tensing in every muscle and the roaring of her heart as he provoked her. With Masters love was different. The aggression and the thrust of his body into hers made her react with her own demands and she realized for the first time how much she had missed being loved, how much her body had resented its long disuse. For a long time they were locked together, their limbs entwined in a ritual fight to the little death. Valentina gripped the carved bedpost as that long-awaited moment burst on her senses. She heard Masters cry out and felt his body dissolve in her own. Then she was silent. Masters held her hand and cradled her in his arms.

"I once had a cat that looked white and fluffy and plain beautiful. It fought like a tiger when it was aroused. I always reckoned she thought she was a tiger and perhaps she was."

"What made you think of her just now?"

"I can't imagine, can you?"

Valentina looked at the barley-twirled bedpost and saw marks where her nails had become embedded in the wood. She smiled contentedly. Then for a while she slept entwined in Masters' arms. The church clock struck ten, eleven, twelve. Valentina woke first and sat up, tracing her lover's face with her fingers, circling his eyes, his mouth, his nostrils. How handsome he is, she thought, how unlike any other man I have ever met. She threw back the bedclothes and looked at his body minutely, tracing her finger over his thighs, the small hairs around his penis, his stomach and chest. She bent to kiss him and then to nibble and devour him. Masters woke and pulled her toward him.

"That's no way to wake a man."

"You taste of lemon and peaches."

Valentina asked herself why Masters had fallen in love with her at all when she had done nothing but be disagreeable to him in the past. She tried not to think of her husband and the scene there would be when she arrived home. Masters looked questioningly at her.

"Those moods of yours change pretty quickly. Are you all right?"

"I'm half dead from bruises and exhaustion."

"Great, now go to sleep."

"I must go home, Alex."

"You really want to go?"

"No, but I must. On weekdays I breakfast with Vasily before he goes to school. He'd be terrified if he came to my room and found me gone. He'll think I've had an accident or run away."

They drove to Masters' house in the Bois and kissed good night under the black lace pattern of the elm leaves. The dew wet Valentina's feet as she hurried back to her home. She looked up at the windows, surprised to see no light. Had the count gone to bed? Surely not. She crept inside and up to her room, wincing at every creak of the stairs. No one accosted her. No sound broke the silence of the night. She put on a nightdress, throwing her discarded clothes on the floor in the bathroom. She was asleep within minutes, tiredness and tension overwhelming her.

The count sat at his desk in the darkness. He was fully clothed and as pale as death. It was three-thirty in the morning and his wife had just arrived home. There was no further doubt in his mind that she had taken a lover. He paced back and forth until dawn, unable to settle for the agony of uncertainty in his mind. It was 6 A.M. now. At seven she would eat breakfast with Vasily, as was her custom on schooldays. By eight he would visit her and state his terms for the continuation of the marriage. With Yanin he had been content to be silent. He was no longer willing to be the cuckold. The count shook his head and asked himself what Valentina would say if he challenged her. She would probably tell him to go to hell with her usual devastating forthrightness. Then he would not lose only her but also his beloved boys when she swept out of his life in a fury. He decided finally to say nothing at all.

## CHAPTER SIXTEEN

### *The Domaine, Autumn and Winter 1921–1922*

At 8 A.M. Valentina heard the goatherd's pipes and the barking of his dog as it herded the flock in orderly formation down the cobbled streets. She was not yet accustomed to the sounds of the new quarter, but they made her feel intensely Parisian. She stretched languidly and thought of Masters, who had left for America the previous day. They had spent a glorious summer together, almost every day from morning to night, supervising the work to be done on the Domaine Russe. They had lunched by the Seine at old inns and faded mansions all over the area and had enjoyed exploring the Rambouillet region from the Domaine to the distant farms of the Ile de France. Valentina had sold her home in the Bois de Boulogne and had moved to the Left Bank, where Masters had helped her find an apartment to rent in the rue de l'Odéon, near the Luxembourg Gardens. His theory was that she needed a change of scene and that it was easier to reach the new property from south of the river. Valentina knew it was nothing of the kind. Masters wanted her away from her husband, if possible. Masters wanted everything his own way and generally got it, except that he appeared unable or unwilling to do anything about his unsatisfactory marital situation. Valentina shrugged. She would not think of such unpleasant matters on a beautiful autumn morning full of smoky blue haze and mellow gold light. She heard her sons arguing in a room across the landing from her own, and wondered if the count would visit them today. He had refused to move to the new apartment because he believed the Left Bank to be full of "waiters, students and revolutionaries." He had taken instead a small suite in a hotel off the Champs-Elysées and there he remained, obdurately refusing to move to be with his family. Whenever the count visited her he brought a small gift. He had confided that he had decided to sell some of his family jewels so he could endow the Domaine Russe, into which they would all be moving before the Christmas holiday. Valentina was touched by her husband's affection and the joy he had manifested when told of the new property. She knew only too well that the count had guessed that she had a lover. News of the estate purchase "at the hands of a rich benefactor" and her plan to adopt the Russian children had made him change his mind about her current activities and he had taken her to Maxim's to toast the new venture. Afterward the count had talked for days about the help he would give the children, the tuition he would provide in hunting, shooting and fishing and the ways of a Russian gentleman. For the first time, Valentina knew, her husband was looking forward to something. At last he had lost the intense depression that had dogged him ever since he arrived in Paris.

On the pavement below the apartment wood sellers were stacking their wares. Charcoal braziers had been lit outside the cafés to warm those who chose to sit on the terraces. Valentina opened the window and looked down on students en route to the Sorbonne and the Medical School, hurrying on their way, their faces pinched with cold. At lunchtime the richer ones would go to the small restaurants of the quarter for a prix fixe meal of beef daube or lapin au moutarde.

Miss Knatchbull arrived, blue with cold. While Valentina made coffee, Miss Knatchbull sat on the edge of the sofa explaining what she had ascertained about financial help for the Domaine.

"My dear, I visited four of the Russians on your list and all of them gave me a piece of jewelry to be sold in aid of the new estate."

Valentina had also been visiting rich people to obtain money for the Domaine. Not only exiled Russians were to be approached, but also French and English residents of Paris. She had organized a ball to be held at the Crillon and had made it known that only the finest aristocrats of the city would be invited. The result had been a clamor for the extortionate tickets and talk all over the city about the elegant fund raising of Countess Korolenko. Miss Knatchbull drank her coffee and looked again at the list.

"I have some even better news, my dear. I visited the house of my friend Masson, the stockbroker. He has a client who is dying. The gentleman is Russian-born and has no one to whom to leave his money. I think you should visit him and see if he would endow the Domaine Russe with his fortune."

"Where does he live?"

"He has a property in Neuilly. I've made an appointment for you to go there on Friday."

"Any other news?"

"I have, my dear. You remember when I went to London I told you that both my nephews are enthusiastic socialists? Well, on sending my will to the executor in London, I was informed that neither boy wishes to be left money. They do not believe in inherited wealth and have told me not to give them a shilling. I therefore propose to leave what I have to Nikolai and Vasily. I shall also sell my stocks and shares and give you what remains of my cash. I shall keep only some gold in case of emergency. I must say I am delighted by the thought of living *en famille* again. I have missed the old days when you needed me."

"I'm obliged to you for all you say, Natty. I shall never be able to repay what you've done for me since I was small."

"No need for thanks, my dear. You always made me feel needed and at my age it's common to feel as needed as a weed in a garden. Thanks to you I have something to look forward to. I intend to set the very best example to those poor children. I have decided also to give up gambling so I shall not let them down."

"Are you telling me that you gamble, Natty?"

"I've played cards in private games for years, but now I shall definitely give up my vice. I shall be sixty on the thirty-first of December. It's time to give up all the old indulgences."

In the streets of Paris the leaves were turning to shades of cinnamon, snuff and amber. The air smelled of wood braziers, roast chestnuts, new bread and a mysterious scent of smoke and overripe fruit that was the essence of autumn. Alone after Miss Knatchbull's departure, Valentina thought of the jewels she had sold. The diamond pendant from Yekaterina, the emerald necklace and the two Fabergé eggs that Yanin had bought her were all gone, sold under their value to an unknown man, whose eyes had gleamed like twin beacons when he realized what a bargain he had. Valentina had never missed the objects until now, but autumn was the time of year when she was inclined to feel melancholy and given to remembering the days in Russia and skating on the lake with her lover. She hurried to her bedroom and opened the lid of the music box: "Say goodbye, my own true lover, as we sing a lovers' song . . . how it breaks my heart to leave you. Now the carnival is gone . . ." Tears fell unheeded down her cheeks and she wished fervently that her mind would release her from the commitments of the past. Outside, a man called his wares: *"Chapeaux à vendre, souliers à vendre. . . ."* The bell of the local church boomed the hour. Valentina did not hear them. She was far away in a locked compartment of memory, riding through the cornfield of summer with Yanin, a wreath of poppies in her hair.

On the morning of her appointment with the rich philanthropist, Valentina looked at her reflection in the mirror. Was she wearing a suitable outfit for her important mission? Did she look like a responsible person? She was about to leave for the house in Neuilly where the elderly millionaire lay dying. She had taken pains with her appearance but still felt uncertain of the old man's reaction. She had discussed the meeting with Miss Knatchbull, had all the figures relevant to the running of the Domaine Russe and estimates as to the future upkeep of the property, as well as budgets for the maintenance of each child she was about to adopt. She had decided to speak the truth, as was her custom. She would tell the man she had become the owner of the Domaine, which was about to be filled with Russian children exiled by the revolution. She had money enough to run her enterprise for some time but in the light of rising prices not forever. She had begged money before, many times, but something told her that this would be different. More money was at stake—indeed the whole future of her enterprise—and she had never met the old man before. Apprehensive, she patted her hair and looked yet again at her reflection in the mirror.

As the cab drew near on the cobbled roadway of Neuilly, Valentina began to feel even more nervous. The driver opened the door for her outside a detached mansion built in the Second Empire style. She looked up at the decaying house and thought of the decaying man inside. Then she rang the bell and was admitted by a maidservant.

Inside a room that smelled of aniseed and ether, Valentina

looked down at the man whose skeletal bones protruded under his pajamas. He had watery blue eyes and a constant dribble of saliva running toward his chin. She nodded a greeting.

"I am Countess Korolenko. I understand my former governess, Miss Knatchbull, has spoken about me."

When he did not reply she waited, looking away from the liver spotted face and the shuddering hands to a room full of crayon drawings by Boucher, English porcelain pieces and finely painted Japanese screens. The old man spoke at last in a breathless voice.

"My dear mother, Svetlova, came from Russia. She was prima ballerina at the Mariinsky Theater in her youth."

"I understand so, sir."

"Where did you live in St. Petersburg? Who were your friends?"

"I lived on the Nevsky Prospekt in the count's palace there and spent a considerable time in my country house near Tsarskoye Selo. Our best friends were the Volkovs and the Imeretinskys and also the Yanin family."

"I met Madame Yanina many years ago when I was a young man. I thought she was the most beautiful woman in St. Petersburg."

"I am sure she was."

"I understand you wish me to leave my fortune to endow your orphanage."

Valentina resolved to be patient.

"It won't be an orphanage, sir. I am adopting all the children who will come to live in the Domaine Russe with my own family. The children have been through so many dreadful and unnerving experiences and have lost all their own families. I do not wish them to think they are orphans and believe strongly that they need to feel part of a large family again, as they did in Russia."

"Well, you may not call it an orphanage but that is what it is."

Valentina held her tongue, stung by the old man's disapproval, becoming increasingly angry when he spoke.

"I will leave you my money on condition that the establishment be called the Svetlova Orphanage for Russian Refugees. If you will not agree to this I shall leave what I have to the cause of the White Russians who are still hoping to liberate our country from the Bolsheviks."

Valentina looked up at a painting by Goya showing a father eating his own child, the blood running down his jaws as he salivated with enjoyment at the taste of his own flesh. She rose and stood looking down at the sick man.

"Thank you for sparing me your time, sir. However, I did not escape Russia to be dictated to by a gentleman who will not listen to reason. My children will live in the Domaine Russe and they will call it *home* for the rest of their lives. Though I shall not be their real mother, I hope to be allowed to be their guide and counselor for always. An orphan is a child who has lost his entire family and who has no one but the government or an institution to care for him. My children will have gained a new family and therefore cannot be called orphans."

"You are a stubborn creature and a fool. Think what you are losing by your attitude."

"Thank you for your time, sir. Perhaps when I have gone you will reflect on the good your wealth could have done for these poor suffering children."

The old man lay back, staring at the ceiling. He was angry that a woman should call on him to beg for money. The countess had a husband. Why had he not come to plead her case? Perhaps the husband was a cad or, worse, a philanderer with no interest in her charitable endeavors. The old man thought of the plan Valentina's governess had outlined for him, a plan that would cost many fortunes to bring to fruition. He called for his maid and asked for a glass of water and his morphia pills. He was exhausted and in pain. Was there time to worry about Russian orphans?

In December it snowed and Valentina wondered whether to postpone moving into the new property with the children. The countryside would be bare. The house, empty of inhabitants for so long, would be bleak. Then she remembered the anxious faces she had seen on her last visit to the orphanage and hurried to dress. Miss Knatchbull joined her at eleven and together they drove in a fiacre to the suburb of Belleville. It was a small, villagelike suburb of terraced houses and lanes full of leafless trees. Valentina was thinking of the count and wondering if he would be waiting for her at the refuge home. As the cab drew near she looked up and saw children's faces pressed against every window on every floor. She rang the bell and handed over the document she had finally succeeded in winning through the courts, giving her permission to adopt sixty-six children, those whose remaining family had not come to claim them. The count was standing in the hall when she entered.

"My dear, I rented two autobuses to carry our party to the Domaine. I fear you will have our work cut out with the children. Some of them never speak, others cry all the time and most of them are terrified of going with us. In the beginning I think they wanted to be adopted. Now they want nothing more than to be left in peace. I have tried to explain your plan but most of them are unable or unwilling to listen."

"Will you wait near the first bus and take Natty to the second so you can show the children to their seats when I bring them out."

"Very well, my dear, let us pray you haven't made an error in this enormous undertaking. I fear we shall never win the children's affection."

Valentina walked into the Assembly Room, where a nun called for silence. She sat on a window bench, watched by the children. When she spoke, some of them began to cry.

"It's taken me many months to obtain a paper which gives me permission to adopt you all as my own sons and daughters. Some of your parents are dead. In some cases *all* your family members have been executed by the Bolsheviks. There are many of you, therefore, who are completely alone in the world. I'm offering you a home, a real home like the ones you left behind in Russia. I shall expect you to behave like real sons and daughters and I shall behave, as best I am able, as your mother. I shall expect you to do me credit when you go out into the world and to remember that the Domaine Russe is your home and that I shall always be waiting for you to visit me or to continue living there for the rest of your days. I don't wish any child to come with me who is not absolutely sure that he or she wants to live in the Domaine. It is your decision, just as it was your decision to leave Russia. May I ask one of the older children to speak on your behalf."

A young boy of twelve rose.

"Vladimir Stepanovich Fortunov, milady. My father was one of the Tsar's advisers."

"Feel free to say whatever you wish, Vladimir, and whatever the children wish you to ask."

"We would all like to share your home, Countess, but we don't want to be adopted until we are quite sure that none of our relatives is alive."

The boy looked down and Valentina thought how like Nikolai he was, with his corn-gold hair and clear blue eyes. Vladimir continued after thinking awhile.

"Some of us cannot believe that none of our family remains, that everyone is dead. We keep hoping and watching and praying that someone will come to claim us and to take us home to Russia."

Valentina took a sheaf of newspaper cuttings out of her purse.

"I've already recognized the fact that some of your relatives could be alive. I have therefore put advertisements in the leading newspapers in London, Berlin, Rome, Paris and New York. If you have any family left they will know where to find you. Is that satisfactory to you all?"

Vladimir looked for guidance to the other children and Valentina saw a show of hands, a unanimous show of hands. She began to tell the children about the house.

"The Domaine Russe is a very old house in a most beautiful area adjacent to the Château de Rambouillet. It was once one of the most magnificent houses in the region, but now it has been empty for many years and I have had to spend a great deal of money making it habitable. We must learn how to make the estate prosperous and I shall need your help and advice. You'll be given lessons there in French, German and English as well as Russian. You will also learn about art and music from the finest teachers, and science, too, in case any of you wish to become doctors."

The children laughed for the first time at this statement and one of them called out.

"Doctors never get paid, milady."

Valentina continued sternly.

"In the old days in Russia doctors were too proud to send out their bills. Now we are in the year nineteen hundred and twenty-one. Soon it will be nineteen twenty-two and even the rich have business interests because life is expensive in Paris. There are very few servants and I shall expect you all to learn how to earn your own living. Have you any further questions?"

A small girl with auburn ringlets rose and stood shyly waiting for Valentina to give her permission to speak. Valentina nodded approval. The little girl spoke.

"Milady, when we grow older where shall we live? Will we have to leave your orphanage and go out into the world all alone?"

Valentina rose and looked down at the child.

"What is your name and how old are you?"

"Tanya Ivanovna Yanina. I am seven, milady."

"Are you related to Colonel Ivan Grigorevich Yanin?"

"Yes, milady. He was Mama's cousin."

"Well, Tanya, and all of you, listen carefully. You are *not* orphans and my home will never, repeat, *never,* be called an orphanage. It is going to be my home and my sons' home and your home too. You will not refer to yourselves as orphans and you will *never* call your home an orphanage. You have a brand-new family, even though you may have lost the old one. You therefore cannot be orphans. Do you understand my views on this matter?"

"Yes, milady."

The children chorused their reply. Then Vladimir Stepanovich Fortunov rose and asked a question.

"Milady, what shall we call you? If we are not orphans and simply a part of your family we'll not call you Countess and we cannot call you Mama."

"When you are in class you will call me Countess. When we are alone you will call me Valentina. The count will still be referred to as sir because he is not yet used to the familiarity of modern times."

"Very well, Valentina."

Vladimir blushed furiously and sat down with a bump. Valentina walked to the door.

"I am leaving now. Those who wish to come with me will form twos and follow me to the autobuses in which we are going to travel to our new home."

She walked smartly from the house, having thanked the supervisor of the children. When she reached the clearing where the buses were parked, Valentina was gratified to see a long line of children holding hands behind her. She guided them onto the first bus and into the charge of the count. Then she filled the second bus and sat at Miss Knatchbull's side behind the driver.

An hour later they were traveling along a road lined on either side with poplar trees. Valentina saw ahead the Château de Rambouillet and in the distance her new home. She was happy to see the sun shining on the snow, making the property look like a fairy tale castle surrounded by shimmering white. She pointed out of the window.

"That is the Château de Rambouillet and behind it is the great forest where the kings of France used to hunt. There, ahead, is the Domaine Russe."

The children chattered excitedly as they looked out and saw the cream of the stone building lit by pale gold winter sun. Valentina whispered to Miss Knatchbull.

"Say a prayer we shall be successful in this, Natty. I do so want these children to be happy."

"They will, my dear, look at their faces. How lovely the Domaine looks in the snow. I do believe it is the most beautiful house you've ever owned. You must tell me someday how you contrived to buy it."

Valentina stepped down and looked up at the house Masters had bought for her and her new and unruly family. Vasily came and held her hand, as if needing reassurance of his own importance in her life. She bent to his side.

"You know this house well, Vasily, because you and I and Nikolai have been here often during the past few months. Will you show the children to their rooms? Their names are on most of the doors."

Zita was in the kitchen with Dubrovsky and his wife Aimée. She greeted Valentina with a jubilant smile.

"Oh, ma'am, I do love our new house and the land around it. I went for a walk this morning and picked the tastiest mushrooms you ever saw. It's like Russia, only ten times prettier."

Valentina noticed the blush on Zita's cheeks and the look of anticipation in her eyes.

"Who did you meet on your walk, Zita?"

"I met a man who used to work in this area for a family who have now sold their house. It's falling to ruin, he says, and he's looking for work. He invited me to lunch with him on Thursday, ma'am, and I'll go if you give me permission."

"How old is he?"

"He'll be forty-two at the end of the year."

"Of course you must lunch with him. Now, tell me, how are things going in the house?"

"I've given some training to the country girls you took on to clean. They'll all live out so they don't take up precious space. The count's new valet is from St. Petersburg, though he came to Paris when he was twenty. He's still very Russian, ma'am, so that will please Sir."

That night Valentina lay in bed listening to the sound of the countryside, owls hooting, a church bell chiming in the distant town and a local man on his way home from the inn singing overloudly in his merriment. She lit the lamp at her bedside and read again the note Masters had sent to her:

I wish I could be there on the day you move, but I'm stuck here in New York and can't change my plans. You know well enough that your success at the Domaine is going to make me very proud, so work hard and don't let the kids down. I'll be in Paris in June or maybe earlier. I'll take you to lunch under the apple trees if you're free. I'm sending you kisses with this letter. I wish I could wheel down and take a look at you and your new army. Take care and don't stop loving me.

## CHAPTER SEVENTEEN

### Paris, Summer 1923

The count had traveled from the Domaine to Paris to register in the same hotel in which he had lived before going to the Domaine Russe. He felt weary and much older than his years. He kept looking at his watch and twisting his wedding ring. Valentina had agreed to meet him at one for lunch.

Korolenko walked around and around the room trying to find some reason for living. He had fallen in love with his wife on first seeing her. He had admired her spirit, her lack of respect, her spark of diamond hardness and the fact that he would never be able to subdue her. After marrying her, he had found himself unable to love her and had been obliged to accept Yanin's sons as his own. Despite the burning jealousy that had tormented him in the early days he had found it easy to accept Yanin and had eventually come to respect the young officer for his discretion, style and breeding. Yanin had been everything he admired. But now, what to do, how to broach the subject of his wife's infidelity, and what to do if she admitted her liaison with the American? The count sat on the bed, his head buried in his hands. For a few months he had been supremely happy at the Domaine. Then, suddenly, life had become a nightmare. From June of the previous year Valentina had traveled to Paris on frequent occasions, giving as her excuse business meetings with rich persons who might endow the house with their fortunes. The frequent trips to Paris had ceased in September, only to recommence this year in May. Valentina was adored by the children, the staff and the locals. In their eyes she could do no wrong. Why then had he been suspicious enough to follow her to Paris that miserable spring day? Was it really only six weeks ago?

And *why* had he waited to watch as she met the handsome diplomat and disappeared to a suite in the Ritz Hotel for hours of love?

Korolenko closed his eyes, the memory paining him so he could not react with his usual sangfroid. In God's name why did he love her so? And why could he not be satisfied with Valentina's promise never to leave him? The visits to Paris had halted a week ago but he knew they would begin again whenever her lover returned. The count remembered his days in Russia, when his wife had been in love with Yanin and asked himself why he could not do what he had done before, remain her friend and her confidant but never her lover. He shook his head. Yanin had been a fine man. The American was nothing by comparison.

Valentina arrived at the hotel at five to one. Promptness was her virtue and in any case she was nervous. Just when she had thought her husband settled at the Domaine he had elected to return to Paris and the hotel where he had once stayed before. She thought of the meetings she had had with Masters, on *bateaux-mouches* or enjoying a luxurious fling at the Ritz. She wondered if the count had learned of the affair and what course of action he had decided to take. She knocked on the door and found her husband about to commence lunch. The count motioned for her to join him and she sat opposite him and began to talk of a new painting she had just purchased.

"Last week I showed you the painting of the lion and the gypsy woman I had bought from the customs officer who paints in his spare time. Well, today I bought another one from him."

"His paintings are a waste of money."

"I like them and believe he is talented."

"You believe that young drunkard Utrillo has talent and also the one who died, the fellow who painted women with lopsided necks."

"Monsieur Modigliani?"

"He was a lunatic. Who next will you patronize?"

The count looked listlessly at the food he had ordered, conscious that Valentina was watching him closely. He flinched at the directness of her questions.

"Why did you return to this hotel? And why did you ask me to meet you here? I had thought our new home would be sufficient for your needs."

"It is a magnificent house. Did Mr. Masters buy it for you?"

"He did, sir."

As always, Valentina's honesty shocked and the count remembered with longing the early days of their life together when her forthright answers had alarmed and diverted him. He poured himself more wine, conscious that he was drinking too much. When he spoke Valentina knew the moment had come, that her secret affair was no longer a secret. The count chose his words carefully.

"Last year I noticed that you came to Paris very often between the months of June and September. This year it began again, from May until approximately one week ago. One day I decided to follow you from the Domaine to your apartment in St. Germain. You said you were coming to buy books but you were coming to meet Mr. Masters. You went with him to the Ritz and were there in suite two-one-five for three hours."

Valentina looked more confident than she felt but she remained calm.

"Where is this line of questioning leading, sir? I met Alexander Masters in St. Petersburg many years ago. I disliked him, as you probably recall. I met him again, quite by chance, here in Paris three years ago and thought differently about him. My aim in the beginning was to enlist his help in obtaining funds for the children. He has many powerful and rich American friends who have been most generous in my endeavors."

"And after he bought you the Domaine you were grateful and allowed him to love you?"

"No, sir, before he told me about the Domaine I discovered I had fallen in love with him. He's married and will never leave his wife. I am married and will never leave you. However, as I am in the prime of my life I want to enjoy these years before I decline into middle age. I began to have an affair with Alex Masters some time ago. I've been discreet. We meet only in my apartment or in the restaurants where your friends would never go. He takes a suite at the Ritz Hotel whenever it is my birthday. When he is not in Paris I remain at the Domaine and devote myself to you and to the children. I don't think you can say you have been neglected."

The count drank his wine and rang for a waiter to serve Valentina's second course. When the waiter had left he spoke firmly but without rancor.

"I cannot return to the Domaine knowing that Masters purchased it for you without my knowledge. I don't need to tell you that he is no gentleman. He is a philanderer and an imposter and his manners leave much to be desired. When you fell in love with Colonel Yanin I was distressed for many months, but gradually I found myself able to accept him as the father of our sons. Yanin was a gentleman. Masters cannot even walk in his shadow."

Valentina ate without tasting the food. She watched a fly creeping up the window of the count's room and looked to her husband, uncertain what he was going to do.

"What are your intentions, sir?"

"I intend to live here. You will remain at the Domaine and I shall be grateful if you will stay away from me. From this day I do not wish to see you again. You may send Nikolai and Vasily to lunch with me when it is convenient but I shall not see *you*. From the very moment of our first meeting your presence was a barb in my soul. I cannot hate you. On the other hand I am man enough to admit that your presence can only be to my ultimate detriment."

Shocked by the hurt in her husband's tone, Valentina spoke softly, as though remembering happier days.

"When we first arrived in Paris you told me you loved me, and I was grateful for your courage in bringing me and my sons out of Russia. For a few weeks we were happy and I tried very hard to do all in my power to satisfy your need for constant comfort and company. Within a short time you were longing for your country so terribly that nothing and no one else mattered. You had no time for me or for my sons. You thought only of the houses you had lost and the homeland you would never see again. You elected to live in the past, sir. You were not willing to come with me to the present and the future. You may blame me for taking a lover, but I am young and anxious to use every day of my life as if it were my last. I don't know why I need to live so intensely. Perhaps I shall never know. You can blame me for loving someone new but you will have only yourself to blame for causing the loneliness that opened the door to Alex Masters."

The count finished his wine and fell silent. Valentina's words had cut him to the heart because he knew she was right. He looked across the table at her and for a moment his dark eyes held hers.

"I'm sorry I became so dejected. I was very conscious of your desire to please me and of our brief happiness when I tried to accept living in Paris. Sadly, I am getting old and I'm tired to the soul. What happened in Russia was not only the end of my country, it was the end of my life as it had always been. Like a wounded animal I wish to retreat to lick my wounds. Like a wounded animal I cannot forget."

"Nikolai and Vasily will be distressed if you don't return home, sir, the children, too. They love you and need your attention."

"And you, Valentina, what will you feel?"

She thought hard before replying.

"I have come to rely on you, sir. Whatever goes on around me, whatever the turbulence of my emotions, I imagine you will always be there supporting me with your wisdom, caring for me and for our sons. I ask a great deal, I know, but you are a man who has proved himself capable of anything you wish to do. I've never found you lacking when I need you. In my way, sir, I love you. It's our mutual sadness that our marriage was not to be one of those ideal unions that novelists write of, at least not in the way I had hoped. However, in my own way I have been happy with you."

"That is one of the kindest and most loving things you ever said and I thank you. I'm sorry to be an imposition on your life, a husband you never desired, a man who took you away from your home in Paris to a country you never loved. I have a great deal to answer for in your life, Valentina."

"If I were to give you time to think on this matter, sir—if I were to promise never to leave you and never to expose you to ridicule—would it be so very different from our life in Russia?"

"The difference is in me, my dear. I am a gentleman, and for a gentleman to feel as insufficient and as unrewarding a person as those of the lower orders is no life at all."

Valentina left her husband at his request and walked alone down the burning-hot pavements of the Champs-Elysées. The rich had deserted the city for seaside houses in Deauville, Etretat and Honfleur. The newspapers were small in size because as many staff as possible had been given their annual holiday. Many of the shops were closed. Even the flower sellers were absent. Only the tourists staring at famous monuments were undeterred by the emptiness and the heat.

Valentina sat for an hour in the small park between the Rond-Point and the Place de la Concorde. Children were playing on the

grass, watched by eagle-eyed nannies in white and gray. Doves
perched on a statue in the sunlight, their fantails outlined against
an azure sky. The only sounds were the drone of traffic and the
gentle cooing of wood pigeons in the trees. Valentina thought of
Russia and the count's generosity in dealing with her liaison with
Yanin. He could have divorced her or exposed her to ridicule. It
was no wonder he found it impossible to countenance her new love
for Masters. Even she had been unable to pinpoint the exact moment when she had begun to love the American. Even she had
been astonished by the depth of her own feelings. Impulsively she
walked back to the hotel where her husband was alone and lonely,
a fate she knew he did not deserve. She decided not to lie to the
count, simply to ask him to come home. Surely he would be unable
to resist her plea.

The count folded his clothes and put them in his suitcase. This
he did not lock, though the keys were at the side of the bed. He
straightened the bedclothes and closed the terrace window. He was
thinking of Valentina in the turquoise-silk suit she had worn at
lunchtime. He was repeating her compliment word for word, grateful that she felt something for him other than mere gratitude. He
thought how beautiful she was, how priceless and different in every
way from other women. In truth she was neither good nor bad but
an intriguing combination of the two. There was fire in her, a fire
that could scorch the unwary. There was also humility and pity for
those less fortunate than herself. The count shook his head ruefully.
He wanted none of her pity! He adjusted his cravat in the mirror
and when he was satisfied with his appearance sat in the armchair
loading his gun. It was unusually silent outside and this displeased
him and made him hesitate. Then, having made sure everything in
the room was in order, he put the barrel of the gun to the side of
his head. He hesitated. It was not easy. It had taken a man to live
through the years of Valentina's affair with Yanin. It would take a
man to rid her of the last impediment to her freedom. Korolenko
was conscious of a thousand memories rolling through his mind
like black-and-white images in the new moving-picture houses. He
saw his sister Yekaterina eating lunch at the Europa Hotel. He felt
Magda, at the height of her beauty, enticing him into her boudoir
and burying his head in the undulating yellow plumes of her
negligée. Finally he saw Valentina skating on the lake outside the

Flower House, a white-fox hood around her head, a scarlet coat around her body. The count smiled sadly. For love of Valentina he had achieved one brief moment of heroism in bringing her out of Russia. The heroism had been sadly unsustained when he reached Paris and he had sunk back into his torpid longing for Russia. Worse, he had tried to imprison a free bird and had made Valentina unhappy. His was the responsibility for her affair with the American. She was right. It would be better this way.

The noise of the shot resounded in the corridors of the hotel. The receptionist ran from his desk to the first floor. A maid dropped her brush and dustpan in shocked alarm. Valentina entered the hotel and walked upstairs unnoticed by anyone. When she reached the corridor outside her husband's room she saw the chambermaid weeping uncontrollably. A stern-faced housekeeper looked accusingly in her direction.

"Do you know the man in this suite?"

"I am Countess Korolenko, his wife. Is something wrong?"

The housekeeper pursed her lips, weighing Valentina from head to toe.

"The count shot himself a few minutes ago. You'd best not go in the room."

Valentina remembered her first dinner with the count and thought of the compliments he had paid her and his promise to allow her to draw a mustache on the portrait of his mistress. She recalled the moment of marriage, when the count's hand had trembled as she put on the ring. The revolution had defeated many, but not him. He had had a hidden well of courage that had finally evaporated in the light of her affair with Masters. Valentina realized that she had clenched her hands so hard her nails had gone through the skin of her palms. Strength returned to her and pushing the maid aside she made her way to her husband's room.

Korolenko lay on his back, his eyes open, his face an upturned question. A pool of blood had formed by his ear and there was a dark-red hole in his right temple. Valentina sat on the bed, her body ice-cold despite the heat of the day. She picked up two letters the count had left, one to her, the other to his lawyer. Time passed. She did not cry or try to stop the memories that kept running through her mind. A gendarme came into the room, followed by two men from the emergency squad. One of them spoke in a kindly voice.

"Madame, I understand this is your husband. Were you here when he died?"

"I was just returning to see him. When I entered the corridor, the housekeeper told me the count was dead."

"You were here at lunchtime, I understand. Why did you return?"

"I wanted to tell my husband something I had forgotten."

Valentina sat on a wooden bench in the local gendarmerie. The walls were painted dull green, the woodwork brown. The sergeant at the desk was sweating profusely, droplets of perspiration falling onto the charge sheet every few seconds with an irritating plop. Valentina heard the sound of a typewriter in the next office, then the scream of an ambulance siren. She looked at the clock. It was 5 P.M. She rose and spoke sharply to the man on the desk.

"I've been here for two hours. May I not leave? I will give my address, of course."

The man disappeared, returning within minutes and shaking his head regretfully.

"I'm sorry, Countess. They say you must wait. Would you like some coffee?"

"You're most kind."

At ten past eight the original officer came to the bench and nodded curtly, dismissing Valentina. She rose wearily and asked when she could collect the count's body. The officer shrugged.

"Your husband will be buried in a common grave. The bodies of suicides can't receive the blessing of the church."

"I wish to bury the count in the grounds of his home."

"I'll ask permission. Where can we contact you?"

"Ask permission *now*, sir. I've been here half the day. I can wait until you have an answer."

Fifteen minutes later the man returned.

"You can take the body from the Central Mortuary at ten in the morning, Countess."

Valentina walked aimlessly down the Champs-Elysées, turning toward the river and crossing at the Pont Alexandre III. For a moment she paused by an orange iron streetlamp of the Belle Epoque and looked down at the dark river gleaming black in the moonlight. Her mind felt blank and she wondered how long it would take to recover from the shock of what had happened. She felt guilty. The count had surely killed himself because of her. Had he done it because of her? In the early days in Paris he had often expressed a desire to see the end of his life. Was this affair with Masters merely an excuse for the inevitable? From the Palais Bourbon she walked down the Boulevard St-Germaine, seeing little of the bustle on all sides and barely feeling the exhaustion that was fast overwhelming her. A young man took off his hat to her. A violet seller offered her a posy. Valentina walked on, her eyes devoid of expression.

After two days filled with handling the arrangements for the count's funeral, and comforting the children, Valentina sat alone in the orchard of the Domaine reading the note he had left her.

> *My dearest one,*
> Forgive me for what I have done. The fact is I love you and am aware that you will be free at last without me. The urge to grant you your desire coupled with my own selfish longing not to see us drift gradually apart has made me decide to take this drastic action. I am getting old, my dear, and old men have far too much pride. They can bear to lose their homes and their wealth and the power that was once theirs but they cannot bear to lose the one they love. The thought that I might eventually become a mere pest in your way is hideous to me.
> If I may presume to offer you some advice, it is that you tell Nikolai and Vasily that they were born as a result of your union with Yanin and that they are not my true sons. In this way they may come to hate me or you or us both but they will be released from the stigma of being descended from a suicide.
> My respects to you, as always, my love enduring and for ever.
> *Vladimir Vasilievich Korolenko*

Tears ran down Valentina's face and she found it impossible to throw off the gloom that had descended on her since the count's death. Nikolai walked toward her through the orchard and she saw that his face was alight with pleasure.

"I love the summer holidays, Mama. Some of the children are helping with the mustard harvest. They're yellow all over and unable to stop laughing. Vasily looks like a clown in the circus. Mama, you're not crying again, are you?"

"You're old enough to read this, Nikolai."

Valentina handed her son the count's last note and was surprised to see his face remained unchanged as he read it. When he had finished the note he kissed her gently.

"I had already wondered if Colonel Yanin was your lover, Mama. I'm not really shocked to learn that I'm his son and not Papa's at all, though I'm relieved by the count's generosity in allowing me to know your secret. Don't tell Vasily yet, though. He's not old enough to understand. As for me, I'll never tell anyone, I promise."

"Does it not matter to you that I had a lover?"

"I was proud to have the count as my father because he was a gentleman and a hero in my eyes. I'm content to be Yanin's son too, because he was an example to us all and I loved him since I was very small."

"I love you, Nikolai."

"I adore you, Mama. Now you're not to sit here in the orchard going over the past. I've decided not to think of the past for at least a week. Won't you come to the field with me and the children? Everyone's asking about you."

Masters arrived in Paris and went to Valentina's apartment. He found a young man painting the walls of her bedroom. The young man was dressed in workman's overalls and covered in pink paint from head to toe. Masters asked how he had gotten into the apartment.

"The countess lent me her key. I do odd jobs for her now and then. I feel obliged to help her because she keeps sending wood and food and cakes around to me and my wife. She knows I'm just starting out as a writer and she worries in case Hadley and me starve."

Masters held out his hand.

"Alexander Masters."

"Ernest Hemingway, sir. Say, is this color even? I thought I'd surprise the countess, get her over the shock a little."

"The shock?"

"Haven't you heard? Count Korolenko shot himself six weeks ago. Paris has been buzzing with the gossip. There was a court hearing and the countess was asked to appear. They put her photograph in the newspapers and wrote an article that was downright rude, implying she had a lover and that she was about to run off with him. All nonsense, if you ask me, but you know how newspapers like that kind of thing."

Masters noted the acute glance of the young man and the deceptive casualness of his manner. He went to the drawing room and unpacked the gifts he had brought for Valentina and the New York papers he had read on the crossing, which she always scrutinized from cover to cover. He went to the kitchen and made coffee, carrying a cup through to the bedroom where Hemingway was busy finishing the wall. Masters weighed the ceiling and the sections already complete.

"How long are you going to be with this?"

"Another fifteen minutes."

"I'll buy you lunch. Michaud's or the Tour d'Argent?"

"How about the Nègre de Toulouse?"

"I'll expect you to tell me all about the countess. I was going right out there to see her this afternoon."

"Go then. She'll be waiting to see you. She told me the count had left her a problem she didn't know how to resolve. Perhaps you can help."

Later that afternoon Masters sat in the apartment, his mind racing back and forth over the news he had learned. He sat down at the window and looked through a pile of old newspapers and magazines. The headline of one made him frown in distaste: "Love countess's husband commits suicide rather than lose her." Masters looked out on the narrow street and the square beyond. People were hurrying home from work. An old woman was dragging a cart along the gutter, a notice saying "Knives Sharpened" wobbling over her head. Two young students were racing back to their lessons, their faces aglow from excitement at a brief encounter they had had with a demi-mondaine in the Place St.-Sulpice.

Masters thought of his wife, Davina, who had once been the prettiest debutante of the Washington season. They had married and made plans for a home in the country and a family of four. When no children came Davina had started to drink and now day and night were the same to her. Her lovers had all been men who were personalities of the day, a jazz musician, a composer, a charleston champion, a movie star, a gigolo, an artist. He had tried to stop her from taking lovers but Davina was incontrollable. Since meeting Valentina he had no longer cared. Davina had fallen in love with the artist, but no means of persuasion would convince her to grant him a divorce. She had found one of Valentina's letters when she searched his briefcase years previously and had become obsessively jealous of the woman she had never met. Talk of divorce provoked Davina to mention his obvious desire to marry Valentina and often she screamed at him when she was less than sober. "I'll never divorce you, never, never, never. You can wait forever for your fine lady friend." When she was sober Davina was contrite and as persuasive and charming as ever. Masters sighed. At first he had remained in the same house for the sake of her reputation. Then he had moved to live in an apartment in preparation for commencing divorce proceedings. Each time he spoke of divorce she took an overdose of tablets. Each time he went to the clinic to collect her and forgot about divorce again for a few painful months. He thought of Valentina, whose loveless marriage was now behind her. He would marry her someday if he had to drag his own name and Davina's through every court in America. But would she want a figure of scandal, especially after her own brief brush with notoriety? Masters thought of Yanin, the gallant young officer with whom Valentina had been in love for so long. Was it possible to make her forget the passion of her youth and concentrate fully on the love of her prime? He was not sure that it was but was resolved to try his damnedest to make her adore him. He took a train timetable from the drawer. He could take the train or could drive there in an hour or so. He strode downstairs and out to his car. Within minutes he was driving out of the city and into the countryside that led to Rambouillet.

Valentina received the telegram Masters had sent and read it again: "Have heard the news. Am on my way to see you, love you a million." She crumpled the telegram and threw it on the floor. Then she bent and picked it up, straightening it painstakingly on the dresser and reading it wistfully again. She had told herself a thousand times she must not complicate her life with Masters. He was married. She was free and she had her children to think of.

She would still see him, of course, but she would force herself not
to long for a future that could never be. She would accept the situation and try to enjoy what little she had of him. It was ridiculous
to hope for the unattainable. Marriage with Yanin had been unattainable and one unattainable man in a lifetime was enough. With
Yanin, thanks to the count's indulgence, she had been able to lead
an existence that mimicked marriage. With Masters she would
spend her life waiting and hoping for him to return to Paris. She
frowned at the idea and told herself adamantly that she must take
another lover, two or three or four, like other women, thus mini-
mizing her constant longing for Masters. She admitted reluctantly
that she loved Masters and no one else and that she had not the nature for promiscuity. She must simply put the relationship in per-
spective. He must not be her life as Yanin had been. He must not
be the only factor in her happiness. She thought of the children
and of her love for them and was almost content.

One of the girls came into the bedroom. It was Natasha, a frail
young girl of ten. Valentina motioned for her to sit on the stool so
she could watch the process of making up. She was conscious of
the wistfulness in the girl's voice as she recalled past times.

"When I lived in Russia, Mama used to let me watch when she
brushed her hair. It was so long she could sit on it, but yours is a
prettier color, milady."

"You must call me Valentina. The French don't say milady nowa-
days. Of course, they are formal, but once they know each other
well, as we do, they call each other by first names. Sometimes it
takes them years to do this, but we've known each other long
enough."

"But you are my lady and I love you."

"Will you do something for me, Natasha?"

"Of course I will."

"I would like you to go and tell Chef Dubrovsky that he may
take the weekend off to go to his father-in-law's farm for the
harvest." Natasha's face lost its color and she looked afraid and uncertain.

"Who'll cook for us if Chef Dubrovsky isn't here? I hate it when
anyone goes away. I feel sure they won't come back again."

Valentina wondered how long it would take before the scars of
the past healed. She spoke patiently to reassure.

"Chef Dubrovsky is going to bring us a side of pork back from the estate. Now go and tell him he can have permission to go. Zita will cook while he's away."

"She's going to get married and leave us."

"Zita isn't leaving. She and Henri are going to live right here. Henri's going to be my gamekeeper and he and Zita will live in the apartment on the ground floor."

Natasha's face lit up with relief.

"I was sure they'd go away and we would never see them again."

Valentina sat at her dressing table looking at the small pieces of jewelry she had left. She was trying on an old earring that matched the yellow-diamond Tartar ring Yanin had given her when Vasily burst into the room.

"There's a man downstairs asking to see you, Mama. He's wearing a hat like riverboat gamblers and he has a big white car with leather seats."

"Did he give his name?"

"Yes, Mama. He said tell the contessa that Alex Masters has come to call for her. Are you going out with him, Mama? Why does he say Contessa?"

"I suppose he likes the sound better than Countess."

Valentina rushed to the wardrobe and took out her green-silk dress with the pattern of white daisies. She stumbled over a shoe and then over her son, who watched the frantic performance with amusement.

"Who is the man, Mama? He isn't French, because he doesn't wear those old-fashioned clothes like lawyers wear."

"He's American."

"Is he a riverboat gambler?"

"No, he's a diplomat. He has a ranch in the American country-side and his brother in Kentucky breeds horses. Now, does that answer all your questions?"

Vasily ran downstairs to the hall where Masters was waiting. Tapping the American on the shoulder, he asked politely, "Do you carry a gun, sir?"

"Only when I'm going out to shoot someone."

Vasily beamed at the response.

"When I'm older I shall come to visit you in America with

Mama. I've always wanted to see real cowboys and their ranch house."

"I'll look forward to entertaining you, Vasily."

Zita peeped out of the kitchen and saw Valentina in her green silk with a new white cloche on her head. She was looking at Masters without saying a word. Goodness, Zita thought, Milady is in love again, and what a fine gentleman he is, with his fancy clothes and his foreign hat. She saw Masters handing Valentina a small box of dark-blue velvet.

"I reckon it's time I gave these back to you. I bought them for you at the auction a long time ago. I got them for near to nothing because all the other Russians were selling their jewels and no one wanted what they had to offer anymore."

Opening the box, Valentina saw the emerald necklace Yanin had given her and the two Fabergé eggs she had missed so often in the melancholy days of autumn. Masters took out another box and handed it to her.

"Just in case you get tired of thinking about the past this will give you something to look forward to in the future. Now let's go get into my car. I'm taking you to dinner at that restaurant near your apartment in Paris and tomorrow we're going to a party."

Valentina looked down at a ring of stark simplicity, a diamond with a pearl set at an oblique angle to the stone. She put it on her finger, removing Yanin's yellow-diamond ring for the first time since she had received it. For a brief moment she felt a pang of conscience. Then she looked questioningly at Masters.

"What does this mean, Alex?"

"It means forever, and don't you forget it."

# CHAPTER EIGHTEEN

## The Domaine, May–June 1924

The chestnut trees were in blossom in the fields that stretched forever and there were men working with plows and horses amid the deep red earth of the Domaine. Valentina looked out on the scene and was content. In the main classroom of the school section of the property, Miss Knatchbull was holding an English class for the younger children. In the other classroom a French mathematics teacher was putting the elder boys through their paces. In the music room the Russian children's choir was practicing for its latest recital. In the courtyard she could see Zita pumping water to her new kitchen garden. At her side there was a pram containing the child just born to the maid and her husband, a boy called Louis, whose birth had united the children and made them really believe that the Domaine was their home forever. The children called Louis "our baby" and there were frequent quarrels as to whose turn it was to wheel the pram around the courtyard. Valentina saw a gig approaching the outer gates. She strained her eyes to see who it was, but only when the gig entered the courtyard did she recognize the young man who stepped down. She examined the epaulettes of the English-style overcoat and then the slim, pale face with its penetrating eyes and silky black hair. The visitor looked appraisingly up at the house before entering the hall. Valentina rushed downstairs, calling to him over the balustrade.

"Dmitry! Dmitry!"

He clicked his heels and kissed her hand, looking into her eyes and seeing that though she was older she was essentially the same countess he had always admired. Her eyes still asked questions he did not know how to answer. Her laughter was still infectious and warming.

Valentina led him into the salon and for some time they sat together drinking coffee and bringing each other up to date. Valentina told him the truth about her husband's death and about the Domaine Russe and her love for Alexander Masters. Dmitry explained that he had been living in England since his escape from Russia with the Korolenko family. He had studied at the Military Academy, passing with flying colors to the delight of his aunts. Disaster had struck when an epidemic of influenza robbed him in quick succession of both elderly aunts, all that was left of his father's family. In her will, the elder of the two left him her home and what remained of the Borshchov money. Dmitry looked appealingly at Valentina.

"What am I to do, Countess? All I was trained to do was to manage one of my father's estates. I was not the eldest son and though I attended the Lycée I was not destined for the army. I did not imagine that I would inherit my father's title. Before the revolution it was unthinkable."

"I hope you'll stay and manage this estate. It will be a hard task, though. The land hasn't made a profit for thirty years. You could take over the dower house if you came here."

"I would rather live here in one of the apartments. But are you certain of this offer, Countess? If I were to sell all I own in England, may I really stay here for the rest of my life?"

"You may stay as long as I stay; forever is only as long as I have sufficient money to run the Domaine. I must tell you that I have a very large loan from the local bank at this moment, and unless the estate becomes more profitable in future I cannot be certain of being able to keep the house. At the present time we live off the interest on the investments I made when I first came to the Domaine and on gifts from Russian families living in Paris. Our biggest income comes from the choir."

"What choir?"

"Our children formed a choir to sing Russian and English songs. They perform in theaters in Paris during the winter season. I accompany them wherever they go and have arranged contracts guaranteeing us a good part of the box-office takings. I feel that is

my greatest achievement, apart from bringing the children here in
the first place."

"Have you no other money at all?"

"I have a fund-raising committee that organizes fêtes, culls rich
companies and individuals for money. The committee manages to
bring in enough to keep the house and land reasonably solvent,
though I have yet to learn how to pay off my bank loan."

"You've come a long way from Russia. Running companies, theatrical events, charitable organizations was not your métier in those
days."

"I would do anything to keep my children safe and secure."

"How did the choir come about?"

"Every Christmas we have singsongs. Soon everyone wanted the
children to sing at their parties. Miss Knatchbull and I decided we
could exploit the children's talent for their future good. So far their
earnings have been my biggest single reliable income."

"How many children do you have here?"

"I have sixty-six. I was going to adopt a hundred but some were
claimed by their remaining relatives. But what of you, Dmitry?
What will you do? Will you return to England to sell your house
and settle your affairs?"

Dmitry looked down sheepishly.

"I already have, Countess. Once I knew where you were and
what you had done, I was certain you'd find a place for me. I'll
make your estate profitable, you'll see; you don't have to worry
about that side of your business anymore."

Vasily entered the room and recognizing his old friend rushed
into Dmitry's arms.

"What are *you* doing here, Dmitry? How do you like our new
home? How did you find us?"

"I had a magic stone that told me where you were."

"Are you going to stay?"

"Forever."

Vasily rushed whooping around the room until his mother covered her ears.

"Enough! Take Dmitry to the yellow room and then show him
around the estate. He's going to be our new manager, so you can
show him all the worst parts of the land as well as the good ones.

We have five hundred acres, Dmitry, but only the kitchen gardens and the orchard save me money."

When Vasily had gone, Valentina went to the piano and sat down to play. Leafing through the music she found a piece that was one of Masters' favorites, a Brahms lullaby: "Close your eyes, my little one, the day is over. . . ." She did not play the piece but sat looking at the words. Masters had gone away in January, having told her that he would be coming less frequently to Paris in the future. The inevitable reassignment loomed ahead, when and if he could settle his marital affairs. Valentina thought of Davina, the woman about whom she knew very little except that she would not divorce her husband. Masters had said Davina led her own life. What did it mean? If she had a life of her own why did she cling to her husband? Was it that she feared the stigma of divorce? Or was she vindictive and possessive, making sure that if she could not retain her husband's affection no one else would either. Valentina began to play the lullaby, at first gently, as it was written. Then, as her anger against Davina mounted, she banged out the melody line and jazzed it up so it became unrecognizable. From the hall Vasily called out that a visitor had arrived. Valentina did not hear. She was shredding the lullaby into ribbons so the melody became a clarion call to battle.

Masters stood looking down at her, aware of her anger and of the frustration she normally concealed. When they had first become lovers, Valentina had accepted that they were both married and that the relationship could never be more than a bittersweet affair. Now she wanted more and he wanted more and was resolved to have his way. But at what price? Would the price be a scandal of such dimension it would cost him her love? She slammed the keys all at once, making a cacaphony of discord. Masters startled her when he spoke.

"Is that how you really feel?"

Valentina looked up, startled to find the object of her thoughts suddenly before her. She rose and without a word walked into Masters' arms, burying her head against his shoulder. She had once said she wanted to be invisible, so she could be assimilated into his body and never parted again. Masters stroked her hair.

"Are you angry with me, Valentina?"

"With you and with myself for wanting so much and not being

satisfied with what I have. I'm so happy to see you, Alex. How long can you stay?"

"For a week. May I stay here? This is a purely private visit, I've nothing to do in Paris."

She sat on the rose-damask sofa that matched the curtains and the upholstery of the bois claire chairs. Masters looked around appreciatively at the cavernous fireplace, the shaded lamps and objects that were precious to her, all displayed on low tables. He picked up a pebble that seemed incongruous by the side of the Russian ornaments and tiny lace fan from Valentina's first ball.

"Where does this pebble fit in with your collection of memories?"

"That's the stone you wedged our unsteady table with when you took me to lunch at La Pêche Miraculeuse."

"I love you, Valentina."

"Why are you sad?"

Masters watched as she ordered tea. When she returned to his side she looked deeply into his eyes.

"You look as if you bring bad news."

"Couldn't be worse."

"What is it?"

"I've been assigned to the Orient, a two-year stint in India. Davina won't be with me."

"Why are you being sent there?"

"This is a short posting so I can make some decisions about the future. They don't realize that it's Davina who needs to make the decisions and that she never will."

"Why don't you divorce her for adultery? She's given you ample evidence."

"I will when I get back, if there's no other way, but I don't like the idea. When you make a fool or an exhibition of someone you also make it of yourself. I'll lose my job and my job means something to me. I'm a patriot, and what I do is important to my country."

"I thought you were a diplomat."

"I'm a diplomat of sorts."

"What if Davina won't agree to a divorce when you return to America?"

"I'll resign. I made that decision a few weeks back."

That night they loved frantically, two people in a hurry to reach the nirvana of ecstasy. As Masters' body thrust into hers, Valentina forgot all the preoccupations and anxieties of the past and allowed herself to drift on a cloud of sensuality that dulled hurt and accentuated her excitement. Masters loved her, possessing even her thoughts and hopes and secrets. When they had loved they rested. Then Valentina began to love him, relishing the scent and the feel and the longing that was intensified with her every touch.

That night Valentina lay awake trying to work out her problems. Masters had said that after two years he would resign if he could not persuade his wife to agree to a divorce. He would have no option but to resign because there would be a terrific scandal. Davina's past would be paraded for the gossips to enjoy. Masters' condoning of her adultery would be questioned and analyzed. He would surely not be able to say that he did not care a damn, that he was in love with someone else and no longer his wife's keeper. Valentina shrugged. She did not care for scandal. She had tasted it and had recovered from its brief malady but it had left a sour taste in the mouth. She began to make plans and almost woke Masters to tell him what she had been thinking. Instead, taking pity on his restlessness, she went downstairs to the kitchen and found Miss Knatchbull drinking coffee at a table overlooking the garden. The Englishwoman's face was pale and she had obviously been deep in thought.

"Couldn't you sleep, Natty?"

"I could not. My dear, who *is* that man?"

"His name is Alexander Masters. He is an American diplomat and I'm in love with him. I've been in love with him for four years and have been meeting him in secret throughout that time whenever he came to Paris."

"Well, that's honest if nothing else. Is he married?"

"Yes, Natty, he is."

Miss Knatchbull pursed her lips and stood with her back to Valentina so she could not see the emotions passing on her face.

"Colonel Yanin was a gentleman, as you know, my dear. Is this man a gentleman?"

"He loves me, Natty."

"A man who wears clothes like that could be a scoundrel."

"I love him, whatever he is."

"Dear me, just when I thought I was settled for life."

"You *are* settled for life, Natty. I shall never sell the Domaine, and now we've taken on some new teachers you'll have to oversee everything for me. When you're here I feel I have no need to worry about anything. The children love you and need the stability you give them. You're settled and everything is beginning to work well. I want to allow myself a little time of my own."

"And this man, does he want you to run away with him?"

"He leaves for India in a week's time. He'll be going alone and has been posted for two years."

Miss Knatchbull looked at Valentina and loved her for her honesty and the way she explained everything she knew about Masters' wife, who led her own life. When Valentina had finished her story, Miss Knatchbull became thoughtful. It was one thing to love Yanin while being married to the count, but what would happen if Valentina persisted in her love for the American? If he was unable or unwilling to divorce his wife there could be a calamity. There could even be more children. And all the while Valentina could only expect an occasional visit, a mere reminder of the happiness for which she longed. Miss Knatchbull gave her best advice.

"I think it's a scandal and I'm not at all sure I shouldn't horsewhip the fellow *and* his big hat. One thing is certain, for two years you must concentrate on your work and your estate and your children. Then, if you're still of the same mind, you must see if you cannot come to some more satisfactory arrangement with Mr. Masters."

"What exactly do you mean?"

"I mean he must give up his job and come here to live with you or you must go to live there with him. A mere day or two of being together isn't enough."

"I can't believe you're giving me this advice."

"I was in love once, a long time ago."

Valentina waited expectantly. When Miss Knatchbull said no more she inquired the outcome of the passion. Miss Knatchbull shook her head wryly.

"The gentleman concerned was married. He suggested an alternative arrangement which I refused, of course. Then I spent the next thirty years wishing I had not. Dear me, I've said too much. I must go back to bed. It's a good job I have no children. The worrying I've experienced on your behalf has often been murderous. I can only think that if I had had a child my worries would have propelled me to an early grave."

The following morning Valentina and her lover rode to Maintenon to eat lunch at the Cheval Blanc. They sipped pastis as they waited for the waiter to bring the meal and talked of things that interested them both. They avoided mention of the coming separation and spoke of the house.

"Does much work remain to be done, Valentina?"

"Not a great deal on the house but the land is being completely reorganized since Dmitry arrived. I'm lucky he and Zita's husband get on. Every morning they go off together like conspirators to devise methods of making the estate profitable. I don't know how long it will take, but I think they will succeed."

"I envy them."

"You should envy them, Alex. They live in the Domaine and are absolutely content. They don't have to travel or to be separate from their family. They're going to spend the rest of their lives with me in my home, while you wander the earth like a rolling stone."

"I love you, Valentina. Try to understand that what I do is important to me. My parents taught me to be a patriot and my work is for my country."

"Is it secret work?"

"Sort of."

They exchanged glances and were silent, content not to disturb the peace of the day. On the way back to the Domaine, Masters picked a bouquet of honeysuckle and handed it to Valentina. She smelled the sweet scent of the flowers and thought how she would press them and look at them with longing in the dark winter days. She frowned, annoyed with herself for thinking of the lonely days ahead. When she reached her own land she walked her horse and they looked over the hillside newly planted with pine trees. Masters admired the stables and the horses she had bought and then walked after her through the avenue of beech trees that led to the escutcheoned front door. There he kissed her and followed her through the endless corridors of the house, pausing to study marble statues, impressionist paintings and open fires already stacked with logs in readiness for the winter nights. In one of the rooms he noticed that the walls had been painted with mustard flowers.

"This is new, isn't it?"

"A local artist did the murals for me."

"Are you planning to re-create the house you used to have in Russia?"

Valentina smiled at the sudden anxiety in his tone. Masters was still troubled by her past, she knew, and rightly so because she had not managed to assimilate all the things that had happened. Like her, he still dwelt on the peaks and valleys of her younger years, weighing their effect on his own relationship with her. She answered tactfully, determined not to upset him.

"No one can ever re-create the past and I don't want to. My aim is to make this house my today home, not my yesterday one. The young man who painted this room is also going to paint scenes of Rambouillet and the forest in the chapel. He's talented and I plan to use his local knowledge to the betterment of the property. In that way the children will feel familiar with their surroundings and a part of them."

The next day they drove to Paris and booked into the Ritz. Valentina laughed delightedly as Masters led her to the suite in which they had often met for lunch. This time there was no orchestra softly playing and they made love to the sound of the traffic of early evening, horns hooting, bicycle bells ringing, autobus claxons calling. At six Masters ordered champagne. Valentina felt a trickle of melancholy seeping into her soul. When Masters and she made love she forgot everything. But after love the sadness came. Usually it was short-lived, but today it did not go away. She watched as waiters wheeled in tables and Louis XIV chairs. Then a procession appeared, holding dishes of everything she most adored. She lifted the lid off the turkey and the candied potatoes and the small green peas. Masters raised his glass.

"To you, my love. I hope you'll be happy during my time away. You haven't realized yet that it's going to give you a chance to get to know yourself deep down. You've not been alone since you were a child. When I come back I expect to find the Domaine prospering and you with all your decisions made."

"My decisions depend on you, Alex."

"Think about it when I'm away. Think hard, Valentina, because if we're going to be together for life we've hardly touched trouble yet. You might decide you'd rather have the quiet life."

They arrived back at the Domaine at 4 A.M. and were told that

Vasily had developed measles. Valentina hurried to her son's room and went to sit at his side.

"I'm here, Vasily, everything's going to be all right."

"Are you sure?"

"Absolutely sure."

Valentina turned out the light and sat holding her son's hand, amused when he spoke of Masters.

"Mr. Masters told me they have wild horses on his ranch in America. I'm going out there when I'm older to work as a hand. Nikolai doesn't like horses much, but I do, and I shall ride them from morning till night. Mr. Masters' brother breeds horses too. He has the finest stud in Kentucky. I could work there, too."

Dawn was breaking when Valentina went back to her room. She stood at the window watching the deep-gold light of morning rising over the fields. There was a sudden stir of people from the nearby village pushing farm carts laden with produce to the Sunday market. She went downstairs and found Masters eating breakfast.

"If I catch measles I'll not be able to leave for India. Shall I go to Vasily's room and have him breathe on me?"

"If you catch measles everyone else in the house will, and I shall have a hospital on my hands. Aren't you tired, Alex? I heard you wandering around in the night."

"I'm taking you to Montfort today. I hear there's a great market there and a good restaurant near the castle."

"I vote we stay at home. I want to stare at you all day so I won't forget a single line of your face."

"You'll come to Montfort. You can stare at my wrinkles another time."

The days passed too quickly and by the end of the week Valentina had her fund of memories, lazing under the willow trees near the old mill stream, visiting restaurants of the area and buying souvenirs in ancient villages, lest she forget a single moment of the last precious days. She tried not to think of the morning when she would walk with Masters to his car and wave good-bye with a smile on her face. Would he return from India? She had heard rumors of fevers that killed those who ventured to the tropics. She looked out at a starry night sky and a wide harvest moon that seemed to mock her premonitions. Masters entered the room and stood behind her, kissing her neck.

"Look what one of the kids gave me."

He showed Valentina a rusty horseshoe.

"Which child gave it to you?"

"Vladimir Fortunov. He said it was to bring me luck in case pirates tried to rob me while I was on board ship."

It was a chilly night with a faint but persistent breeze. Masters put his jacket around Valentina's shoulders and drew her into the doorway of the dovecote.

"Let's walk to the river and I'll show you the wild flowers I found today. I'm going away tomorrow, Valentina. When I come back you'll have had plenty of time to see what life's like when you're alone. I don't want you to regret anything once we're together. Have a taste of freedom and see if you still want me when I come back. I don't think you realize what's going to happen once I'm out of the way. Every man in Paris is going to want to make love to you or marry you."

Valentina considered this unexpected thought.

"I shall tell them I'm in love."

"They'll want you all the more."

"I'll go out with all of them and see if I really *do* love you best."

"God damn it, Valentina, I'm leaving tomorrow."

"Kiss me again."

"Let's get back to the house; kissing's not enough right now."

At dawn Valentina walked downstairs to join Masters, who was breakfasting in the conservatory, surrounded by passion flowers and vines. They barely spoke. Both were distressed by the imminent parting and less than usually confident about the future. As the clock struck eight Valentina followed Masters to the courtyard, where his car was parked. He stepped inside and looked up at her.

"What do I say? Thanks for everything. I'll see you when I come back."

"Say 'I love you, Valentina.'"

"I love you, Valentina. I love you and you'd better know it. I'll leave the car outside your apartment. Use it while I'm away but remember it will break down if anyone else steps inside—any man, at least."

Valentina ran to the boundary wall and stared after the car until it was a chalk-white dot on the pathwork of green and gray. When she could see it no longer she walked back inside the house, feeling emptier than she could ever remember feeling. There were two ways to make time pass quickly. She could work like a dog to perfect the estate, concentrating hardest of all on the children she adored. Or, as Masters had said, she could play harder than she had ever played before, attending parties, séances, theatrical performances and flirting outrageously with men. She thought of the stories of Zelda Fitzgerald, who boasted she had "kissed" a hundred men and to whom kissing meant something more than a mere touching of lips. Could *she* allow her body to be used by the hunger of the men she met? As she ate breakfast Valentina realized that she knew nothing of her capabilities and incapabilities. Her body had been loved by two men and never touched by any other. Her mind was virgin territory. She remembered Masters' last lingering kiss and the wave he had sent from the far side of the mustard field. She knew she had everything she wanted in him, if only he could stay by her side. If he did not, she must do her best to forget him until he returned.

Nikolai joined his mother as she sat drinking endless cups of coffee. He looked anxiously at her.

"What are you going to do now that Mr. Masters has gone away, Mama?"

"I'm going to work hard at being alone. I haven't been alone before, not since I was a very young girl. I shall learn a great deal in the next two years."

Nikolai shook his head ruefully. Did his mother mean she was going to work hard at being alone by going into seclusion? What did she mean by speaking of herself as being alone when there were so many people and children in the house? He shrugged resignedly. He could never tell what she might do next. He resolved to keep a firm eye on her until Masters returned.

# CHAPTER NINETEEN

## Kentucky, Spring 1927

Valentina was sitting on a rocking chair on the ranch-house porch of Brett Masters, Alex's brother, and going over the events of the past two years. During Alex's absence in India she had spent three days each week traveling from the Domaine to Paris to seek bequests that would secure the future of her property. It had been hard work and she had not been entirely successful. The children had settled down at last. They no longer had nightmares and screamed the nights away. They had a home and had realized it at last. Valentina patted her pocket, where she kept the letters she had received that day asking when she would be returning home. Dmitry, her dear estate manager, had written to say that at last the estate was beginning to thrive. He had taken on a master viticulturist to create a new wine for the Château Russe label and was hopeful that it would be a great success. Valentina thought of the day when she had received an invitation to bring her sons to America. What a reunion she and Masters had had and how Nikolai and Vasily had taken to America. Then Brett had contracted polio and the invitation that had been for six weeks had extended to six months. Valentina's mind turned again to the children of the Domaine and she knew she must soon go home. In the meantime she would enjoy Kentucky and all the different and wonderful things she had discovered there.

There were white board fences all around and groves of cedar, hickory and willow. Waxen magnolias welcomed the spring and there were lawn parties and trips to the horse auctions. During the winter Valentina had photographed snow geese migrating to warmer climates and in the early spring egrets and herons on the lake. She had learned to enjoy carrot cake and blue point oysters and even Yankee pot roast steaming with red cabbage. It was a different world and one where they had been made truly welcome.

Valentina thought lovingly of her sons. Nikolai was working on a newspaper in Washington, thanks to Masters' influence. He had shown her a book *in embryo,* fed from his experiences in Russia, set down in a journal meticulously kept from childhood. She felt sure success would lie ahead for him. Her mind turned to Vasily and she thought how radically he had changed since arriving at the ranch. He had always wanted to work with horses and Kentucky offered the best. She had mulled over Masters' advice: "Let the boy stay here with Brett. My brother can teach him more in a year than he would learn in ten at school." And so it had been.

Vasily was sitting by the sawmill looking out at an empty expanse of fields and hills. He had been to the basketmaker's shop and then to the carpenter, leaving messages from Brett as instructed. He was idyllically happy in the new country. He thought of his mother and how everyone had been excited that morning because one of Alex Masters' friends was due to arrive for a week's stay en route to New York and then Spain, the country of his origin. Vasily rolled the foreign name around his mouth, Don Francisco Ortiz Vidal de la Pedrugada. He preferred the simple names of America, like Job and John and Chad and Dan. He was walking through the mud near the duck pond when he saw horsemen approaching. He ran to the top of a hill and stood straining his eyes to assess the visitors.

In a four-wheeler surrounded by men from Brett's estate, Don Francisco and his daughter were wiping dust from their clothes in readiness for being presented to their hosts. They had traveled by train from Jefferson City, Missouri, and had been picked up at the station. They were planning to stay for a week in order to rest before their journey across the sea. Don Francisco was thinking of the ship that would take them home and what would be waiting when they arrived. His mind returned to the day when he had learned that his brother was dying. Don Francisco and Elena had crossed the ocean to stay with his brother during the long illness, and to help manage the ranch. The funeral had been followed by an auction of the estate. This had given him a new fortune, one he had never expected as he was considerably older than his brother. He turned to look at his daughter, Elena, and was displeased by what he saw. She was sad to be leaving America. She did not want to go home. The old man felt furious and frustrated because he had never understood the enigmatic creature who was his daughter.

Elena was thinking of Spain and how strange it would be to live the old life again, perpetually told to behave like the lady she was, chaperoned at every turn and never allowed to ride astride a fast horse as she had secretly done during their long stay on her uncle's estate. She looked out of the carriage window and saw a tall young man with jet-black hair watching her intently. Elena's heart quickened and she frowned, because the young man was obviously a ranch hand, if his clothes were anything to go by. Disappointment clouded her mind, because her father had decreed that she mix only with those who were her social equals and had even gone so far as to forbid her to speak with men on the ranch where they had been living for the past eighteen months. Don Francisco's words echoed in Elena's mind: Once we return to Spain you will no longer ride unchaperoned and sitting astride a horse like a man. Don't think I do not know what you have been doing. I am ashamed that my brother permitted such behavior. He had become too American for his own good. When we arrive in Spain you will put up your hair and you will behave as your late mother did, with decorum and gentility. I do not wish to have a wildcat for a daughter. Wildcats stalk the plains intent only on having their way. They know nothing of the obligations of inheritance. . . . Elena forced her eyes away from the handsome young man on the hill and tried to concentrate on her father.

"Are you feeling better, Papa? You're still very pale and I fear you may have caught cold."

"I long to be home. If Cayetano had not insisted on my presence I should never have come to America. I fear this visit will have changed us both forever."

Alex welcomed the guests and introduced them to Valentina and then to his brother, who was confined to a wheelchair. The two women weighed each other as the men were chatting. Elena saw a tall, slim woman whose age was difficult to judge. The lady was dressed in a blue suit patterned with cornflowers. Her limbs were brown from the sun and she was sophisticated in a way that Elena found both modern and yet not. Elena thought sadly, Papa will not like the countess but I shall and I shall not care if he chastises me. Valentina saw a girl with petal-soft skin and shiny black hair. Her eyes were almond-shaped and dark, her mouth curved like a bow. Elena was eighteen, petite and eager for life. Valentina approved of the proud gaze and the nervousness well concealed, betrayed only by a tenseness in the hands. She led Elena upstairs to the guest suite and showed her the living room she would share with her father and the private bathroom only she would use. Elena's dark eyes widened as she sat on the bed and touched the shimmering satin spread.

"After the ranch where I have been living, this seems very grand. Papa told me about the horse-breeding estates of Kentucky, but I had not expected them to be so beautiful. I also saw tobacco in the fields. Is this another famous product of the area?"

"This is a horse-breeding estate primarily but they grow tobacco in the far fields, as you saw. On windy days you can smell the scent of the flowers. It's like nothing else on earth and I shall miss it when I go home."

Elena looked down and Valentina realized that she was apprehensive. She tried to be reassuring.

"You and your father can stay as long as you like. You've had a very long journey, so do tell Don Francisco to rest. When you travel to New York I shall be traveling with you."

Elena's face lit up with pleasure.

"I have not been looking forward to the journey to New York. Papa is troubled by the change America has made in me. He keeps telling me to be how I was before I came here, but I cannot. We left Spain only a year and a half ago, but I was a child then and I am a woman now."

"All fathers want their daughters to remain little girls. We have to teach them very gently that we're women."

Elena walked to the window and looked out at the paddock. Vasily was approaching the front door. She looked closely at him and then turned to Valentina.

"The countryside around here is very beautiful. There is no grass where I live in Spain. At the end of each season the ground is so dry we must feed the horses and bulls by hand. The sun in Andalusia devours the surfaces of the land so we have learned to do without grass. May I ask who that young man is who uses the front door of the house? I saw him as I was approaching this property and thought he was a ranch hand."

"That's my son, Vasily. He's learning about horse breeding from Brett. He'll be staying on here after I leave, unless he changes his mind."

"He has adopted the American way of dressing, like a servant."

Valentina tried not to laugh at Elena's manner.

"My sons are descended from the very finest aristocracy of Russia. They're both aware of that and don't feel the need to dress up and adorn themselves. In Russia we say that only the newly rich dress up to work."

When Valentina had gone, Elena sat for a long time thinking of what had been said. Vasily Korolenko was descended from the finest aristocracy of Russia, yet he dressed like a ranch hand. She wondered if her father was one of those newly rich about whom the countess had spoken with disdain. Elena brushed her hair till it shone and then selected two of her dresses for pressing. She had no modern clothes and was conscious that she might appear ridiculous in her archaic outfits. She looked at the scarlet dress that reached to her ankles. The other was emerald green and even longer, with a boned waist in the old-fashioned style. Elena held them against her body, swaying from side to side as she contemplated their faults. Then she had an idea and sat with a pair of scissors, cutting off the hems.

Vasily ran upstairs two steps at a time and hammered on the door of his mother's room. She hurried to let him in.

"Is there a fire, that you need to make so much noise?"

"Mama, my gray pinstripe suit doesn't fit me anymore. I'm afraid I've grown again and the evening jacket is also too small. I need new clothes immediately."

"We've been here for six months and all you've worn are your working clothes. May I ask why you suddenly need new things?"

"Alex says we're going to have a ball tonight to welcome Don Francisco and his daughter. They're planning it in the old-fashioned style and I must wear evening dress. What am I to do, Mama?"

Valentina looked at the scarlet face, the anxious eyes, and tried to understand the change in her son.

"I'll ask Alex if his brother can lend you a dinner jacket. You're about the same size as Brett used to be. He can also lend you or give you his tweed jackets and that lovely gray suit of his. He isn't going to be wearing them again. He's lost so much weight since he became ill; Alex says he's half the size he used to be."

"Can we ask Alex's tailor to call later? I can wear Brett's clothes till my own are ready. How long will they take?"

Valentina sat at the dressing table spraying scent on her neck. Vasily walked up to her, held her lightly from behind and kissed the top of her head.

"Mama, one other thing. There's going to be an orchestra tonight and they're going to play all the old-fashioned tunes. Will you teach me to waltz? Nikolai knows how to do all the dances but I never wanted to learn. I just need to know how to waltz, nothing else."

Valentina had the good sense not to laugh and without further ado she put on a gramophone record and began to count to the music. She showed Vasily how to approach an old-fashioned girl, how to hold her so close but no closer. She counted firmly, one-two-three, one-two-three, relieved to find that her son was light on his feet despite his height. After a few turns around the room the lesson ended and she gave Vasily her best advice.

"Sometimes you forget to count when you begin to dance and then you tread on your partner's toe. Until you're quite sure of yourself, remember to count, Vasily. Come back later this afternoon for another lesson if you like."

"Yes, Mama, thank you for your time. I do love you."

He dashed out, his face wreathed in smiles, and was last seen waltzing back to his room, turning gracefully in correct time and counting softly under his breath, one-two-three, one-two-three. Valentina closed the door of her room and turned off the record. Her eyes were thoughtful as she went over the conversation, thinking of the jerkiness of Vasily's movements, the coltlike eagerness of his demands. He was in love or thought he was and he had not yet met Elena. Like most mothers she found it difficult to imagine her sons in love or married. Nikolai was diligent in his work and ambitious to be an author. She had never seen him with a woman and he had never confided his innermost thoughts. Vasily had always been so contrary she had thought it impossible that any woman could thrill his churlish soul, let alone set it on fire. But Elena's appearance had lit a flame that could be difficult to extinguish. They were too young to marry and in any case Elena was older than Vasily. They came from different worlds and cultures. Valentina thought of Masters and admitted that coming from different worlds was not important if love was involved. She shrugged. She would not think of problems when the two young people had not even met. She would watch and wait and try not to be the worried mother, apprehensive about her young.

Elena appeared for lunch in the red dress, its hem decorously reaching the middle of her calves. Her father took one look at the length of the skirt and ordered her back to her room to change into something more suitable. Elena fled, her eyes full of tears. A heavy silence filled the room and no one spoke for some time. Valentina saw Vasily glowering fiercely in Don Francisco's direction. She hoped he would remain quiet and not start arguing, as had often been his way. It was half an hour before Elena returned, her eyes red-rimmed from crying. Valentina did her best to remedy the situation by asking about the family property in Córdoba. Don Francisco replied while his daughter toyed with her food.

"Our home is in an area that was once a stronghold of the Moorish occupation in Spain. The estate is of a modest size, unlike the estates of America. You used to have a million acres, Alex, until you sold them all and resettled in France. Your brother has half that amount. I have barely a million square meters, a mere fraction of the size."

"And what do you grow?"

"I breed bulls and horses, Countess. The bulls of Don Francisco Ortiz are the bravest and most tenacious bulls in Spain. The people of our province are like the fighting bulls. We don't give way, we go always forward. We know how to fight and we die bravely."

Another long silence followed this formal speech. Then Alex apologized for his brother's absence.

"Brett's been overdoing it these last few weeks. First he went to the tobacco auctions, then he rode in my car to see a foal at the Main Chance Ranch. The illness has worn him out and made him weak. He decided to rest so he could be sure to join us tonight."

"I hope your brother will soon recover his health, Alex. I remember well his great strength when he came to visit you on your ranch in Missouri. He was almost a fighting bull himself. But tell me why you sold your property. My brother was truly astonished to hear that you had decided to do so."

Vasily looked across the table at Elena and was surprised to be given a smile as their eyes met. Valentina watched her son in his smart gray jacket with his hair almost tidy for the first time she could remember. She had been right. Vasily had fallen in love. How long would it take before the malady was over? She looked again at Elena and knew that though she had lived a sheltered life she had a sophistication Vasily would not yet understand. Boys always seemed less knowing than girls and Vasily was less knowing than most.

After lunch the Spaniards retired for the traditional siesta. Soon Don Francisco's snores could be heard through the open windows of the house. Vasily went to his room and changed into the red-tartan shirt and tough blue-cotton trousers he wore for work. He went to the stables and was currying his favorite horse when he felt someone watching him from the door of the stable. Turning, he saw Elena in the scarlet dress that had caused her such embarrassment at the lunch table. His heart leaped with fright and he had visions of being challenged to a duel by her old-fashioned father. She came toward him with an impish smile and sat watching as he groomed the horse. Her voice was low and full of secrets. Vasily felt goosepimples rising all over his body as she spoke.

"When I first saw you, Vasily, I thought you were one of the ranch hands."

"That's what I am."

"You are well bred, you cannot be a servant."

"I can be whatever I like, unlike you."

Elena looked down and for a moment Vasily thought he had made her cry. He had a flash of inspiration and held out his hand.

"Would you like to see one of the most beautiful things in the world, Elena?"

She took the hand, clutching it anxiously.

"I should like that very much."

"Come with me."

Vasily took her to see the new colt, a stylish pure-white Kentucky thoroughbred so lovely its presence took her breath away. Elena was silent for a moment. Then she bent down and nuzzled the horse, her hands patting and fussing, her face transported. Feeling like an intruder, Vasily stood by the open door of the stable, trying to control the panic her presence aroused. Nikolai had been right, as always. Love was an illness to be avoided like the plague. Vasily left Elena with the colt and hurried back to the house. He was nearing the porch when Don Francisco came out, his face puce with rage. The Spaniard stepped out into the garden. Vasily moved to delay him.

"Could you not sleep, sir?"

"I sleep very well, but when I wake and go to visit my daughter she is not there. Now when I find her I shall have to discipline her. Women are impossible to train."

Elena stood in the doorway, listening to the exchange. She heard Vasily's pacifying tone and was pleased by his courage.

"I think Elena's with Mama, working on the dress she's going to wear this evening, sir. Women love gossiping about clothes. It bores me and my brother to death."

Don Francisco followed Vasily out toward the fence and they stood together watching one of the hands working a new horse. The old man was relieved that nothing had happened to his daughter. He had imagined that she and Vasily might be together unchaperoned. Don Francisco wiped his brow with a red-silk handkerchief and tried to make up for his suspicions with politeness.

"I'm getting old, I fear, and Elena is too much for me. Her dear mother died giving birth, but I still loved the baby at once because she was the child of my autumn years. I was already fifty when Elena came into the world. I thought she would be like my other children, who are boys, but she has remained a mystery to me from that day to this. When I think she will be happy she is sad. When I think she will be sad she is happy. I am ashamed that I embarrassed her at lunchtime."

"You thought you were doing the right thing, sir."

"And I was not?"

"Mama's skirt was four inches shorter than Elena's. I think your daughter's clothes are very old-fashioned. My father used to dress in the style of the past when he left Russia and went to live in Paris. Everyone thought it very funny, but some thought him mad because he longed so much for the life he had lived in St. Petersburg."

"Elena's clothes reach to the ankle. That is how I like them to be."

"Girls haven't worn skirts to the ankle for some time, sir. It doesn't mean that they're not ladies, like Elena. It just means they want to be fashionable, like Mama."

Elena slipped from the stable to the house and went at once to Valentina's room. She stumbled to explain her presence.

"Papa thinks I am with you, Countess."

"You are with me. Would you like to try on some dresses for this evening?"

"I should like it very much."

That evening, Vasily tied his tie once, untied it and tried again. Then he threw it on the floor and stamped on it. At the fifth attempt he went to his mother's room and begged her to help him. Valentina tied the bow in seconds.

"As you know, Alex has decided that tonight dinner will be as old-fashioned as possible for the benefit of Don Francisco."

"He's not just old-fashioned, he's archaic."

"He's Elena's father and don't forget it."

"I'll remember, Mama."

"Elena and I are going to wear two of the ball gowns from the Masters collection. Brett's late wife kept clothes in a family room that's almost a museum, with wonderful gowns and riding clothes and traveling habits from as far back as the days of the Civil War. Elena and I have found two beautiful ones and Alex is joining in the plan. The men will wear evening dress, but the whole decoration of the room, the choice of dishes and the servants outfits are to be old-time. We're going to show Don Francisco that he isn't the only one to know about style and tradition."

Don Francisco joined the men in the main hall of the house, where dinner was to be served. He was impressed by the flower-bedecked arena and the men dressed in black tails, their suntanned faces contrasting elegantly with their white shirts and diamond studs. He looked from Alex to his brother, impeccable though in the wheelchair. Then he looked to Vasily and saw, in his mind's eye, himself when young. He weighed the rigidly straight back, the jet-black unruly hair, the eyes full of passion and fire, and sighed for the days of his youth.

Masters greeted Don Francisco and admired the silver embroidery on his jacket, the elegant black boots with silver thread pattern. They drank French wine and watched the servants running back and forth like ghosts in the candlelight. The table was set with the family silver burnished to a sheen and dark-red glass goblets that had once belonged to a doge of Venice. There were red orchids strewn on the floor and favors for each of the ladies wrapped in satin ribbon. Don Francisco turned to Masters and expressed his surprise.

"I had not expected such a magnificent show, Alex. I did not even imagine such existed in America."

"You'll be surprised, Don Francisco. We're not all that different, you know."

Don Francisco turned to wait for the ladies and was struck to silence by the appearance of Valentina at the top of the sweeping staircase. She was dressed in a gown of black floating chiffon with a crinoline skirt decorated with jet and silver lace. Her hair was in an Edwardian roll studded with diamonds and she was holding a black-lace fan. Don Francisco stepped forward and bowed, kissing her hand.

"Dear lady, I have not seen such elegance since the days of my youth."

"We thought it would be amusing for you to celebrate your arrival with a party in the old-fashioned style."

The Spaniard handed Valentina to Masters, who signaled for a servant to pour her some wine. At her side Don Francisco bowed his head. He was thinking of his rebellious daughter and wondering if Elena would shame him by disdaining the Old World clothes of the evening. He was holding out his glass for one of the servants to fill when he saw Brett's face light with pleasure and Vasily blush with longing. Following their gaze, Don Francisco looked to the top of the stairs and saw Elena in a gown of fragile white lace beribboned in pink. Her shoulders were bare, a deep frill covering her breasts and exposing a tiny waist. The skirt undulated around her like a vast gossamer aureola. In her hand she carried a white-lace fan. In her hair, which was raised in an intricate chignon, there was a wreath of forget-me-nots interspersed cunningly with Valentina's best sapphires. Don Francisco felt tears forming in his eyes as he walked forward to kiss his daughter's hand.

Elena joined the party, conscious of the sensation she had caused and grateful to Valentina for arranging it. She smiled conspiratorially at her new friend and then glanced at Vasily. What was he thinking as he stood there staring at her as if she were a ghost? She smiled enchantingly at him and fluttered her fan. Vasily's face turned scarlet and he hurried from the room and stood on the terrace breathing deeply, as if he were ill instead of in love.

Vasily felt as if his legs were paralyzed, like Brett's. He told himself firmly that he was the son of Vladimir Vasilievich Korolenko and a descendant of one of the finest families in Russia; his legs would soon recover their firmness and his heart would stop banging like a gong in his ears. He looked up at the moon and saw that it was a lover's moon. He walked back to the assembly and handed Elena a glass of champagne.

"I used to think the elegant ladies of St. Petersburg were very boring."

"And now you have changed your mind about elegant ladies?"

"You and Mama have made me realize what a silly child I must have been."

He led Elena to the table. Valentina took Don Francisco's arm and Masters wheeled his brother to the head of the table. Candles flickered, white-gloved waiters poured imported French wines. The meal combined the best of American food with the subtlety of Europe. They ate gulf crabs sautéed in butter and served with a Béarnaise sauce. Fried chicken buried in a golden crust followed with baked potatoes and red Savannah rice. Steaks marinated in tequila and coriander melted in the mouth and the service was unobtrusive and gentle.

Don Francisco watched as course followed course. In his brother's house there had been food aplenty, but nothing like this. He began to view the country differently, admitting for the first time that his own country was not unique in her ability to create quality and style. He raised his glass and proposed a toast.

"To you, my dear friend Alex, and to you, Brett. To our new friends, the countess and her son Vasily. May God bless you all."

Valentina ate cherry pie with lashings of cream and tried to ease her body within the restricting bones of the bodice. Vasily was staring at the vision across the table and drumming his fingers in impatience. Valentina listened as Don Francisco questioned her son.

"And what do you intend to do in life, young man?"

"I shall breed horses, sir."

"Here in America?"

"No, sir. I'll be returning with my mother to Europe in a few weeks' time. I intend to continue my studies in France and then to find a breeding establishment somewhere in Europe where the horses have sufficient quality to interest me."

"Where do you live in France?"

"I live in Rambouillet, sir, some distance from Paris. Mama owns the Domaine Russe, where we all live."

Don Francisco found it impossible to stop asking questions, though his daughter was frowning across the table at him. He turned back to Vasily.

"Do you have many brothers and sisters? I ask because you said *all*."

"I have one brother, Nikolai, who works as a writer in Washington, and sixty-six other brothers and sisters, who live in the Domaine."

Don Francisco stared aghast at Vasily and then across to Valentina.

"Sixty-six brothers and sisters! Surely I do not understand."

"Mama adopted the refugee children who came from Russia to Paris after the revolution. We all live in the Domaine."

Don Francisco mopped his brow, relieved to be reassured.

"How noble to adopt such a number of orphans."

"They're not orphans sir. Mama doesn't allow anyone to call them orphans. They're part of our family, you see. We can all live together in the Domaine, if we want, for as long as we like. We're a real family."

"And what if these children marry someday?"

"They can remain at the Domaine or they can go and live somewhere else. They'll always be our family and they know it."

The table was cleared and some neighbors arrived for the dancing. They had joined in the spirit of the party and were dressed in their family heirlooms. Don Francisco danced with Valentina and then with his daughter. Masters danced with Maisie Johnson, a near neighbor of his brother, fending off the stream of questions Maisie aimed in his direction: "How's Davina? . . . Where's Davina? . . . And who is that divine countess whose clothes are the talk of the neighborhood? . . . How long is it she's been staying as a guest? . . ." The questions continued and Masters explained with a serious face that Valentina was his adopted daughter. Maisie fell silent, furious to be so brazenly mocked. Alex Masters had always been a real bastard. Now he was positively ornery.

The orchestra played the old tunes. The staff walked around with trays of champagne. Vasily sipped his with all the calmness he could muster. Then he walked over to Don Francisco and asked if he could dance with Elena. The old man consented. Vasily stepped toward the object of his adoration, bowed with a click of the heels and looked hopefully at her.

"Elena, may I waltz with you?"

"I shall be delighted, sir."

A faint whiff of cigar smoke filled the air. It was a warm night so the doors to the terrace were open, allowing the musky scent of blue grass and tobacco to drift in. Vasily thought of the yellow flowers that would always remind him of Kentucky. He would never smell that elusive fragrance again once he left America. He would never ride toward the Blue Ridge Mountains that framed the horizon so the landscape looked like a painting never to be forgotten. Vasily accepted that he would miss the country he had come to love. But Elena lived in Spain and he must be near her. He would not lose her, no matter what the opposition. He felt her slim body enticing him. He had been dancing with her at arm's length, as if she were a rare china doll. Now, as the champagne gave him courage, he pulled her closer, then again as near to his chest as the billowing skirt would allow.

Elena was conscious only of the man holding her so tightly. Other people in the room, the perfume of flowers, the drone of voices and the thump of the big bass drum, all faded into insignificance as Vasily looked down at her, smiling that curiously elated smile of his. Ever since childhood Elena had known that being Don Francisco's daughter and heir to his fine estate would make her a desirable match. From the moment she had arrived in America men had been more open in their admiration. Whenever her father turned his back someone presented his compliments and sent her a note or told her he was mad about her. Until now all men had bored her and those who had not had been obvious in their interest in her inheritance. But Vasily Korolenko was different. Elena knew he was only sixteen, but she dismissed this immediately. The countess had told her that Vasily had packed more into his sixteen years than some men put into a lifetime. She looked up at him and knew he had already experienced sadness, revolution, the loss of his home and loved possessions, tragedy and the renewal of his belief in himself. His eyes were dark blue, not brown as she had thought at first, and there was something in the hardness of his mouth that excited her. She felt him squeeze her hand and was aware of a weakening sensation within her body, a longing she had never before experienced. She looked down, her cheeks blushing at her own wantonness. Vasily spoke sharply.

"If your father sees you blushing like that he'll think I've been making advances."

"You have."

"I didn't say a word."

"It was not necessary to speak."

"What would you do if I asked you to meet me in the stables after everyone's gone to bed?"

"I should slap your face and go at once to tell Papa."

"Then I'll not ask you."

Valentina distracted Don Francisco's attention from the young couple waltzing around the floor. Twice she caught Masters' eye and each time he inclined his head toward Vasily, who was bending down, lower and lower, toward his partner's face. A roll of drums signaled the end of the waltz. With a start Vasily remembered himself and bowed, as his mother had taught him. Elena curtsied and hurried to kiss her father's cheek.

"I have so enjoyed myself this evening, Papa."

"Enjoy yourself while you can, *reina*. Tomorrow we shall be back in the present day and you will never again be able to taste the age of mystery."

The guests went home at two. Members of the household had one last drink before retiring. Valentina took off the ball dress and grimaced at the red marks the whalebones had made on her skin. The past was romantic, the dresses a dream, but the present was synonymous with freedom. Corsets brought confinement and claustrophobia. She was glad there was no longer need for them. She put on a wrap and let down her hair. It was longer now and less easy to manage. She brushed it thoughtfully. She could have it cut again, but Masters liked it long. Would she have it cut? She postponed making a decision. Outside her room there was a soft footfall on the landing. Valentina prayed her son was not doing anything foolish.

Vasily sat in the stable on a bale of hay. He had brushed his hair and put on his best pajamas and a silk dressing gown borrowed from Masters. He put two mugs of hot chocolate down on a nearby bench and waited in the moonlight, listening to the song of a mockingbird. Would Elena come? He had no idea what she would do. He only knew about his mother and his sisters at the Domaine. They all copied Valentina and were forthright in their manner. Elena looked different and felt different in his arms, but her character was a mystery. Vasily wondered if her father was the only man she really wanted to please. He sipped the hot chocolate thoughtfully. Then he saw something white fluttering in the doorway. Elena was dressed in a high-necked nightdress and wrapped in a dark-red shawl. Vasily beckoned and she came and sat at his side, sharing the hay bale and drinking the warming brew. She did not speak and Vasily imagined he could hear her heart beating with excitement in unison with his own. Then she looked anxiously into his eyes and whispered.

"I have never been alone with a man before. I told myself I should not come to you but here I am. Why did you ask me to meet you, Vasily?"

"I wanted to kiss you so you wouldn't forget me when you went to sleep."

She drank more of the chocolate and Vasily could see her hands shaking like aspens in the breeze. He rose and pulled her toward him, looking down in wonder at the sheen of her waist-length hair. The moonlight shone silver on her face and sparkling into her eyes. Then he kissed her, merely tasting her lips at first. Discord turned to harmony in his mind and Vasily knew he had lit the flame of her sensuality and of his own. He kissed her again and Elena put her arms around his neck and returned the kiss.

Valentina stood in the doorway and saw her son's eagerness and the limpness of Elena's body as the two kissed. She spoke softly, afraid lest the girl cry out.

"I heard you going downstairs and minutes later Don Francisco asking for bicarbonate. The meal was too rich for him. He's awake and likely to look for you."

Elena clung to Vasily's hand.

"I must return to my room. Please forgive me, Countess."

"Go up the servants' stairway, no one will see you. I'll follow in a moment."

Valentina looked up at Vasily and saw tears in his eyes.

"What now, Vasily?"

"I'm going to marry Elena, Mama."

"Did you ask her?"

"No, but she'll accept me, I'm sure she will."

"You're too young to marry. Don Francisco will certainly refuse your proposal. Even I think it's unwise."

"Then we'll marry without permission, Mama. All my life I felt malcontent until I came to America. Then I began to realize that I just needed to feel wanted and useful, really useful, as I do in Brett's stables. Since I met Elena I've had the ambition that was always lacking in me. I want to keep her in style, Mama. I want a family and a future together. Please don't be angry. Help me because no one else will."

"I'll always help you, Vasily, but we all have to wait for some things in life."

"I can't wait."

"You're as impulsive as your father and as full of romance."

Vasily thought of the count and how well his father had concealed his true nature. He walked upstairs with his mother and left her at her door.

"I'll leave with you for New York, Mama."

"On Monday?"

Vasily looked inexplicably sad.

"Only five more days to be with my favorite horse. Only five more days to make myself unforgettable to Elena."

In her room Valentina found a branch of magnolia blossoms and a card on which Elena had written: "Thank you for being my friend." She put the magnolia in water and looked at the clock. It was four-fifteen. Soon the estate workers would arrive and go about their tasks. It was almost time to go with Vasily to inspect the stables and watch the horses work out. She thought of Elena descending the staircase, as she had descended that staircase in Paris at her first ball. It was meant to be. Vasily was in love and his feelings had always been intense and never shallow. Whatever the future held, he would fight to have his way, and Valentina knew she would help him. She made her way to Masters' bedroom to tell him what had happened.

Three weeks later Davina was successful in opposing Masters' divorce petition. Valentina sailed back to France, resigned to the impossibility of ever marrying again. Only the jubilant welcome of her children and the party they threw for her prevented her sinking into a deep depression of despair.

# CHAPTER TWENTY

## *The Domaine, September 1929*

Masters succeeded at last in obtaining a posting back to Paris. He took an apartment next door to the embassy and saw Valentina for dinner whenever she was in the city. The weekends were spent with her and the children of the Domaine. The future was still uncertain. They were not married and Masters knew his work could keep them apart at any time. They had agreed not to debate the future anymore, simply to enjoy every moment together.

Since her return from America, Valentina had taken time to get to know the children again. Like all young people they changed rapidly, and she was astonished to find some of them almost adult. Vladimir Fortunov was twenty, Tanya a glowing fifteen, Natasha, who helped Zita manage the house, was sixteen and Dmitry twenty-seven. He would marry in the autumn. The youngest children were now eleven, the oldest twenty-three. Two of Valentina's sons, the Romanov brothers, were already married and living in Rambouillet nearby. She was proud of the way they came each week to see her and the way they took it for granted that they would help with the harvest. Valentina gazed out of the window to the yellow field of mustard dotted with red poppies. The pinewoods were no longer mere nurseries for saplings but new woods, green and healthy. She owed Dmitry a great deal for all his work and thought over the years. She considered the girl he was going to marry, one of the eldest of her Russian family, Irina Demidova. Irina was the only surviving child of Field Marshal Demidova's family. She was twenty, a beauty with long flaxen plaits and laughing blue eyes. What a handsome couple they would be. Valentina racked her brain to think of a suitable wedding gift. She had long

considered renovating the gatehouse of the property and making a
gift of it to Dmitry when he married. She picked up the telephone
and called the local builder, Monsieur le Breton. An hour later he
came to take her instructions.

Tanya crept into the room while they were discussing the
gatehouse and listened to the plans for rewiring and replumbing
the property. She waited until le Breton had gone before speaking
to Valentina.

"You're going to give Dmitry the gatehouse for his wedding
gift?"

"It's a secret, don't tell anyone."

"Zita would like it better than Dmitry. She goes there every afternoon for a bit of peace. Last week she bought some material for
the curtains of one of the rooms, the one she likes to sit in. You
should give *her* the gatehouse so she can live there with Henri and
Louis. Five rooms isn't enough for Dmitry. He's a gentleman and
he and Irina should have more. Why don't you give them the hunting lodge in the woods, the one that was once owned by the King
of France? It has twelve rooms and it's a very nice house and not
too far away from home."

Valentina phoned le Breton again and requested his wife to ask
him to return. Then she turned to Tanya.

"That's a very good idea and I shall take your advice."

"Tell me about Nikolai's book and the work he's doing in
America."

"I told you all about him yesterday."

"Tell me again, Valentina."

Valentina thought how all the children called her Countess, except Tanya. She had expected them to call her by her familiar
name, but tradition decreed that they address her by her title. She
watched Tanya's face growing dreamy as she described Nikolai's
work. She knew her daughter was visualizing herself working at
Nikolai's side as his stenographer, typing his notes and being his
right hand at all times. She hugged Tanya's slim shoulders and
kissed her.

"How are your typing lessons going?"

"Very well. I'm also learning bookkeeping and business-letter
writing in English."

"You'll be able to get a very good job with all that knowledge."

"When will Nikolai be coming home?"

"I think he's planning to stay in America."

Tanya fell silent and when she spoke Valentina understood the loneliness and longing within her.

"I love Nikolai. I've always loved him, but he just thinks of me as the little girl I was when I first saw him. Sometimes I can't stop thinking of him and I write to him every week, but he never replies."

Valentina made a mental note to write to her son: Why haven't you replied to Tanya's letters? Did I not teach you to reply to correspondence from your friends? Have you forgotten your manners? She left Tanya mooning over her son and went out into the kitchen garden. Zita approached her and begged a moment of her time.

"It will only take five minutes, ma'am."

"I have all the time in the world, Zita."

Zita closed the kitchen door and sat at Valentina's side on a green iron bench overlooking the herb garden. She adjusted her new spectacles and fidgeted with her plait while she sought words to explain her predicament.

"Ma'am, my husband's very ill."

"I wasn't aware that Henri was unwell. He always looks so healthy and he's young."

"He'll be forty-nine at the end of the year."

Valentina rubbed her palms with mint and sniffed the fresh green scent. When Zita spoke she felt unaccountably sad. Zita had had so few years of happiness and now, at forty, was about to be widowed. Zita's voice broke as she explained.

"Henri's been having stomach pains for almost a year. I give him a special mixture when he's bad and up to now it's worked. A few days ago though, he was so ill in the night he went straight to Dr. Martin in the morning. I just had a phone call from the doctor. He says Henri has cancer. He doesn't know if my husband will see Christmas."

Tears fell down Zita's cheeks as she spoke but she remained calm. Valentina held her hand.

"We've been through so much, you and I. We'll just have to weather this storm too. The main thing is to make sure Henri is never in pain."

"They're going to give him morphia, ma'am, but when he took

the first dose it made him sleepy and a bit drunk. He doesn't know whether to take it regularly. He'll have to, I suppose, but I haven't told him yet what Dr. Martin said."

"For the moment don't tell him. Doctors are often wrong in their diagnosis. I'd best ask Alex to find the very best specialist in Paris and we'll take Henri to see him."

"What if it's true and he dies?"

"Then I'll have to find a new gamekeeper and you'll have to settle down here with your son. Zita, I've decided to make the gatehouse over to you. I shall be signing the deed next week. I want you to be independent of us all in the future and as a house owner you'll never want for money. You can house some of the summer workers in your spare rooms and I'll pay you additional money for each one. Or you can take in guests who come to the agricultural school at Epernon."

"I don't know what to say, ma'am."

"Say nothing. I hope you'll always work for me, at least until Natasha is more experienced. I don't want to think of you retiring any time soon."

"Retire! Oh, ma'am, I've no intention of leaving your employ. Natasha will just have to wait for my keys of office."

Valentina found a letter waiting for her in the post the following morning.

*Dearest Mama,*

Don Francisco has decided to give me work on his estate. He's promised me a partnership when I'm twenty-one if I continue to work hard and to study each day. I'm taking lessons in bull breeding and winemaking (because Elena will inherit Don Francisco's sister's vineyard someday). Yesterday I proposed to Elena and she accepted me. I'm writing this a week before my birthday, Mama. Please send me all the latest books from Paris on the subjects mentioned and some fashion magazines for Elena. She says not to bother you about this but I would like to please her with the magazines. She has never seen anything like the ones you read. It's so hot here I am black as a Negro. My feet are blistered from walking on the earth. There is no grass and sometimes the sun is so cruel even Don Francisco's workers keep in the shade as much as possible. I love it despite the heat. It's the most beautiful place in the world, even if there is no grass. Don't trouble to send me any lotion for my blisters. Elena has some and puts it on for me every night. I love you a hundred, Mama.

*Your son Vasily*

Valentina went to Paris and bought all the books she could find on viticulture, stock raising and bull breeding. There were few on the latter subject, so she chose a book on the history of Spain, with sections on the customs and fashions of the past and present. She bought copies of *Vogue* and *Style* for Elena and packed them with a gift of her own choosing, a massive volume on the great houses of Europe.

When she had finished this task Valentina went to see her bank manager. She had been receiving irate letters for some time and it was obvious he was displeased by her long absence in America and the resulting drop in the recent revenue from the patrons of the estate. When she left his office Valentina was depressed beyond all measure. The Domaine cost a great deal and more each year. The monies vouched by wealthy Russian and French supporters were never enough and she was constantly fighting a losing battle against debt and, worse, the loss of the estate altogether. She was too proud to ask Masters for money. He had said from the start that the running of the property was her work. She knew he had also had to finally sell his ranch in Missouri to repay the bank loan taken out to cover the original renovations to the property. The problem of money was now so familiar Valentina's mind had long given up the battle to find a solution. She was surprised, therefore, to have a brilliant idea. The children who had originally formed the Russian choir were now almost grown up. It was time for them to give their farewell performance.

Within a week Valentina had rented the Empire Theater, calculating that it would give her the greatest profit from its size and popularity with the rich. Within a month bills were posted all over the city, invitations sent out and the choir rehearsed in its final program. Valentina had decreed that the children should be dressed in white against a deep red backcloth and that the only decoration be a giant Christmas tree, lit and decorated in the old Russian style.

At last the day dawned and at five on a dark winter evening Valentina led her children to the theater. There, amid the now-familiar smell of chalk and greasepaint, they put on their new clothes and sat silently waiting for the call. It was the end of a long and prosperous career, the end of the choir that had saved the Domaine so often in time of need. Each child knew this and felt sad because of it. There was also uncertainty. Without the choir to help the Domaine's financial affairs, would they even have a home within a year or two? The usual tumult of noise in the dressing room was silenced as each thought his own thoughts.

Below, Valentina was backstage, looking through a hole in the velvet curtain to the audience. The theater had filled, the critics were in place, the orchestra leader about to enter. The lights dimmed and offstage a voice announced in Russian and then in French:

"Ladies and gentlemen, for the last time, we present the Russian Children's Choir of the Domaine Russe."

Applause filled the auditorium and there were resounding cheers. The orchestra leader tapped his baton, the overture began and then the curtain rose slowly, revealing the children standing in a semi-circle, the youngest in front, the older ones forming the outer edges of the crescent. They were singing one of their favorite songs, "Kalinka," with its soft beginning and gradual crescendo to a peal of clear young voices and then the gradual fading into the distance until only one voice remained.

For an hour the children sang every song beloved by Russian expatriates, every traditional folk song of their country, every song of love lost. The merry followed the sad, the martial followed the lullaby. Then, as the audience applauded wildly and threw flowers, bank notes and gifts, the choir burst into a spirited rendering of the "Marseillaise," the much-loved French national anthem. The audience rose and sang with the children. Then, as the curtain fell, they filed out, having left onstage a pile of money and gifts that would take the children over an hour to sort.

Valentina was in the box office, counting the profits of the evening. Tears were running unheeded down her cheeks and she felt that an episode in her life was ending. With the choir disbanded after its short but successful career, she had come to the end of all things Russian. She wiped her eyes and tried to tell herself that she must be happy. The Domaine's finances had been augmented, yet again, by the golden voices of the children. She went backstage and watched as the money and gifts were put into sacks. She was about to take the children outside to the bus when one of the smaller boys approached her.

"Countess, now that we are no longer a choir, does it mean we must leave the Domaine?"

"Of course not, the Domaine is our home."

"But if money is short I heard one of the other boys saying we should not be able to stay at the Domaine, that it would be sold."

"We shall find money, Gregori, that is all. No one is ever going to make us leave the Domaine."

Gregori held Valentina's hand tightly and walked with her to the waiting bus. She looked around and saw Tanya clutching one of the sacks and two of the smaller children holding another between them. She smiled happily. Again the choir had given her a respite from financial worry. She began to sing softly and soon all the children had joined her.

A week later, as she looked through her appointment book, Valentina realized that this was the day she must take Katrina to her audition at the Conservatoire in Paris. Katrina would be nervous, very nervous. Valentina resolved to buy her some new clothes. There was nothing like a shopping spree to cheer a woman. They would eat lunch together at the Polka des Mandibules and they would visit the silk shop in the rue du Colisée, and buy everything that caught their fancy. Valentina took her emergency money out of its hiding place, determined that nothing should prevent Katrina feeling confident enough to win one of the coveted places at the Conservatoire.

They went together to St.-Cyr, Valentina's current favorite dress shop, and then to order a new black dress for Katrina. Valentina bought her daughter new shoes and an expensive suit of deep-blue silk. They had a café crème at the zinc bar of Emile's and a walk through Les Halles, which reminded both of the weekly markets in Russia. In the window of an exclusive shop in the Faubourg St.-Honoré a silk blouse in cyclamen caught Katrina's eye. Valentina purchased it without hesitation.

"When you're a great concert pianist you can buy *me* silk blouses when I'm old."

"You'll never be old to me, Countess, and not to the others, either. We shall always remember you that day when you came to collect us from the home and sent Vasily to take us to our rooms. I was proud when I saw my name on the door. It was the moment when I really knew I belonged again."

Valentina sat at the rear of the audience of tutors, sponsors and members of the governing body of the Conservatoire, listening as would-be entrants played three pieces as their entrance examination. Two were so nervous they achieved nothing but discord and fled the room weeping. One was sensational, if lacking in technique. Valentina wondered if that would be Katrina's competition for the coveted place. She watched as her daughter entered and with a formal nod to the judges sat down and began to play a Chopin polonaise. The pale face with its sea-green eyes and soft blond hair became transformed. The slim body commanded and the hands were master of the keys. Valentina could not take her eyes off the young woman she had brought up during the formative years of life. A playful Russian folk song followed and for a brief moment Valentina saw the Flower House and the cornfields of summer. Only in Russia had there been such heat, such beauty, such rainbows after a storm . . . only in Russia had there been wealth and security in the days before the revolution destroyed everything. Katrina finished with a ponderous piece by Rachmaninov, an ambitious choice for one so young. Valentina saw one of the judges looking at her. She recognized him as the Comte de Vaux, one of the patrons of the Conservatoire. He was younger than she, a tall, slim, handsome man with dark eyes and black hair framing a thoughtful face. Valentina watched Katrina take her bow, touched by the rapturous applause that filled the room. She wiped tears of pride from her eyes and rose to meet the count as he came to speak to her.

"Madame la Comtesse, I am enchanted to meet you. I have heard all about the choir you used to have at the Domaine. I gather the little ones are all growing up and that they have disbanded now so they can concentrate on their studies. You are not without talent, though. Your daughter is quite the most wonderful pianist I have heard in the last ten years. She is assured of a place in the Conservatoire, of course, and I would like to pay the cost of her tuition. I look upon this as a small gesture and a means of being able to congratulate myself on being part of her background. Someday she will be a great star of the musical world."

"I'm so glad she wasn't nervous."

"She has great talent, there was no need to be nervous. Say you accept my offer, Countess."

"I accept on Katrina's behalf, and thank you."

"I understand you are farming the land of the Domaine Russe. You have five hundred acres, have you not?"

"You're very well informed about me, sir."

"I once planned to buy the Domaine, many years ago. The plan was shelved, but I have always retained an interest in the property."

"Do call if you're in our area."

"I shall be passing on Saturday, Countess."

"Then I invite you to lunch."

Katrina and Valentina drove to the station in silence. Reaction had set in and neither could concentrate on her surroundings. Katrina kept going over the pieces she played for the judges and frowning at the mistakes she had made. Valentina was going over her conversation with Count de Vaux, remembering his dark eyes on her face, his intent gaze as she spoke. Katrina spoke quietly, as if to herself.

"It was the silk suit that made me play so well. When I put it on I felt beautiful. Usually I feel ugly because my hair is rather orange and I'm far too thin. The children tease me about my lack of shape but when I wore the suit I felt like a real beauty. I can hardly wait to tell Tanya what has happened."

"She'll be waiting by the gate, if I know her."

"Who was that handsome man you spoke with, Countess?"

"That was Count de Vaux. He's going to pay all your tuition fees and he's coming to lunch on Saturday so all the children can meet him."

"He was nice, just like a knight in one of the picture books Mama used to read to me from . . . in Russia."

That night Valentina lay awake, listening to the sounds of her home, workers trundling carts along the road as they finished a long day in the fields, a church clock chiming the hour, owls hooting in the yew trees. She thought of Count de Vaux, whose eyes had shone with interest on sight of her. She was forty-three. He was not more than thirty. Age did not matter up to a point, and then it mattered more than anything. At this moment men still

wanted her. Did she want them to stop? Was she looking forward
to a peaceful old age? She shook her head. She did not want to
have a peaceful old age, alone and without admirers. She wanted
to be happy and loved and able to flirt like a demon once in a
while. She thought of Masters, who was jealous of other men and
who denied vigorously that he was ever affected by that emotion.
Then she put him to the back of her mind and began to plan what
she would give the count to eat on Saturday. Perhaps he would
give her a donation for the Domaine bank account. Dear Monsieur
Chambord would be relieved if he did. She smiled sheepishly. It
was nice to have something to look forward to.

On the fourth of December a lawyer, Monsieur Laval, came to
visit Valentina. He had a dry manner and wore clothes as old-
fashioned as those the count had once cherished. He looked at her
from behind thick spectacles that hid his blue eyes, pursing his kit-
tenish mouth and coughing nervously every few seconds. Valentina
waited patiently for him to speak.

"I am in charge of the will of one Nikolai Mikhailovich Svetlov
whose mother was Krizia Leonidovna Svetlova, the Russian star.
The said person, Nikolai Svetlov, died some years ago—eight, to be
precise—and left all his money to a cause which has since disinte-
grated, in short, a cause which no longer exists."

"To the White Russian Army, if I recall from my visit to Monsieur Svetlov?"

"Yes indeed, Countess. I forwarded a small part of the bequest to
the armaments division of that army in nineteen hundred and
twenty-two. After that nothing was heard so I sent no further
monies. The capital has therefore accrued with interests and stock
sales. The various properties and accounts are now managed by
myself and Monsieur Vannier, the accountant, and more than the
requisite period of years has passed since I last heard from my contact in the White Russian Army. I came here a year ago to see you,
but you were away."

"What did you want?"

"I wanted to ask you a question. Monsieur Svetlov insisted that
this be done only if the Domaine Russe were still functioning and
that it should not be done until five years after my last contact with
the true inheritors of this will."

Valentina watched icicles dripping in the winter sun outside her window. The lawyer coughed and coughed again. She tried to sit still but felt increasingly uneasy. He began to speak in a hesitant voice.

"The estate of Svetlov comprises one house in Paris Neuilly, one house on the outskirts and another in Madrid. There are gold deposits in the Banque de Paris totaling one million francs, gold deposits in the Bank of England totaling forty-five thousand pounds sterling, gold deposits to the value of seven hundred thousand Swiss francs in the Banque de Lucerne and other small items including a row of houses in Chantilly, an apartment in the Marais district of Paris and a farmhouse in Vire in the Calvados region. These are unimportant properties; probably the inheritor will wish to sell them. There are also pearls given by Tsar Alexander the Third to a relative of the dead man who was his mistress, and emerald earrings valued highly by Monsieur Cartier. The mother of Monsieur Svetlov always taught her son to save his money in gold and one of the conditions of the will is that the gold be left in its present form and not converted to currency as it lies on deposit, only when required to be used. There are no further conditions, except the question."

Valentina sat very still, shocked by the revelation. In the courtyard, outside the window, she could hear the younger children playing snowballs. Above her head Miss Knatchbull was banging the logs on her fire with her favorite brass poker. Valentina looked closely at Laval, wondering why he kept dabbing sweat from his brow. She made her voice sound as normal as possible.

"You came here to ask me a question, sir; ask it please."

"The question is this, Countess. If the fortune were to be left to you, are you willing to change the name of the Domaine Russe to the Krizia Svetlova Orphanage?"

She felt a pulse ticking in her temple, and feelings of rage so intense she feared she would faint. That this carrot should be dangled before her nose when the Domaine was short of funds was nothing short of cruel. She frowned at the lawyer's expectant gaze, asking herself a dozen times what to do. From the very moment she had taken guardianship of the children she had instilled into them the fact that they were *not* orphans, that they were her sons and daughters, an adopted family as dear to her as her own. She had even threatened to horsewhip the schoolmaster who had put it about that the children were orphans. The townspeople had accepted her ways and the word orphan was never used in connection with her children. Inwardly Valentina damned the egotistical old man who in a last message from the grave had tried to tempt her to change her mind and betray her children. There was no decision to be made. She had made that decision when she first met Monsieur Svetlov all those years ago. She answered clearly, unable to move an inch from her position like Don Francisco's bulls.

"I have no intention of changing the name of the Domaine, sir. This is the home of my children, their real home for all their lives. It is not an orphanage, as I told your client many years ago. Now if you'll forgive me I must be about my work. I would be obliged if you would never trouble me about this matter again."

"Then may I congratulate you, dear lady. The inheritance is yours. It was specified that if you were willing to change the name of the Domaine you would not be able to inherit. Monsieur Svetlov would have considered you a woman who could not keep her word in the face of money. As it is, you are the sole inheritor of what remains of his estate."

Valentina sat motionless on the chair. Laval looked down at the papers before him and then to the courtyard where the children were playing. He thought what lucky young men and women they were to have such a steel-willed creature at their disposal, to love and honor them, to protect and guard them from others less strong than herself. Seeing that Valentina was too stunned to speak, he took his leave gently.

"Drop into my office during the next few days, Countess. I am at your disposal at any time."

The following morning Valentina received a letter from Masters saying that he had been posted to Madrid and that Davina had died after an orgy of drink and drugs. Through tears, she read his proposal:

This is no time to ask you to marry me, but will you? We've waited so long for this, my love. I'm getting on the next boat and coming right back to wed you at the Domaine, under the apple tree in the meadow. One thing's certain, we shan't be short of witnesses!

# CHAPTER TWENTY-ONE

## Córdoba, May 1932

Seats for the bullfight were sold in the *sol* or *sombre* positions. The cheap seats were in the full sun, the expensive ones in the *sombre,* or shade. In the shaded half of the arena, the most expensive were those at the barrera, behind a wooden fence that kept the events in the ring from coming too close to the audience. Don Francisco had regular seats at the center of the barrera of the Tejares bullring. He was proud of his bulls and the recognition they had brought him. He was proud also of the greetings he received as he led his party toward the barrera. Around him women in bright dresses and elegant combs were watching the empty sanded ring with deep concentration, as though willing the matadors to appear. Don Francisco looked at his daughter, content that Elena had eyes only for Vasily. He handed Valentina down to sit beside her son, placing himself on her other side so he could explain the intricacies of the performance.

Masters took a seat beside Elena and looked toward his wife. He had seen bullfights before, in Mexico, and was uncertain how Valentina would react. He had learned to avoid trying to put her responses into categories, because though she called herself a Parisian he knew she was Slavic by nature and given to extremes in everything. He smiled reassuringly as she stared at the empty ring. She returned his smile and then looked away when a trumpet call sounded to silence the cacophony of noise in the arena. The bulls for the feria of Córdoba were from Don Francisco's ranch. Valentina felt a mild excitement as the afternoon's performers entered the ring.

To the sound of an out-of-tune but enthusiastic band the matadors paraded toward the center of the ring. There were three of them, each with his entourage of picadors, banderilleros, men to wave protective capes when needed, others old enough to advise their masters on the bull's ways. Valentina admired the matadors' satin suits, one violet and silver, one poppy-red and gold, one opal-beaded on white. On their heads the men wore the traditional black hat, on their legs pink stockings to fill the gap between feet and tight satin breeches. Ladies around the ring placed silk shawls over the red-painted barrera and the air was silent with a strange expectancy, as if two thousand people were waiting not for a display of skill or a moment of excitement at the kill, but for the catch in the throat that comes on sight of death. Like audiences at the circus waiting for the tightrope walker to slip, they had come to see men die and would go home disappointed if only animal blood were spilled. The only sound in the hot dusty arena was the sound of fans clicking, like the flutter of a thousand cicadas.

Valentina watched the darkly suntanned faces of the matadors and saw solemnity. They had joined the parade from the chapel behind the arena and had no time at all for the sensuous glances of the habitués at the barrera. Each was wondering if God had been listening to his prayers for protection, or if this would be the day when death would stretch out her hand to claim him. The matadors bowed to the president of the corrida in his box high above the ring. The discordant music ceased as they passed with their entourages to a position between the barrera and the wooded frame that protected water carriers and dressers from the bulls. The matador about to fight crossed himself and stepped forward to watch the gate through which his adversary would enter. Valentina was so close to him she could have touched his cheek. She saw a nerve twitching in his neck and a small red spot on his forehead. She followed his gaze, starting violently as a black bull careered through the gate and looked around menacingly at the watchers. A notice announcing the bull's weight was placed in a frame on the sunny side of the arena. Valentina's heart began to pound as she looked from the bull to the slight man who stepped forward, capote in hand to challenge.

As the matador put the bull through its paces the crowd called approval at moves stylishly accomplished. Valentina did not join in the *olés*. She was trying to assess what chance the matador had of killing the beast before him. Gradually she became accustomed to the passes, when the bull charged the cloak and not the man. Then the matador stepped back behind the guard fence and left a picador to do his work. Valentina watched the matador mopping his brow with a red handkerchief. He took a mouthful of water, swirled it around his mouth and spat. The picador was piking the bull's shoulders. Valentina watched blood oozing down the strong black back. Ignoring the pain, the bull continued to charge.

Don Francisco leaned forward and whispered.

"That is one of my finest bulls. Nothing will stop him charging, nothing but death."

The picador rode out of the ring, his place taken by men who would place banderillas in the bull's neck. The matador watched intently, frowning when his men placed the darts too high or too far back and when one of them received a round of enthusiastic applause.

Valentina gazed at the blood running down the bull's back and wanted to leave at once. If she did she knew she would shame Vasily in front of those who considered bullfighting an art. Don Francisco leaned forward again to tell her something.

"When the bull first enters the ring he is *levantado,* he holds his head high and charges everything because he wants to show his power. Now he is *parado;* it means slow and cautious. At this moment he is dangerous. He will charge the matador if he can because he has realized he must kill."

Valentina felt sweat on her brow and a sense of unreality. Why, if this was Don Francisco's favorite bull, had he allowed it to come here to be slaughtered? She glanced at Vasily, who was watching the matador intently. Elena was gripping Vasily's hand and gazing with rapt, almost sensuous attention at the man in the ring. Valentina turned back to watch as the matador tired the bull with more elaborate passes. The bull was brave, always coming forward, unlike some who disdained to charge once hurt and ran for the gate through which they had entered the ring. This was a bull from Don Francisco's ranch. Valentina was relieved it was doing him proud. She looked around the arena and saw the faces of the crowd, silent and watchful. She remembered the vultures she had once seen at the zoo and thought how alike they were. The matador was making the bull less strong. Blood from its neck dripped onto the sand but its attention never wavered from its enemy. The matador walked back to the barrera and exchanged the wooden sword on which he had been suspending the smaller red cape for the sword that would kill. Then he walked purposefully back to take another long look at his adversary. The bull's head was low but he was still pawing the ground. Don Francisco spoke proudly.

"Now the bull is *aplomado*. He is heavy and tired and feeling like lead. He is no longer fast but he is still dangerous. He does not like what is being done to him and wants his revenge."

The matador made the final passes, to make sure his prey was still charging in a straight line. The last pass was received on the knees. The crowd applauded and called wild *olés*. The bull watched in puzzlement as the matador turned and took a bow. Silence fell on the arena as the matador pointed his sword and prepared to make the pass of death. The bull did not move. The matador continued to measure precisely the distance and the angle. Then, without warning, the bull charged. Bedlam erupted in the arena. Don Francisco rose and roared with delight at his bull's courage. The matador's body rose on the horn and fell to the ground, the white suit stained with red. A dozen men rushed out to distract the bull's attention but he would not be distracted. He knew his enemy and charged again, scattering them all. Then, as though pleased with himself, he galloped away and did a tour of the ring. Doctors ran to the man on the ground. A stretcher team appeared and the sand was scuffed over.

Valentina turned to Don Francisco.

"What will happen to that bull?"

"He will be returned to my estate to live his days in peace. Such a bull must always be respected, that is our tradition. He will never fight again. He has earned a happy retirement."

The buzz of crying, shouting, gossiping, calling, died down when the second bull ran in. The tall slim matador in violet stepped forward and earned ecstatic praise with a combination of turns and passes that had the bull dizzy and the crowd on its feet. The picadors did their work well. The banderillas were placed. The matador stepped forward to complete the domination. The bull charged. The matador placed himself for the kill. Don Francisco turned to Valentina.

"This young fellow knows how to kill, watch him closely."

The matador stood sideways to the bull, weighing the angle of the charge. The bull's head went down. Valentina could feel the electric atmosphere in the arena as the matador lunged, the bull's knees crumpled and he fell, four legs in the air in ignominious defeat. The crowd cheered. The president awarded two ears. The matador did a tour of the ring. She felt unbelievably distressed as she watched the bull being dragged from the ring to be skinned, cut up and sold to eager waiting women. Valentina looked at her hands, puzzled to have felt so elated when the first bull triumphed and so deflated when the matador did. Don Francisco turned to her and beamed.

"Did you not think that a wonderful kill, Countess?"

"I liked it better when the bull was allowed to go home to a happy retirement."

Don Francisco turned to Masters.

"Your wife prefers when the man is tossed to when the bull is killed, imagine!"

"She's Russian, sir, never forget it."

Valentina left the bullring with Masters and Don Francisco and drove back to her hotel in a carriage beribboned for the fiesta. She and Masters had come to see the spring fair in Córdoba and had enjoyed every moment of their visit. Only the bullfight had been disagreeable, but Valentina said nothing of this to her companions. In their hotel she asked for wine and tapas. Don Francisco explained his plans.

"Once the feria is over you will come to stay with me until the wedding. I was most relieved that you gave Vasily permission to marry, Countess. Elena and Vasily have been in love for so long, and I am impatient to have my first grandchild."

Valentina took out a list and handed it to Don Francisco.

"This is a list of presents bought by Vasily's brothers and sisters for the couple. I will be giving my son a small house in Madrid, which is part of an inheritance I understand I am to receive in the next few months. I have not received full details of the inheritance, but I do know it includes this property."

"You are most kind, Countess. For my part I have bought Elena and Vasily the land next to my own and a small property on it. Elena is enjoying supervising the restoration of the house so it will be habitable for them after their wedding. When I die she will inherit my land and my own finca and they will be able to join it onto their own land and make a most superior estate."

"Have you had any difficulties with the Republican government since the King left Spain?"

"Of course; everyone has had difficulties. I hear they are going to pass a new law which will oblige landowners to sell some of their land so it can be used by the peasants. The government cannot and will not pay us the correct value of the land, so who will sell willingly? Not I. Then the peasants will try to take what is ours. There has been nothing but trouble since the King went away, and to be truthful a great deal before he went."

Valentina thought of the peasants who had wanted the Flower House and its estate and wondered if her son was going to suffer as she had suffered when the villagers came to take what was not theirs. Don Francisco patted her hand.

"Don't worry, Countess. I am not one of those landowners who have fled to his town house in Madrid or Seville. I shall stay, and if anyone tries to take the land I have worked all my life, I shall fight."

That night there were fireworks and an orgy of flamenco dancing. Valentina and her husband followed a procession through the streets of Córdoba, past churches of great antiquity and white houses, their façades covered with climbing geranium and bougainvillaea. In the Plaza del Potro she sat at Masters' side at a table on the pavement near a fourteenth-century inn. They were drinking rough red wine and eating a fricasee of giblets and a stew of aubergine, asparagus and bulls' tails. Valentina thought of the corrida that day and wondered if this was the tail of one of the bulls she had seen. Masters kissed her ear.

"Are you happy?"

"I've been happy ever since I came to Spain. These are the happiest years of my life, Alex."

"And mine."

"When we go back to Madrid we'll furnish Vasily's house for him, shall we?"

"Sure, why not. You're lucky to have had such a legacy. I was relieved you didn't care for the bullfight, Valentina. Women usually go for bullfighters, and that guy in purple must have had you followed back to the hotel. He sent you flowers."

"I didn't see them."

"I threw them out of the window."

"What will you do if he comes around to see me?"

"I'll throw *him* out of the window."

"The woman doesn't exist who can make you jealous."

"Dammit, Valentina, don't remind me."

That night the young matador sang outside Valentina's window.

> *"Una mujer malagueña*
> *Tiene en sus ojos un sol*
> *En su sonrisa la aurora*
> *Y un paraíso en su amor."*

Valentina woke to the sound of bells in the *giralda* nearby. Masters had already gone out. She wondered if he would be buying her flowers or a shawl she had admired in a shop near the main square. She wrinkled her nose at the early-morning smells of garlic, lemon and overripe fruit, smells alien to her experience. She rose and put on a wrap and stood at the window looking down on the square. A parade of mounted Córdoban aristocrats was passing. The men were wearing the traditional flat black hat and elaborate frogged jackets of the feria. The women were sitting behind their men on the rump of the horses, dressed in frilly pink, red and yellow dresses coin-spotted in white. Their hair was pulled back in coils at the nape of their necks and there were small kiss curls at their ears. This was the final day of the fair and the mounted men and their ladies were en route to the Grand Parade. Valentina thought they looked like something out of a Velázquez painting.

Masters had gone out to take a stroll and to drink coffee at a pavement café in the first light of the new day. At the counter there were market traders, abattoir workers and men whose only job during the feria was to sweep the streets clean of silver paper streamers, horse manure and discarded *turrón* boxes. Masters was keeping an eye on his wife's window when he overheard a gruff voice nearby.

"That's her, the mother of the bridegroom. They say she's Russian and a countess."

Masters saw Valentina on the terrace of her room, looking down on the square. She had not seen him. He raised his morning paper to cover his face. The two men nearby continued.

"What time are we meeting?"

"At five A.M. Then we ride to the Las Chapas ranch and confront Don Francisco."

"And the other fellow, his neighbor."

"He's gone away to Madrid. He went as soon as the troubles started. There are rumors Don Francisco's bought his land for the couple to work."

Something was whispered that Masters could not hear. Then the two men walked away toward the horse dealers' market. Masters put down his paper and looked intently after them. They were ranch workers or horse breakers, of that he was sure. He rose and returned to the hotel. They would have to miss the final day of the feria. They must go at once and warn Don Francisco that men were plotting to visit him the following morning.

The fields around Córdoba were arid, sand-colored and barren of vegetation, except for agaves, thorn bushes and a few giant cacti. The only sign of life was two *guardia* on mules searching a rocky outcrop for smugglers. Masters drove on, avoiding cockerels strutting on the rough road and a little boy on a donkey. They paused for a drink in a bar by the wayside and were offered coffee and *izarra,* a liqueur made from flowers, sugar and sun. On the wall of the bar, faded into near-illegibility, was a notice as old as the aged owner: "NO DOGS, NO JEWS, NO GYPSIES." They proceeded, noticing that the cottages were becoming smaller and lower with no windows to let in the light or the cruel heat of the midday sun. Valentina looked across the rolling brown plain and saw nothing but oscillating reflections and small hills burned to the rock beneath them by the sun. She thought this the most forbidding place she had ever seen. A few miles farther on she saw a corral full of horses and another in the distance. She was pleased to find grass as they descended into a valley more fertile than its surroundings. In a dried-up riverbed two black bulls were eating gillyflowers. Ahead, to her right, she saw a one-story property and then another much larger on the skyline. She turned to Masters and asked what he thought.

"Is that Don Francisco's house? I imagine the smaller house is the one he's bought for Elena and Vasily. His own house looks very strange. There are no windows at all."

"There'll be windows on the inside of the courtyard. The Moorish style has a lot in common with the haciendas of Mexico. They were both built to withstand the heat and for protection against marauders. You'll see, it won't seem so strange once you're inside the house."

They drove through twenty-foot-high gates into an inner courtyard of such beauty that Valentina caught her breath. The shimmering white walls of the exterior were mellowed inside by a double set of arches that ran around the entire property, keeping the sun off the downstairs rooms and providing a terrace around those of the upper floor. The arches on the ground floor were covered with shiny green ivy, trained to follow their contour. The upper part of the house, inside the arches, was painted Greek blue. In the center of the courtyard there was a fountain of blue and green mosaic. Looking down, Valentina saw goldfishes swimming in the pellucid water and mysterious fernlike underwater plants undulating in the sunlight. Two men on horseback were about to leave. Another opened the gate and the two rode out at full gallop to remind the estate workers of the celebration feast after the wedding.

Don Francisco came out to greet his visitors.

"I did not expect you until tomorrow. You have missed the parade of the feria. Carmen, Pepita, come, take our guests to their rooms."

Valentina and Masters walked along corridors white painted and heavily beamed. Underfoot, woven-silk carpets lay on shiny tiles of dark brownish red. On the walls, saddles inlaid with silver were hung next to somber ancestral portraits. On the floor, copper pots held ferns next to chests of Córdoban leather stained with primitive designs of animals and fruit. Valentina looked askance at the bedroom into which she was led. It was at least forty feet long and furnished with a four-poster hung with tapestry and chairs of ebony inlaid with bone. On the wall there was a colorful painting of a mounted bullfighter reining in his horse before the charge. Seeing her gaze, the maid explained that the *rejoneador* in the painting was the don's late father.

When they were alone Valentina and Masters looked at each other and then at the tiger lilies in a vase on the dresser, the scented herbs in pots at the bedside. Valentina spoke for them both when she expressed her surprise.

"I thought from outside that this was an ugly house, rather primitive and dark."

"I told you it'd be different inside but I didn't expect a palace. Let's go look at the bathroom."

The bathroom was white and silver with a bath so large and so old-fashioned they burst into peals of laughter. Masters kissed Valentina's cheeks and held her close to his chest.

"You realize we could both get in there and it would still leave room for Don Francisco's best bull."

They went back to the bedroom and Masters disappeared to tell his host about the conversation he had heard that morning. Valentina looked out through the window to the terrace outside her room. There were chairs of carved cedarwood and a low table holding more of the greenery that filled the house. The air smelled of jasmine, carnation and grass-of-Parnassus. She sat on the bed and thought how lucky her son was and how unlucky too, to live here and to be threatened by those who wanted what would someday belong to him. She brightened when she thought of Vasily, who was obviously old enough to know his mind and to decide his own future. Vasily had told her that he would never leave Spain. He would fight for what belonged to his new family and never allow anyone to take what was theirs. Valentina was content with this and settled that the couple would lay solid foundations for their future. She took a turquoise-studded box from the bedside and opened the lid. There was a knock at the door and Elena entered. She saw Valentina listening to the music from the box.

"Vasily told me you liked music boxes, so I bought that for you when I visited Seville. It plays the music of the feria. You will remember us and our strange customs when you listen to it."

"How are you, Elena?"

"I am well and happy. I can hardly wait two more days to be married."

"We saw your new property as we drove here."

"I have been restoring it so Vasily and I can live there after the ceremony. I shall take you to see it tomorrow and afterward we shall have a picnic by the river."

"I didn't see a river."

"Long ago there was a river, but now for one hundred years it has been dry. Only when there is a storm does it fill and look as it once did. We call it the Río Seco, because to us it is still a river."

The morning of the wedding dawned, a hot, sunny June day full of the scent of lemon blossom. Valentina rose and went to Vasily's room. He had already eaten breakfast and was dressed in a gray suit with frogged jacket and frilly white silk shirt. She thought how like Yanin he looked, how handsome and bold. He kissed her and then continued pacing the room.

"I'm worried, Mama. I don't remember being as worried and scared as this since I got lost in the snow and Ivan Grigorevich came to find me."

"You look very handsome and quite the Spanish gentleman. Don Francisco will remember himself forty years ago when he sees you."

"He often says I remind him of himself when young. Have you seen Elena yet, Mama?"

"I came to you first."

"Go and give her some encouragement, Mama. She was terribly upset by those men who came to see her father yesterday. She's afraid they'll kill Don Francisco if he doesn't give them some of his land. I'm afraid it may spoil our wedding day for Elena. She didn't eat any lunch yesterday when the men had gone and she only had an apple and a glass of wine for supper."

"I'll go and talk with her."

Valentina looked up at the handsome sun-bronzed face and kissed her son on both cheeks.

"Good luck, Vasily. I hope you and Elena will be the very happiest couple in the world."

"We just want to be together, Mama, for always."

Elena was dressing in a blue underskirt with an old pair of silk stockings underneath. Maids lifted the wedding dress over her head and Valentina saw that it was a crinoline in the old-fashioned style of gleaming ivory satin, the skirt gathered in parts to reveal the blue frills of the petticoat. The bodice was tight, the shoulder frills lavish. Elena would be wearing a wreath of cornflowers over her black hair and a necklace of sapphires at her throat. She turned to Valentina with a smile.

"I had this dress copied from the one I wore in Kentucky when you helped me to impress Papa."

"You look absolutely wonderful."

"I'm glad you're here, Countess. I feel safe when you and your husband are near."

"There's nothing to worry about."

"There is, but I shall not think of it today. I shall be a happy bride and make Vasily happy also."

When the religious ceremony was over there was dancing to the tune of guitars and drums. Guests drank the best wines from Don Francisco's cellars and men from the estate sang traditional love songs. As dusk fell fires were lit and wild boar, oxen and lambs basted with mint and honey. The guests ate doves with black olives, rabbit in garlic, fish in vinegar and heavy slices from carcasses turning on the spit.

Vasily sought out his mother with a plate of choice bits. Then he rushed back to Elena's side and looked into her eyes.

"This is the best wedding I ever had."

She kissed him delightedly.

"How lucky we are, Vasily. You are all I want in the world."

Don Francisco's servants carried in tables with the dessert and Valentina saw pancakes, candied pine kernels, quince jelly and Córdoba cakes made from flour and cider. She walked over to where Don Francisco was standing.

"When will the young ones go to their new home?"

"They are to stay here tonight, Countess. I had to change my plans for allowing them to move to the new property."

"Is something wrong?"

"Men have occupied some of my land, Countess. I do not like to risk sending Vasily and Elena away in case the peasants do them harm."

"What will you do?"

"I shall wait and hope the law will help me. I cannot and will not run away. This is my home and my land and my daughter's too. We must remain here."

"Is there anything Alex and I can do?"

"Your presence here is enough. You and your husband remind Elena of the days when she and Vasily first met. She is a romantic and madly in love with her husband. Your presence here has made her forget the threats of the men who came to see me yesterday."

While the guests sang and danced in the firelight glow, Vasily carried Elena to the bedroom of the suite her father had prepared for them. They were not upset that the move to their new home had been delayed. They were young and in love and in a hurry to be one. The clocks were chiming three as Vasily undressed his new bride. He felt her trembling under his touch and was suddenly conscious of her dependence on him. He had never made love before, but Masters had explained how it was and that he must be gentle. Vasily felt he had come a long way since the days of childhood, when his whining had driven his family wild. He carried Elena to the bed and told her not to be afraid. Then he loved her like the passionate man he was and in the dawn of the new day made promises that warmed her heart. As the sun rose, Vasily lay holding Elena in his arms, watching a butterfly trapped inside the room. He got up and let it out into the cool air of morning. He was happy and in love. Nothing else mattered.

Two days later Valentina and Masters left for Madrid. Though Don Francisco had lost a small part of his land, the young couple were radiantly happy and this had settled Valentina's mind. Elena had given her a gift to take with her, a carved chest to remind her of her stay in Córdoba. She thought how lucky she was to have such a daughter-in-law. There were women who loathed their sons' wives and waged war on them from the moment of first meeting. She and Elena were different. Both remembered their first hours together and the triumph of Elena's appearance at the ball in Kentucky. Valentina looked out at the road skirting the far periphery of Don Francisco's land and saw horsemen moving people into some of the long-derelict farms. She spoke sharply to her husband.

"Are more people moving onto Don Francisco's property?"

"If he doesn't stop them every landless peasant for miles will come to take what's his until there's nothing left."

"And if he does oppose them?"

"He'll be killed or they will."

"Shall we go back and warn him?"

"He knows. Don Francisco posted men to watch his land. He was only waiting for the wedding to be over and for us to get away safely before he moved to evict the squatters."

"What's going to happen, Alex?"

"Who knows and we mustn't start worrying all over again about something that isn't part of our life together."

"Vasily's my son!"

"Vasily's chosen Spain and Elena. He's a man and he knows the trouble Don Francisco's in. We talked for hours about the range wars and what *we* do when someone tries to take our land."

"I don't want to hear anymore. I thought everything was settled. I thought Vasily and Elena were going to be happy forever."

"Close your eyes and go to sleep. I'll drive so fast we'll be in Madrid in a moment."

Valentina linked her arms with his.

"I wish I weren't going away."

"I've told you a hundred times, Valentina, we have our life and your sons have theirs. Ours is to enjoy each other and theirs is to live their lives independently. They're men; you can't treat them like children to be watched over forever."

Valentina fell silent. She was thinking of the rousing music and the dancing on Vasily's wedding night. She resolved to return to Córdoba soon to hire men to fight for Don Francisco if need be. She would tell Masters nothing of her plans if he continued to advocate aloofness from Vasily's problems. She closed her eyes and whispered an Andalusian song. Masters knew exactly what she was thinking.

## CHAPTER TWENTY-TWO

*Córdoba, June–July 1936*

———————
———————

Valentina and Masters had hurried from Madrid to Córdoba on receiving a letter from Vasily.

> *Dearest Mama and Alex,*
> I write with very good and very bad news. First, our second child is thriving. We have named her Lisabette Valentina. Sasha is not yet jealous of his new sister. He just keeps peering into the cradle in wonder. He says he will train Lisabette to help in the fields as we have no workers left. They all ran away for fear of reprisals. You will be shocked to hear that Don Francisco was murdered one week ago, when men tried to storm the finca. They are not content with having occupied our land, now they wish to take the finca too. We do not know what to do. All our neighbors have fled and no one would dare buy the estate if we tried to sell it. Please write with your advice.
> *Vasily*

Now Valentina was sitting under the arches of the inner courtyard, fanning her face and listening to the buzzing of bees in the climbing geraniums on the white wall. Their color and the pristine beauty of the daisy bushes with their fernlike leaves calmed her, despite the tension of the day. That morning, as she was eating breakfast in bed, peasant workers had come to ask for Vasily. They had been accompanied by a communist deputy from the city, a man anxious to please the mob. She had explained, as she had on their previous visits, that Vasily and Elena were in Seville and that they might not be back for some time. They had then asked if the estate had been deserted by its owners. Valentina had replied disdainfully, "Of course not. I am here and as Vasily's mother *I* am in charge. You may address any queries to me." The men had gone away stony-faced. It was one thing to confront Vasily Korolenko, who had repulsed them when they had tried to storm the finca for the second time. But to attack a woman who faced them unarmed and who had little connection with the land or the bulls or the horses of the Ortiz ranch, that was another matter. Spanish pride and gallantry won the day and the men had gone away.

Masters had gone through the tunnel that led under the house to the caves where Vasily and his family were hiding, to warn them that the peasants had again been to visit Valentina. Alone, she could only conjecture what else had been said. Before long, Valentina knew, men would come and occupy the hacienda. Perhaps they would be polite, perhaps not. They would come with guns to kill because killing had become a habit. She cooled herself with an esparto-grass fan and longed for her home in France. She kept thinking of the look on the faces of the men who had visited her that day. They had longed for Vasily's blood. It was not only his land they craved.

For two weeks after the peasants' visit Valentina and her husband lived under the burning summer sun in a house deserted but for two maids, their brother and father, an old retainer who had remained to look after those he had served for decades. Masters went out frequently to finalize deals on Vasily's instructions and soon there were no black bulls grazing on the Ortiz land. Only one had been kept and it was hidden on the estate of friends who lived many miles from Córdoba. Until now Masters had acted willingly as Vasily's deputy and transporter of animals to be sold. He knew no one else could be trusted to do what must be done. He also told himself with increasing certainty that the situation was coming to a climax. Vasily could not live forever with his family in the cave hideout, fed and watered by his mother. They were all living at great risk and Masters had decided to take Valentina away shortly. He had said nothing of his decision to her. Only to Vasily had he pointed out gently that a decision must be made. He must either come with them to the Domaine or he must stay and fight for what was his. If he stayed and fought he would certainly be outnumbered and killed.

Vasily was setting rabbit traps on a burning July day when he saw soldiers riding through the fields. He ran back to tell Elena what he had seen. She listened wide-eyed to his description of the soldiers.

"But some of those are surely Moors and men of the Foreign Legion stationed in Africa. Why would they come here to our estate?"

"I'll go and speak with Alex. Perhaps the soldiers came to overthrow the government. They might have called at the house. You know what rumors there have been."

Afraid to appear suddenly within the house, Vasily ran over the parched, dusty ground on his way to speak with his mother. He paused to look sadly at the empty fields where Don Francisco's bulls had once grazed. Then he scanned the rocky outcrops for a sign of his enemies, the peasants who were determined to take over what was his. He was almost at the gate of the finca when he saw a line of unkempt riders approaching from the riverbed. Vasily ran back to the cave, praying the peasants had not seen him. His heart was pounding as if it would burst and as he reached the spot where Elena was hiding he called out to her.

"Peasant riders are following me. I'll lead them toward the road and then come back over the old bull field. I love you, don't be frightened."

Elena ran to kiss her husband but he was gone, dodging and racing over the hard sand-colored earth, his red shirt the only patch of color in a monochrome landscape. She thought as she watched her husband, Take off your shirt Vasily, if you take it off they will not see you. But he did not hear and seconds later Elena cowered back inside a hollow in the wall of the cave, holding her children against her, as a band of riders galloped by. They were whooping wildly. They had seen their prey. They would soon be rid of Vasily Korolenko.

Valentina saddled a horse and rode out of the hacienda in the direction of the cave. She had seen Vasily from her bedroom window and had watched as he ran from the approaching riders. In her hand she carried a rifle and looped over her shoulder a bandolier. She did not know what she was going to do, only that somehow she must help her son if she had to kill every peasant in Córdoba. Masters was in town, buying fuel for his car. He was restive and she knew that soon he would take her away. She leaped down outside the cave and hugged Elena and the children.

"I saw men riding after Vasily. I brought your father's rifle. I know how to use it, so don't be afraid."

Elena pointed to the plain below, where the peasants made a sudden turn and were galloping away from Vasily.

"Look, Countess, the men are turning back!"

Vasily ran on, blinded by dust and choking with dryness and exhaustion. His clothes were filthy, his hair matted from long weeks of living in the cave. His hands and boots were covered in mud. He slowed his pace, suddenly conscious that he was hearing the sound of horses' hooves from a different direction. He squatted down near a clump of prickly pear bushes, resting his exhausted body and trying to work out what had happened. He could see the red-and-yellow bandanas of the peasants who had pursued him disappearing into the distance. Confused, he rose and began to walk slowly back to the cave. It was then he realized that there was a second troop of horsemen in the area. He looked over his shoulder and realized that they were gaining on him. He stood his ground and was soon overtaken.

The commander of the troop looked down at the young man. Vasily looked up at a darkly tanned Spanish face with a hooked nose and thin black mustache. The officer held himself like an old-fashioned cavalry man. Vasily scowled at the sardonic smile on the colonel's face as he spoke.

"Did you fall off your horse, young man, or did your peasant friends leave you behind deliberately to slow my progress?"

"I wasn't on a horse, sir, and those men were pursuing *me*."

"I am Colonel Diaz-Estellencs of the Nationalist Army."

Vasily was silent. There was no such thing as a Nationalist Army, so what did the man mean? He began to fear that these were government soldiers come to share out his land with the peasants. He weighed the colonel and tried to decide whether to run for safety. The colonel looked him over from sweat stained shirt to dirty boots.

"At which estate do you work, young man?"

"I own the estate which used to belong to Don Francisco Ortiz."

"You are one of the peasant squatters?"

"No, sir, I own the ranch. Don Francisco left it to me and his daughter Elena, who is my wife."

The colonel looked at his deputy and they laughed at the joke.

Soon the entire troop was laughing at this seemingly outrageous statement. Vasily glowered at them, furious to be ridiculed in this way. The colonel began to speak.

"You must answer me one question. Do you support the Nationalist Army?"

"I have never heard of the Nationalist Army."

"That is not what I asked."

"I'll answer none of your questions. I am Vasily Korolenko, husband of Elena, daughter of Don Francisco Ortiz. I own the ranch on which you're riding, though those peasants are trying to drive me out. I shan't leave for them and I shan't leave for you, either."

"Your name is not Spanish, is it?"

"I'm Russian. I was born in St. Petersburg. My father was the Count Korolenko."

"Now I understand why you cannot vouch your support to the Nationalist Army. You are one of those Russians who have been infiltrating our society and teaching our people the Bolshevik way of life."

"I'm no Bolshevik! My father was dispossessed of everything he owned and I will be too if I cannot find a way to deal with these peasants."

The colonel's smile faded and he looked sternly down.

"You are a fool to tell such lies. I am not a fool, however, and I do not believe you."

Valentina and Elena watched as Vasily spoke with the hawk-faced officer of the strangely dressed regiment. Now the peasants, who had been pursuing Vasily, had fled the two women were beginning to relax. Then, without warning, they saw soldiers seize Vasily and stand him against the leaves of the prickly pear bush. Valentina leaped to her feet, watching in horror as a line of men marched into position facing her son. The officer in charge seemed to be asking Vasily something. Valentina shouldered the rifle and took off the safety catch.

Vasily narrowed his eyes to look up through the rays of the sun to where Elena and his children were hiding. He knew he could not involve her with the colonel, but surely there was something he could do to convince the old man. A sense of unreality filled him and he tried in vain to remain calm.

"If you will take the trouble to check my story, sir, you'll find my mother, Countess Korolenko, in the finca of the Ortiz estate. I am speaking the truth, I swear on my son's life; if you kill me you will be a murderer."

"I do not have time to check the story of every lying peasant in Andalusia."

Valentina watched as the soldiers raised their rifles. She fired her own into the air. The colonel looked up in the direction of the cave, then brought down his sword. Five rifles fired and Vasily fell to the ground.

Elena let out a shriek of animal horror that would remain a nightmare in Valentina's mind for years to come.

Valentina aimed her rifle and fired again and again and again. The colonel fell. Two men from the firing squad dropped at his side. The others took cover and began answering the fire. The wounded colonel ordered his adjutant to help him back on his horse. Then he gave the order to advance and search out the dead man's accomplices.

Elena looked down at Vasily's body, at the red stain on the brown ground and the red shirt that matched the blood exactly. Already a mass of flies was buzzing around Vasily's head. Loud voices shrieked in her tormented mind, screams of agony and anguish that her husband was dead. She took the rifle from Valentina's hands and handed over her children.

"Please go back to the house at once, Countess."

"We must leave at once, Elena, come with me."

"If you recall, Countess, I once told you that all I ever wanted was to stay with Vasily for always."

As Elena walked to the edge of the stony outcrop, the baby began to cry. Valentina clutched Lisabette in her arms and held Sasha against her hip. Then, turning, she ran as fast as she was able back toward the house, through the rock-hewn corridor that had so recently seemed like Vasily's salvation. Behind her the sound of firing continued like the raging of the gods.

Elena fired the rifle once, then darted behind a rock and fired again from a different position. She saw men climbing toward her and knew in her heart that these were the troops of the Foreign Legion and that she had no chance at all. She looked over her shoulder and saw Valentina hurrying down the tunnel that led to the house. Sasha looked back briefly and Elena saw her son's face lit by the light as the trapdoor was raised. He was not crying. She smiled wistfully; Sasha was his father's son. His would be the future. She ran out and stood like a white-clad madonna, her long black hair billowing in the wind, her brown legs firmly astride the uneven rocks. She fired again and again and again.

One of the soldiers looked up and seeing the tears running down the woman's cheeks hesitated to return her fire. Another, less sensitive than his companion, took out a machine gun. The white dress became spotted with blood. The rifle fell from Elena's hands. For a moment she knew she was dying. Then, like an eagle, she lifted her arms as though in flight. Her body crashed from the ledge to the ground below. She landed not more than a foot from Vasily.

The colonel glanced at the woman and knew immediately that this was no peasant or revolutionary. Behind him his men were mounting their horses and preparing to leave. Two or three were still searching the hill to see if any opposition remained. At that moment a boy walked by carrying a wild turkey under his arm. The colonel called out to the child.

"Boy, come here and tell me if you recognize these two people."

The boy's lips trembled as he looked down on the bodies. Then he spat at each one before answering.

"That is Elena, daughter of Don Francisco Ortiz and that is the Russian, Vasily Korolenko, son of Count Korolenko."

"Where do they live?"

"They lived in the hacienda of Don Francisco after my parents took their own home and burned it. We would have burned Vasily Korolenko, too, if he had not hidden in the caves."

"Do you know what happens to those who dishonor the dead?"

The boy stared up at the officer and shook his head. The colonel's black eyes were terrifying and the boy cringed in the face of such loathing. The colonel spoke derisively.

"They die and go to hell, where their eyes and their bodies are eaten by rats. Remember it, boy. Now go away."

When the child had gone the colonel covered his face with his hands. He had been hasty and had killed without cause one of the very landowners he had come to save. He ordered his men to bury the dead and when it was done took the chain from around his neck and threw it to the ground where the couple lay. Then, with a mournful salute, he rode away to take Córdoba for General Franco and the Nationalist cause.

Valentina bundled the children into the car and followed them without a word. From what little she had told her husband he knew enough to realize they were in danger. A force of Nationalist troops was riding on Córdoba, to take the city out of government hands. Civil war had come to Spain and Vasily had been one of its first victims. Masters loaded what valuables he could find in the house, including Elena's jewels and the hidden Ortiz treasure chest. Then he locked the door and secured the gate. Faint echoes of the music and laughter and feasting of Vasily's wedding came into his mind and he looked at Valentina's tear-stained face and knew what she was thinking. He drove them away at speed. If it was a rebellion the Nationalists would have to take Madrid and all provincial capitals. He tried desperately to work out a suitable route, aware that he must skirt Valencia and Barcelona on his way to the frontier. Ignorant of the Nationalists' plans, he set himself to reach France within twenty-four hours. He said nothing to comfort his wife, conscious that she was still in a state of deep shock. Mercifully the baby was silent and Sasha already asleep. Masters stopped at Bailén to buy pans and a camping stove, bottled water and some wine, ham, cheese and fruit. Then he drove on into the night.

Valentina was thinking how tall Vasily had stood and how Elena had accepted his death with a fatalism that was eastern in its origin. She remembered how Sasha had looked back with longing at his mother and how he had since refrained from asking questions, as though instinct told him there were no answers to the questions he wanted to ask. She looked out of the window at black windmills outlined against a pale rose evening sky. Vasily's love for Elena had augured well for the future but had ended in tragedy. Now, at forty-nine, she was left with a boy of three, a baby of nearly one and the responsibilities of the Domaine and all those who lived in it. Suddenly she felt very tired. She longed to be selfish, to do only what she wanted to do and to leave responsibility behind. She held the baby close to her heart and kissed Sasha's head. The boy turned to her and asked gravely, "Where are we going, Nana?"

"We're going to my house in France."

"Will Lisabette and I live with you forever?"

"Of course you will and there'll be children for you to play with and lots of fields to run and ride in, just like there were at home."

"Is there grass where we're going?"

"Lots of grass, enough for a hundred horses."

"I shall like it and so will Lisabette."

The boy fell asleep. Valentina looked at Masters and then at the road ahead. They were driving on into the night and the Sierra de Alcaraz. She thought how black the mountains looked and how silent. She spoke to Masters for the first time in hours.

"How long will it take before we're out of this country?"

"It depends on what we meet. I reckon we have seven or eight hundred miles to go. With luck we could hit the border by tomorrow night or the day following."

At dawn they saw corpses floating like bloated sacks on a river. Valentina looked ahead, determined to ignore her surroundings. She knew Masters was exhausted because they had barely stopped since starting the journey, except to make food and drink for themselves and the children and to shelter when they saw troops riding through the countryside. They were now approaching Almansa. After the winding mountain roads, Masters had decided to follow the coast. Valentina rested her hand on his shoulder, longing to nestle in his arms.

Masters felt cinders in his eyes and knew he could drive no further. He pulled into an inn a small distance outside the town and led Valentina and the children through a pergola covered with bougainvillaea to a bare room furnished with a wooden table, six chairs and a collection of crucifixes. Masters explained to the owner that they were traveling toward the border with France. She rose and led him to a bedroom furnished in the same simple style, with a bed, a candleholder, two religious pictures and a chair painted red. Outside the window there was a terrace with a view to the flat fields of Albacete. The woman looked down at the baby and spoke in a whisper so as not to wake her.

"You are my first guests for three weeks. I was beginning to think there were no people left in Spain."

"Are you alone, señora?"

"I have my mother and my sister and her son."

Valentina put the child down on the bed. The owner asked the baby's name.

"Her name is Lisabette and her mother is dead."

Tears welled in the woman's eyes and she hurried out of the room, returning minutes later with an antique chestnut-wood crib. She and Valentina prepared the crib and the woman, Maria, hurried back to the kitchen to make food. She gave Sasha a basket and told him to go and collect eggs from the fowl hut. She did this because she felt that the boy needed something to occupy his troubled mind. She wondered what could possibly have happened to upset such a young boy so dreadfully. When Valentina came into the kitchen Maria poured her a glass of sherry and showed her the contents of the pans on the stove, soup made of onions and pigs' feet, a stew of chick-peas, mutton and pimiento, a stout casserole of turkey with garlic. She poured Valentina another glass of sherry and then bustled outside to show her guest the patio and the bamboo chairs on which she could rest.

Sasha collected the eggs and walked past his grandmother to the kitchen. Maria gave him a bowl of soup and another of fresh milk. The boy was very young but he was strong and sure of himself. She was therefore astonished when he dived under the table on sight of a soldier who had arrived to ask for water. Maria gave the soldier water and agreed with his complaints about the heat. When he had gone she called Sasha.

"You can come out now. The man did not see you."

"Is the soldier going to shoot us like they shot Papa and Mama?"

Maria was stunned for a moment. Then she went to the wall and blew the dust off an ancient blunderbuss, which she brandished before the boy.

"If anyone tries to harm you I will kill them. You need not be afraid while you are in my house."

That night Valentina and Masters sat on the terrace under the vine eating Maria's food. As night fell and cicadas whirred in the trees, Tomás, Maria's nephew, sang a soft and sweet lullaby as he played his guitar. A giant centipede waggled along the ground near the table. Valentina watched it and the candles flickered in a lazy breeze. She thought how peaceful it was, how very far away from what she had seen the previous day. Would she ever forget

it? She knew she would not and that both she and Sasha would be
scarred by the tragedy forever.

Masters raised his glass to her.

"To us, Valentina, to Sasha and Lisabette and all the kids of the
Domaine. It's funny, isn't it: these folks know nothing of the troubles. We'd best not tell them."

"They'll know soon enough."

"I can't wait to be home at the Domaine."

"Alex, how long will it be before we can be out of Spain?"

"Who knows? I don't know what we'll meet on the way. All I
know is I'll get us back to the Domaine as soon as I can."

"I'll never leave it once I arrive back."

"Of course you will, you'll come for holidays with me."

"No, I shall stay there; the children need me there and I need
the Domaine."

"Valentina, they're not children anymore. Some of them are married and have kids of their own."

"They need me, however old they are."

When Valentina and her husband had gone to bed Maria and
her family sat talking in the kitchen. Tomás had heard that soldiers
had landed that day in Alicante.

"They came from Africa and they call themselves the Nationalist
Army. They take each town on their way to Madrid and they shoot
everyone who refuses to support their cause."

"What are Nationalists?"

"I don't know, Mama. I think they are allied with the church and
the Fascists. Certainly they kill on behalf of the rich and not the
poor."

Maria ladled herself more stew.

"I shall say I am a Nationalist so as not to get shot. Then I shall
think as I have always thought. I hate soldiers. Soldiers always
bring death."

Throughout the following day Masters drove swiftly along the
road leading to the city of Valencia. He took a by-pass avoiding the
center of the city and proceeded on the road to Tarragona. In the
main square of that city a traveling circus was the entertainment of
the day. Masters stopped the car and watched a blowsy redhead in
pink tights prancing around, cajoling men and boys to follow her.
A clown with a shiny red nose and threadbare orange suit was link-

ing arms with the little girls of the area and leading them and their mothers to the big top, a giant red-and-yellow-striped umbrella under which a fire-eater was mesmerizing the crowd. Masters remained at the side of the road as a troop of soldiers rode by. The people of Tarragona fled. They had no idea who the soldiers were, but history decreed that soldiers were synonymous with suffering. The clown continued his banter. The lady in pink tights looked everywhere for someone to lead to the rickety wooden seats. And under the big top the fire-eater continued his act, oblivious to his surroundings.

Valentina was beginning to think they had left behind all the areas where Nationalist Troops might be and were therefore out of danger, when they neared the inland border and found their way blocked by a group of armed men. A polite elderly man informed Masters that he could not pass. Masters inquired why. The man replied, "This is Cataluña, señor. We are defending it against all opposition."

Masters showed his diplomatic passport. The man shook his head regretfully. Masters reversed and drove instead to the main road and on it to the main border. He was a hundred meters from the customs post when another line of rifle-bearing men blocked the road. This time they were not so polite.

"Get away, you can't pass."

"I have no quarrel with you. Why can't I go through?"

"We are letting no one in or out of the province, sir. We have been ordered by the Council of Cataluña to prevent all passage between this area and France in order to prevent undesirables from entering and leaving."

"I *have* to get to Paris."

"Turn back or we shall fire."

Masters spoke sharply to Valentina and her grandson.

"Get your heads down and, Sasha, hold on to your sister so she doesn't fall off the seat."

He revved the engine and to the surprise of the men drove directly on toward the customs post. When he did not stop, as they expected, the men began to fire. With bullets whistling around his head Masters drove forward, crashing through the flimsy barrier and continuing on the long, winding mountain road that would lead them to France. At the French customs post he stopped and offered his passport. He was passed through with barely a glance.

Valentina kissed her husband's hands.

"We're in France, Alex. Soon we'll be home."

Masters drove toward Perpignon. Sasha sat quietly on the back seat of the car, one hand on his sister, the other on Valentina's shoulder. He was thinking of the house about which he had been told, where there was grass enough for a hundred horses.

# BOOK III

## Paris, 1940-44

*. . . I would like you to know that Paris
has never been more beautiful. . . .*

Colette for *Paris Mondial* broadcast, 1939

# CHAPTER TWENTY-THREE

## The Domaine, June 1940

It was the twelfth of June. The Germans were in Evreux and closing in on Paris. Valentina was on the roof of the Domaine, looking down on the road. For miles and miles there were people streaming away from the capital. It was 11 A.M. on a bright spring morning and it was now known to be inevitable that the Germans would occupy Paris. Valentina saw people walking aimlessly into oblivion. On the horizon ominous black clouds pinpointed the enemy advance. Orange sparks and a dull red blotch in the sky showed where the villages had once been. She looked down again at the people on the road. There were no longer rich or poor. There were only refugees fleeing the capital. She saw elegant women inappropriately dressed in mink coats, riding in limousines by the side of cyclists, buses, carts and hearses, all loaded with people. Even the ambulances had been requisitioned and filled with the old who would be unable to walk such a great distance. Pale-faced children shuffled next to their parents. Babies were carried close to the heart and all the while the people looked upward, squinting against the sun, afraid of the planes that could come at any time to end all hope of a safe refuge.

Valentina reentered the attic and locked the window behind her. She had done all she could to prepare for war, storing food in every cupboard and hidden place in the Domaine and moving gold from her bank in Paris to others in London and Geneva. For a moment she stood looking at the dust-covered floor. How quiet it was here, a world away from the panic below and the panic within. She scanned the accumulated objects of her past, a parasol last used in the garden of the Korolenko Palace in St. Petersburg, an old picnic basket last seen in Kentucky, a leather trunk of out-of-date clothes, a silver lace lovers' knot from the wedding cake of Tanya, her daughter, and Jean-Jacques Laval, the lawyer's son. She had kept everything, because everything in the room was a minute of her past. She picked up a turquoise-studded music box, remembering the day in Córdoba when Elena had given it to her. On her return home to the Domaine she had put it away, so it could not remind her of the saddest day of her life.

Valentina walked downstairs to the second floor of the house, where most of the children were lodged. Laughter echoed from one of the rooms and from another there was the sound of the youngest children singing Russian songs. The schoolrooms were deserted, because Miss Knatchbull had given everyone the day off. She was now in the kitchen helping Zita, Nikolai, Louis and Masters stack food in a newly built false ceiling designed to keep their current supplies out of the way of any acquisitive eyes. Valentina went to the kitchen and watched as the food was placed in the new hiding place. She felt thankful that Louis was too young to be sent away and that Nikolai's eyesight was so bad he was considered no help in any army. Dmitry's age and his occupation had precluded him, at least for the time being, from being sent away and so they were still intact, to a degree, the same few members who had escaped Russia together, all except for Vasily. Valentina shrugged. She must not start thinking of Vasily. She put water on the stove and began to cut slices of ham and cheese and brown bread and put them on plates in the center of the table. She brewed tea to quench everyone's thirst when they came down from the ceiling and set the samovar on the table with slices of lemon and cubes of sugar.

As they ate Valentina watched Louis cutting himself extra slices of bread. She and Zita exchanged glances and the housekeeper laughed delightedly.

"My son's going to be a giant, ma'am. If all the bread he eats each day were put end to end it would reach the moon."

Masters consulted the list he had been making and then reported to his wife.

"If we eat carefully we'll have enough food there for a couple of years."

Valentina looked from her husband to the plates piled with ham and cheese and bread. Then she remembered Miss Knatchbull and asked where the old lady was. Louis answered with a broad smile.

"She's in her room hiding things."

"What kind of things?"

"Food, money, jewelry and souvenirs of the past. She has a wonderful scrapbook of pictures of you when you were young, Countess. She says you were the most beautiful young lady in St. Petersburg."

"That was a long time ago."

When they had eaten they went to their separate duties. Left alone with Zita, Valentina leaned against the wall of the kitchen. It gave way under her weight and she fell into total darkness. Above her head she could hear Zita calling for Masters to come at once. Then, as she looked up, she saw them both looking incredulously down as she lay at the foot of a staircase hewn out of stone.

Masters took a torch from the dresser and ran down the steps toward his wife.

"Are you hurt, Valentina?"

"Only bruised from head to toe, I think."

He followed her gaze and saw that she was staring at a long narrow passageway that led under the kitchen and below the wine cellar. Where it ended Masters could not imagine. He raised the torch and shone it down the passage. Then he turned to Valentina.

"Can you walk, let me help you up. Can you move all your fingers and toes?"

"I'm fine, Alex. Where do you think that passage ends?"

"Shall we go find out?"

Masters called for Zita to lock the outer and inner doors of the kitchen and to tell no one of their discovery. Then, holding out his hand, he led Valentina down the passageway and on and on until they turned right and came face to face with a carved-wood wall. Masters pushed but nothing moved. He tried to slide the wall but it did not slide. Then, remembering how Valentina had fallen through the kitchen wall, he pushed the top and bottom to see if they were weighted. The wall did not move.

Valentina looked at the door, which was carved with designs of griffins and unicorns. First she pushed the lemon wood eyes of the animals. Then she pulled the unicorn's horn. A hollow sound echoed in the silence as the door swung open and she stepped forward with her husband into an ornate bedchamber. Together they looked around, their eyes wide with astonishment. The walls were of royal-purple velvet stamped with gold in designs of ancient France. The chairs and bed hangings were in petit point, showing battles won in times long past. On a table in the far corner there was a French vermeille tea set and in the other corner a painted Venetian chest, a spoil of war for one of the kings of France. Masters hugged her to his chest.

"You realize where we are?"

"I've no idea."

"This is the Château de Rambouillet. One of the kings of France in times past must have had a jealous wife so he had the passage excavated. That way he and his mistress could exchange visits without anyone knowing. Look out of the window and you'll see the Domaine."

"I remember Monsieur Laval once telling me that a king's mistress had lived at the Domaine."

"Let's go back and tell Nik."

On the night of the thirteenth, the French Tenth Army withdrew from Dreux to Brittany. The Paris Army abandoned the capital and moved around the city along a line marked by the Rambouillet Forest and the Chevreuse Valley. Telephones ceased working. The postman did not call. And on roads between the Domaine and Paris men of the French Army were trapped, unable to escape the advancing Panzers because every outlet from the city was blocked by refugees. Throughout the night the battle raged and explosions were all around the house and no longer a distant tumult to be forgotten in sleep. The children began to cry. Their mothers ran to comfort them and were comforted in turn by Valentina. At 3 A.M., she asked Zita to make hot chocolate and to bring out the Dundee cakes Miss Knatchbull had recently ordered from England. The novelty of this took the children's minds off their troubles and soon they were sitting together in the banquet hall dressed in nightgowns and pajamas, gleefully enjoying their treat.

At 5 A.M., after a singsong of traditional Russian tunes, the children went to change. An uneasy silence had fallen on the countryside and no one wanted to be the first to remove the black screens from the windows to see what was happening outside. Valentina asked herself if this was the silence of death or the silence that comes after conquest. She was unaware that at this moment every German tank within miles of the Domaine was hurtling toward Paris to take part in the victory parade.

At ten Masters ordered the gates opened. What he saw outside shocked him so harshly he ordered the gates to be closed behind him. Then he rode around the estate on horseback, looking in anger at broken fences, trampled vines, shell-marked cottages and the undertaker's van outside the woodman's house. Having tethered his horse he ran inside the cottage and came face to face with Yvette, Jean's fifty-year-old wife. She nodded a greeting.

"I'm obliged for your visit, sir. How did you know Jean was dead?"

"I didn't know, Madame Yvette. I left my wife at home and rode out to see what had happened on the estate. I never saw such a mess in my life."

"Their tanks came from the direction of Dreux, at least thirty or forty, I should say. Jean and I were in bed but as they came nearer he got up and went to the window to see what was happening. They drove over the vineyard, knocking down the walls you'd built to keep the wind from the vines. They fired their guns in all directions though there was no oppostion in these parts. One of the bullets hit Jean as he was standing at the window. How shall we tell the countess about the vines, sir?"

"Leave that to me, madame."

"And what about the cottage? It goes with the woodman's job. I'm strong but I can't cut down trees."

"I'm sure we both want you to stay on, madame. Where's your son at the moment?"

"Serge is in the army, sir. He was the first to enlist from Rambouillet."

"If Paris is taken by the Germans some of the French forces will be sent home. Then Serge can carry on his father's job as he always planned."

"The Germans would send him away to work in their factories. That's what they do with all the men of the conquered countries who are in the right age group."

"I must go see the rest of the estate. I'll be back, madame."

Valentina climbed to the attic room and looked out on the land she loved. The woods had not been touched by the tanks. The mustard field was a mash of green and yellow, its colorful crop ruined. On the left of the field the vineyard with its once-neat stone walls was now a mass of rubble, vines, granite stones, spilled oil and petrol pushed into deep furrows in the ground. Valentina stood like a statue turned to stone, her eyes hard, her face pale with rage. In the distance two of the estate cottages by the river were in ruins and nearer home the woodman's cottage chimney lay on the ground in his front garden. She saw Masters riding toward the winery and leaving minutes later to go to the hunting lodge to see if Dmitry and his family were safe. She tried to make sense of the conundrum. All that had been built over two decades had been trampled into the ground. Anger white-hot in its ferocity filled her heart and for a while she remained at the window, trying to control her urge to shout distressed, angry accusations at the wind.

At last she walked downstairs to wait for something to happen. She found herself constantly looking at the clock. It was almost midday. Would the Germans arrive by the end of the day? A little boy came in crying because he had helped to cultivate one of the now-ruined fields. Valentina comforted him.

"The field will be resown and reworked when the war is over, Charles. You and your children and their children will keep the Domaine in good condition. We're lucky none of the bombs came into the house, remember that. Just think how horrible it would have been if we'd found ourselves sleeping next to a tank."

"If the Germans come I'll set my dog on them."

"Of course you will. Now go and fetch your mummy and bring her down to lunch."

They ate in the main hall, a silent assembly uncertain how to react to the happenings of the night. Masters eyed his wife and saw that Valentina was taut with anger. He hoped ruefully that no German would arrive to receive the brunt of her distress. He tried to act as though unmoved by the events of the previous night. He spoke of pleasanter things and was conscious that his wife answered, though her eyes were full of that distant expression that cut out personal contact and shared emotion.

At three-twenty on a hazy summer afternoon a large black car was seen speeding toward the Domaine on the road from Rambouillet. It stopped outside the gates of the house and an adjutant rang the bell. From her room Valentina saw one of the women letting in a low black Horch, which stopped in the courtyard close to the wall. The adjutant leaped out and opened the rear door for a tall hawk-faced officer in the uniform of a Waffen S.S. Oberführer. His face was suntanned, his body athletic, his bearing aristocratic. She could not see the color of his eyes but his hair was black and graying prematurely at the temples. She judged his age to be about forty. She watched as the adjutant came at his command and hammered on the door. She had thought a great deal about this moment and had discussed what to do when it arrived. She had discussed it with her husband, with Miss Knatchbull, Zita and other women in the house. She thought how glad she was that Masters was at the hunting lodge, helping Dmitry move his family to the main house. It was easier to say what had to be said when alone and unencumbered by Masters' protective instincts. She heard a voice calling from the hall.

"Oberführer Schuller, please bring the owner of this property to me at once."

Zita rushed upstairs to Valentina's room and opened the door.

"They're here, ma'am. An Oberführer and two others and a driver and lackey to open doors for them. Good luck, ma'am, God bless you."

Valentina descended the great staircase at a leisurely pace. The three men looked up and saw a tall, slim woman in elegant black lace. Her hair was dressed in a silver halo-like roll around her head. Her violet eyes were watchful, her manner aloof. The Germans stood to attention and clicked their heels. Oberführer Schuller weighed the woman more curiously than his companions. He had just read her dossier and knew she was fifty-four years old, though she looked little more than forty, a woman who had lived more lives than most. Valentina came face to face with him and nodded brusquely. Schuller's heart beat a little faster because he could feel her hate burning like acid into his consciousness. He made the necessary introductions.

"I am Hanspeter Schuller, Oberführer. This is Standartenführer Koch, Hauptsturmführer Wengen."

"I am Valentina Masters. I own this property. May I ask what you want, sir?"

Schuller saw women and children on the stairs and landing of the house. All were watching him intently. He turned to Valentina.

"May we speak privately with you, Countess?"

"I was Countess Korolenko before my second marriage. My son Nikolai is now the count. I therefore prefer not to use the title, though people still call me Countess after all these years."

"The title suits you, perhaps that is why."

Valentina looked into the green eyes and risked a polite smile. In the library she sat behind her desk and motioned for the men to sit one step below her.

"What do you wish to discuss, gentlemen?"

Schuller rose and paced the floor.

"We wish to occupy a suite of rooms in this property for an indefinite period. I came here as a courtesy to ask you to arrange this, Countess. If you do not I can, of course, requisition the entire property."

"Of course."

"You agree then?"

"No, sir, I do not. It would distress my sons and daughters far too much and their children also. It would be quite impossible to have men from the army which desecrated the estate on which we have all lavished money and hard work for almost twenty years. Follow me, gentlemen. Let me show you what the power of the Nazi Army did to us in a single night."

Koch and Wengen looked at each other and then to their superior. Oberführer Schuller nodded. Valentina walked ahead of them to the courtyard and motioned for them to follow her, first to the cottages razed in the previous night's bombing, then to the mustard field, now a muddy quagmire after a shower. The rain began to fall again, only this time heavily. Valentina raised her umbrella and took from her pocket a small book of photographs. She handed this to Schuller, sheltering him under her umbrella as he flicked through the pages. She explained the significance of the photographs.

"This is a photograph of the Domaine before your army passed in the night, and this is a set of photographs of my former home, the Flower House at Tsarskoye Selo, near St. Petersburg before and after the revolution. You will see that the communists and the Nazis have a great deal in common. Both take what is not theirs and both know only how to destroy. My adopted family of sixty-six Russian children was originally composed of aristocrats who had all been forced to leave the great estates, owned by their families, by the communists. Though they are now adults with children of their own, they remember well the fear and the agony of the years in St. Petersburg, when their entire families were murdered and their homes destroyed. That is why I don't wish to offer you rooms in my home. You may take them, of course, but I couldn't guarantee your safety for a single night. We Russians know well how to be rid of our enemies."

Valentina took back the album from the silent officer and, having nodded curtly to him and his companions, made her way back through the rain to the house. She was wishing fervently that she were still young and beautiful. There had been a time when one look from her had been any man's command. Now all she had left was the strength of her will. Would it be enough?

Schuller stood in the rain watching the figure in ebony lace holding the large black umbrella over her head. Her legs were mud-stained, her shoes ruined, but still the countess was a figure that commanded obedience. He had been right. Hate had been the emotion he had seen in her on first meeting. The countess and her family equated him and his officers with the communist rabble who had taken everything she had owned, the rabble who were now ruling Russia. Schuller thought of his own home on the banks of the Rhine and the vineyards his family had tended for generations. He looked at Wengen and saw the same confusion he was feeling. Wengen's family home was on the German-Austrian border. Koch's father had been administrator of the Black Forest region for twenty years. Everything that most opposed what each of the three believed was contained in the communist doctrine. Schuller turned to his companions and spoke his innermost thoughts.

"The coordinator of Abwehr Intelligence in Paris is to establish his operations here with us three to guard his work. The countess said we can take the accommodation if necessary, but I personally find it unacceptable to be considered in the same breath as the Communists of the revolutionary brigades in Russia. We are friends as well as fellow officers, I ask you to speak freely."

"I agree, sir."

"I too, sir."

"We shall return to Paris, then, and I propose we bring back the men who will assist us in guarding the coordinator and also all that will be necessary to create an atmosphere of calm within this house. In that way we may be given hospitality and not hostility by our hosts. It is going to be a long war and we shall be here until the end of it. I prefer that we sleep easily in our beds and that this most vital undertaking be successful."

"May I ask why this location was chosen?"

"The coordinator is too important to be billeted in Paris. The Allies may bomb the city at any time. This location is one of seven chosen for use by members of the High Command and that of Military Intelligence. The others are all great houses around Paris. We chose them because we do not think the Allies will bomb them. The English in particular venerate monuments and castles."

The following morning Valentina was wakened at six by the sound of Miss Knatchbull calling along the corridor.

"There will be no laughing, shouting of rude words or rude gestures. You will behave like the ladies and gentlemen you are and will not, repeat not, antagonize the enemy while they are working on the countess's land. Do you understand?"

Valentina opened her bedroom door and looked out.

"What's happening, Natty?"

A roar of information greeted her. Valentina silenced the children and told them to go to breakfast. Miss Knatchbull came to her side with a broad grin on her face.

"A lorry arrived an hour ago with a squad of big strong German soldiers. They're rebuilding the walls of the vineyard and doing their best to set things to right. There are others in the mustard field. They've removed all the plants that were destroyed and are planting seedlings. That hawkish fellow who came yesterday is sitting outside the gate with his two colleagues. I should have thought they'd have been ringing the bell and asking to come in before now, but they just sit there watching those poor young fellows sweating it out. They'll be hungry by lunchtime. You'd best advise Zita to get some stew on the stove."

"Those are German soldiers, Natty!"

"They are soldiers who are rebuilding your estate, my dear. I don't know what you said to the Oberführer yesterday but he's doing his best to right the damage that has been done. He can't do anything about the lost vines and the mustard harvest, but he's doing what he can. Accept it graciously or we may get someone infinitely less sensitive than he billeted in your house."

Masters rose at seven and looking out of the window saw a squad of blond young Germans working in the fields. He went downstairs for breakfast. Valentina and Miss Knatchbull had already eaten and were sitting with Zita making lists of food that could be used to provide a substantial midday meal for the soldiers. They settled on rabbit stew with garlic and potatoes with jugs of wine and water and a heavy apricot pudding. Masters smiled wryly at his wife's expression.

"Yesterday you were ready to shoot the Germans. Now you're planning to give them lunch."

"Yesterday they ruined my crops. Today they're here to mend the damage."

"You've just learned one of the great lessons of war, Valentina: bend with the wind."

At one Zita walked with Louis and one of the other boys to the field. First they opened the gate and let in the Oberführer and his companions, having invited the Germans to lunch. Then they put up trestle tables normally used for the annual garden party in the grounds of the Domaine. When the tables were erected jugs of wine were placed at intervals along their length with baskets of bread and tureens of stew. The field workers looked enviously at the table. Then Zita shouted and banged a pan with her spoon.

"Lunch is served. Lunch! Come for lunch."

In the dining room of the Domaine Nikolai took his place at his mother's side. Masters sat at the other and Oberführer Schuller and his two men at intervals along the table. The children and their mothers filed in and sat as though this were a day like any other. Wine was served with a meal of terrine, salad, boiled chicken and chocolate mousse. Valentina spoke to the Oberführer.

"You won't have food like this all the time you're billeted with us, but today we decided to celebrate the fact that your soldiers have started the restoration of the estate. I'm very grateful to you, sir."

Schuller raised his glass.

"To you, Countess, and your very large family."

The Oberführer became aware that he was being watched

closely by a small girl sitting opposite him at the table. She had spun-silver hair and large blue eyes and looked uncannily like Valentina. He looked closely and saw that her hand was being clutched by a handsome young boy with jet black hair and dark eyes. Curious, he spoke for the first time to one of the children in the house.

"May I ask your name, Mademoiselle?"

"I'm Lisabette Valentina Korolenko. This is my brother Sasha."

"And which is your mama?"

A hush fell over the assembly and Sasha answered quickly.

"Mama and Papa were killed at the commencement of the war in Spain, sir. That is why Lisabette and I live with the countess, our grandmama."

Anxious to change the subject, Schuller looked around the vast table and asked each person to state his or her name. A procession of voices answered: I am Ariane, Vladimir, Marina, Eloise, Michel, Madame Fortunov, Madame Yurbatov, Katrina, Natasha, Nina, Dmitry and my wife Irina, our twins Ivan and Boris and Tousia and Amala and our daughter Anya . . . Nikolai Korolenko, the countess's son.

Schuller weighed a handsome, strongly built man in his thirties with blond hair and deep-blue eyes behind thick gold-rimmed spectacles.

"You were not enlisted into the French army, Count Korolenko?"

"No, sir, my vision is bad and getting worse. I was rejected by the Military Board."

"No doubt you find plenty to do here in the country where food growing will become more and more important to us all."

After the introductions there was an awkward silence. Then Lisabette spoke to her brother's alarm.

"Why do you wear a gun at the table, sir? Are you going to shoot us like the other Germans shot Monsieur Jean, the woodman?"

"No, Lisabette, I am planning to do my best to be an invisible guest. I have no wish to upset any of you. I have my work and you and your parents have yours. We shall meet only at mealtimes, with the countess's permission."

Everyone looked to Valentina to see what she would say. She looked to Masters and when he nodded turned to Schuller to reply.

"After lunch I'll take you to the suite of rooms you and your officers will occupy Oberführer. I think we should all prefer to have you billeted in the house rather than someone less willing to understand our wishes. Isn't that right? Do you all agree?"

Everyone agreed.

# CHAPTER TWENTY-FOUR

## Paris, Winter 1941

The winter was the coldest Paris had known in many years. Valentina shivered despite the fur coat she was wearing. At her side Masters was grim-faced and tense. They were walking from the Arc de Triomphe down the Champs-Elysées, neither speaking, each appalled by the new Paris before them. Small sentry boxes painted black, white and red had sprung up all over the city. Black, white and red flags with the swastika emblem decorated major buildings and monuments. Most of the beautiful bronze statues that had for decades graced the squares and leafy boulevards of Paris had been torn down and taken away to Germany to be melted and used as shell casings. In their place there were yet more sentry boxes and signposts stating in German the direction to Wehrmacht and S.S. and Propagandastaffel offices.

At the stroke of twelve a regiment of German soldiers marched from the Arc de Triomphe to the Place de la Concorde. Ahead of them a military brass band played tunes of German glory. At first Parisians had lined the pavements to watch this daily manifestation of might. Some had spat on the conquerors and had been arrested for their trouble. Now the boulevard was empty, because Parisians of all ages had decided to shun the daily exhibition. Let them goosestep and sing and play their discordant marches. We do not have to act the victims for their benefit. This was the feeling that made Masters draw Valentina into the doorway of a nearby arcade and turn her face with his own to the wall. He was conscious of tears falling down her cheeks and saddened by the droop in her shoulders, the resignation in her eyes. He tried to make light of the new order.

"Someday, when the Germans have gone, we'll drink champagne and only remember our first days in Paris together. We'll put all this right out of our heads."

"I should have stayed at home."

"They've gone, Valentina, let's move on."

There was a big red flag with a black swastika emblem flying over the Crillon Hotel. Others flew from the Claridge, the Bristol, the Meurice. As Masters led her toward the Ritz, where they were planning to have a drink, Valentina was hoping that by some miracle Monsieur Auzello's patriotism would have prevailed and that there would be no swastika flag over her favorite hotel. She paused on entering the Place Vendôme, shocked to see the same flag waving over the Ritz and German sentries standing at attention outside the Vendôme entrance to the hotel. Others could be seen in the hall. She turned to her husband.

"The Ritz is occupied by Nazis. We don't want to drink there, do we?"

"The Cambon side is still running as usual. The Germans only managed to requisition half the hotel. Come on, put a brave face on it, we don't want to disappoint the Auzellos."

They drank a martini that tasted less than usually elegant and talked for some minutes with Blanche, the manager's American wife. Despite her loathing for the occupation, Blanche's sense of humor prevailed and she recounted how her husband had insisted that his German guests produce ration books, just like everyone else. When they refused, Auzello had served them a meal of vinegar and cabbage soup. Now officers on the Vendôme side of the hotel ate food collected each day in Wehrmacht vans from the supply depot in Passy. Naturally some of the priceless supplies found their way into the normal guests' kitchens. As Blanche laughed, Valentina thought she looked terribly thin. She ventured to ask why Madame had stayed in Paris.

"Would it not have been wise to return to New York, Madame Auzello?"

"Call me Blanche, and no it wouldn't. My home's here in Paris. What would I do in New York if I went back? All my friends are dead or married and there's nothing there for me anymore. How about you, Mr. Masters, don't you think of going home?"

"I think about it but I don't go. My home's in France too. There's a lot of work to be done to keep the Domaine going and the kids eating all they should."

"I wish you luck. Having that place and all those mouths to feed is almost as bad as running the Ritz."

Valentina and her husband were surprised to find their apartment on the Ile St.-Louis unoccupied and in perfect condition. She rang the bell of her neighbor Madame Bandol's apartment. There was no reply so she rang the bell of the apartment on the other side. Monsieur Duchêne, director of the Banque de France, opened the door. Valentina was shocked to see that he had aged almost beyond recognition since their last meeting. She handed him a packet of smoked gammon, brought with her from the Domaine.

"I brought you some eggs and brown bread too Monsieur Duchêne."

He looked at the gifts and then back to Valentina.

"Come in, Countess. I'm living alone since my wife died, two weeks after the Germans came. Thank you kindly for the ham and the other food. I've certainly been hungry these past months."

"Are things well with you, as well as can be expected?"

"This apartment stayed free from German occupation despite the shortage of accommodation because of Madame Bandol. Your apartment is also free from their odious presence thanks to her."

"How did she manage it?"

Duchêne put the gammon steaks on a plate and locked them in his food cupboard. Valentina wondered why he was so ill at ease. When he spoke she understood.

"Madame Bandol is beautiful and famous, even though she's not exactly young. She was one of the first of the actresses to go back to work on the order of the Commander of Gross Paris. She did *La Dame aux Camellias* at the Théâtre Matignon and while she was appearing there one of the *boches* fell in love with her; at least that is what she told me. He visits her on Tuesdays and Thursdays at five-thirty precisely. His brother, who is aide de camp to the commander, visits on Monday at the same time. Neither stays the night. It's like a visit to the dentist for them. Madame Bandol used her influence to keep the other two apartments on her floor unoccupied and for that we must be grateful to her, whatever we might think of her liaisons."

Valentina watched as Duchêne prepared coffee from a nearly empty container.

"How are things at your bank? Are your affairs much hindered by the occupation?"

"Hindered? My business affairs have been taken out of my hands by the Devisenchutzkommand. As you know they've taken over all the banks and issued Reichskreditkassenscheine in place of the deposited notes. They do as they like with everyone's transactions. They even opened safes in the Paris area and blocked foreign accounts. You had good advice from your lawyer Laval. I don't know where you keep your gold these days, but wherever it is it's safer than with me."

"I owe Monsieur Laval a great deal."

"You know he's a Jew, of course?"

"That hasn't entered into my dealings with him, Monsieur Duchêne."

"Don't misunderstand me, Countess. I mean Laval could be deported at any time. The Germans hate Jews and their poisonous loathing is fast spreading in our own country. It would be best if you advised Laval and his family to leave France."

"He wouldn't listen to me."

"He might. God only knows how you'd get them out of Paris, though. They say one cannot get a raft through the cordon of security at the Channel Ports."

Valentina returned to her apartment and sat looking out of the window at the Seine and the barges gliding by. An old fisherman was there at the quayside, his face calm, as though unmoved by the conquering grip on his city. A barge captain called to the old man, who raised his cap and waved a reply. Valentina held Masters' hand.

"Duchêne says we should advise Laval to get out of France."

"Because he's a Jew?"

She nodded, unable to bring herself to think of what might happen to Tanya if Laval and his son were arrested. She looked anxiously at Masters.

"Will Tanya be affected by her marriage to Jean-Jacques?"

"They'd all be better out of France."

Darkness fell and the curfew came, emptying the streets of all but German patrol cars and sentries. Seeing Valentina's distress, Masters tried to cheer her.

"Don't worry too much. When all this is over we'll have good times again. We had good times before, didn't we? Just keep on thinking of them. Don't dwell on the present. Think of the day I first showed you the Domaine and the inn where we had dinner under the apple trees. Think of Kentucky and the time you danced the Charleston, when you'd always said you wouldn't."

"It seems such a very long time ago, Alex."

"It sure was. In those days I could dance all night. Now I'm always tired."

They held hands and finished the last of the bottle of wine. Then they went to bed because the apartment was cold and there was no oil for the stove. Valentina lay awake, unable to take her mind from thoughts of those who lived in fear in the Marais. She thought of Laval, whose thoughts had always been for her good and for the good of the children who had lived their lives in the Domaine. She whispered to Masters but he had fallen asleep. She spoke more loudly.

"Alex, how would you get someone out of Paris if you needed to, someone like Laval?"

Masters did not answer and Valentina resigned herself to a sleepless night of making plans that might never come to fruition. At seven she rose and in the gray light of dawn stood looking out of the window at the dark waters of the Seine. The windows were frozen on the inside and through the filigree ice patterns she saw a barge slowing down at the Pont St.-Louis. A crew member jumped off and ran up the stone steps to the road. The barge continued on its way unnoticed because it was one of the sights of Paris that even the German sentries took for granted. Valentina continued to sit at the window, counting the number of barges that passed by. By 8 A.M., when Masters woke, there had been six. She felt certain that she had found a way to get the Laval family out of France.

The spring of forty-two was unusually dry. As a result there would be little grain and virtually no fruit to pick in June and July. Valentina was in her bedroom talking with Zita.

"How are our supplies lasting?"

"I've made a list for you, ma'am."

Valentina looked down at the list and then at Zita.

"If it weren't for the supplies the Oberführer brings we'd be having haricot beans for breakfast, lunch and dinner."

"Louis brought his hidden supplies back from that cave near the river. They'll help for a while."

"What were they?"

"Tins of tomatoes, hams, tongue and chicken in aspic. Miss Knatchbull still has her hoard too."

"What does she have?"

"I don't know, ma'am. She gets more and more secretive as she gets older."

"Leave her be for the moment."

Valentina looked again at the list. They had plenty of flour, salt, dried beans, peas and lentils and coffee. Oil, soap and sugar were almost gone and they had only two more cases of tinned meat. She shook her head as she studied Zita's neat writing and her estimate of their needs over the coming year.

"It's fortunate we have our own land and potatoes planted, apart from those we grow for the Germans. I never thought the children would take to the land as they have."

"They love it, ma'am. Even Lisabette goes with them to the fields and she screamed blue murder the other day when Miss Knatchbull tried to stop her."

"Have you anything interesting planted?"

"I have tomatoes, herbs and lettuce. The hens are laying and the turkeys are growing bigger every day. Don't worry, ma'am. We have our land and that makes everything worthwhile. Folk in Paris are trying to keep themselves alive by growing vegetables in their wardrobes!"

"I shall speak with Oberführer Schuller and see if he can help."

"He's a good man."

Valentina looked sharply at Zita.

"I never thought I should hear you say that of a German officer."

"No, ma'am, neither did I."

Valentina walked to the field, where Schuller and Nikolai were shooting with Koch and Wengen. She stood watching for a few moments as the men made one last attempt to increase the bag. Then Schuller handed a pouch to Nikolai and another to Wengen and the two went back to the house to give the rabbits to Zita.

Koch passed by carrying the guns. Valentina smiled at his sweating face.

"You had a good morning I see, Standartenführer."

"We did, Countess. We shall all have a fine dinner tonight and tomorrow, too. It reminds me of home when I go shooting."

Schuller turned to Valentina and weighed her slim body and the ethereal halo of hair. How clean she looks, he thought, as if nothing in the world could ever soil her. She led him from the meadow to the stream where the family had enjoyed a picnic the previous Christmas. He helped her over a rough patch of ground, smiling at her directness.

"Before the war was declared my husband and I went to Paris and scoured the shops for food. We spent a great deal of money and hoarded the supplies we bought. I foolishly expected my stock to last for about two years. However, the room where we store our food is now almost empty. We have buckets and bicycles and hardware in plentiful supply with flour, dried peas and beans and two boxes of tinned meat. When we finish that we shall have to eat the potatoes and turnips we grow on the land and the eggs our hens lay, nothing else."

"I didn't realize that four Germans ate so much, Countess."

"You don't eat so much, Oberführer, but the soldiers who restored the damage to the property ate a great deal during their four months with us and the children who are staying here with their mothers also eat from morning to night. They are growing children and I don't like to stop them. Is there anything you can do to help me?"

"How is Mr. Masters getting on with the food growing on your fields?"

"My husband and Nikolai have been working twelve to fifteen hours every day in the fields with Dmitry and Louis. All the children and some of the mothers have also been planting, once the men turn the ground. We have potatoes, turnips and cabbage for ourselves and also for the supply depot in Rambouillet. We can't plant any more because it would be requisitioned for German restaurants in Paris."

"Wengen and Koch will shoot each morning, I too when I am free."

"How are you getting on with the new coordinator?"

Schuller looked away to the river. The new coordinator was a fanatic of the worst possible kind, unlike the previous officer, who had just been posted back to Berlin. Schuller shrugged.

"To be as direct as you, Countess, I do not care for our new coordinator. It was only with the greatest difficulty that I persuaded him not to search this property. He insists it must be searched each month as a matter of security. He is very keen on security because he was previously an intelligence coordinator in Poland and there came into contact with the men who worked at a local detention camp. He was most impressed by their efficiency."

"What does he expect to find?"

"Guns, ammunition, enemy agents, who knows? I shall try to use my authority to dissuade him, but he came here on the highest recommendation—the Führer's personal recommendation, I believe —so I may not be able to control him."

"Why does he eat his meals in his room? The previous coordinator ate with us."

"He does not wish to fraternize with the enemy."

"Why not? We're all quite happy fraternizing with you."

"He does not wish to be friendly in case he must discipline the members of this household. He has some difficulty in understanding that this is a home and not a battlefield."

Valentina was silent. Since the arrival of the new coordinator, with his skull-like head and empty black eyes, there had been an imperceptible change in the atmosphere of the house. Fear was their new and unwelcome companion, felt by even the youngest children, who tiptoed past his office, fearful of disturbing him. Valentina thought of Masters, who had known at once that the new arrival would bring with him danger and disruption. She counted herself lucky to have Schuller to act as a go-between with his colleague. Fearful that they might be being watched, she moved to the shelter of the trees. Schuller followed.

"Don't be afraid, Countess. The coordinator cannot see us from his window."

She turned to face Schuller, searching his eyes for some sign as to his feelings.

"I don't like the coordinator, Oberführer. From the moment he arrived in this house we've all feared him. As you know, this is a house of women and young children who are not involved in any way in anything that could be considered detrimental to your work. I'm sure you have a file of information on all of us. If you've read mine you'll know that my life has been a turbulent one and that I am now of an age to need peace and tranquillity. I have no intention of doing anything to disturb our situation at this time. We all know we're lucky to have you and your officers and not men who would destroy everything that is precious to us. I don't know what I shall do if the coordinator upsets the children."

"Do nothing, Countess. I shall do all I can to protect you and your family. As for food, I will bring back whatever I can from the supply depot. You know, of course, that there is no butter in Paris, also no real coffee, fruit or vegetables, and that even the black marketeers cannot provide milk."

"I've heard that things are worsening every day."

"How did you hear that?"

"I send food to a neighbor in Paris, just a few eggs, a chicken or a sack of potatoes whenever I can. He wrote last week and said that he'd lost ten kilos in weight. He's Monsieur Duchêne, our friend on the Ile St.-Louis, you've heard me mention him often."

"How do you send the letters, Countess?"

"Through the post, of course."

Schuller was silent for a moment.

"I worry too much on your behalf. There can be no harm in writing through the official mail."

"Did you think someone would see harm in it?"

"The coordinator has ordered that all letters sent from this house be opened as a matter of security."

"I shall train carrier pigeons in the future!"

"I believe you would, Countess. I should not like to have you as an adversary, that is for certain."

Valentina smiled despite herself. Schuller continued thoughtfully.

"You realize, of course, that the coordinator has also read your file. Perhaps that is why he is so cautious about everything to do with this property."

Valentina went to the field where Masters and Nikolai were working with the others. She carried with her a jug of lemonade and a tray of onion tarts. The men downed their spades and crowded around her. Dmitry spoke angrily.

"Our quota of potatoes has been increased, Countess. We'll have to plant another field in order to be able to send as much food to the depot as the Germans are demanding."

"Will we still have enough for ourselves?"

"Only if we plant the new field at once."

"I'll send the women out to turn the ground."

Dmitry stared at Valentina and then looked questioningly to Masters.

"Women can't turn the ground. It's all right for them to plant things with the children's help, but women cannot be asked to dig."

"Of course they can. If they can give birth to children they can dig. I shall send them out at once. Can you spare me a moment, Alex?"

Valentina walked back to the house with her husband. In the kitchen she asked Zita to make some milky coffee, remembering how Schuller had told her there was no milk to be had in Paris. They drank the coffee in the conservatory, amid tomatoes, lettuce and cucumbers, where once there had been exotic flowers. Masters was preoccupied, as he had been for days. Valentina waited until he was rested before telling him what Schuller had said about his new intelligence coordinator. Masters took the news calmly, not surprised that his suspicions had been proved right.

"He's a Nazi to his fingertips, Valentina. He's everything a guy like Hitler would admire and he was appointed to be Abwehr head of this area because he's trusted. Now all that bull about being friendly with the French is over Hitler needs someone he can trust."

"Is he the reason for your being troubled, Alex?"

Masters shook his head.

"I never think of him. To me he's invisible like a germ and I'd rather he stayed that way."

Masters knew he would have to confide in Valentina and spoke resignedly.

"I was hoping to keep this from you, but it's your house and our family and I need your advice. Two days ago Laval was arrested by the Gestapo. Before he was taken away from his office he managed to tell his secretary to warn Tanya. Jean-Jacques had just come back on leave from the munitions factory where he's been working in Germany. When he heard what had happened he brought Tanya and the baby here. Then he went to the jail at Gazeran, shot three Gestapo guards and two S.S. officers and brought Laval back here too. They're all in the passageway leading to the Château de Rambouillet. I kept them there the first night but I had to move them this morning when some Germans searched the place."

Valentina thought of Laval, Tanya, Jean-Jacques and the tiny baby only two months old. She remembered how she had told Schuller she was not involved in anything illegal. Only an hour ago she had said that and he had believed her. Now she would have to become involved because they could not leave the Laval family to rot under the ground. She looked at Masters and saw lines of exhaustion on his face. For weeks he had been working like a laborer in the field. He had joked that the digging and plowing had firmed his muscles, but each night he tossed and turned, suffering from cramp and backache because he was too old for such harsh exercise. She kissed his cheek tenderly.

"What have you thought of doing, Alex?"

"I'll have to take them out later. I'll be able to try that harebrained scheme of yours about putting them on a barge going south from Paris."

"You'll do nothing of the kind. You have to plan these things carefully. I'll go to Paris after lunch and arrange passage south with one of the barge captains. Then, when I've done all I must do, you can travel to Paris with the Laval family. It will be best if you and Laval travel together and separate the others. The Gestapo will be looking for the entire family."

"Better still if you and Tanya and the baby were to go to Paris today and stay there until we can join you. No one's going to be taking much note of a woman and her daughter and grandchild."

"What will you do with Laval and Jean-Jacques?"

"They'll have to stay in the cellar until we're ready to get them out. Best if you take Tanya out now though. I've been scared to death someone might hear the baby crying."

Valentina took Tanya upstairs to her old room and sat on the bed watching as her daughter put clothes into a case. Tanya looked longingly at the trinkets in her old jewel box, the paintings on the wall, the pressed flowers she and the other children had placed under glass during the long winter evenings of their youth. The baby gurgled on the bed. Valentina picked it up and nursed it while Tanya changed her clothes.

"You know, Countess, I still dream of this room and of being at home with you."

"You're happy, aren't you?"

"I'm happier with Jean-Jacques than I ever thought possible."

"Take this, it will keep you and make sure you're free to travel. The key fits the front door of my house in Monte Carlo. The smaller key fits the safe that's under the floor in the living room. There's gold there, enough to keep all of you until the end of the war."

Valentina handed Tanya a thick wad of notes and a key. Tanya looked at it as if it held the secret of her whole future.

"Will we really be safe in the South of France?"

"I think you will, safer than here for sure. It's no paradise, of course. Folk there are short of food and the ground's stony so they can only grow olives, but you'll get by. If you feel you're in danger hire a fishing boat and go to Corsica or Sardinia until the war's over. You have the maps I gave you and you have money. That's all we can do for the moment."

Valentina led Tanya into the dining room, having primed everyone not to appear surprised by her presence. As lunch was served Lisabette beamed across the table at Tanya and was only prevented from making one of her forthright comments by the appearance of Schuller, Koch and Wengen.

On seeing Tanya, Schuller spoke to Valentina.

"How lucky you are, Countess, to be visited so often by your sons and daughters. I wish mine came to see me as often. How is your baby, Tanya?"

"She's well, sir. She had a bad start in life and kept losing weight but now she's better and we're hopeful she'll survive and be strong. She's certainly tenacious."

"Like her mother?"

"The countess taught us all to be tenacious, sir."

They ate rabbit cooked in mustard and garlic, boiled potatoes and the last of the winter cabbage. There was enough for second helpings, which left Schuller in an expansive mood.

"I'm going to Paris this afternoon. May I bring you anything back, Countess?"

"You could give me and Tanya a lift to Paris, if it wouldn't cause you any difficulty. I have to go to the dentist and Tanya has to see her doctor."

"I shall be delighted, of course."

"I'm going to comb the shops for some food."

"I doubt you'll find very much."

Wengen took money from his pocket and handed it to Valentina.

"Please buy a stylish birthday card for my mother, Countess. She likes those with lace and a sentimental verse."

Schuller leaned forward to speak to Masters.

"And you, Mr. Masters, what can I bring you back?"

"A Havana cigar if you can find one."

They all laughed delightedly at Masters' longing for a cigar. Whenever anyone went to Paris he told them to bring him back a Havana. No one had yet managed to fulfill the order, though he persisted in asking. While Zita served an apple pudding, Valentina chatted with one or other of her adopted daughters. Schuller watched their animated faces and was content. He was going to Paris and taking the countess with him. It seemed like something to look forward to. He was curiously at home in the Domaine and had been from the very moment of first arrival. He often thought of his wife back home in Germany and was shocked to feel remote from her. Then he admitted that they had drifted apart over the years, so gradually that he had barely noticed the change. He thought sadly that in war one's family was whomever was at one's side.

At ten past three Valentina and Tanya stepped into the back of the Horch and were driven off in the direction of Paris.

From an upstairs window the coordinator watched them. When the car had disappeared he telephoned the local garrison at Gazeran and asked for a party of soldiers to search the entire property.

Olga, one of Valentina's Russian daughters, was returning to her room with her two children when she heard the coordinator speaking on the telephone. She put her children to bed for their afternoon nap and went immediately to warn Zita of what had been said. Together they went from room to room warning everyone that the house was going to be searched.

Three cars appeared with the search party of Gestapo officers. They saw children working in the fields, women hanging out washing in the orchard and young boys sweeping the courtyard. Masters invited them in and asked for an authorization signed by the instigator of the search. The coordinator's voice startled him from the stairs.

"I ordered the search, Mr. Masters. Please step aside and let us see if your home is as innocent as I have been led to believe."

# CHAPTER TWENTY-FIVE

## The Domaine, May–September 1941

———————

———————

Three days after the search of the property Valentina was still in Paris. It had proved harder than she had imagined to make contact with a barge captain, and the old fisherman who had unwillingly agreed to act as intermediary had made no promises at all. Unable to watch Tanya's anguished face any longer, Valentina made her way to the quayside and berated the old man.

"Do I have to beg for your help?"

"I shall make contact in due course, Countess."

"I can't wait any longer, I must make contact myself."

When the next barge passed by traveling south, Valentina hailed the captain and spoke with him. He shook his head and passed on. The old fisherman, taking pity on her, called out.

"Your man won't be by until two this afternoon. Come down then and I'll introduce you."

Valentina returned to her apartment and found Tanya sitting by the window holding the baby and staring fixedly at the river.

"Did you and Alex make an arrangement for Jean-Jacques and his father to meet us here in Paris?"

"I was supposed to be back at the Domaine on Tuesday morning, after arranging with a bargemaster to take you all south. If I didn't return, Alex said he would bring Jean-Jacques and his father here today at noon."

"It's already twelve-thirty. Does Alex have a key to the apartment?"

"Of course he does, now do calm down."

"How can I be calm? My whole life is at stake. I must love Jean-

Jacques and I never realized it. I love him, Countess. It's been worth all this to make me realize it."

"You remember that small hotel on the Quai d'Anjou where we once ate lunch some time ago."

"We had moules marinière in the courtyard and some young guitarists came and serenaded us."

"Let's go and eat there again."

"It will be full of Germans."

"All the better. They'll not think you're a fugitive if we eat among them."

At five minutes to two Valentina hurried with Masters, Jean-Jacques and Laval down to the water's edge. She was desperately anxious to be sure the Lavals were clear of the island before the 2 P.M. patrol passed the bridge. It was a risk to take them all down, but if the bargemaster said yes he would take them they would all be ready to leave. If he said no, Valentina passed her hand over her brow and wondered what on earth they would do then. She was grateful to see that Laval had on a straw boater, as if he were going for an afternoon outing on the river. Jean-Jacques was dressed in a fisherman's jersey and Tanya was carrying a lace parasol. They had chosen to go during daylight hours because there was little option. The only other friendly barge captain passed the Pont St.-Louis at four in the morning, a time which would involve them all in curfew dodging.

Within minutes the deal was done and Valentina stood by the side of the river with her husband, waving good-bye to Tanya and her new family.

"Write to me as soon as you arrive safely and don't forget to write to the island and not the Domaine. They open all our letters there, as I told you."

"Thank you for all you've done, Countess. Good-bye, Alex."

Jean-Jacques disappeared below with Tanya and his child. Laval stepped forward and raised the old-fashioned straw hat.

"I shall never forget what you've done for us today, Countess. It has been a privilege knowing you both."

He went below and the barge drifted forward, passing under the bridge and out of sight. Valentina and Masters walked arm in arm back to their apartment. Old Ducros resumed his fishing, his eyes scanning the nearby bridge for any unfamiliar faces. Satisfied that all was well, he called his grandson and together they baited more lines and sat gossiping in the sun.

Inside the apartment, Masters was telling Valentina what had happened since her departure.

"The place was searched from the attics to the wine cellar. Miss Knatchbull's room was clean. They didn't find a thing and Zita's been buzzing with curiosity ever since to know where the old bat's hidden all her food. The Oberführer's still in Paris and Koch had a blazing row with one of the search party for smashing your Dresden shepherdess. I thought he was going to shoot the guy. The co-ordinator's been sulking in his office ever since because nothing was found."

"What did you tell them about my absence?"

"I said you had a swollen face after your visit to the dentist."

"Did they believe you?"

"Sure, why not? Women don't like looking ugly after the dentist. Anyway, Wengen's had a toothache for days so he's sympathetic."

"Are you going home at once or can you stay for coffee?"

"I'll have to leave right now if I'm to be there before curfew. I don't want to get caught by a patrol and I can't ride that cycle as fast as I used to, at least not without a dozen stops for drinks and rests."

"I'll come on the morning bus at nine."

"We were lucky, Valentina. They got away and we didn't get caught. We've been damned lucky."

Valentina put on flat shoes and went out to look for food in the shops. There were no taxis and few cars on the roads, which made walking around Paris easy but dismal in the strange silence. At the corner of the rue des Jardins and the rue Charlemagne she paused before a poster printed in red and black and white. On this black-bordered announcement were the names of fifty men. Valentina read from top to bottom, where the words "*Ils ont été fusilés aujourd'hui*" ended the notice. She walked on and saw other such notices with their ominous black borders. For a while the Germans billeted in Paris had been friendly by order of the Führer. Then, with savage swiftness, the reprisals had begun against mis-demeanors imagined or real. Fearing to read any more names, she hurried on and found herself near Katrina's apartment. She rang the bell. There was no answer so she opened the door with her key and walked from room to room. She put on a kettle of water and searched the shelves for tea or coffee. There was nothing of any kind to eat. After the massive food-buying expedition she and Masters had done before war was declared she had thought they were safe from hunger at least for a while. But now she needed the tins of chicken, ham and tongue that had been stored in Katrina's attic. Valentina wondered where the tenant, Rebecca, was, if she had returned to her parents' house. She had taken a lease on Katrina's apartment until the end of the war. Why then was she not here? Why was there no food on the shelves, no blankets on the beds?

Valentina went downstairs and found a pair of steps in the cellar. She carried these upstairs and climbed up and peered into the roof space. It was completely empty. She stepped down, discouraged that the supplies had been stolen. She had been counting on them. She had been so sure they would be there. She turned off the gas and was about to let herself out of the apartment when she saw a sheet of music fallen to the ground. She picked it up and read the hastily scrawled message that had been written on the edge: "Germans came today, searched, took food, arrested me." Valentina read the note again. There was no date and the writing was almost illegible. Katrina was safe in the Domaine, so who had written this? Had Rebecca been arrested? If not, who had been in residence when the Germans called and what would the consequences be for the owner of the apartment, Katrina? Valentina locked the door behind her and hurried down the street to the glassblower's shop. It was closed and barred, with no sign of life in the upper windows when she rang Isaac's bell. Tired and discouraged, she looked for a taxi to take her home. She paused at two shops on the way to the square, to try to spend her precious coupons, but they had nothing to sell that she could not already obtain. She forced her aching feet on and walked to the Place de la Bastille. Again and again she went to food shops but all she gained for her pains was a small jar of tomato purée and a piece of inferior Parmesan.

At five-thirty, when Valentina had bathed and poured herself a glass of wine, someone rang the doorbell. She opened it and found

Oberführer Schuller outside. In his hand was a spray of yellow roses. In his pocket was a bottle of champagne. He smiled hopefully and she let him in.

"How is your tooth, Countess?"

"My tooth is perfectly well, thank you."

"I thought it might be."

"Have you been following me, Oberführer?"

"Not precisely, Countess."

He handed her the flowers, whose color and perfume reminded her of Yanin and the Flower House. She went to her bedroom and put on a black-velvet housecoat, pinning one of the roses to her lapel. When she reappeared Schuller had poured out the champagne. He offered her a glass and clinked his own with hers. She motioned him to a seat facing the river.

"Explain yourself, Oberführer. How precisely have you been following me?"

"On the day we came to Paris I believed that you really were planning to visit your dentist. I was delayed here in Paris until this morning, when I telephoned the house to tell you that I should be returning very late tonight. You were not there and I was told that you had a swollen face from your visit to the dentist. I decided to bring you some flowers and champagne to cheer you. At two this afternoon I was crossing the bridge leading to this apartment."

Valentina looked closely at the man before her, at the dark-green eyes, the sensuous mouth, the silver hairs at his temples. He was calm and almost conspiratorial. She held her breath when he spoke.

"I saw everything, of course."

"Why have I not been arrested?"

"You have not been arrested because I could not find in my heart to betray you. You were seeing Tanya and her husband and his father onto a barge traveling south. No doubt they will try to reach the Mediterreanean and take a boat to free territory, perhaps to Sardinia or one of the other islands."

"Yes, Oberführer."

"Your family loyalty is commendable, Countess, and I must admit that I should have done the same. I shall say nothing of your having assisted the Laval family to escape. If, however, you do anything illegal under the terms of the occupation while at the Domaine and I find out, I shall have no option but to order your arrest. You understand, Countess, it would be a case of my life or yours."

"I understand and thank you for your—"

"My friendship, I think you were going to say?"

"I wasn't sure what to say."

"My affection would have been appropriate."

Valentina looked again into the mysterious eyes and thought of Zita's comment: He's a fine man, a fine man. She held out her glass for more champagne.

"Are you planning to return to the Domaine tonight?"

"That depends on whether you would care to dine with me."

Valentina hesitated and Schuller hastened to explain his invitation.

"I have jars of pâté in my car with chicken in aspic and some of the finest ice cream in Paris."

"Bring it in at once."

"I thought you would say that."

He hurried out and returned with a bulging box of food. Valentina set the table with flowers and candles and her best silver. Schuller took his place, watching her all the while. They ate the pâté with brown bread he had appropriated with the other things and a green salad he had put in a wooden box. All the while they told stories of their youth and their life in the Europe of the years before the war. Schuller seemed completely at ease as he remembered the days of his youth.

"My great interest was riding. My brother and I were show jumping champions of Europe for fifteen years."

"You never told me that before."

"Would you do me the favor of calling me by my name when we are alone, Countess?"

"Very well."

"And you, what was your interest in life, Countess?"

"Mine was the Domaine and my adopted family. Before we had the inheritance I had no idea if I could keep the estate running forever. My husband had bought it for me and had paid for the restoration and all the furniture and furnishings. He hadn't enough money left to endow it forever. The children learned about money by working out our accounts each year in the days before we had an accountant. They also had a choir that performed all over Paris and brought in considerable money for the estate. I owe them a great deal; without them there wouldn't be a Domaine."

"Did you live in America ever, in your early days of marriage?"

"We spent some time in Kentucky with my husband's brother Brett. He had one of the finest stud farms in Kentucky."

"You won't believe this, Countess, but one of our finest horses was bought from him. I won the championship of Europe and an Olympic gold medal on Major. Imagine, what a coincidence."

Late that night they stood on the terrace looking out on the moonlit river. Schuller wrapped his great coat around her and placed his hands gently on her shoulders as she stood with her back to him.

"I am forty-three years old, Countess. I have been a soldier all my life and have often dreamed of being posted to Paris. Tonight for the first time I have understood the magic of this city. I would like to thank you for a wonderful evening. I almost forgot that there was a war."

They closed the windows and put up the blackout curtains. Schuller made himself a bed in the living room and after a last glass of champagne they parted. Valentina lay awake in her cold bed, thinking of all she had told him during the evening and all he had confided in her. Schuller lit a cigar and propped himself up on the feather pillows thinking of the vivacious way Valentina had talked, the jokes about her life she had told, the sad stories too, of Vasily and Elena. He patted his pocket. He had at last found a Corona cigar for Masters. It would make the countess laugh when it was presented after all these months of Masters' longing. He closed his eyes but could not sleep. How wonderful it had been to be with a friend for a few moments, to forget that he was the conqueror and hated by everyone in sight. Schuller rose and walked to the balcony, surprised to find Valentina standing outside looking at the Seine.

"The champagne has made our brains too lively, Countess."

"I shan't sleep tonight."

"I am sorry my presence has disturbed you."

"Not at all. I enjoyed every moment of your company."

"Shall we drive home to the Domaine?"

"Can you pass the patrols?"

"Of course, I am a German officer, if you recall."

"You make it very easy to forget, Hanspeter."

They drove through the blackness of night, the car's hooded headlights revealing only the patch of road immediately before them. Twice they were stopped by patrols. Each time the Oberführer's identification was enough and he was saluted on. When they were a few kilometers from the Domaine Schuller began to speak.

"I should like to ask a very special favor, Countess. My uncle, Admiral Canaris, will be in Paris in one month's time. He is head of all Abwehr operations in Europe. He will therefore visit the Domaine to have meetings with the coordinator. May I invite him to have lunch with you and the family?"

"Of course, will he want to stay in the house?"

"I imagine he will stay in Paris but I am not sure."

"I shall enjoy meeting him and so will the children."

"Thank you, Countess. By the way, I brought back some soap, sugar, coffee and tinned meats. I have no idea if they are of good quality but they are what our officers are eating in Paris. I also brought some sacks of dried vegetables and onions. I thought they would be useful for soup making."

"I don't know what we'd do without you."

"You would manage, Countess, you always have."

They entered the Domaine as dawn was breaking. Having placed the car where the coordinator could not see it, they went together into the house. Zita was in the kitchen making tea. Valentina looked at her pale face and red-rimmed eyes and knew at once that something dreadful had happened.

"What's happened, Zita?"

"Monsieur Masters has been arrested, ma'am. I've been waiting to tell you about it. He was coming back from Paris when he had a flat tire. He mended it and was pedaling as fast as he could when he was stopped, just after curfew, by a German patrol. He's in the prison at Gazeran and they're questioning him. Oh, ma'am, I think they're trying to link your husband with the death of the Gestapo officers. They've been searching every barn and estate in a circle around Gazeran, trying to find out if anyone's hiding out hereabouts. I heard about all this from Madame Yolande at the dairy. Her son heard everything as he was delivering the milk at the village."

Zita carried in a pot of tea and left Valentina and Schuller together. Then she went to the kitchen and took fresh bread rolls out of the oven and hurried with them to the breakfast room, noting that the two were still sitting in silence, stunned by the news she had given. Zita went back to the kitchen and stood looking out at the fields and the stone walls Masters had ordered built. Was the peaceful life at the Domaine coming to an end? Was it all going to go bad, as it had at the Flower House? Had the countess's luck finally run out?

Valentina spooned black currant jam on the roll and grimaced at its sourness. There was not enough sugar left to make more jam and what was left was bitter as gall. She sighed. Masters had been arrested. Curfew dodgers were usually imprisoned for the night and made to clean the boots of the soldiers who were guarding them. At best they were released the following morning. At worst they were herded out to be lined against the nearest wall and shot in retribution for attacks the previous day on German personnel. Then their names were listed on the black-bordered notices she had seen in Paris. But Masters was not a simple curfew dodger. The Gestapo were suspecting him of complicity in murder. Would they even bother to question him? Behind her the sun rose on a brilliant June day. Valentina heard Zita opening windows and shutters to let in the cool air of morning. Later they would be shut to keep out the heat of midday. Shut like the door of Masters' cell.

Shocked by the realization of the depth of her feelings for her husband, Valentina wondered when she had really first loved him. Had it been that first day in St. Petersburg? She shook her head. Until now the specter of Yanin had reared before her constantly, preventing total commitment. Masters knew it. She knew it and could do nothing about it. But now, what was she going to do? She wanted her husband back. She knew she loved him above all else and could not carry on without him. She told herself she must concentrate. Then she poured more tea and turned to Schuller.

"Do you know anything about the officer in charge of the unit at Gazeran?"

"I know nothing, but I will inquire."

"I must go there at once."

"I would not advise it, Countess."

Looking at Schuller, Valentina saw apprehension in his eyes and fear, something she had never seen before.

"Why should I stay away Oberführer? They may move Alex or shoot him if someone does not intervene."

"If that is their intention they will do it whatever you might say."

"What do you suggest?"

"I suggest you let me find out about the officer at Gazeran. I will do so immediately and return to tell you what I have learned."

"I'll wait in my bedroom."

At ten Schuller knocked on the door and Valentina called for him to enter. He seemed less troubled than before and this made her hopeful.

"I have telephoned the commander of the unit at Gazeran and personally vouched for your husband, Countess. I imagine he will be released shortly."

"Does the coordinator know what you've done?"

"I hope not."

"Thank you, Oberführer."

They smiled conspiratorially and Schuller looked around, pleased to be here in this most private place. He took in the Empire bed with its raw silk hangings and the Russian samovar on a low ebony table.

"This is an enchanting room, Countess. On entering it one can imagine that the ugliness of war is left far behind."

"Aren't you tired of fighting, Oberführer? Don't you ever feel ill at ease in places where your uniform makes you an enemy and not a friend?"

"I am your friend, Countess."

"And I yours, Oberführer. I wasn't meaning here in the Domaine. I was meaning in Rotterdam and Sebastopol and other cities of Europe. You're a good man. Does your conscience never trouble you?"

Schuller rose and kissed her hand.

"My conscience will have to wait. I must go to see the coordinator at ten-thirty. I hope your husband will soon be back, Countess."

The clocks struck eleven, twelve, one, two, three. Valentina went to the coordinator's office and asked him to help her secure

Masters' release. His coal-chip eyes looked icily down at her. His face was pale and there was tension in his manner that she had not seen before. He cracked the knuckles of one hand and then the other and gave her permission to sit opposite him. Valentina smoothed her skirt and tried to compose herself.

"My husband has been arrested. He had a flat tire on the way back from Paris and was unable to get here until shortly after the curfew hour. A few hundred meters from the gate of the Domaine he was arrested by a Gestapo patrol."

"Which was there at my bidding, Countess."

"Why was it there?"

"I suspected your trip to Paris, which coincided with the disappearance of a Jewish family from Rambouillet."

"Is coincidence your grounds for arresting my husband?"

"It is. My suspicions will now be confirmed by the Gestapo, who will interrogate Mr. Masters."

Valentina had a sudden urge to damage the man before her. Instead she rose and walked to the door.

"My husband and I went to Paris to buy food on the black market for you and your fellow officers and our family to eat. We shall not go there again and you will all eat turnips when there is nothing else left. And for your information, sir, the postmaster of Rambouillet goes to Paris every Monday, as do at least fifty other residents of the town. Some of them go every day of the week. Have you arrested all of them?"

The coordinator remained silent as Valentina continued.

"You have searched my home and will no doubt search it again. You found nothing and will find nothing in the future. You know well enough that all those I love most in the world live within these walls, yet you persist in believing me guilty of crimes against the occupying authorities. I shall visit the commander of Gross Paris to report you and I shall discuss your obsession with Admiral Canaris, your superior, when he comes here next month. Perhaps he will show you the error of your ways."

Valentina walked out of the office slamming the door so hard the sound echoed throughout the unusually silent house. First she went to the kitchen and told Zita what the coordinator had said. Zita bustled about making coffee and pouring brandy.

"I shall give him nothing but turnips in the future, you'll see, and

the worst wine, the stuff we throw out each year. We'll save it for
him in the future."

"Where is Oberführer Schuller?"

"He came out of the coordinator's office white with rage, ma'am.
He went immediately to the telegraph office and sent a wire to his
uncle, Admiral Canaris. Then he collected his gun and went shooting in the woods. Dmitry says he's shot everything in sight, even
sparrows."

"I shall go to Gazeran at once."

"Is it wise, ma'am?"

"I see no alternative."

Dusk was falling when Valentina drove the trap out of the
grounds and onto the road. One and a half hours remained before
curfew, barely time to reach Gazeran, get back and have an inter-
view with the commander. She chivvied the horse to go faster and
reached the adjacent town at five. German soldiers were sitting
under the chestnut trees of the square, being served foaming mugs
of beer by the sullen-faced daughter of the innkeeper. The jail was
in a cul-de-sac guarded by S.S. sentries. Valentina stepped down
and secured the horse. Then she walked past a leather-coated Gestapo officer into the jail. She had put on her Balenciaga black suit
with a Reveillon wrap of silver fox that trailed luxuriously behind
her. Her hair was dressed in its usual Edwardian roll and there
were black pearls at her ears and throat. She had heard persistent
rumors that the commander of the unit at Gazeran was obsessed
with money and had done her best to look as wealthy as possible.

She was ushered into the commander's office and invited to sit
down. The German offered her a sherry. Valentina accepted, noting that it was the very cheapest sherry money could buy. No
doubt the commander took home the rest of his entertaining allow-
ance. She looked intently at the German's face, at the thin lips and
anxious eyes, the fingers constantly drumming the table. Schuller
had said the commander was not suitable for the job and had only
been fourth choice from those officers remaining in Paris, a substitute for a substitute after his predecessors had been killed in air
raids or posted to the front. She began to hope.

The commander looked in awe at the cascades of pearls, at the
lavish fur negligently thrown to one side, the violet eyes hard on
his, the unusually large purse of shiny lizard skin. He spoke in a

sibilant voice, hesitating now and then to choose his words more carefully.

"You are come to ask about your husband, Countess. Mr. Masters was arrested early last evening and is awaiting transport to Fresnes Prison."

Valentina's heart beat uncomfortably fast. She had not expected this. Fresnes was the prison of no return, where members of the Resistance, spies and other celebrities of opposition were tortured to death, shot by firing squad or transported on trains to mysterious destinations, never to be seen again. She spoke with a confidence she did not feel.

"I've come to take my husband home, sir. As you must be aware, he'd been to Paris to see me and to buy food on the black market to feed the German officers in our home. I've spoken with the coordinator who lodges with us and have informed him that I shall complain personally to Admiral Canaris when he comes to visit us next month. I shall also visit the commander of Gross Paris, to inform him that you are now arresting innocent people without proof of guilt."

The officer rose to pace the room.

"I am in charge of the unit here in Gazeran and also, unfortunately, the prison, which is a Gestapo interrogation center. I cannot release your husband, Countess, not unless I have Gestapo authorization. I am a Wehrmacht officer. I do not control the Gestapo."

"Could you release my husband without Gestapo authority once he is on his way to Fresnes Prison?"

"I do not accompany prisoners to the prison, Countess."

Valentina was silent for a moment. Then she looked quizzically into the officer's eyes.

"How much would it cost to make you change your mind, sir?"

The German sat behind his desk looking fixedly at a report before him. A violent scream filled the building, followed by others that faded gradually into low animal moans. Valentina felt the color draining from her face. She thought again and made her offer.

"I will pay you one hundred thousand Swiss francs to release my husband."

The pale blue eyes glazed with shock, greed and fear. One hundred thousand Swiss francs was worth ten million German marks,

probably double; it was the passport to a future of wealth and security. He could even obtain a forged passport and escape the
damned war and make a new life in Argentina. But what of the
risks? He would have to tell the countess to tell the coordinator
that he had checked with Canaris on receiving her visit. Would the
coordinator then phone his superior? The commander of Gazeran
thought not. He picked up the telephone and spoke to the prison
officer. Then he turned to Valentina and explained.

"I shall say, if asked by your coordinator, that you insisted I contact Admiral Canaris and that when I did he ordered Mr. Masters
to be released. You will have no trouble with Oberführer Schuller,
and if the coordinator asks further questions you will tell him to
contact his superior. I do not think he will do that, Countess, but in
case he does it would be wise to ask Schuller to send some message
to his uncle to bear out what you say. They are the very best of
friends. Admiral Canaris will not doubt Schuller's word."

"The money will be delivered to you within one month."

"I would prefer gold."

"Then gold of the same value will be delivered to you within the
same time. In the meantime you may take this."

Valentina took a huge wad of notes from her purse and handed
it to the sweating man. He spoke anxiously.

"How do I know you'll keep your promise?"

"You don't, sir. However, you may be assured that my husband is
more valuable to me than one hundred thousand Swiss francs are
to you. That can be your guarantee."

When Valentina reached her trap she found Masters already in
it. She covered him with a blanket and drove away at a gallop,
avoiding looking again at his face, with its closed eyes and broken
teeth and purple swellings that distorted everything. She held his
hand.

"We'll soon be home, Alex. I'll prepare a bath for you and serve
you dinner in bed. Zita's making something special to celebrate."

"How'd you fix it, Valentina?"

"One hundred thousand Swiss francs in gold fixed it."

"God, I was glad to see you."

"Was it very bad?"

"Bad enough. I wasn't there for a holiday but they only questioned me for two hours. They've had an Englishman there since

yesterday morning and they've been beating the hell out of him ever since."

Valentina drove into the coach house and handed the reins to Louis. He took the horses to the stables and ran back to help her get her husband to his room. Shocked by Masters' appearance, Louis knew better than to ask questions. Masters had been arrested and tortured and was inexplicably back home. Louis looked toward Valentina and saw that her face was as white as snow, with pale-violet shadows under her eyes. When he had maneuvered Masters to the bed Louis went to the kitchen to tell his mother what had happened.

On Valentina's advice Schuller went to town and wired his uncle a request to confirm her statement, if asked by the coordinator. Then he returned and with Wengen helped lift Masters in and out of the bath. The two officers were appalled by the injuries they saw, the toes without nails, the back scarred from beating. When Masters was settled in bed they retired to the smoking room, leaving Valentina to feed her husband his supper. The Germans sat alone discussing the matter in hushed tones. For them too war had come uncomfortably close to the deceptive peace of the Domaine. To each man war had meant fighting for the Fatherland, not torturing innocent civilians in ways at best medieval. They fell silent, conscious that they had not understood what means would have to be used to keep the citizens of France under control. They wondered how to face the rest of the household when news of Masters' injuries became known.

That night Schuller lay awake thinking of Valentina. As he could not sleep he read until the small hours, conscious of intermittent footfalls on the stairs. Who was walking around at this hour of the night? What was going on? He rose and went downstairs to the kitchen, were he found Valentina and Zita drinking tisanes.

"Forgive me, Countess, I heard people walking back and forth. The stairs creak, as you know."

"Have something to drink, Oberführer, and thank you for all you did last evening."

"Is your husband feeling better?"

"Alex became ill after dinner and I had to call Dr. Martin. We were anxious not to be caught again after curfew so we were all tiptoeing around like phantoms."

"What did the doctor say?"

"They've taken my husband to the local hospital. Dr. Martin thinks he may have a ruptured kidney. We shan't know until morning."

"I'm so sorry, Countess."

They talked until three, when Schuller and Zita went to their rooms, leaving Valentina alone with her thoughts. She went outside to the rear of the house and picked some mint and parsley from the herb garden. At the stable door she nuzzled her favorite horse, taking comfort from his pleasure at seeing her. It was a dark, moonless night and Valentina was glad she was as invisible to the coordinator as everything else. She looked up at the tower room where he slept, smiling grimly because his blinds were drawn and he was for once not following her everywhere. A twig cracked somewhere behind her. Valentina held her breath. Gradually she became conscious of the sound of men approaching. Fear made her breathless as she strained her eyes to see. Then she heard Dmitry calling her.

"Countess, come here, please."

Valentina ran toward the trees and felt Dmitry take her hand.

Valentina peered into the wood to where two men were standing. One was young and blond. The other looked considerably older and was stooping with tiredness. Dmitry whispered, "The older man says he's a friend of Alex's and has met you in Paris. Is it true, Countess?"

A familiar voice greeted her.

"Hi, Valentina, Jack Stevens here. This is my son Tim. He was in a prison camp and he escaped and got word to me that he was trapped in Paris. I came over to take him home. Can you help us get to London?"

"I'll try."

"How's Alex?"

"He's in hospital. The Gestapo interrogated him yesterday and injured him very badly."

"Don't worry, Valentina, he's as tough as a grizzly. Can you help Tim and me right now? We've nowhere to go and we haven't eaten in three days."

"Come with me."

When she had led Stevens and his son to the underground tunnel that led to the Château de Rambouillet, Valentina sat in the kitchen trying to shut out what was happening to her. Unwittingly and unwillingly she had become involved despite her instincts for self-preservation. If she was going to help people reach the Channel Ports she must do it alone, relying only on her immediate family. The alternative was to trust strangers and be betrayed. She began to plan an escape route to London.

As she walked upstairs to her bedroom she heard children shouting and playing in the second-floor rooms. Valentina smiled wearily. Life must go on and she must concentrate on seeming content, relaxed and confident. She closed and locked her bedroom door and fell on the bed. She was asleep within seconds.

# CHAPTER TWENTY-SIX

## London, January 1942

_____
_____
_____

In January Masters was asked to call on an old friend with whom he had once worked at the American Embassy in Paris. Dan Long was sixty-six and retired to live with his French wife in St.-Germaine. Masters was surprised to be taken aside by his former colleague, who was observing the most rigid security measures.

"How are you feeling, Alex? I heard you'd been ill."

"I had a kidney removed a few months back but I'm fine now. At least it got me out of all that hard work in the fields."

"How's Valentina?"

"She's great, if it weren't for her I wouldn't be here at all. They had me down for Fresnes Prison and you know what that means."

"I need your help."

"You have it."

Long went to the cabinet and took out a long, slim file.

"This is so important I can't send it via normal channels. You've done a lot of undercover work in the past in this area and other parts of the world. I thought of you when they told me someone had to take it to Churchill."

"What is it?"

"It's a plan for the Allied invasion of France."

"What the hell are you doing involved in all this? You retired before I did, if I recall."

"I never retired at all, I just seemed to. Will you do it? The lives of so many Allied soldiers depend on this plan reaching its destination."

Masters looked at the papers and then back to his old friend. He wondered how to tell Long that he could not become involved.

"I'm sorry, Dan, I've got responsibilities right here in France. The Domaine takes all my time and Valentina and I aren't getting any younger. A lot depends on us keeping the place going until the end of the war."

"There won't be a Domaine in a few years if the Germans aren't driven out of France."

Long took another paper from the safe. It was a communication from the President of the United States. He handed it to Masters, who read the decoded translation. It was a priority appeal to Long, as head of Covert Operations in Paris, to liaison with the head of the O.S.S. and arrange for the message to reach Churchill at once. Masters passed the message back to Long.

"What happened to the three couriers who tried to take the message to London before?"

"The Germans shot them. They were young guys, Alex. They looked like soldiers and the Germans took them as easy as pie. They should have been picked up by an Allied plane at Compiègne. The Germans shot the first as he neared the pickup spot, the second as he was stepping on board the plane and the third when he tried to run away on hearing gunfire. That's why I need you, Alex. You're too old to raise suspicions easily and you're the only guy in Paris that has experience of covert operations in war conditions."

Masters looked again at the last paragraph of the letter:

I cannot stress too strongly that the future of our country could depend on the outcome of the operations envisaged for spring, 1942. Give this matter your most urgent priority.

Suddenly Yanin came into his mind and Valentina's words of admiration: Ivan loved Russia more than anything, even me and his sons. As time goes by I admire him more for that. Masters handed the message back to Long.

"I'll deliver your message for you, on one condition."

"I agree, whatever it is. You could ask for the Chase Manhattan Bank right now and I'd give it to you. What's your condition, Alex?"

"That I go on my own and return my own way. I want no pickup by plane from a field in Compiègne on the night of the full moon like it says in the message. That's just when German patrols would be increased to look out for enemy agents."

"Whatever you say, but for Christ's sake hurry."

"After this I don't want to hear from you or your department again, Dan."

"You won't. You liaise with the Swedish consul-general, by the way. Contact Raoul Nordling."

Masters went from Long's house to the Swedish Embassy and had a meeting with Nordling, who was still operating as consul for a neutral country. The consul-general poured him a whiskey and explained how he could be of help.

"If you'll not go by the normal pickup from Compiègne you could perhaps go to London on my behalf."

"It wouldn't stand up, sir. Your country and mine have no possible connection that the Germans would believe."

"I have another suggestion. Can you fly?"

"I have a pilot's license."

"And I have a friend with a collection of First World War planes."

"If I weren't shot down by the Germans the English might get me, sir."

"What then?"

"I'll have to think about it."

"There's a great urgency as you know, Mr. Masters."

"I came here to ask you to call my wife at seven tonight, sir. Get her here and then tell her the truth of my journey."

The consul-general rose and paced the room.

"Are you telling me that you mean not to go home to tell your wife what you are doing?"

"If I see Valentina I shan't go at all."

"I do not approve, but I will do as you say. I will telephone the countess tonight and frequently during your absence."

"All the telephones in the house are tapped, sir. Our mail is also opened. Tell her nothing unless she is here in your office. Do you know her, by the way?"

"The countess and I once won a tango contest at an embassy party. She is a delightful lady."

"Tell her I'll bring her and Miss Knatchbull some English muffins when I come back."

"May I ask why you agreed to go on this most dangerous mission, Mr. Masters?"

Masters hesitated. From the moment when he had first been

arrested and tortured by the Gestapo he had known that if given
the chance he would do all he could to see Germany crushed. The
seemingly innocuous papers he carried to Churchill detailed the
sites for Allied landings to northern France and more, he guessed,
perhaps even of the entire Allied invasion. That was why they had
to be delivered to Churchill personally, not even to the military
heads of combined operations. Since his illness he had not been allowed to work in the field. He had been given the best food and
the best wine and was sent upstairs for a nap every afternoon while
women and children slaved in the fields till they fell exhausted on
the ground. He had always been a man of action who had never
counted the risk and he knew that despite his age this was something experience qualified him to do, something others might not
be able to do. He was needed and it felt good. Masters thought of
Valentina and shook his head, puzzled by his own attitude. He
made a reply that provoked a smile from the Swedish consul.

"You ask me why I'm going on the trip. Perhaps I just feel like a
change."

"I don't believe you, but let's work out what I can do for you. I
can give you a car full of petrol with a laissez-passer that will take
you out of Paris. After that you will be alone."

"How far will the pass take me?"

"As far as Pontoise, perhaps farther. In which direction will you
be traveling?"

"I don't know, sir."

Nordling looked hard at the noncommittal face.

"You are obviously a professional intelligence agent, Mr. Masters,
and trained not to share your plans. I will therefore give you four
passes, one to the north, south, east and west of Paris."

"I'll bring the ones I don't use back to you and we'll split a bottle
of champagne."

"For your information, it is impossible to get over the Channel.
The Germans allow French fishing boats to go out, but often a German soldier goes out with them in case they are tempted to pick up
unauthorized cargo. Only the crew can go aboard and each man
has been registered at the local town hall. The trains to and from
Paris are all guarded and even Vichy ministers are having difficulty
obtaining passes to and from the Free Zone."

"I understand, sir."

"May I wish you well, Mr. Masters. Here are your passes. They were signed by General von Stülpnagel and were intended for diplomats traveling under my aegis and taking food to the Red Cross."

Masters drove out of Paris on the road that led to Chantilly. He met three roadblocks before he was clear of the city and was waved through each of them without difficulty. In late afternoon a violent storm broke. Masters smiled with relief. The roads ahead would be virtually empty. He had been lucky so far.

He reached Chantilly at nightfall and went at once to the home of Katrina and her husband Jacques. They rushed into his arms and hugged him. Then, while Jacques put Masters' car away, Katrina brought her baby to show him. She could not resist inundating him with questions about the Domaine.

"Is the countess well? Are Zita and Miss Knatchbull well, and Nikolai, too? Have you heard from Tanya? And did the soldiers really rebuild all the walls before they left?"

"They did, every last bit of broken fence."

"Jacques didn't believe it when he heard, but I told him you'd make them do something. I forgot to ask you what you're doing here, Alex, what brings you away from home?"

"I have to go to England."

"To England! That's impossible."

"I have to be in London by Thursday."

Katrina fell silent. She knew well that every port was watched by German guards and forbidding gun emplacements. She looked at Masters' eyes that seemed to demand something from her. She thought how he had purchased the Domaine and how his encouragement had supported them all through the hard times. She kept asking herself if she dared tell Masters about Malik, another of Valentina's sons, who owned two fishing boats and ran them with his brother and two retired French Navy men. Malik was fishing out of Dieppe. Masters' eyes continued to bore into her consciousness and Katrina wished her husband would return.

"I'm doing a concert in Dieppe tomorrow. You could travel with my party. I doubt if we'll be asked for passes as the Germans are grateful I'm to play for them."

"Thanks, Katrina, I'll do that. I could try for a fishing boat to England from Dieppe."

"Malik's running two boats from Dieppe. He's registered officially and is known there by everyone."

"What else does he run? If I know Malik he'll be making money."

"He runs Jews to the beaches of Sussex and refugees from all over Europe."

Masters looked askance at Katrina, shocked that she should know so much and speak so freely.

"Never, ever, say that to anyone!"

"But you and your wife are like parents to me."

"Don't even say it to your reflection in the mirror."

Katrina sat by the fire and looked sadly at the blaze.

"I found out about all this because Malik took one of Jacques's friends and his family to England. They sent us a postcard from Bognor Regis via an English agent."

Jacques appeared with a loaf, two tins of beans and a small box of biscuits.

"I got these from the priest, Alex. He got them from one of the English officers who parachuted into a field on the other side of town. The curé guided him to the manor and the owner took him to Survilliers. The English come every time there's a full moon."

"Don't the enemy wait for them?"

"Sometimes they do. If a patrol comes by everyone hides in a ditch. Sometimes they shoot it out and everyone's killed. Other times, especially when the weather's bad, the Germans don't bother to come."

"How'd you know all this?"

"I'm one of the helpers who hide English servicemen when they've landed. Katrina and I receive coffee, butter, baked beans and fine paper on which she can write her music. The English are very polite and not at all demanding and I am proud to do what little I can for France."

"Why aren't you in Germany working in a factory?"

"I was drafted there but when I contracted tuberculosis they sent me back to France. Hurry and make dinner, Katrina, Alex and I are hungry."

They ate a frugal meal of turnips stewed with meat bones. Masters retired early to write a letter to Valentina. Outside, staccato shouts somewhere to the right of the house indicated that a German patrol had caught someone out after curfew. Masters struggled to put into words what he was feeling, why he had come on this mission and how much he was longing to be home. He addressed the letter to the apartment on the Ile St.-Louis. Uneasy but exhausted, he dozed for an hour. Then a dog began to howl nearby. He rose and walked to the window. Tethered to a post in the garden of a neighboring house, the dog was howling a lament to the night. Masters continued to watch the silent street. Minutes later a German officer left a house three doors from Katrina's. Masters thought of the risks she and Jacques were taking by volunteering to hide English officers. He shook his head. His was the risk. Tomorrow he would meet Malik again and entrust his life to the young man from the Caucasus. He remembered Malik as a young boy of fourteen, selling seats in the Domaine garden for performances of his own conjuring act and later setting up a vegetable stall by the roadside. Well-born Malik might be, but he had the instincts of a fixer, a streetwise operator more at home in Manhattan than in northern France. Masters closed his eyes and thought of Valentina. He would buy her a gift in London, a gift so splendid she would forget her anger at his sudden departure. He opened his eyes and thought dejectedly that there was not a gift in the world that would make her forgive him. Or was there? He sighed despondently. He had not wanted to upset her and from the moment of first meeting had done all he could to make her life happy. The trip to London was something he knew he had to do. Was it patriotism that had fired his desire to go there? Was the specter of Yanin still haunting his life? Or had he missed the danger of his old profession?

Masters arrived safely in Dieppe with Katrina's party. He kissed her good-bye outside the hotel in which the Germans had booked her.

"I plan to be back at the Domaine by Sunday. Get a pass and come and stay with us for a while."

"We'll try, Alex. Jacques and I have been talking about it for ages."

"Which is Malik's boat?"

"It's the one painted blue and green. You'll find him and Ivan on the boat or in the café on the quayside."

"Thanks for everything, Katrina."

"Good luck Alex, take care."

Masters walked to the quayside and stood looking down at Malik and his brother Ivan. They looked up at him and then incredulously at each other.

"What on earth are you doing here, Alex?"

"I have to be in London by tomorrow, can you take me there?"

There was a moment's hesitation, then Malik called out, "Come down. Of course we'll take you to England. We're going out on the tide at eleven."

"Shall I come down right now?"

"The Germans might search the ship before we take off. You'd best wait for me in the café over there."

"I've no papers."

"Come aboard Alex, if they search we'll say you're our guardian. It's true anyway."

Masters sat in a small cabin under the deck, listening to the sounds of the quayside, gulls screeching, men shouting, engines chugging. The suspense was straining and he poured himself a glass of wine from a bottle in the cupboard. Minutes later he heard Malik answering questions put to him by a German officer on the quayside. Masters closed his eyes, willing himself to be calm. The German came on board, the sound of his boots clonking ominously on the deck. Then, to Masters' surprise, he heard the German returning to the quayside and disappearing into the distance. Above him Malik cast off. Masters relaxed at the welcome sound of the engine coming to life. He waited awhile before standing at the porthole and looking out at a choppy sea and the gray houses of Dieppe fast disappearing from view. He opened the cabin door and went up on deck. Malik threw him a sweater and an oilskin coat.

"You heard the German come on board?"

"I sure did. I was scared to breathe."

"I gave him some halibut and he went away. Sometimes they go back to the barracks if you give them something sufficiently valuable. Sometimes they don't. Last week they came on board and searched the ship from stem to stern."

"You were lucky not to be carrying anything unusual."

"I *was* carrying something unusual. The family who were going to England jumped overboard and waited underneath the ship until the soldiers had gone. I had to give the daughter artificial respiration. She was pretty. I'll go and see her if I'm in London."

"How long will it take to reach the coast?"

"We should be there by late afternoon, depending on the weather."

"I'm in your debt, Malik, how much do I owe you?"

Malik's eyes glistened, and he turned away. Then, as he guided the boat expertly, he spoke.

"I was nine when I first arrived at the Domaine with my brother. We had lost our home, our parents, our grandparents and our two older brothers. We were all that was left out of the entire family in St. Petersburg. At first we cried all the time. Then the countess told us that we weren't orphans, as we'd thought, but that we were all to be her new sons and daughters. From that day we began to believe that we really were part of a family and we started to laugh and fight again. Remember the time when the schoolmaster in Rambouillet kept calling us the 'Russian orphans' and your wife went to his school and told him that if he continued doing it she was going to blow off his head? I was so proud of her when she told him to keep his ridiculous statements to himself. You can travel on my boat anytime, Alex. Ivan and I are always trying to think what we can do to make you and the countess proud of us. You seem to have everything, the Domaine, the sons and daughters who still live near enough to visit you often. . . ."

"We're proud of you, Malik, as proud as hell."

At ten-thirty the following morning Masters was ushered into his meeting with the British Prime Minister. There were no witnesses to hear what was said, but the priceless lists were delivered and the two talked for over an hour. At the end of the meeting the Prime Minister walked to the door with his visitor.

"I am deeply grateful to you, Mr. Masters, for coming here with these most valuable lists. It won't go unrecognized, believe me. Someday you will learn that your dangerous mission was well worth the risk."

"I'm sure it was, sir."

"How will you return to France?"

"By fishing boat, I leave tomorrow at three."

"Where are you staying?"

"At the Clarence."

"Try their Yorkshire pudding; there may be no beef to eat with it, but at the Clarence it's worth trying for its own merits."

"Thank you for your time, Mr. Churchill."

"Thank *you*, Mr. Masters."

Masters walked from Downing Street to Trafalgar Square and then to Regent Street. The sun was shining but it was freezing and there was an icy wind coming from the Thames. Despite the gray skies and the cold, Masters was content. In London there were no German soldiers, no swastika flags or German signposts to familiar landmarks. Above all, there were no constant demands for identity cards and passes. He found the jeweler's shop he was looking for and stepped inside to speak with a director of the establishment.

The man's face seemed to glow when he heard what Masters wanted.

"It's true, sir, that we at Wartski's are famous for our Russian objects. However, I am not quite sure we will have what you have in mind."

"I have until tomorrow morning. Will you call me?"

"Better still, sir, I'll show you what we have in our vaults."

Masters examined each piece until he found one he wanted. He handed over a check on his Swiss bank and asked that it be cleared immediately. The director agreed to send the piece around to the hotel the following morning and Masters left the shop content. He was unable to buy the muffins he wanted to bring to Valentina and Miss Knatchbull because he did not have an English ration book. He thought awhile and then stopped a woman to ask if she would buy him some on her ration card. She handed him the muffins, squealing with joy when he handed her a five-pound note. Masters made some other purchases for the family before making his way to the American Embassy for lunch.

In the evening Masters called the jeweler.

"Alex Masters here, did you clear that check?"

"We did, sir, and we've arranged the export license for the piece. We require one or two more details for our own files. We need to know the address of the purchaser and the name and address of the person for whom it has been bought and if it will go into a museum, a private collection or will be resold."

"It's for my wife, Valentina Masters, for her personal use. Our address is the Domaine Russe, Rambouillet, France."

"I'll send everything with the piece in the morning. What time will be convenient?"

"Can you come at nine? I'm leaving at ten."

"Very well, Mr. Masters, and my thanks for your custom. I hope we'll be able to meet again when this awful war is over."

Masters overcame the temptation to call his wife. He returned to his hotel, where he drank a martini in the bar. The staff were putting up the blackout boards and the manager was altering the menu to avoid supplies he had been unable to obtain. Masters watched the man's effete movements and the fussy way he rubbed out the original item on the menu and replaced it with bold copperplate writing. The fellow might seem effete but the hotel was running with most of its renowned efficiency in the midst of the London blitz and no one even mentioned the war. He smiled at the understatement inherent in the English character. He had ordered a bottle of claret to help him sleep. He took his place in the dining room and asked for the wine to be brought. He thought grimly that he must preserve his strength. Coming to England had been all too easy. Returning to the Domaine could be a nightmare. He thought again of the German soldier on the quayside at Dieppe, praying silently that he would not be there when they returned.

At 8 A.M., as he and Masters had arranged, Malik went by taxi to the Clarence Hotel. The streets of London were loud with the sounds of fire engine bells ringing, police sirens sounding and the cries of London, alien to his ears: "Violets, lovely violets, buy a bunch of violets, lady." At the end of the street, a cordon prevented the taxi from going any farther. Malik walked past the cordon, holding the address of the hotel before him and looking up at the numbers on the doors. When he came to the place where the Clarence Hotel had been he found a pile of burning rubble. The remainder of the street was in ruins, bombed in a German raid the previous night. Malik hurried to speak with a policeman.

"I'm here to meet my guardian, Alex Masters, he was a guest at the Clarence Hotel and due to leave England this morning. Can you tell me where the guests were taken at the commencement of the air raid?"

The policeman found a chair salvaged from the hotel and motioned Malik to sit down.

"The hotel was destroyed in the night, sir. There was no air raid warning, so the guests had not been taken into the cellar, as was the custom. No one survived here or in any of the other establishments in the street. It was a direct hit, you see. I'm sorry, sir, can I get you a cup of tea?"

Malik looked from the officer to the smoldering rubble and back appealingly to the young man. Tears began to course down his cheeks and he let them, unashamed to cry for the man whose money had bought a home and security for him and his brother and all the other children without hope. He walked forward and stared helplessly at the desecration before him. Then he had a thought and turned hopefully to the officer.

"It's possible Alex was out when the air raid took place."

"It happened at three-thirty this morning, sir."

Malik wanted to argue but he knew there was no point. Masters was dead. He dropped down on the chair and buried his head in his hands. A polite English voice broke through his painful reverie.

"I heard what you said, sir, about your guardian. I am Mr. Buckingham from Wartski's, the court jewelers of Regent Street. May I speak with you about Mr. Alexander Masters?"

The two men walked from the street to a café in Piccadilly. Buckingham put a cup of tea before Malik and then, as an afterthought, two slices of toast.

"Drink this, sir, it will settle your stomach. I didn't quite catch your name."

"I'm Malik; they call me by that name, though I am Andreas Malik to be exact."

"Mr. Malik, your guardian came to our establishment yesterday and requested a piece of jewelry by a particular designer. He paid by check and after he had gone I cleared the check with his bank in Switzerland. I also arranged an export license for the piece. At eight forty-five this morning I came to deliver the package to Mr. Masters at the Clarence Hotel. While I was waiting there you arrived and I overheard your conversation with the constable."

"You want me to deliver the piece to the countess?"

"To Valentina Masters."

"She was formerly the Countess Korolenko. We always call her Countess because that is what she was when we first met her. She adopted sixty-six Russian children who had fled the revolution to Paris."

Buckingham's face lost its staid complacency for a brief moment. Then he inquired of Malik what exactly he was to the countess.

"Do I understand that you were the adopted son of Mr. and Mrs. Masters, of Countess Korolenko as she was?"

"That is correct. I don't know how I'm going to tell her what has happened to Alex."

"My only advice is to keep the lady busy. When we are occupied we tend not to think of the destructive things in life. With reference to the piece Mr. Masters purchased, I don't need to tell you its value. It is insured with Lloyd's, of course. I must therefore ask you to produce some proof of your identity—just a formality, you understand."

Malik produced his French passport, his fishing license and a photograph of himself, his brother, Valentina and Masters and two other children.

"That is the countess, that's Mr. Masters and me and my brother Ivan. The other two are my sisters, Nina and Natasha. The document is my license to fish out of Dieppe and it's signed by the German officer commanding the area."

Buckingham saw that Andreas Malik, educated at the Domaine Russe, Rambouillet, and resident in Dieppe, had been authorized to fish off the coastal waters. He handed the package to Malik.

"May I wish you a safe journey back to France, Mr. Malik."

Sunday came and went. Valentina could not remain for more than a few moments in one spot. Schuller hovered nearby, watching her every move. He had been the one who had told the coordinator that Masters had not returned from a lunch date in Paris and that he was presumed injured in an accident. Since then the coordinator had questioned every man, woman and child in the house repeatedly in order to ascertain Masters' whereabouts. Valentina had told Schuller that she had no idea where her husband was and that he had gone to lunch with friends with whom he had once worked. He did not believe her entirely but was doing his best to support her endeavors in her husband's absence. In truth Valentina had been told by Nordling that Masters would be back home on Sunday. It was therefore with the greatest anxiety that she paced back and forth on the terrace.

On Monday Wengen went out to Rambouillet and returned with
an antique scale from the local dealer, an object he had often heard
Valentina admire. Not to be outdone, Koch visited Paris on his day
off and brought back a pile of oranges taken from the officers' club.
Valentina received these small tokens of affection with gratitude,
but only half of her was concentrating on the everyday incidents in
the house. The other half was wrestling with the ever-increasing
panic she was feeling at her husband's continued absence.

On Wednesday morning, a bitter-cold day when snow fell thickly
around the Domaine, Valentina saw a figure approaching the house
from the north. She put on a wrap and ran outside to meet her husband, halting, askance, when she saw Malik, one of her Russian
sons. He was ghastly pale and stumbling as though drunk. She held
out her arms and almost carried him back to the house and upstairs
to her room. At each step she thanked God that the coordinator
was in Paris lunching with General Gehlen. She rang for Zita and
asked for food and wine to be brought. Then she put Malik on her
bed and peered anxiously into his face.

"My dear Andreas, whatever are you doing here? Have you a
pass to travel so far? Is something wrong?"

Before he could answer, Valentina saw red stains spreading over
the coverlet of her bed. She ran to the telephone and asked Dr.
Martin to come immediately. Then she went to Malik and held him
in her arms.

"What happened?"

"I went to England with Alex. He had a package to deliver personally to the English Prime Minister. They wouldn't trust it to be
delivered to anyone else. Other men had tried to deliver the papers
and were to have been picked up by the British from Compiègne,
but the Germans shot them. That's why Dan Long asked Alex to
deliver the material. He traveled from Paris to Chantilly on the first
day and stayed the night with Katrina and her husband. Then he
came to Dieppe and we took him to England. I went to London
with Alex and was due to meet him on Friday at nine in the morning. We were to go together to Newhaven for the journey back to
Dieppe. Alex wasn't there when I went to call for him."

"Why not?"

"His hotel had been bombed during the night, Countess. There
was nothing left of it and nothing left of the whole area around it."

Valentina heard herself cry out. She bit her hand to stifle the tears as she held Malik close to her heart.

"Is Alex dead?"

"No one escaped, Countess. There was no warning of the air raid so they had no chance to evacuate the guests at the Clarence Hotel. I checked and rechecked before I left London. The raid took place at three-thirty in the morning. Alex would have been sleeping. I can't believe this has happened, but it has. Alex bought you this before he went back to his hotel. The jeweler gave it to me to deliver to you."

From a fold in the blood-stained jacket Malik took out a box wrapped in brown paper. Valentina pushed it aside.

"And you, what happened to you?"

"I got ashore all right and made my way out of Dieppe. I traveled at night so I could dodge the patrols. Then I made the mistake of walking from Nogent this morning in the daylight. I was two miles from here when I was stopped. I had no pass so I ran for it. The German patrolman fired."

"And you walked two miles in this condition?"

"I wanted to deliver the package, Countess. Alex would have wanted it."

The doctor arrived and for some time was locked in the bedroom with Malik. Valentina went to her dressing room where she tore off the brown paper and found inside a royal purple velvet box on which was written "CARL FABERGÉ, Imperial Jeweller." She opened the box and looked in wonder at the piece inside. It was a Fabergé egg that opened to reveal a woman with silver hair driving a trap pulled by a chestnut pony. The woman's hair was made of diamonds. The horse was made of topaz, the clothes of emeralds and rubies. Behind the lady was a property that looked uncannily like the Flower House. A note fell out of the box. It was in Masters' handwriting:

> I couldn't resist this lady because she looks like you. Now I've bought you a Fabergé egg. You see I'm still competing with Yanin.
> Love you always, Alex.

Valentina looked at the bejeweled egg with its magnificently wrought interior and read the note again and again, stroking the paper as though it would bring Masters back. Was it possible he was still alive? He could have been dining at the Embassy. She picked up the telephone and called Raoul Nordling.

"Valentina Masters here."

There was a long pause then Nordling answered in a somber voice.

"I invite you to lunch, Countess. Does tomorrow suit? I have so much to tell you."

"I'll come at twelve-thirty."

"I look forward to it."

Valentina put the phone down, her hand trembling violently. She was having lapses of concentration when she thought she was talking with her husband. She started when the doctor entered. He spoke briskly to reassure her.

"Your son's as strong as an ox, Countess, otherwise he'd be dead. He has two bullet wounds which are superficial and another in the back of the neck which is not. I've arranged for him to be collected by an ambulance. He'll recover in Chartres Hospital. Please don't look so distressed."

Valentina did not answer and, seeing the strangely vacant look in her eyes, Martin guided her to a chair.

"Countess, is something wrong? You seem to be in shock, if I may say."

"I've just been told that my husband is dead."

The doctor crossed himself.

"My most sincere condolences, Countess. If there's anything I can do . . ."

Dr. Martin paused in the kitchen on the way out of the house to tell Zita what had happened. Zita burst into tears. Miss Knatchbull hurried to Valentina's room. She said nothing of what she had heard and only held her former charge close, as she had when Valentina was small. Men came with an ambulance to take Malik away. The local priest arrived and waited downstairs to see members of the family. Schuller, Koch and Wengen, having finished their work for the day, went to the kitchen for tea. There they found many of the women and children crying openly. Alarmed, Schuller hurried to speak with Zita.

"What is happening? Why are the women crying?"

"Mr. Masters is dead, sir. The countess is in her room with Miss

Knatchbull. She'll be terribly distressed. I don't know what this will do to her."

Schuller ran upstairs and knocked on Valentina's door. There was no reply. He opened it a fraction and saw Miss Knatchbull sitting on the window seat with Valentina. The old lady was stroking Valentina's head. He listened as Miss Knatchbull spoke.

"You've suffered a most terrible loss, my dear, but don't give up. You and Mr. Masters bought the Domaine to be a refuge for your children. You must keep it safe until the war is over and give courage to everyone, as you always have. Don't cry so; your tears will distress everyone and make them forget the hope you've instilled in them for the future."

Schuller closed the door and stood helplessly on the landing. Nikolai came out of his room.

"I heard an ambulance. Is someone ill, Oberführer?"

"Come, Nikolai, I have something to show you. You said last week that you needed some binoculars. I have found some in my trunk."

Once in his room Schuller handed over a pair of binoculars and asked Nikolai to sit down for a moment.

"There has been some very bad news, I'm afraid."

Nikolai tried to gauge the German's expression, but all he could see was tension and sadness. He flinched when Schuller explained.

"Mr. Masters is dead. I know nothing of the circumstances but I gather it happened some days ago. Miss Knatchbull is with your mother, trying to comfort her."

Nikolai took off his glasses and wiped them absentmindedly. He was unable to envisage life without Masters' silent strength to see them through. Schuller ventured to offer advice.

"Allow your mother to cry until she has spent her grief. Tell her you are now in charge of the Domaine and show her the truth, that you are quite capable of being in charge. She needs someone to take away the burden of her responsibilities. Your mother has suffered much, she is no longer young and we all expect too much of her. For my part I shall do all I can to help in any way I can."

"We're lucky to have you, sir. No one is ever going to replace Alex in Mama's eyes, but I can try to be her right-hand man, as I was when I was young at the Flower House."

Schuller sat alone in his room thinking of Alex Masters. The American had been clever. He had fallen in love with a pampered aristocrat and had made her into a most formidable woman, by means of giving her the Domaine and encouraging her to adopt the children. A lifetime of devotion had strengthened her and taken away any frivolity that might have remained. Schuller looked at the wallpaper patterned with ivy and the solid oak furniture of his room. Everything in the house was typically French and made to last a lifetime. In the Domaine he was happy. He would remain in the house as long as he could. His stay with the family had taught him something he had never had the opportunity to learn before, either from his father, a military man whose wife had died on the day of his birth, or from an unloving wife preoccupied with making money. From Valentina and her husband he had learned the value of a home and family. He had also learned that love has to be nurtured, like a rare orchid. He fastened his uniform jacket and combed his hair. Then he strode to Valentina's room and knocked on the door. Miss Knatchbull had gone, and when he entered and saw Valentina standing before him, her eyes red from crying, it was all he could do not to sweep her into his arms to tell her how much he admired her. Instead, he spoke formally.

"I have learned of the death of your husband, Countess, and wish to express my condolences."

"Alex was killed in London during the blitz. Apparently he was persuaded to play the hero by one of his former colleagues at the American Embassy. I knew nothing of it. He didn't even come home here to say good-bye to me and the children. I suppose he knew I would try to dissuade him from going."

"You must tell no one that your husband died in London."

Valentina rose and snarled her anguish at Schuller.

"I don't care who knows. I don't care about anything anymore."

"Of course you care. Do you want every woman and child in this house to be interrogated and tortured by the Gestapo? I expect the greatest self-control from you at this moment. That's what I expect from the woman whose dossier so impressed me before I had even met her. It is too late for you to start letting down all those who love and trust you. This is the moment for you to start showing your true courage and worth."

Schuller's eyes lit on the Fabergé egg, with its exquisitely jeweled interior. Valentina had placed it next to the ones Yanin had bought her. The Oberführer touched the objects with reverence.

"Though you may not think it, Countess, you are a very lucky woman. During your life you have been loved by many people. Remember it whenever you are tempted to indulge in self-pity. I have never been loved. I am not one of those who attract strong emotion. I therefore envy you."

Valentina sat on the window seat and looked out on the estate. After a while she spoke.

"How shall I explain Alex's disappearance to the coordinator?"

"I advise that you go to Paris at once. I will drive you there myself. You can return in a few days saying that your husband had had an accident as you had suspected. You can also say that he died in the hospital. The coordinator believed that your husband was missing and that he had not traveled out of France. He checked to see if Mr. Masters had applied for a travel document; that is why he thinks he remained in France. It is very fortunate that the coordinator was away when you first learned the news of Mr. Masters' death."

"I'll pack my case."

"I'm at your service, Countess."

Valentina looked up, struck by the gentleness in Schuller's voice. He smiled down at her.

"I too love you, Countess. It can only cause me distress because my feelings can never be reciprocated but it is best that you know it. Whatever I can do for you I will do, now and always."

At 4 P.M. Valentina stepped into the Oberführer's car and drove with him to Paris. In the mailbox of her apartment on the Ile St.-Louis she found a card from Masters posted from England. Inside an envelope it showed a view of the English city, with its historical Tower of London and view of the river. She read it through tears.

Lovely one,
Here I am holding two packs of muffins and wishing I were sitting in front of the fire at home toasting them for you. London's cold and the hotel has no heating but I'm leaving in the morning so it doesn't matter. I sent you a letter from Chantilly explaining my feelings about this trip. I hope you understood. I also want to tell you that I miss you every minute and that I'm going to love you until you're old and deaf and a

menace around the house. I miss you every minute. See you put on a big smile when I come brandishing the gifts I've bought you.

Love you, *Alex*

Valentina sat alone in the darkness, thinking of the wonderful times she and Masters had had together. She remembered their trips to the Ritz Hotel for lunch and love in the afternoon, their elegant Kentucky ball in the style of times past, that had brought Vasily and Elena together. She took pleasure from the memory of their years of restoring the Domaine and the dinners they had enjoyed under the apple tree in the valley of Chevreuse. It was over. From now on life would be black-and-white. There would never be a rosy-gold morning again.

Valentina slept until six, when there was a knock at the door. Answering it, she found Schuller pale with anxiety outside.

"Have you received a visit from the Gestapo, Countess?"

"I've had no visits at all."

"There is a warrant out for your arrest."

"Why, what am I supposed to have done?"

"I don't know, but we must leave at once for the Domaine."

"I'll go and dress."

"Please hurry, Countess, there is no time to be lost. I'll be waiting on the Quai d'Orléans in my car."

Valentina dressed, collected two tins of coffee left over from a previous visit and was putting her keys into her purse when a Gestapo officer approached along the corridor.

"You are Valentina, Countess Korolenko?"

"I am Valentina Masters."

"The same, I understand. You will come with me."

"Where are we going?"

"Never mind, you will learn soon enough."

Madame Bandol, always an inquisitive soul, closed her door and caught her breath. She had heard Schuller's voice and had eavesdropped on his conversation with Valentina. She had also heard the summons of the Gestapo officer. She ran to her bedroom and put on her dressing gown. Then she rushed to the Quai d'Orléans. In a low black car she found Schuller waiting for Valentina.

"You're waiting for Countess Korolenko, aren't you, sir?"

"Who are you?"

"I'm her neighbor, Madame Bandol. A Gestapo officer has just arrested the countess. He drove away over the bridge, you'll catch them if you hurry."

Schuller drove away at once, following the Citroën toward the rue des Saussaies. His heart was thudding ominously because the rue des Saussaies was one of the two main Gestapo interrogation centers in Paris. Schuller knew he was involving himself and that this could be fatal. He shook his head defiantly and pulled up outside the dark building where Valentina had just been taken. He held out little hope that he could help her.

## CHAPTER TWENTY-SEVEN

*Gestapo Interrogation Center, Paris, 1942*

———————

Valentina was put in a cell with a young woman who had been tortured for many days. There was just room for them both to lie on straw pallets or for one to lie and the other to use the primitive toilet tin in the corner. Valentina bathed the woman's face and tried to encourage her to speak but her lips were swollen and she could barely sip the water. Her eyes were puffed and purple, blue and red and one of her wrists seemed broken. Valentina sat on the pallet, stroking her companion's hands and trying to learn something about her.

"Are you French?"

"English."

"How long have you been here?"

"A week."

"What is your name?"

The woman began to vomit blood. Valentina sat on the edge of the bed looking into space. Was this what happened when one tried to toe the line set by the occupying powers? Was this what determined noninvolvement had brought her. She heard screams coming from rooms below her cell and fear stark and terrible filled her mind. She remembered Schuller's words: This is the moment for you to start showing your true courage and worth. She asked herself how one showed courage when faced with the madmen of the Gestapo. Would they torture her to tell what she did not know? What would she do if they did? Were they knowledgeable enough to know when one spoke the truth and when one did not? Did they care? Or were the rumors right and did they just enjoy their grim work? The cell was dark and she had no idea if she had been there an hour or a day. Confusion was the only emotion she felt, confusion and blinding fear. She held the injured woman close, not caring about the stench or the fleas or the body-racking sobs of animal hurt. To comfort the woman she talked of the only thing she could think of that might interest an English girl.

"My name is Valentina. I live in Rambouillet at a place called the Domaine Russe. It's a beautiful house with five hundred acres of vineyards, mustard fields and gardens. My second husband bought it for me. He was American and I loved him dearly. We bought the house twenty years ago when it was in poor condition and we've been restoring it and the estate around it ever since. Alex went to London a few days ago and was killed in an air raid on the city. I didn't even know he'd gone to London. Isn't it funny, you can live with a man for two decades and never know how much he longs to be a hero."

"Was your first husband a hero?"

Valentina thought of Yanin. Was that why Masters had gone to London? Was he still competing with Yanin, as he had so many times in their life together? She continued her story.

"My first husband was Count Korolenko. He brought us out of Russia in the face of the revolution, so he could be called a hero. Alex was a diplomat. He often told me he felt the need to compete with the first love of my life. Now all I have left is my home. I love the Domaine more than anything in the world, apart from the children. I adopted sixty-six Russian boys and girls who were left without parents after the revolution."

"Have you children of your own?"

"I have a son, Nikolai, who's the new Count Korolenko. I had another son who was killed at the beginning of the Spanish Civil War. I also have a lady living with me who is English. Her name is Miss Knatchbull and she used to be my governess when I was young. She comes from Tunbridge Wells, though she's been living in Paris for decades. I also have my maid from St. Petersburg at the Domaine. Her name is Zita and she has a son called Louis."

"Tell me about your son Nikolai."

"He's a writer and he's blond and blue-eyed like an Englishman. He used to live in New York but now he's come home to help manage the estate. I think he wants to live in France forever. He's thirty-six now and it's time he settled down. May I ask you your name?"

"My name's Mazarin, and that's all you'll get out of me."

"Well, Mazarin, you and I are in trouble. I've heard about this place, and most of the prisoners die here and those who don't are sent to Fresnes Prison."

The Englishwoman's hand clutched her own and Valentina told her more about Miss Knatchbull and about the Domaine. She was dozing against her new companion when the cell door opened and the guard dragged her outside and upstairs to one of the interrogation rooms. She was alarmed to find two S.S. officers, two Gestapo thugs in shirt sleeves and the coordinator from the Domaine Russe sitting before her. He began the questioning.

"You are Valentina Masters, formerly the Countess Korolenko."

"I am."

"You live at the Domaine Russe in Rambouillet, a property you acquired in nineteen twenty-one."

"That is correct."

"Your husband, Alexander Masters, was an American spy?"

"He was an American diplomat attached to their embassy in Paris when I first knew him."

"That is the American title for a spy."

"That is your opinion, not mine, sir."

"Obviously you must have known about your husband's work."

"I knew he went to the office in the morning and returned in the evening, that he was posted to various locations and that he retired officially in Madrid in nineteen thirty-six. He's been at home ever since until last week, as you know, when he went to London. I now know that he went to London."

"Are you saying you did not know that he went to London?"

"Alex went to Paris to have lunch with some of his friends. He told me he would be back at six. When he didn't return I assumed he'd had an accident and I notified the police and asked them to check their lists. Today when I came to Paris I found a note from my husband. It had been sent from London and spoke of another note sent to me from Chantilly, but I haven't received that one. I also had an anonymous phone call telling me that Alex was dead."

"You learned of your husband's death how?"

"I received an anonymous phone call. I don't know for certain if it was true, but I imagine it was."

Valentina thought of Malik and knew she must continue lying. She sat very stiffly in her chair, answering as quickly and clearly as she could. She was surprised when the coordinator repeated all the questions at least twice. Then he progressed to a new line.

"Mr. Masters had friends in Paris; who were they?"

"They were people with whom he had previously worked."

"Do you know them?"

"I used to, but I haven't seen any of them since nineteen forty when they returned to America."

"Tell me their names."

Valentina repeated the names of two or three men who had returned to the States long before the war. Again the questions were repeated. Then the coordinator startled her.

"Were you aware that your protégée, Katrina Yelensky, has been involved in work forbidden by the occupying powers?"

"What kind of work?"

"She and her husband have been harboring Allied spies who parachute into France to cause disruption to the Fatherland."

"I don't believe it."

The coordinator waved a sheet of paper before her eyes.

"This is the confession of Jacques St. Roche, Yelensky's husband. He was shot this morning at Fresnes Prison."

Valentina's expression did not change, though her face paled and her eyes hardened as she gazed at the coordinator. She clenched her fists, trying not to shout questions at him. Was it true? Was Jacques dead? And what of Katrina, had she managed to escape? She heard the coordinator giving an order to the guard. The room was so silent she could hear the sound of her own heart beating. She continued to sit upright, determined to preserve her dignity for as long as possible. She concentrated on a small patch of green-painted wall above the Gestapo officer's head. There was a stain on the paint that had been wiped, making it more noticeable. Valentina wondered if it was blood and if hers was soon to mingle with the other. The coordinator watched her closely as Katrina was led in. Valentina turned to her daughter and nodded. The coordinator sounded gleeful.

"During her interrogation Yelensky has revealed that your husband resided in her house overnight before traveling with her to Dieppe, where he intended to take a fishing boat to England. I have checked the identity of those authorized by the authorities to fish off the French coast and find that two of the boats are owned by your adopted sons. One of these men, Andreas Malik, has vanished. The other, Ivan Malik, took his fishing boat out yesterday afternoon and did not return. I believe he has fled to England. The other Malik, Andreas, is surely still here in France. I want him and you may soon discover that you know where he is."

Valentina risked a look at Katrina, whose face was almost as swollen as that of the woman in her cell. She felt a profound hatred for the coordinator and endless self-regret that she had not done whatever she felt like doing since his arrival. She could have led the men who called frequently at the Domaine begging help in getting to England. She could have formed a real escape route, not just the flimsy one through which she and Nikolai had led Jack Stevens and his son to the Channel Port. She replied as calmly as she could.

"I have no idea where Ivan and Andreas Malik are. I know they have fishing boats because I was the guarantor for their loans in purchasing the boats. I have not seen either of them for over a year."

"I do not believe you, Countess."

"Why should you doubt me?"

"Because it was on one of the Malik ships that your husband went to England."

"I knew nothing of my husband's visit to England and nothing of his plans. He did not tell me he was going and you will no doubt remember my distress on the night he did not come home to the Domaine."

"I believe nothing you say or do, Countess."

The coordinator nodded to one of the guards, who tied Katrina to a chair and stretched her hands out before her on the table. Valentina began to feel the agonizing hammerings of panic. The coordinator spoke with obvious enjoyment.

"Yelensky and her husband were captured on the night of the full moon as they were leading an Allied spy to their home. They revealed Mr. Masters' visit and what they knew of his intentions. I believe you when you say that you knew nothing of Yelensky's involvement with the English spies. I do not believe you when you say you know nothing of Mr. Masters' visit to England."

"I assure you I know nothing at all."

"I have seen your dossier, which proves to any reader that you are defiant of any personal injury and discomfort but that you care in an exaggerated fashion for your 'children,' as you are so fond of calling them. Hecht is going to break Miss Yelensky's fingers one by one if you do not reveal precisely the information I require. Now let us begin. Where is Andreas Malik?"

"I have no idea; you know I have no idea and that I cannot make up a story that will satisfy you."

Valentina turned away as Katrina screamed hysterically. There was an ominous crack and the sound of frenzied sobbing. Valentina leaped out of her seat in the direction of the coordinator.

"You know I know nothing! My husband went to England without telling me."

She clawed at the colorless face, bringing blood in stark red lines down the coordinator's cheek. One of the guards leaped toward her and smashed his fist into her face. There was another crack and an agonized scream from Katrina. Valentina dropped onto her seat, shocked that her clothes were soaking wet with sweat. The cracking and screaming went on until one of Katrina's hands hung limp at her side. Valentina concentrated hard on holding on to her consciousness. She heard the coordinator speak as if through a haze.

"Take the girl away. The countess can know nothing or she would have saved her protégée's precious fingers. Send the girl to Fresnes in the morning and don't waste your time dressing the hand."

Valentina was half carried, half dragged back to her cell and thrown down beside the Englishwoman. When the guard had gone, slamming the door of the cell behind him, Mazarin knelt at Valentina's side and whispered.

"Let me help you onto your bed. There are rats in these cells; you mustn't lie on the floor."

With a practiced hand the Englishwoman felt Valentina's neck and then her jaw.

"Your jaw's broken; during the night it will swell and you're going to be in bad pain. You need a doctor."

"Don't call the guard."

Valentina felt herself held in the firm young arms. Then Mazarin began to speak.

"My name is Claudine Pontchardet. I'm English, of English parents, though my father and mother had lived in France all their lives and I was born here. After the occupation some Germans were billeted in our home in Dreux, which isn't far from your house in Rambouillet. One of the Germans got drunk and shot my father and mother as they were trying to hide from him in their wine cellar. I went to England immediately afterward and volunteered to be trained as an agent. I'd done fifteen jumps into enemy territory when I was betrayed and brought here. All the resistant groups are fighting among themselves, as you probably know. The communists want power and so do those who support De Gaulle. I don't know who betrayed me, but I suspect it was my landlord and not one of the French counterparts to my work. The landlord's daughter was in prison. Perhaps the Germans promised to release her if he gave information on me."

Valentina felt herself being covered with a ragged blanket. Then Mazarin settled on the opposite pallet. The darkness became so intense that she could not see the rats, though she could hear them in the walls and in the straw below her. Her jaw began to throb and swell to such a size she thought she might have difficulty in swallowing. She sat up and cast her mind back to the days of her youth. For hours she went over every moment that had ever given her pleasure: her love for Yanin, the birth of her sons, the gradual narrowing of her differences with Korolenko, the first meeting with Dmitry, the triumph of their flight from Russia. Then she thought of Masters and saw him in her mind's eye, his broad shoulders and swinging step striding through the vineyards and away toward the woods. She imagined herself running after him and linking arms and kissing him as she had so often done. Then she buried her head in her hands and thought of Schuller, praying he had stayed out of all this and that his benevolent attitude would keep those who lived in the Domaine safe now she was gone.

A faint gray light showed under the door. Was it already morning? Valentina rose and took off the silk blouse she had been wearing at the time of her arrest. This she washed under the tap and hung up to dry from the hook in the ceiling. Then she walked to the door and listened to the noises in the corridor outside. In the

distance she could hear men talking and the sound of a metal trolley scraping on the ground. For a few hours the screaming of the
prisoners under interrogation had ceased. Soon, she knew, it would
start again.

Mazarin rose and yawned.

"At five they bring tea round with some black bread. Then the
prisoners for Fresnes are put on a lorry that waits outside in the
courtyard."

"I'm hungry; I won't be able to eat, but I'm hungry."

"I'll help you drink your tea, Valentina."

The guard put tea and moldy black bread on the table. Then,
looking up, he saw the blouse hanging from the hook on the ceiling. He laughed heartily.

"Still anxious to look smart, Countess."

Valentina huddled in the blanket, ignoring his taunts. When he
had gone she tried to drink some tea, spilling more than she
swallowed, though she persisted. When she had drunk as much as
she could she put on the damp blouse and sat on the edge of the
bed waiting. What if she were not sent to Fresnes? What if she
were asked to witness Katrina's agony again? Her thoughts raced
back and forth on lines of ever-increasing alarm. Her anguish
ended when two guards arrived and pushed her and Mazarin out
of the cell and into the yard.

Twelve gaunt men and women stood or lay in the snow, their
faces swollen, their limbs bandaged or bloody. Valentina kept close
to Mazarin as they were herded into the truck. It was then locked
and bolted for the journey. Mazarin's bruised body shielded Valentina's against the metal side of the truck. Valentina tried to accustom herself to the pain in her jaw by thinking of times past.
Then she heard the driver enter and take the truck to the first sentry post on the main road. Half an hour later there was another
halt for a sentry and then, only a few minutes later, a third stop.
This was much longer than the others, at least five minutes. Then
the truck trundled on. Valentina thought of Nikolai and what he
would do when he found out what had happened to her. He would
surely continue leading those in the Domaine on a moderate
course. He would do his best to keep its affairs in good order, but
how lonely he would be. She closed her eyes on the intense pain in
her face, conscious that she must not fall and be trampled by the

weight of the others. She must concentrate on staying well, in case
a miracle occurred and she could go home. Sweat ran in rivulets
down her face, soaking the blouse and skirt. She clung onto the
side of the truck and grimly, determinedly, closed her eyes on her
agony.

Suddenly the side of the truck was thrown open and a staccato
order came for the prisoners to step down. Blinking in the wintry
sunlight, they found themselves in dense woodland that Valentina
recognized immediately as her own. She looked around and saw
Nikolai, Dmitry and Louis looking in shocked alarm at her injury.
She fell weeping into Nikolai's arms.

"Whatever have you done, Nikolai?"

"We commandeered this transport, Mama. Is something wrong
with your mouth?"

Mazarin stepped forward.

"The Germans broke your mother's jaw. She must try not to
speak. Now where are the driver and guard?"

"We buried them in a field on the other side of St.-Rémy."

"Have you a plan?"

"I've come to take Mama home. You can come too, if you wish,
or you can go on alone."

"What about the other prisoners?"

"They can come too."

Valentina tried to speak but her jaw was agony and she took to
writing her questions down: "Whatever will Oberführer Schuller
say? . . ."

Nikolai smiled and kissed her.

"Everything is going to be all right, Mama. Now, if any of you
men can dig, please assist with the burial of this truck. Then you
can come to the house for lunch. If anyone wishes to go on to their
own home they may do so. If you are questioned in the future
about this escape say you were set free by the communist resistance and that you have no idea where they put you from the
transport."

Valentina and Mazarin walked arm in arm ahead of Nikolai. He
was admiring Mazarin's blue-black hair and broad-shouldered
figure. Even the terrible injuries she had suffered had not detracted
from her majestic beauty. He thought of the candid look in her
dark, knowing eyes and was suddenly overwhelmingly happy. He

smiled at his mother, who had stopped at the side of the mustard field to look up at the house. Nikolai knew that she was wondering for how long she would be free. When the coordinator arrived back from Paris they might all be arrested or executed. Nikolai sighed. Everything would depend on whether the rest of his plan worked. He looked again at Mazarin and was cheered by her resolute manner and confidence. He knew instinctively that she was a woman to be relied on.

Valentina was stumbling up the steps to the house when she felt a firm hand on her arm. Looking around she saw Schuller. She swayed with shock. Schuller caught her and carried her into the house, leaving Mazarin alone with Nikolai, who turned shyly to find out more about the woman who had fascinated him from the moment of first meeting.

"What's your name?"

"You can call me Mazarin."

"I called Dr. Martin and asked him to wait in case you had any wounds that need dressing. Zita's made a cake for us all; it's not a very good cake because she doesn't have much fat, but it's better than nothing. Are you French?"

"I'm English."

"And beautiful."

"Are you a flirt, Count Korolenko?"

"I don't think my worst enemy would call me that."

"Good, now let's go and organize the others. One of the men is really seriously injured."

Schuller put Valentina down on the bed and held her hand.

"You are at a disadvantage, Countess. You cannot speak and therefore cannot interrupt me so I can say whatever I wish. I was waiting for you on the quayside the other evening when your neighbor, Madame Bandol, came and informed me that you had been arrested. I followed the Gestapo car to the rue des Saussaies and waited for a while to see if they released you. I thought there might have been some mistake as to your identity. When I realized there had not, I entered the building and asked to watch your interrogation through a two-way mirror. I found out afterward that you were to be taken to Fresnes the following morning. I returned to the Domaine, had a meeting with your son and Dmitry and

Louis. We then took charge of the truck in which you and the other prisoners were traveling. My uniform and my authority were enough to make the driver stop though there was no authorized checkpoint there."

Valentina felt tears falling down her cheeks. She made to speak, conscious of the ugliness of her injury.

"What will happen to you?"

"That depends on the second part of our plan. One thing is certain. I am an officer with twenty years' experience of military operations. I am willing to fight the enemies of the Fatherland. I am not willing to stand by and watch women and children being tortured."

"Katrina?"

Schuller went to the telephone and asked Dr. Martin to come up.

"I regret to inform you, Countess, that your daughter, Katrina, committed suicide in her cell. My grief is so great I cannot even express it. I can only pledge you my loyalty and my protection, for what it is worth."

Lisabette tiptoed away from the room and ran all the way from her bedroom. She had seen her grandmother's swollen face and black eyes and had heard every word of the conversation with Schuller. When she reached the room she asked her brother the meaning of the words committed suicide.

"Does it mean Katrina's dead like Mama and Papa?"

"Don't talk like that, Lisabette."

"But, Sasha, what does it mean?"

"It means she's dead, but Nana's alive and that's all that matters."

"Oberführer Schuller got her out of prison, I heard him say so."

"You'd better not tell anyone what he did or *he'll* be arrested too and maybe all of us. Do you understand, Lisabette?"

Later, Lisabette went downstairs to the room where Schuller wrote his letters. He was there, his head inclined over a pad of cream paper. He looked up as she entered the room.

"How are you, Lisabette?"

"Very well, sir."

"Are you glad the countess is back?"

"I knew she'd come back."

"And how did you know?"

"Because Nana can magic things. I knew she'd come back to look after me and Sasha."

Schuller smiled at the description of Valentina magicking things. She had certainly cast a spell on him and Wengen and Koch. He looked back to Lisabette in her frilly white dress and patent leather shoes.

"I am writing to my daughter in Germany."

"Can I be your daughter, too?"

Schuller looked into the bright blue eyes and saw a fierce longing there.

"Why do you wish me to be your father?"

"Because all the other children have fathers except me and my brother Sasha. Nikolai's my uncle and Dmitry's my friend but they aren't my father. I want to choose my father so I can have someone I love like a father."

"And do you love me?"

"Yes, I do."

"Do you know why?"

"Because you brought Nana home and looked after her, because you bring us food every day and because I like the stories you tell me before I go to bed."

Schuller rose and picked Lisabette up in his arms.

"If I were to be your father I should have to live here all the time to guard and love you."

"You do live here all the time."

"Someday I shall have to go away. Germany is my home, not the Domaine Russe in Rambouillet."

Seeing her distress, Schuller took a sweet from his pocket and popped it in her mouth.

"I could be your uncle. Then I could come to visit you someday long after the war is over."

"You can be my father. Even if you go back to Germany, you can be my father. I love you and want to belong to you."

Lisabette skipped happily from the room. It had been decided. She had decided. Schuller would be her papa and that was that.

Schuller signed the letter to his daughter and sat gazing out of the window at the peaceful fields of the Domaine. At six the co-ordinator would return from Paris. What was he going to do? How could he do what had to be done and not throw suspicion on the inhabitants of the house? Suddenly he felt very tired. He had not slept that night and had been going over and over the hideous scene in the interrogation room. On enlisting in the S.S. he had vowed obedience in all things to the Führer. Had that meant obedience even where acts of a criminal nature were concerned? He had never even imagined that he would be obliged to condone torture, brute force by men who were sadists, perverts, who simply enjoyed killing and torturing those who could not defend themselves. Koch and Wengen had been decorated many times in battle, he too. Now he had disgraced his uniform and he was glad to have done so. Schuller wondered how long it would be before he was arrested. He sat in the fading light, conscious of the unusual silence in the house. They all knew about Katrina's death and were hiding their grief as best they were able. He watched Dr. Martin riding away on his bicycle and looked up as Zita appeared with a glass of wine.

"You're very pale, sir."

"I am as well as can be expected, thank you, Zita."

"Where are Hauptsturmführer Wengen and Standartenführer Koch?"

"They went out to clear their heads. They are uneasy, as I am. It is very likely we shall all be arrested if we cannot carry out our plan."

"Don't worry, sir. Everything will turn out fine now Madame's home. She's feeling better already; all she ever needs is to be home."

Schuller saw a black car approaching on the road. Zita followed his gaze and helped him into his jacket.

"The coordinator's on his way, sir. I'll go and tell Madame and Nikolai."

The coordinator strode into the hall and fixed Schuller with a baleful gaze.

"You will come to my office at once, Oberführer."

The two men disappeared upstairs. Zita saw Koch and Wengen galloping back to the house and the coordinator's treacherous adjutant smoking a cigarette outside by his car. Upstairs the sound of the coordinator's rage echoed in the house.

"You were there watching that woman's interrogation. I wish

they had broken her neck and not her jaw. You pitied her, admit it, Schuller, you pitied her."

"I pity anyone who is in the hands of those madmen in the rue des Saussaies."

"They are professional interrogators."

"They are nothing of the sort. They are perverts and totally unprofessional in all they do."

"I shall order your arrest. You too can be interrogated. I do not need to tell you that the transport to Fresnes, which held the countess and other malefactors, never reached the prison. No doubt you will feign ignorance of all complicity in the countess's escape."

The coordinator picked up the telephone and tapped to get a line. The telephone was dead. He rose and called Wengen and Koch, who marched smartly into the office and saluted.

The coordinator turned to Schuller.

"You were chosen for this post because of your distinguished record in battle and because you had also had experience of intelligence work and because you satisfied our security requirements. From the very beginning, since you came to this house, you have showed sympathy to the inhabitants of the property. You have not neglected your duties but I believe you are guilty of a most serious error which will destroy your military career. I believe you helped Countess Korolenko escape from the transport to Fresnes. Koch, Wengen, accompany Oberführer Schuller to Gestapo headquarters at Gazeran. No doubt they will prove able to make him talk about his recent activities."

Koch and Wengen marched Schuller to the hall. The coordinator went over to his wireless set and sat down to tap out a signal to Berlin. Behind him the door opened. He did not hear it because of the earphones. A sharp crack on the head fractured his skull. Then, swiftly, he was wrapped in blankets and dragged to Miss Knatchbull's bedroom. Nikolai handed her back her lead-handled stick and put the coordinator's body in the priest's hole she had just revealed to him. On the floor of the room there was a pile of food that had previously been hidden there. Nikolai looked in wonder at tinned foods of every dimension, bottled fruit, flour, sugar, coffee. He stuffed the coordinator's feet into the hole and brought down the double oak wall over the incriminating evidence.

"I should feel pain, but I feel nothing at all. I've killed a man, Natty. I should feel something, surely."

"He's your enemy and would have had the lot of us arrested. Why should you feel pain?"

"Is that really where you hid your valuables, Natty?"

"It is, and no one's found it despite all the searches. I reckon this house is as full of holes as a Gruyère cheese. The lady of the house must have hidden her royal lover there on occasion."

"What were you saving the food for?"

"I was saving it for a night like this. Help me get it downstairs. We'll ask Zita to make some gooseberry pies."

"Mama will be furious she can't eat the pies."

"I've saved some fruit for her when she's better."

Nikolai carried the food downstairs, then went back to the coordinator's office to check that nothing looked amiss and that he had left no traces of blood in the corridor. As the clock struck the half hour he went to his mother's room and found her writing notes for Sasha and Lisabette. She looked up at Nikolai and wrote, "Has the coordinator arrived yet?" Nikolai took the note and threw it on the fire.

"I haven't seen him yet, Mama."

Valentina wrote to Sasha to take Lisabette to change for dinner. Then she rose and indicated to Nikolai to help her put on a dress of chestnut velvet. He stood behind her as she smoothed her hair in the mirror.

"You're beautiful, Mama; not even two black eyes and a fat jaw can alter that. Now you're not to worry about anything. Zita's made a special dinner and I've found some straws so you can drink your wine through them. Shall we go now and have a drink before our meal?"

Dinner was trout from the stream, chicken in garlic sauce and gooseberry pie. Valentina sucked soup through an improvised metal tube and champagne from an invalid's cup. She seemed so calm and in control of her situation that no one asked what was happening and how she had returned so miraculously from her ordeal.

Lisabette sat on the opposite side of the table to Schuller, smiling shyly and blushing with pleasure when he told her how like her grandmother she was. After dinner she sang for the assembled family and one of the young women played Katrina's first composition as a tribute to the dead. At ten, members of the household retired, leaving Nikolai alone with the Germans. They drank coffee and crème de menthe. Then Nikolai asked for help.

"Gentlemen, I need something from you."

Schuller smiled at the indirect appeal.

"I'm sure you do, Nikolai. May I ask where the coordinator is?"

"He went away, sir. Have you seen his adjutant?"

"He also went away."

"Thank God Mama didn't see the car. I need it to be abandoned far from here. I have no pass to travel at night and wouldn't wish to apply for one. Have you any idea where the adjutant is?"

"He went away and will not be back."

Nikolai looked hard as Schuller continued calmly.

"We will see that the car is placed in a suitable site. You need worry no further for the moment."

"Thank you, sir. I shall cover for your absence if you tell me what to say."

"If anyone should telephone from Paris or Berlin you will say we went out to search for the coordinator, who has disappeared with his adjutant. I trust he is well hidden and not able to get free."

"The possibility of his getting free is virtually nonexistent, sir, and he is very well hidden."

"The adjutant also."

At 5 A.M. Schuller returned to the Domaine and walked outside on the terrace. He was smoking a cigar when Valentina joined him, taking his arm as he paced back and forth.

"Are you feeling better, Countess?"

She nodded and wrote on her notepad, "The telephone wires have been mended and the telephone in the coordinator's office has been ringing."

"I will see to it, Countess."

Valentina let him lead her back to the house. She watched as Schuller took the pages from the pad and burned it on the fire. Then he helped her to her room and told her to go to sleep. She waited until she knew he would be well on his way to the coordinator's office. Then she ran to the door and listened as he spoke in rapid German to the headquarters in Paris.

"We cannot find him, sir. Wengen, Koch and I have been

searching all night and have gone as far as Paris on the road he would have traveled from the Gestapo offices in the rue des Saussaies. . . . He has been in the best of health, sir. . . . He likes his work, of course. . . . He is always most secret about his affairs. . . . A woman? . . . I imagine not; money interests him more than any woman. . . . I know nothing of the details of his bank account. . . . I cannot say, sir. . . . I will call Berlin in the morning and speak with Admiral Canaris, his superior. . . . Yes indeed. . . . Yes I will. . . . I will inform you immediately when he returns."

Schuller sat in the coordinator's office blowing smoke rings at the ceiling. Had the coordinator told anyone in Paris of his decision to arrest Schuller, the man sent from Berlin to guard him? In the previous twenty-four hours he had arranged the murder of the guards and driver of the prison van, the concealment of their bodies and the burial of the van. He had compromised his own military career and that of Koch and Wengen, but they had been given a little time, a moment or two of peace. He felt no remorse for what he had done.

Schuller went to bed and lay on top of the bedclothes, too tense to rest, too weary to undress. He was trying to work out how long it would be before the coordinator's car were found. He smiled grimly as he thought how Wengen had left the car outside a notorious homosexual brothel in the rue de la Lune, a place frequented by the coordinator's adjutant. The crime would be discovered the moment someone reported to the Gestapo that the countess was back home, or until the coordinator's replacement checked the dossiers of everyone in the house, if checking was in his nature. Until then Schuller decided to enjoy the Domaine and the family who lived there. He would shoot in the early hours of dawn. He would go adventuring in the wine cellar and would watch Zita making the pigeon-and-garlic pies he loved so much. By the bed he noticed a bunch of winter roses. There was a card nearby in Lisabette's childish hand: "To Papa with love." He smiled at the note and put it in his pocket. Then he fell asleep until morning.

As spring came and turned slowly to summer Nikolai and Mazarin adventured the estate. She had almost recovered from her experiences in the rue des Saussaies, though one hand had been slightly paralyzed as a result of her injuries. Nikolai held the hand and kissed it often.

"In wartime there's so little time to say the things one wants to say, you know that, Mazarin. I live every day as if it were my last, because it might be my last. I don't know how long Oberführer Schuller can keep all this going. I want to tell you that I'm in love with you. From that first moment when I saw you in your torn gray suit with blood in your hair I was in love with you. I know you'll have to leave soon, and I'll be taking you to St.-Malo myself, but before you go I wanted to tell you my feelings. Say something, for heaven's sake!"

"You have odd taste."

"Don't joke about it."

Mazarin stepped out of bed and put on a wrap Valentina had loaned her.

"I always joke about things that are too serious to think about. I don't want to be in love. I don't want you to love me. It's wartime and I would be dead by now if it weren't for your mother and you. In a few months I'll be sent back to France to parachute into a field and perhaps be caught again by the Gestapo. I don't know any more than you if I'll be alive by the end of the war."

"I'd like to ask you to marry me, Mazarin."

"You can't know you love me enough for that!"

"Do you not feel anything for me?"

Mazarin looked down.

"I feel—I feel too much."

"Then say you'll marry me."

"You might change your mind by the time the war ends."

"I'm too old to change my mind."

Nikolai took from his pocket a box containing one of the remaining pieces from the Korolenko family jewels. It was a ruby ring so large and dark it radiated many colors in the sunlight of morning. Mazarin looked at the ring and then back to Nikolai.

"If I accept you I'll be very serious about it. I'm very serious about everything and you'll not be able to brush me off when I come back a few years from now."

"You talk too much."

They were still kissing when the air was disturbed by the sound of a squadron of Allied bombers en route to Berlin passing overhead. Nikolai looked through the window at the circles of red, white and blue. Then he closed his eyes and concentrated on Mazarin.

# CHAPTER TWENTY-EIGHT

*Fresnes Prison, New Year's 1943*

———————

Valentina was in a cell at Fresnes, listening to the forbidden shouted greetings of the prisoners: "Jack calling François, good morning, how did you sleep?" "François calling Jack, I'm fine, thank you." *"Marignon demande les nouvelles de Balzac." "Balzac ici, tout va bien, merci."* "Brigitte asks news of Tatin." "Tatin here, I'm well enough." Each morning this parade of voices cheered those incarcerated in the prison. Each evening they bade each other good night. Sometimes one of the voices did not reply to the inquiry about his health. Then there would be a moment of silence before the solicitations began again.

Valentina saw the guard looking at her through the spyhole of her cell door. She turned her back and sat staring up at the sky through the small window. How long had it been? How long had she been away from the Domaine? Was Nikolai still alive? Had Schuller, Koch and Wengen reached the comparative safety of the South of France, after their escape through the same tunnel Tanya and the Laval family had used? These were questions Valentina asked herself constantly in the hours of her interrogation. When she had not answered the questions, despite all that had been done to her, the Gestapo had sent her to Fresnes to await death by firing squad. For the first two months she had been locked in solitary confinement in one of the underground cells. Unable to lie down fully stretched, sodden with water that leaked in through the ceiling and bitten by rats, she had been fed once every three days and would have died if it had not been for the kindness of a doctor who did not believe in torturing the older women. Even there the prisoners had kept in contact with her. Valentina smiled wanly as she heard her name called: "*Marignon demande les nouvelles de la comtesse.*" She rose and called through her window, "I am well, thank you."

Valentina heard the wheels of the coffee trolley coming toward her cell. A mug was pushed toward her, then the door was slammed. She flopped down on her cot. Until December she had had no idea how long she had been in the prison, only that winter had come and that she was very cold. Then, at Christmas, the greetings of the prisoners had made her realize the length of her stay in Fresnes. Yesterday they had wished her a happy new year, in the middle of a dark, starry night. She heard an English voice singing "God Save the Queen." On this New Year's Day the Englishman had informed them all that his resolution was to sing his national anthem every morning. The French prisoners had replied with a spirited rendering of "The Marseillaise." Valentina looked out and saw that it was snowing. She went to the wall and struck off another day from the calendar she had scraped with a rusty nail. She began to count the days of her detention. She had arrived in Fresnes on the first of October. It was therefore her ninety-third day in the prison and her hundred and thirty-second in captivity. She had come here defiant and able to withstand all that had been done to her. She was now physically broken. Only anger kept her counting the days to the moment when she might return once more to the Domaine. She cast her mind back to the moment when the new coordinator had arrived, after months when Schuller had done the work previously accomplished by the dead man. The new coordinator had been surprisingly young and mercilessly efficient. Valentina shivered as she recalled the day when he had questioned Schuller. "I have checked the files of everyone in this house and according to my records the countess should be in Fresnes Prison. How exactly did she come to return home?" Valentina and Nikolai had led Schuller, Koch and Wengen to the secret passageway to freedom. She had given Schuller money and a note to give to Tanya when he arrived in Monte Carlo. His last look still lingered in her mind. Then he had kissed her hand formally and marched to his unknown destiny. She had been arrested by the Gestapo two days later. Valentina closed her eyes, thankful that only she had been taken. Obviously the Germans had believed it impossible that the entire household had been party to the deception.

On the twentieth of January a great storm almost drowned the sound of the morning greetings: "François calling Jack, how are you?" "Jack to François, I'm still here, keep your chin up." "*Marignon demande les nouvelles de Balzac.*" "*Balzac va bien, merci.*" "*Marie-Hélène demande les nouvelles de la comtesse.*" "The countess is well, thank you." "George sends his English friends greetings. God Save the Queen." The sound of the breakfast trolley stopped outside Valentina's cell but instead of receiving a cup of ersatz coffee, she was pulled out and taken to the courtyard to join the day's transport to Compiègne. From there she would be sent by cattle train to Buchenwald. Unaware of this, Valentina was profoundly relieved to be leaving Fresnes. As she was led to the yard she called one last greeting to her friends. "The countess is leaving. She bids all her friends good-bye." A guard hurled her into the van, but not before she had heard the chorus of good-byes and the sound of "The Marseillaise."

Valentina found herself next to a tall, fair-haired young man with lazy blue eyes. His teeth were broken and his clothes were caked with blood. He held out his hand.

"George Armstrong, Countess."

"You're the Englishman who keeps singing his national anthem."

"The same, Countess."

Two other young men closed in around her to keep her from being squashed in the mass of bodies.

"I'm Tiny, the Australian who serenaded you with 'Waltzing Matilda,' Countess."

"*Enchantée, Tiny.*"

"I'm Jack Hannegan from Boston, Countess."

"Pleased to meet you, Mr. Hannegan."

Valentina almost laughed that Tiny was at least six feet six tall and that the young man from America looked like a perfect German officer.

The interminable journey began. They were allowed one stop when water was given out, and two prisoners who had died were thrown out of the wagon into a ditch. The convoy continued through the snow to Compiègne. The Englishman held Valentina to his chest, whispering to her about his home as she had once whispered to Mazarin about the Domaine Russe. She made him laugh out loud when she spoke.

"George, do you speak German?"

"A little; why?"

"I was thinking that when we escape we shall need a man who speaks German to get us through the checkpoints. We shall also need a German uniform."

The three men looked at each other and then back to the frail woman within the circle of their bodies. They smiled despite their pain and exhaustion. They were in good company. There was still hope.

Nikolai was alone in the study of the Domaine, looking out on the snowy fields. There was no food in the house, except the eternal turnips, cabbage and half-rotten potatoes. There had been a sharp decline in their fortunes after his mother's arrest and the departure of Schuller, Koch and Wengen. At that time he had been called before the new Oberführer, who had replaced Schuller and had been told that the house was to be vacated by the Abwehr. Relief had been short-lived when he learned that he was to be fined heavily for disruption caused by the plotting of his mother. If there had been proof of his complicity, and that of his family, in the disappearance of the previous coordinator and his adjutant and the further disappearance of Schuller and his aides, every man, woman and child in the house would have been executed. As it was, it had been decided to fine him a sum that amounted to two thirds of his entire fortune in gold. This would be used to finance Abwehr operations in Europe. The ailing German exchequer had saved his life. Nikolai gritted his teeth when he remembered his argument with the new Oberführer.

"How do you know what savings we have?"

"We know everything about you, Count Korolenko. We have lists of all your assets. There is nothing we do not know."

"We shall be unable to continue here if we do not have money. The money and gold to pay your fine is not mine anyway; it is my mother's and for use in the future to keep the house and estate secure."

"You also had gold of great value deposited in the Banque de France. That was withdrawn immediately before the declaration of war. Use that and be glad you were not fined everything."

"My stepfather buried that gold when it was withdrawn. I don't know where it is. He was killed some time ago and you'll have been informed."

"Are you trying to tell me that you do not know where one third of your fortune is?"

"Sir, my mother asked her husband to remove the gold from the Banque de France and to bury it. She also told him not to tell her where it was."

"And then he was killed. Had the countess not thought of that possibility?"

"It would appear not, sir."

"The fine set by the commander of the Abwehr stands regardless of what you have told me, Count Korolenko. You have one week to make the payment in full."

Nikolai looked out of the window and saw one of his sisters returning from a trip to Paris. Valerie was the youngest of the women in the house. It had been her idea to pool all the jewelry given them at various times in the past twenty years by Valentina and sell this so they could buy food and keep the Domaine out of debt. Nikolai saw tears pouring down his sister's face as she ran up the steps to the door. He went to meet her.

"What happened?"

"No one wants the jewels. What in God's name are we going to do?"

"Ask Natty to come down, will you? I can't help feeling that Alex wouldn't just have hidden the gold. He must have left some record somewhere and Natty's the person most likely to know."

Miss Knatchbull came into the room and fixed Nikolai with a penetrating gaze.

"What can I do for you, Nikolai?"

"Do you know where Alex hid the gold Mama asked him to take out of the bank at the commencement of the war?"

"Of course I do. Your mama didn't wish to be bothered with the information. She felt it might make her feel nervous, so Mr. Masters told me."

"Where is it, Natty?"

"Mr. Masters told me to tell the countess when the time was right. That is what I shall do."

"But Mama isn't here. She may never be here again!"

Miss Knatchbull glowered at Nikolai.

"Then you had best find her and bring her home, my dear, because I shall tell no one except the countess unless I am given proof of her demise."

"And if you were to die in the night. At your age anything could happen."

"In my youth no gentleman referred to a lady's age."

Miss Knatchbull stalked from the room and sent a message down via one of the children that she would loan Nikolai money until such time as the gold could be retrieved.

Nikolai sat in his study, staring out of the window. Zita came with a tisane and stood by his side.

"Can I be of help, sir?"

"Only if you know where the gold is."

"You don't need the gold now that Miss Knatchbull's agreed to help. What we need is the countess. Everyone's stopped hoping since she was taken away. The children sit around like frightened animals and even Louis has lost interest in the vineyard."

"I got Mama out once before but now I don't even know where she is."

"You could find out if you really wanted to, sir."

Night came and Nikolai walked around the estate in the darkness, as was his custom. Until this moment, when he knew he could lose the Domaine, he had never realized how much the land meant to him. The disproportionate fine had ruined the entire financial future of the estate. Miss Knatchbull's money might pay the bills and current food costs, but how were they going to rebuild the estate houses and keep it endowed in the future? He thought of Miss Knatchbull, who at eighty-two was still the dragon she had always been. He would go and speak with her in the privacy of her room. He must persuade her to tell what she knew. Nikolai walked purposefully back toward the house.

A cat miaowed near the vineyard. A startled bird flew out from the trees. Nikolai paused as another bird flew out from cover, in surprise at the sound of the strange footfall. He heard it too and stepped behind an oak tree. The footsteps came nearer and a familiar voice called out

"Nikolai, Hanspeter Schuller here. I can't see a thing. Will you step a little closer please."

Nikolai stepped out and hugged Schuller as if he were a long-lost brother.

"Whatever are you doing here, sir? I can hardly believe it's you."

"It is, I assure you. I hope you have something to eat in the house because I am undoubtedly the hungriest man in France."

Nikolai led Schuller via the back of the house to the kitchen. There he found the remains of a vegetable pie. He set this with a bottle of wine before the man who had done so much for the occupants of the house. Then he tried to bring Schuller up to date, without being too alarmist in his statements.

"We are no longer used as a base for Abwehr operations. Your colleagues moved out some weeks ago. I was fined two thirds of our entire fortune for having been involved in some way in your disappearance and that of the previous coordinator. They were not sure if I was guilty and so preferred to fine me."

"Obviously the money will pay for their operations in Europe. The Abwehr, like all German organization and military operations, is short of money. You are very fortunate in that. I am certain they would have executed everyone in the house if they had known of your involvement and the extent of it. Be thankful they preferred the gold to your dead body."

"The new Oberführer told me we should all have been executed if he had had proof of complicity."

"And now what are you going to do about your mother? Have you heard anything of her physical condition?"

"Mama was a prisoner of the Gestapo at the rue des Saussaies until the end of September. Then she was taken to Fresnes Prison. After that I have been unable to find out anything about her fate."

"She was removed from Fresnes this morning and taken to Compiègne with a convoy of prisoners."

Nikolai looked uncertainly at Schuller.

"How do you know that, sir? And why did you come back here from Monte Carlo?"

Schuller tried to explain feelings he could not even explain to himself.

"I found I could not stay there knowing that the countess was in danger. I returned yesterday and have been watching this house ever since. I was not sure if there were German officers inside or not. My last letter from Zita arrived two months ago. As for your mother, I telephoned Fresnes Prison this morning and gave orders that she be sent to Compiègne."

Nikolai stared incredulously at Schuller.

"How did you know Mama was still there?"

"Monte Carlo has taught me to gamble, my dear Nikolai. I gambled that she was and that they would believe me when I gave the order."

"What now? Compiègne is even farther away from the Domaine than Fresnes. How can we get Mama out?"

"I have a plan. We shall need two men; perhaps you'll ask for two who will be willing to take such a risk. Then I shall need the telephone number of the Francs Tireurs Partisans."

"The communist resistance."

"Exactly; they are undoubtedly the best organized of all the groups operating in Paris. They were already well practiced in subversive activities before the war began. They will do the hard work for us. We will take the risk of getting the countess back to the Domaine."

Valentina looked around the camp of Le Royal Lieu, outside Compiègne. She thought how impossible escape would be from a place like this. Eight low buildings in the compound were surrounded by searchlights and machine guns manned by S.S. troopers. The previous day George and his two friends had reconnoitered the camp and pronounced even the drains to be too narrow for a man to pass through to the outer field. Valentina thought of Nikolai and the women and children of the Domaine. Would they have lost hope? Did they even know she was alive? She walked back to the crowded hut and took her place on a bunk underneath the Australian. He handed her down a bar of chocolate. She called up to him.

"Where did you get this?"

"I took it off one of the guards at the station."

"On the train you 'took' a sandwich from the counter as we were passing through. Were you a pickpocket before the war, Tiny?"

"I was a surgeon, ma'am. You have to have nimble fingers to be a surgeon, I'm just keeping mine in practice."

The Englishman leaned over his bunk.

"Any idea how they'll move us, Countess?"

"If we are going to Germany they will probably take us from here to Chalons-sur-Marne, to link up with the train that leaves Paris from the Gare de l'Est."

"Where does it go to in Germany?"

"It goes via Verdun to Saarbrucken."

"That's a hell of a way to walk back to England. We'd best try to escape from the bus."

"I wish you luck."

"I shan't go without you, Countess."

At eight the following morning they were put into heavy leg irons and led to a waiting cattle wagon for the first part of the journey. Through the slats at the side of the wagon Valentina could see the fields around Compiègne and scenes of French life so idyllic it was impossible to believe that she and a hundred other prisoners were en route to Germany on a journey of no return. She looked longingly out at a young woman feeding her baby in a house by the side of the road. In a field nearby two little boys and an old man were forking hay onto the snow for two thin cows. Valentina looked up at a pale-pink sky and knew that there would be more snow by the end of the day. She shivered violently. George took off his jacket and put it around her shoulders. She shrugged it away.

"Take it back. You're young and must look after your health."

"Don't deny me the pleasure, Countess. This is the first time I've felt like a human being since the Gestapo arrested me in January."

At the station the leg irons were taken off and they were handcuffed in pairs and herded on to the platform to wait for the train traveling in an easterly direction. Valentina sighed. She was right. They were going to Germany. Each step away from the Domaine chilled her, though she did her best to talk and laugh with her three stalwart friends and to show defiance of the guards.

At noon they were put on the train, not in compartments like other travelers, but in open cattle trucks. Valentina took off her underskirt and tore it into strips so she could wrap something around her head to keep her ears from freezing. She handed other strips to the three men.

"When the train moves we'll be frozen. It's best if we sit together in the corner. Wrap those around your ears."

They had been traveling for some time when a violent explosion shook the ground and hurled the front compartments of the train over an embankment into the Meuse. George looked out and reported back to his companions.

"I can see Verdun in the distance. God, what a disaster there is on the line. The French Resistance must have blown up the track ahead. Three compartments or more are in the river."

Valentina smiled for the first time in weeks.

"What of the others?"

"They're wrecked, Countess. German soldiers are carrying bodies out onto the embankment."

A burst of machine-gun fire made the Englishman duck. German soldiers in the remaining part of the train returned the fire and a short battle ensued. When George looked again over the rail of the cattle truck his incredulous voice came back to the prisoners who cheered wildly.

"Crikey! Most of the Germans are dead and some fellow is taking our travel orders out of the guard's pocket. The Germans won't know who they've lost now, thank God. He's coming this way. He doesn't look French. I'd say he looks damned dangerous."

George dropped down beside Valentina as the back of the wagon was thrown open. A gruff voice called for them to get out and on frozen legs they stumbled forward. A French blacksmith cut their handcuffs as they dropped to the ground. Then, like magic, women and children appeared and led some of the men away. Valentina looked questioningly at the blacksmith.

"Who are you and who are these women?"

"They're wives and mothers. They've come to take their men back home, madame."

"How did you know this train would be derailed?"

"We planned it, madame. Now start walking in that direction and never forget that it was the communists who set you free."

Valentina held George's arm. On her right side the Australian fell into step with Hannegan guarding the rear. They had walked only a few hundred paces when a black car shot out of a side street. Valentina flinched as a man in German uniform stepped out of the car. His voice silenced her three companions as they made ready to move against him.

"Get inside the car and don't argue. Help the countess. She looks faint. Hurry, please, this is not a Sunday outing."

Valentina rubbed her sore eyes in disbelief. Then, as the three men lifted her into the back of the car, she looked up at Schuller and saw a tear falling down his cheek. She felt a tightness in the chest and a weakness in the legs and that was the last she knew for some time.

Louis drove via lanes and back roads to Vaux le Vicomte. Then, he proceeded on a route Nikolai had drawn for him back in the direction of the Domaine. Schuller was behind him, ominously silent. Louis thought he knew what the German was thinking. He concentrated on the road ahead, not allowing himself to dwell on the shocking change in the countess's appearance. When they were stopped at a single roadblock, Schuller produced an S.S. identity card in a name that was not his own. Louis grinned despite everything. It was going well. He had been chosen to drive on this most important mission because driving was his talent. He had acquitted himself well and had not burst into tears on first sight of Valentina and knew he would not until he was safe in the silence of his own room at the Domaine. Louis thought with longing of the dinner his mother would have ready for them, whatever the time of night.

Schuller turned to look at Valentina, who was asleep in the Englishman's arms. Then he returned to gazing at the road ahead. The shock of seeing her in her debilitated condition had so distressed him that he could barely concentrate on the dangers ahead. He thought of Valentina's sticklike arms and legs and scant hair around a face of grayish color. Only the violet eyes remained of the woman he had so admired. The hair had been cut to the scalp, the hands and cheeks bore unhealed scars from the torture she had endured. Schuller sat rigidly at attention, focusing his mind on the past. That was how he would remember the countess, in her black-lace dress with the big black umbrella shielding her from the downpour. He paused twice at farms along the route and requisitioned supplies of ham, cheese, smoked fish and flour. On reaching the Domaine he put Valentina, the prisoners and Louis down and drove on with Dmitry in the direction of Dreux, where he made himself known by requisitioning a van and a whole shopful of supplies intended for German officers. They drove on then to Chantilly, turning when they had scoured the town for food toward Paris and calling at various farms on the way. Schuller had planned well. If their trail were followed it would lead north on the periphery of Paris and then back to the capital.

Miss Knatchbull and Zita looked down at the figure on the bed and then in shock at each other. Miss Knatchbull dropped down on the chair by the bedside and buried her face in her hands.

"That it should come to this."

"We'll make the countess better. Don't give in, Miss Knatchbull."

"We must cut off those disgusting rags she's wearing and burn them."

"I have scissors and Louis's going to bring lint and dressings for the countess's feet."

Louis appeared with cotton wool and the first-aid box. He looked down at Valentina as she lay asleep, then at his mother and Miss Knatchbull. Seeing how distracted they were, he spoke sharply.

"If the countess wakes and sees you both with such long faces she'll be upset. You're not to let her down after all she's been through."

"Have the young men finished eating yet?"

"Yes, Mama. I gave them the rabbit stew, like you said, with the bread and biscuits. That Englishman ate four bowlfuls and then asked for more."

Miss Knatchbull spoke gently.

"Go and rest, Louis. We need you to be up early in the morning."

They washed every inch of the emaciated body, put disinfectant on the rat bites, unguent on the marks where Valentina had suffered beatings and torture. There were scars everywhere on her body, some old and healed, some still puckered and red. Zita took one of Valentina's silk nightdresses from the drawer and slipped it over her head. Miss Knatchbull removed everything that might remind Valentina of her experience, the tattered clothes, the number taped to her wrist, the coarse wool socks given her when her shoes rotted in the flooded cellar. She threw all these on the fire in the kitchen, returning with a bowl of beef broth. Zita disappeared to the woods and returned with a bunch of snowdrops for the vase by Valentina's bed. Miss Knatchbull had been unable to wake the sick woman to eat. She took the soup back to the kitchen and sat resignedly by the bed.

"She's too tired to eat. I'll bring the broth back in the morning.

Go to bed, Zita, I'll watch her during the night. We all need you to be alert and energetic during the daytime."

Zita went to the kitchen and sat by the fire, warming her hands. She was thinking of Miss Knatchbull's statement, "We all need you to be alert and energetic during the daytime." Miss Knatchbull's great age made everyone around her seem young. Zita knew better. She was getting old like her mistress. She was thinking with increasing frequency of retiring to the house by the gate, to dream away the winter of her life. Natasha, her assistant of many years, brought a shawl for her shoulders.

"How's the countess?"

"As thin as a skeleton and scarred all over from rat bites and beatings. I never saw such a horror in my life."

"Will she ever recover?"

"Of course she will! She'll look lovely again, too."

Natasha moved to Zita's side and sat looking into the fire.

"Oberführer Schuller's in the cellar with Nikolai and Dmitry. Isn't it wonderful that he's back."

"We have a lot to thank him for. It's a debt we shall never be able to repay."

The two women were still talking when Schuller appeared in the kitchen and looked intently down at Zita.

"How is the countess?"

"She's asleep, sir. She didn't wake when we scrubbed her and put her in her nightdress and dressed her injuries."

"She'll be exhausted for some weeks."

"Will you stay on here, sir?"

"I haven't decided yet."

"Stay, please. The countess needs you and so do we."

Schuller went to his old room and lay smoking on top of the bed. Nothing had changed. The occupants of the Domaine might be anguished at its owner's injuries, the war might rage outside, but inside nothing had changed. He listened to the tick of the clock, the hooting of the owls and the occasional creak of the stairs. He put out his cigar and closed his eyes. He was home, at least for the present.

Valentina woke to the sound of cockerels crowing, children shouting and Zita telling them to be quiet. She opened her eyes and saw Miss Knatchbull dozing on the chair by the side of the

bed. There was a thin layer of snow on the sill and a glowing log
fire in the grate. From the heart of the house the smell of coffee
came with the scent of smoked ham and toasted bread. Valentina
shook her head in confusion. Had it happened? Of course it had
happened. She went over the events of the previous day, the appearance of Schuller, the way Louis had driven all day and all
night without complaint, the moment of arrival home. Tears fell
freely, and she reached to the bedside for a handkerchief. She was
home. She touched the gossamer silk of the nightdress and smelled
the elusive scent of the perfume Zita had put behind her ears and
on her wrists. She was home. She would never go away or even out
of the grounds until the war was over. She heard footsteps and sat
up to receive her visitors.

Zita had put on an old uniform from the trunk in the attic. It was
too tight, but she had covered the gaping buttonholes with a white
frilly apron. Natasha was in blue and Nikolai had on a silk shirt, a
shirt that reminded Valentina of the days before famine became
commonplace in her life. She looked in wonder at the breakfast
tray, at fresh fruit and golden croissants with creamy farm milk. A
pile of paper-thin slices of ham lay next to eggs served *en cocotte*.
She looked from the snowdrops at the bedside to the tray and then
again to each of her visitors.

"This is the most beautiful sight I ever saw."

"Mama, everyone wishes to call on you. When you've eaten and
combed your hair, will you see them? I told them you were tired
but . . ."

"I'll see them, of course."

Zita watched as her mistress drank a bowl of coffee and ate the
eggs. She spoke gently to Valentina.

"It's wonderful to have you home, ma'am."

Miss Knatchbull woke with a start and looked at Valentina.

"Welcome home, my dear. You slept like a log and so did I. I'll
go and wash now, and then I shall return to guard you."

When the others had gone, Nikolai sat on his mother's bed, sharing her coffee and eating some of the ham. He moved the tray
when she had finished and passed her a brush and mirror.

"Will you see them in bed or by the fire, Mama?"

"I'd best sit by the fire or they might think I'm very ill."

Nikolai saw that his mother was spraying perfume on her neck and that she had put a little lipstick on the white lips that had so shocked him. She motioned for him to bring her pink-ostrich-feather wrap. Then she received a steady line of visitors, Sasha and Lisabette, Dmitry and his wife, the Rodmanovs, the Imeretinskys, the Yurikovs, Natasha, Marina, Valerie and on and on until everyone had been to see her.

Alone again, Valentina reflected on the visit of those she loved. Shock had been their first emotion, followed by tears, kisses and encouragement. She looked in the mirror and sighed. Who would have thought she would ever look like this, old and frail with sparse hair and too-large eyes in an emaciated face? She touched the scars on her face, the others on her neck and chest, trying to shut out the memory of the day when they had been inflicted on her.

The door opened and Schuller entered the room. He had discarded his uniform and was dressed in gray. Valentina thought he looked like an English gentleman.

"Are you feeling any better, Countess?"

"As better as I'll ever be."

"When you're feeling stronger I want to show you something."

"Show me now."

He picked her up as if she weighed nothing at all. Upstairs in the attic that was full of souvenirs of her past he pointed to the vineyard, where Louis was working. Valentina saw vines growing through the snow, mere dark twisted stumps at this time of the year, but vines all the same. Louis had tended the entire vineyard on his own and was tending the vines with all the skill of an experienced viticulturist.

"How did Louis manage to keep the vines so well?"

"He's done it for you, Countess. Give him the praise he deserves when you are feeling better."

"I'll do more than that."

Valentina thought to herself that she would make Louis a partner in the vineyard at once. She turned to Schuller.

"When will you be returning to Monte Carlo?"

"I shan't, Countess. I believe I am needed more here than there. When I am old I shall be able to go there to sit on a bench in the park watching the passersby."

Valentina smiled up at the suntanned face.

"What if you're recognized?"

"I shan't leave the grounds of the Domaine and neither will you."

"Don't you care about the risk?"

"It would seem not, Countess."

Seeing that she was tired, Schuller picked Valentina up in his arms and carried her back to her room.

"Now you are not to worry about anything, Countess. We have food which I commandeered from here to Paris and up as far as Chantilly. You and your family will not be hungry again. The good days have returned. You are home and safe and loved."

Valentina thought of the past few months and knew that there had been a change in the war. The Germans had been halted at El Alamein and the siege of Leningrad had not succeeded, despite the terrible privations of the inhabitants. The beleaguered Russians had clung tenaciously to their city, starving, freezing, dying by the tens of thousands but all the while refusing to yield to the Germans outside. Now Allied forces were bombing France and the Germans were protesting about the terrorism in the skies. Valentina smiled contentedly. She was home and the tide was turning. Outside her room she heard Lisabette arguing with another small girl.

"Nana is *not* a skeleton. She's a bit thin because she walked all the way home from Germany. She'll be better by tomorrow, you'll see."

In April, two English fliers appeared at the Domaine and asked to be guided to the Channel Port. Nikolai took them to the Fortunov house in Vire. Vladimir would then guide them to the Malik house in Dieppe and they would be taken from there to England. This was the route Valentina had designed and one that had been put to the test many times in the past few months. Two days after Nikolai's departure a Canadian pilot arrived and asked for help in getting to Bordeaux. Miss Knatchbull agreed to take him by bus to Chartres and there to hand him over to yet another of Valentina's sons who would in turn guide him to Bordeaux. Day after day men arrived at the Domaine and one or another of the household ferried them to one of the safe houses where escaping Allied soldiers spent their nights en route to freedom. No one considered the risk, though each was aware that in helping these men they were taking their own lives in their hands.

One morning Valentina looked at Schuller and asked the question everyone had been wanting to ask.

"Why are so many men escaping from the prison camps these past few weeks?"

"I believe they are being allowed to escape, Countess."

"But why?"

"Germany has surely lost the war. As a soldier I can see that. As a man I must mourn what is happening to my country. I cannot mourn the deterioration of the Führer's chances of success. I decided some years ago that he was insane."

"What made you think that?"

"Something my uncle once told me. I understand the Führer will not allow the doctors to examine him."

"Have you heard from Admiral Canaris recently?"

"I have not. I have sent him various letters but he does not reply."

"You sacrificed a great deal for me and my family."

"On the contrary, Countess, I found myself, here in the Domaine."

That afternoon an Allied plane, being chased by German fighters, unloaded its bombs into the field nearby. Three of Valentina's adopted daughters were killed with two local men, seven children and her grandson, Sasha. Members of the household were stunned by shock and horror. All work ceased, children screamed inconsolably. The village priest came and went, followed later by a Russian Orthodox father, who had traveled to the house from Paris on being summoned by Nikolai. Lisabette refused to leave Schuller's side, screaming each time he withdrew his hand from hers.

Valentina retired to her room with Miss Knatchbull and Zita. Somehow she spoke rationally.

"All the dead must be buried within the grounds of the Domaine. The ground must therefore be consecrated. I must leave that to you, Natty. If necessary contact the Bishop of Chartres."

Zita stepped forward as Miss Knatchbull left the room.

"I shall increase everyone's work schedule until after the funeral. It's the only way to take their minds off this terrible tragedy. They'll need as much food as they can get. I want you and your son to pack potatoes from our fields into sacks and hide them in the cellar. Tell the food supply officer they were destroyed in the raid."

Valentina closed the door when Zita had gone and took out a photograph album from her locked drawer. She had not allowed herself to look at this album for many years, but now needed the bittersweet joy it would bring. She leafed through pages of photographs of Vasily and Elena at the christening of their children and on their first visit to Madrid. The pages revealed Sasha and his sister on first arrival at the Domaine, sitting outside the house under Masters' loving and affectionate care. Valentina looked at their wan faces and compared them with the suntanned children sliding off a hayrick at the end of their first season on the estate.

She turned the pages and saw the last photographs taken at the end of the previous winter. The children looked like children who knew they belonged. She closed the book and locked it away, turning over in her mind the events of Sasha's brief life. Then she drew the curtains and got into bed, but she could not sleep. Pictures sad and serious kept passing through her mind, of Sasha at school and work, helping his sister through her life and answering questions for her, as had always been his custom. She thought of the Allied plane that had dropped bombs on her land. She could not blame the pilot. He had his own mission and his own life to save. The Allies were bombing every approach to Paris, every railway line, every German supply factory, every German position with German soldiers guarding German munitions dumps. Every night planes droned over head on their way to Paris. Valentina thought she would not have it any other way. Her mind turned constantly to Sasha, the child she had adored, and she tried to equate her feelings for him with her longing for the Allies to bomb the Germans out of France. She was relieved when the sun lit the sky with the uncertain pink of a stormy morning. She rose and dressed in a heavy wool skirt and blouse. She would go to the kitchen to drink her morning coffee with Zita. She would preserve routine at all costs and through it the stability of those who lived in the Domaine. She saw Schuller coming out of his room as she went to the landing.

"It's early for you, Hanspeter; did you not sleep?"

"I slept very little. I am fortunate you have such an excellent library, Countess."

"Why don't you call me Valentina?"

"Because you and I will always be a little formal. I shall call you Countess because it suits you best."

While they were eating lunch after the funeral Lisabette sat alone, looking out of the window at the wood near which her brother was buried. Alive Sasha had guided her every move, answered her every question and made her angry in the process. Now that he was gone she wanted to sob because she was lonely and uncertain about the future. She was almost eight years old, not old enough, she knew, to live her life without parental care. She looked at Valentina and knew in her heart that her grandmother was old and frail. Miss Knatchbull too was aged and even Zita had white hair and a worn face. Lisabette walked outside to the edge of the garden and stood before the simple white-painted crosses at the entrance to the wood. The flowers over Sasha's grave had fallen forward onto the soil. She picked them up and put them gently into position. Then she sat looking fixedly at the cross.

Schuller came up on her from behind.

"What are you thinking, Lisabette?"

"I'm wondering."

"What are you wondering?"

"I'm wondering who'll look after me when Nana dies."

"You have many, many relations in this house."

"They're adopted relations. They won't want me."

"Of course they're your real relations. They are your aunts and uncles and cousins. They love you dearly and would die for you, as I would."

Lisabette ran to Schuller and reached up to kiss him.

"I love you, sir. You'll stay here forever, won't you?"

"I shall stay for as long as I can. When I am gone you will have a large and wonderful family to care for you in life."

"Promise you'll come back."

"I will come back someday, perhaps for your wedding or your graduation. You are not to be sad, Lisabette."

On a summer's day, Valentina was lying on a hammock under the pear trees when she heard a shout of joy from Louis.

"The Americans are in Rambouillet."

The previous night Louis and all Valentina's sons and daughters had stayed up to encircle the vineyard in case the advancing tanks tried again to use the Domaine as a highway. Only one tank had passed by. Inside it there had been a French general. He had stepped out of his tank and inquired Louis's reason for mounting armed guard on the vines. On hearing that the young man, newly a partner in the vineyard, had worked for years to restore the damage done by the Germans in nineteen-forty, the General had taken a pin from his collar and had attached it to the rough shirt he was wearing.

"What is your name, young man?"

"I'm Louis Verneuil, sir."

"How old are you?"

"I'm twenty, sir, almost."

"Remember me, Louis Verneuil. I'm General Philippe Leclerc and I'm on my way to Paris with the forces of Free France."

Tears came to Valentina's eyes as she recalled Louis's stunned acceptance of the pin and his joy at the news that confirmed the rumors of the past few weeks. The Americans were in Rambouillet. Valentina ran inside the house, calling to Zita as she made her way to her bedroom.

"Put whatever wine and food we have into baskets so we can take it to the Americans in Rambouillet."

"We have no food good enough to give them, ma'am."

"Then give them some strawberries and vegetables and some champagne."

Valentina put on a white-silk dress and a blue hat. At her collar she put a red rose from the garden. She was too old to fight anymore, but at least she could wear the colors of France on one of its finest days. The women of the Domaine took their lead from her and dressed in red, white and blue, with cornflowers in their hair. Then, having collected their baskets of wine and fruit, they walked with Valentina from the Domaine to the town and the Grand Veneur Hotel, where American soldiers were sitting in the garden drinking mineral water and eating everything the patron put before them. Valentina spoke for the others as she put her basket down at the soldiers' feet.

"We hope you will enjoy these, sir."

"Thank you, ma'am."

"Will you be in Paris tomorrow?"

"We'll be in Paris today with a bit of luck, but there's a way to go yet and a lot of hard fighting ahead."

"May we wish you godspeed, sir."

Valentina and the women and children walked back to the Domaine in the heat of a summer's day. From the Château de Rambouillet, a man looked down at the tall thin woman leading the unruly procession of children and young women. He looked at a list that had been compiled for him and knew that this was Valentina Masters, formerly Countess Korolenko, who, with her family, had regularly taken Allied officers to the Channel Ports. The man knew also that Masters had delivered the plans for the

D-Day landings to the English Prime Minister, Winston Churchill, and that he had posthumously been given the George Medal by the British. He looked again at the list and was thoughtful.

Valentina stood looking up at her home, ecstatic that it was safe. Every field had been cherished, every cottage preserved, though some would need restoration and rebuilding. She knew now that the war would soon be over and with it the active part of her life. She bowed her head. It would be good to enter the final years surrounded by those she loved in the house for which she would have sacrificed everything. She touched the creamy stone of the balustrade as she walked slowly up the stairs to the entrance. Her eyes caressed the majestic door of centuries-old oak studded with iron. How good it was to be home and safe and well.

That night, in the luminous dusk of a summer evening, a line of tanks ground into Paris from the Porte d'Italie. They settled in a half circle around the Hôtel de Ville, the municipal building and center of resistance activity in the city. At first there was a stunned silence. Then someone noticed a white star on the side of one of the tanks and screamed out of his window.

*"Les américains! Les américains!"*

People rushed from locked apartments in streets and alleyways nearby. The French radio, long forbidden to play the national anthem, played it loud and clear and strains of "The Marseillaise" rung out over the rooftops of Paris.

Nikolai had returned by barge after delivering two Allied soldiers to Dieppe. He was in his mother's apartment on the Ile St.-Louis when he heard the noise. He opened the windows so he could luxuriate in the forbidden sound. Below, above and on either side, others were doing the same and in the cacophony of victory people were singing.

> *"Allons, enfants de la patrie,*
> *Le jour de gloire est arrivée . . ."*

From the cathedral of Notre Dame the great bell began to boom, joined by that of the cathedral of Sacré-Coeur in Montmartre. In quick succession church bells all over Paris began to ring. Nikolai wiped tears from his eyes. It was over. No doubt there would be fighting again tomorrow and more would die, but the might of the

German fighting machine had been broken here in the city of his mother's dreams. He picked up the telephone, dialed his mother's private number and held the phone so she could hear the bells and the singing of the people of Paris.

Valentina sat in bed listening to the sound of victory. She clutched the telephone, unable to believe what her son was sharing with her. Nikolai's voice came over the line.

"The bells of Paris are ringing, Mama. The radio is playing 'The Marseillaise' and the tricolor is flying from the *préfecture* and from almost every window in Paris."

"I'm so glad you're safe. When will you be home?"

"As soon as I can get there, Mama."

"*Vive la France, Nikolai.*"

"*Vivent les américains, Mama.*"

Valentina walked downstairs in the darkness and took a bottle of champagne from the cellar. With this in her hand she went through the tunnel to the Château de Rambouillet. It was her intention to leave the champagne in the bedroom of the kings of France, to be enjoyed by the next occupant in the room where so many Allied men had hidden. When she opened the bedroom door she was surprised to find a man sitting in bed reading a book of Molière. By the bedside was a kepi.

The general looked up and saw the woman he had watched through field glasses earlier in the day. He glanced at the clock by his bedside. It was 2:30 A.M. He would be leaving at five for Paris. He rose and put on a dressing gown, towering over Valentina as he bent to kiss her hand.

"Countess, I am honored to have this opportunity to thank you for all you and your family have done for France. I know all about the escape route you organized and the soldiers who passed through it. We are well informed about the risks you have been running."

Valentina glanced wistfully around the room.

"This is the room where the soldiers slept before they left for the Channel Ports."

"This is the bedroom of the kings of France."

"The men were tired and ill. I didn't think the kings of France would have minded."

De Gaulle risked a twinkling smile.

"I see you have brought me some champagne, Countess. Have you any glasses?"

"There are glasses in the cupboard."

Solemnly De Gaulle poured the champagne and raised his hand in a toast.

"To France, Countess."

"To the heroes of France, General de Gaulle."

On the twenty-sixth of August Charles de Gaulle paraded through Paris in triumph, ignoring the German officers who had remained to snipe from the rooftops. The people put on their best clothes and took out their tricolors and waved them enthusiastically in the breeze. It was a march of celebration and joy unequaled in history and one the inhabitants of Paris would never forget. The war was not over, but Paris was free again.

The following morning Zita took in the breakfast tray and drew the curtains. Looking down at her mistress's face, she saw that the cheeks were flushed and that there was sweat on Valentina's neck and forehead.

"Are you a bit feverish, ma'am?"

"I think I've caught a cold or perhaps all the excitement was too much for me."

"It's never been too much before!"

Zita poured coffee and handed the tray to Valentina, who shook her head.

"I don't feel hungry. Will you bring me a bottle of mineral water instead?"

By noon Valentina's temperature had risen to a hundred. By nightfall it was a hundred and three. Zita recalled the doctor, who appeared in his shirt sleeves and examined his patient of so many years.

"The countess must go to hospital. She has influenza and it could easily turn to pneumonia at her age."

"She won't go, sir."

"Where's Nikolai?"

"He's waiting in the drawing room for you, Doctor."

Nikolai went to speak with his mother to try to persuade her to go to the hospital. He returned to the drawing room shaking his head wearily.

"Mama wishes to be treated at home, Dr. Martin."

"I can't answer for the consequences."

"She won't change her mind, Doctor."

Within a week it became obvious that Valentina was gravely ill. The inhabitants of the Domaine went about their business as usual, determined that she should hear all the old familiar sounds and not the hushed silence that comes when one waits for death. Tanya and Jean-Jacques arrived back from Monte Carlo with Laval. He had traveled with them despite the risks involved, because he wished to pay his last respects to the woman who had saved his life. Andreas Malik and his brother, on being notified about the gravity of Valentina's illness, came from England and settled in their old rooms. And from all over France Valentina's absent sons and daughters came, one by one, to wait and watch and pray for the woman who had adopted them.

Nikolai ordered the two remaining cows killed so he could feed the huge assembly. Then he went to his office and explained to Laval what was happening to the Domaine's finances.

"We were fined two thirds of our fortune for illegal activities. Others in this area were shot, whole families of them, so I cannot mourn the loss of money."

"What you have left will keep the Domaine running in a normal condition for about ten years. After that it will have to be sold. The wine and the mustard and every other crop you grow will not keep the house solvent. These great houses are no longer practical. They are a part of the past and no one can afford them."

"The estate houses need restoration, Monsieur Laval."

"If money has to be spent on building or restoration, then what you have will only last for about eight years, depending on the taxes that will be levied after the war and the level of inflation in France."

"I shall give it some thought when Mama is better."

"Dr. Martin doesn't seem to think she will get better."

"He doesn't know Mama and how much she wants to live."

On the ninth day of her illness, Valentina began to have difficulty in breathing. The infection in her lungs had not reacted to the medicine and she knew she was dying. She was lifted onto three high pillows, her forehead wiped by Miss Knatchbull and Zita, in turns with others in the household, throughout the day and night. She pitied their efforts and cast her mind back to the day when her grandmother had told her she must leave at once for Russia. Gradually she went over the events of her long life, chiding herself occasionally for her actions and smiling at the memory of the great occasions, her first ball, her first sight of St. Petersburg, her outings with Yanin and their illicit love, her return to Paris and her meeting and marriage with Masters, their acquisition of the Domaine and the large and loving family. It was well done. She closed her eyes and dozed fitfully.

As dusk fell on a warm summer evening Nikolai opened the windows of his mother's room so she could smell the scent of the flowers. Then he sat by her bedside, listening as her sons and daughters paid their own final tribute. The children's choir of the Domaine was now a choir of mature voices. They sang their goodbye softly from the lawn. . . .

> *Say goodbye my own true lover*
> *As we sing a lovers' song*
> *How it breaks my heart to leave you*
> *Now the carnival is gone.* . . .

Valentina opened her eyes and smiled at Nikolai, who put the old music box into her hand, opening it so it tinkled with the melody of the voices below.

> *Now the harbor lights are fading*
> *This will be our last goodbye*
> *Though the carnival is over*
> *I will love you till I die*

The voices rose. The music box fell from Valentina's hand.

> *Though the carnival is over*
> *I will love you till I die*